T0028261

Praise for *The Lost Flowers of Alice Hart*

'Reading *The Lost Flowers of Alice Hart* is like finding a rich and resonant bouquet – of words, feelings, and experiences.' – *Canadian Living*

'Ringland's storytelling is driven by an undimmed sense of wonder at the darkness and light, the damage and love in people. It makes for a determined investigation of abuse and survival accomplished with profound sensitivity.' – *Sydney Morning Herald*

'A magical coming-of-age novel.' – *Good Housekeeping*

'This story about family, love, and reinvention is defiant in its sweetness and is stirring to its end.' – *Foreword Reviews*

'An engrossing novel imbued with passion and reverence for the Australian natural world, with a cast of characters that inspire affection in the reader even as they make mistakes.' – *Books+Publishing*

'At its heart, this book is about finding a way to care for yourself, in a world that sometimes likes to step on its flowers.' – *Courier-Mail*

The
Seven
Skins
of Esther
Wilding

HOLLY
RINGLAND

ANANSI
INTERNATIONAL

Published in Canada in 2024 and the USA in 2024 by House of Anansi Press Inc.
houseofanansi.com

House of Anansi Press is committed to protecting our natural environment. This book is made of
material from well-managed FSC®-certified forests, recycled materials, and other controlled
sources.

House of Anansi Press is a Global Certified Accessible™ (GCA by Benetech) publisher.
The ebook version of this book meets stringent accessibility standards and is available to readers
with print disabilities.

28   27   26   25   24   1   2   3   4   5

Library and Archives Canada Cataloguing in Publication

Title: The seven skins of Esther Wilding / Holly Ringland.
Names: Ringland, Holly, author.
Identifiers: Canadiana (print) 20230495761 | Canadiana (ebook) 2023049577X |
ISBN 9781487012748 (softcover) | ISBN 9781487012755 (EPUB)
Subjects: LCGFT: Novels.
Classification: LCC PR9619.4.R55 S48 2024 | DDC 823/.92—dc23

Cover and internal design by Hazel Lam, HarperCollins Design Studio
Cover illustrations copyright © 2022 by Fumi Nakamura. Reprinted by permission of Curtis
Brown, Ltd.
Internal illustrations of shells and feather by Edith Rewa Barrett
Author photograph by Daniel Boud; kanalaritja, shell necklace, by Vicki-Laine Green
Illustrations: pages 2, 126: courtesy of Holly Ringland; pages 70, 200: art by John Bauer (page 70
courtesy of Uppsala Auktionskammare); page 262: Dmitry Pistrov/Alamy Stock Photo;
page 336: courtesy of the estate of Charles Folkard; page 416: courtesy of the National Gallery of
the Faroe Islands

Every reasonable effort has been made to trace ownership of copyright materials. The publisher will
gladly rectify any inadvertent errors or omissions in credits in future editions.

*House of Anansi Press is grateful for the privilege to work on and create from the Traditional Territory of many
Nations, including the Anishinabeg, the Wendat, and the Haudenosaunee, as well as the Treaty Lands of the
Mississaugas of the Credit.*

Canada Council   Conseil des Arts
for the Arts   du Canada

ONTARIO ARTS COUNCIL
CONSEIL DES ARTS DE L'ONTARIO
an Ontario government agency
un organisme du gouvernement de l'Ontario

With the participation of the Government of Canada
Avec la participation du gouvernement du Canada | Canadä

*We acknowledge for their financial support of our publishing program the Canada Council for the Arts, the Ontario
Arts Council, and the Government of Canada.*

Printed and bound in Canada

MIX
Paper from
responsible sources
FSC   FSC® C103567
www.fsc.org

This book is dedicated to the love of family,
especially those we choose.

To Myf, sister, keeper of light in dark woods.

And this book is for Sam, my Space Club.

Contents

Some would say that any story of water is always a story of magic, and others would say any story of love was the same.

HEATHER ROSE, *THE RIVER WIFE*

The first skin:
Death

If you want change, raise your sword,
raise your voice.

1

On the afternoon that Esther Wilding drove homeward along the coast, a year after her sister had walked into the sea and disappeared, the light was painfully golden.

It was March, a liminal time on the island when the tides began to change. Cooling sea breezes blew through the blue gums. Bobs of bull seals left their summer ~~haul-outs~~ ~~and~~ ~~bands of black~~ swans began building their nests for winter hatching. By March the Cygnus constellation shone low on the horizon, hidden by daylight. Esther shifted down a gear and eased her foot off the accelerator to watch the sun cast tips of the sea in gold. This had been Aura's favourite time of year. When they were teenagers she'd called it *the golden in-between*. Her voice full of wonder. *We can immerse ourselves in the sea and float our bodies between what's above and below, Starry. This is when the veil between worlds is thin and everything you can dream of is possible.* Whenever Aura talked about it, she got a mischievous glint in her eyes. Whereas Esther couldn't stop herself from protesting that there was no veil because there was only one world, this one – why didn't Aura get that? *My little scientist*, Aura would inevitably tease, rolling her wrists as she spoke, wooden bangles clacking. *I'll find the dreamer in you one day.*

A gust came through Esther's wound-down window, carrying the blended scent of home. Eucalyptus, salt and wood smoke. She tilted her face away, as if she might be able to escape it. Beside her, the turquoise sea shimmered; bull kelp danced rhythmically in the push and pull of tiny waves curling clear on the white sand. *Our bodies, our bodies.* Esther gripped the wheel as she drove over a rise and around the corner that brought her into full view of the seven granite boulders in the far distance, covered in striking orange lichen and algae. Aura singing, *Our bodies, our bodies*, as she twirls through the shallows, her ankles embraced by fingers of kelp. Esther jiggled a knee. Bit her thumbnail down to the quick. At the taste of blood, she pressed her thumb into her fist and squeezed, sighing with irritation. She flicked the radio on and, after a moment of tinny pop music, switched it off.

For the last twelve months, Esther's life on the west coast of the island had been an escape; living and working on ancient river and rainforest country had been the life of oblivion she'd gone there in search of. It was a place of no memories other than the ones she made and remade every day. On the western edge of the island, on the edge of the world, Esther had found a place where she could breathe. But after she'd set off that morning and turned at the intersection where the dirt road met the national highway and the rainforest began to thin and open into dry pastoral country, Esther's chest had tightened. Even when the clean scent of coastal eucalyptus started to come through the air vents in her ute, she still couldn't breathe easy.

All day Esther had felt outside her body, as if she was watching herself drive. She'd learned the topography of the coastal road when she was fifteen and Aura, eighteen, had taught her to drive. Esther watched again as her hand moved the stick through the gears while her feet worked the pedals around the bends. Watched herself lean into the corner which prompted her to look for the giant blue gum on the cliff with the swing hanging from its bough. Slumped inwards to clatter over the low bridge, leaned back to see the sail boats moored around the rockpool with the pink shells and green seaweed in its folds. She sat forward before the next unseen hill, eased her foot off the accelerator before the next hidden dip.

This was the way they'd always come home. Together. Windows down, salty air in their faces. The floor of their ute littered with Chupa Chup wrappers and Aura's Tally Ho papers. Seashells and banksia seed pods lining the dash. Stereo loud, singing Stevie Nicks, Janis Joplin, Melanie Safka. Esther's heart contracting and expanding with such yearning and awe for her big sister, though she'd been sitting right beside her.

Esther pressed her foot down on the gas and inwardly cringed at her childlike inability to accept how the sea, wind, trees and stars could still exist without Aura. And, yet. All the wild waves rolled in. Black swans dabbled along the marshes. And there they stood, the seven boulders huddled together, holding the warmth of the day's sunlight deep inside like a secret. Despite her emotional resistance, Esther's body remembered the way home. To where she had always been, first and foremost, Aura Wilding's little sister.

As she came over the last rise, Esther glared at the sight of a sculpture by the road, next to the sea, of a bikini-clad woman, hands on hips, hair flying, smiling. She didn't have feet: both of her legs disappeared at the knees into a stone semblance of the sea, engraved with a shouty WELCOME TO BINALONG BAY. The sculpture had been in place welcoming and farewelling people for as long as Esther could remember. Growing up, being prone to a touch of claustrophobia, seeing the 'Binalong Bay Girl' always gave Esther sweaty palms and shortness of breath; her frozen smile, hair, bikini and legs in a stone sea, forever trapped. Esther hadn't known how to manage her reaction to the sight of the sculpture until she was a teenager, when Aura had taken her out in the ute for one of their driving lessons.

'I know how the sculpture could make you feel joy,' Aura had said as she drove.

Esther shook her head. Scowled.

Aura looked sidelong at her, one eyebrow raised, afternoon light pouring over her shoulders. 'What if I do this? How about now?'

As they drove past the sculpture, Aura wound down her window and thrust out her arm, hand gripping an imaginary sword hilt. 'Sisters of Seal and Swan Skins! Séala and Eala!' she crowed. 'Raise your swords and your voices!' A peal of Aura's laughter carried on the wind. 'C'mon Starry, your turn.'

Esther tightened her grip on the steering wheel. Sitting where her sister had sat. Hands where her sister's had been. The Binalong Bay Girl shrank in her rear-view mirror.

As she neared the headland and Salt Bay, Esther's head pounded. The blinding hangover she'd awoken with that morning and had been fighting off with paracetamol was gaining on her. She'd been on the road for nearly seven hours, including breaks she'd had to take when she couldn't suppress the nausea any longer. As much as she just wanted the drive to be done, she resented every shrinking metre that separated her from the awaiting homecoming. Her vision started to prickle at the edges, dark spots of fatigue and blurry anxiety. She glanced across at the bags on the floor of the passenger side, trying to remember which one held the paper packet of mixed lollies that she'd picked up at her last servo stop. A sugar hit would keep her going. She eased off the accelerator. Took her eyes off the road for seconds.

Everything happened at once.

Something exploded against the windscreen, which shattered but held. The sound of the explosion made Esther scream; the weight of impact and the fright of it caused her to swerve off the road, press her full weight on the brake and fishtail on the gravel. A sickly smell of something primal, bloody. Of rubber, something burning.

Esther lurched to a stop in a cloud of dust and grit. She breathed fast, heart pounding, body shaking. Confused and disorientated, she reached for the door, pushed it open and stood up on wobbly legs. Her mind couldn't take in what she was seeing: the wreckage of her windscreen, the bowl of crumpled metal where moments ago the roof of her ute had been, as if it were no more solid than wet clay being moulded by light fingertips. She stared at the front ruins of her ute. The windscreen glass was still popping, still shattering. Still holding. In the middle of it a black swan lay dreadfully still, blood-covered, its graceful neck slack, drooping.

She cried out in horror. Pressed her palms against her temples and looked around to get her bearings. Slowly came to recognise the sheltered grove of blue gums by the headland, where she'd spent most of her teens scrambling over the seven silver boulders with Aura to dive into the hidden lagoon within. The car park was empty. Esther was alone. She tried to think calmly and give herself clear instructions. Check the swan. Call the police. Do you call the police if a swan falls out of the sky and hits your ute? If not the police, who do you call? *Aura.* Her sister's name came unbidden. Esther's stomach cramped. She doubled over, nausea and bile overwhelming her. Reached out to steady herself against her ute.

'Esther?'

She startled at the familiar voice shouting her name; a car skidded to a stop on the gravel behind her. Esther blinked in confusion as Tina Turner, all hair and black pleather, fishnets, denim and dazzle, got out of the car.

'Esther?' The woman gently braced Esther's arms, searching her face. Her eyes flashed with alarm. 'You're alright? You're alright.'

Esther stared blankly at the woman's face under the make-up and wig.

'I saw kylarunya fall. I saw it happen,' the woman said, gesturing at the fallen black swan on Esther's ute and at her own parked car, engine still running, door hanging open.

Beneath the teased, caramel heights of her wig and the assault of blue eyeshadow, pink blush and coral-red lipstick, Esther suddenly recognised Aura's best and oldest friend.

'Nin?' she asked in bewilderment.

'You're alright, Starry.' Nin's voice softened. 'Just a bit of shock. You're alright.'

Esther made a strangled sound, something between a wail and a laugh, fear mixed with relief to be in Nin's soothing, familiar presence.

'C'mere. You're shaking like a sea snail.' Nin rubbed Esther's arms.

Esther became aware that she was shivering. The sun had vanished behind thick clouds, turning the sea from turquoise to slate. The cold wind stung her eyes.

'Get into my car; I'll put the heater on.'

'What about …' Esther looked at the swan, struggling to bear the sight of it, unmoving. She wrapped her arms around herself.

'I'll check; let's just get you warm first.' Nin bundled Esther into her car and blasted the heater. She reached into the back seat for a blanket that she wrapped around Esther's shoulders. Shut the door and tottered over the gravel in her red patent leather heels to Esther's ute for a closer look at the swan.

Watching her, Esther blinked hard against her welling tears, against the shock of how good it felt to be steadied by Nin's big eyes and firm hands, to be reassured by the defiant set of her shoulders. It was how she'd grown up, braced between Nin and Aura, a pup certain of her place in the world. For a time.

Esther reached up to touch her forehead and winced as she felt a painful, swelling lump. Closed her eyes and leaned her head back on the seat. Esther watching Nin and Aura, on the beach, arms entwined, strings of iridescent shells around their necks. Esther, always a stride or two behind, running after them. *Wait for me. Wait for me.*

'Must have been terrifying,' Nin said as she opened the door and sank into the driver's seat. The wind slammed the door after her, buffeting the car with its strengthening howls.

'I don't know what happened,' Esther mumbled. 'I was driving, and then it was like a bomb went off, and then I wasn't driving anymore. I was stopped, in my smashed ute, with a black swan on my windscreen.' As Esther heard herself speak, she looked at Nin's face, which was radiant with empathy. A bubble rose in the back of her throat. 'I killed a swan.' Esther choked up.

'It was just a random accident.' Nin reached over to squeeze Esther's hand, her pleather dress squeaking.

Esther narrowed her eyes at Nin. 'You've never believed anything is random. Or an accident.'

'We don't need to get into all the ways you could interpret this, right? Not with what you've already got on your plate.'

Nin's words hit Esther like cold water. She remembered why she was there. What was ahead of her. She took in Nin's Tina Turner costume, realising where Nin was headed.

'You're on your way,' she said flatly. 'To the "party".' Esther made air quotes with her fingers. 'Tina Turner.' She pointed at Nin's outfit. 'I get it now.' Nin and Aura dancing down the hallway of the Shell House and out the front door to their first high school fancy dress party. Tina Turner and Cher, hand in hand.

'Mum's already there, helping set up. I said I'd go early and join her.' Nin adjusted her wig. 'We need to get you to a doctor.'

'I'm fine.'

'It wasn't a question.'

'I'm fine,' Esther said again. 'It's enough dealing with tonight. And now—' Esther took a moment.

'Yeah, but I'm here, aren't I. You're not doing this alone,' Nin said.

Esther could only nod. The wind nudged and tugged at the black swan. 'We can't leave her here,' she said.

'We won't.' Nin started to put the car in gear.

Esther gripped her arm, panicked. 'Nin.' Her face crumpled. 'A black swan just flew into my ute. On the afternoon of my sister's memorial.' Esther heaved for air. 'I can't do this.'

Nin placed one palm on Esther's chest and the other on her own, breathing deeply and steadily. In, then out. In, then out. 'One breath at a time.' She breathed in sync with Esther until she settled. 'One step at a time.' Nin put her hands back on the steering wheel and inched her car towards the ute.

Esther fought the urge to lean over and hug her, to apologise for being gone, to ask Nin how her life was now, did the black hole pull her towards it too? How did she bear it? Did she still make necklaces from shells the colour of opals with the women in her family? The same women who'd once taught Esther and Aura they could call to swans and sing to seals?

'Thank you,' was all Esther said.

Nin left the engine running while she gathered Esther's belongings from her ute, carrying them back to her car in one hand while using the other to hold her wig down against the force of the wind. After she'd opened the door and put the bags on the back seat, Esther offered her the blanket, warm from her body.

'Starry,' Nin began to protest.

Esther motioned again for Nin to take it. As Nin walked back to the ute with the blanket in hand, Esther looked away. Chided herself for cowardice. A few moments later, she felt the weight of Nin placing the swan in the boot.

'Is that everything?' Nin asked when she got back into the car. Esther looked over her bags on the back seat and nodded.

'We'll sort your ute out tomorrow. It'll be fine here. Now,' Nin said, taking the handbrake off, 'let's get you to the doctor.'

'No medical centre is going to be open now,' Esther argued, her forehead pounding.

'You know I'm not taking you to a medical centre.' Nin pulled out onto the coast road and drove away.

Esther's stomach pinwheeled with nerves.

Nin glanced over at her. 'The swan's not a sign,' she said, tenderly. 'Don't make this harder on yourself than it is.'

2

Esther kept her eyes closed for most of the drive, opening them occasionally to glimpse streaks of sunset mirrored on the twilight sea. When she felt Nin slow to a stop, she kept them closed.

'We're here,' Nin said.

Esther reluctantly looked across the dirt driveway and lawn to her parents' house, the home she and Aura had grown up in. Its oyster-white and grey façade. Smoke spiralled from the chimney. The pearlescent windows shimmered in the low light. A year that felt like ten since she'd left, so much chaos in her mind about the thought of ever coming back. So much fretful, anticipatory noise. Yet in the moment it was quiet and simple. Coming home. To the place that had made her. The Shell House.

'It's exactly the same,' Esther murmured.

'And nothing like it,' Nin said.

Esther nodded. Nothing was the same.

The curtained windows down the side of the house were all dark, except for the one in her father's office, dimly lit. A winter afternoon inside, the bare fingers of the Selkie Tree tapping on the window. Her father's voice. *A black hole is a region in space where gravity is so strong that nothing, not even light, can escape it, Starry.*

'I can't see them like this.' Esther traced her fingertips lightly over her bulging, swollen forehead. 'I don't want any fuss.'

'Just as well,' Nin said.

Esther looked at her, quizzical.

'Freya's in her studio with an appointment running over time, and one of Jack's clients had a panic attack this arv and needed an emergency session in their home.' Nin's voice was gentle and matter of fact. 'That's why Mum came early, to help get things underway for when they're good to go. That's why I came early too.'

Esther looked down into her hands. Despite her reluctance to return, she hadn't imagined her homecoming would be without her parents. 'Exactly the same,' she whispered.

'C'mon, Starry.' Nin opened her door. 'One step at a time.'

'Can you pop the boot?' Esther asked.

'What?'

'I'm not leaving her in the boot. In the dark.'

'Starry—'

'Fuck,' Esther blurted out. 'Sorry. Just pop the boot, Nin, please.'

Nin held up one hand in surrender and reached for the lever by her seat with the other. Esther ignored the concern on her face.

They got out of the car, took Esther's bags from the back seat and went to the open boot. Nin reached for the swan, still wrapped in the blanket, but Esther intervened. Slid her hands underneath and lifted it, feeling the strain of its dead weight in her arms. Feather softness, bones and edges. She wondered how Nin had arranged its neck. Irrationally, she worried about hurting it.

'By the laundry?' Nin asked. To avoid passing Freya's tattoo studio, Esther intuited. She agreed and followed, cradling the swan in her arms.

They walked around the front veranda, down the side of the house. Esther's body shook under the weight of the swan. Shook from carrying the memory of a life that no longer awaited her inside: Aura's footsteps running down the hall. *Is that you, Starry?*

She clenched her jaw. Took a deep, slow breath.
'You're alright.' Nin held the laundry door open.
Esther stood at the threshold. Adjusted the weight of the
swan evenly between her aching arms and walked inside.

Esther sitting in the lounge room of the Shell House on an
autumn afternoon, a year earlier. She's picking her fingernails
down to blood. Waiting. She asked her parents for the family
session separately, since the three of them hadn't been in the
same room since the search party was called off. Once the
appointment for their session was made, Esther built her nerve
to tell them. About the note.

The psychologist, a colleague of Jack's, waits with Esther.
He's been polite since he arrived, a calm expression on his face.
The four cups of tea Esther made for them all have gone cold
on the coffee table; the plate of Kingston Cream biscuits sits
untouched. On the hour, the kitchen clock ticks and stutters.
Golden light ripples down the walls. Esther excuses herself. Says
she's going to the bathroom. Watches herself stand, walk into
her bedroom, pull the bags she'd pre-packed from beneath her
bed and walk out of the house through the side door to her ute.
She doesn't look back.

Nin opened the door to Esther's old bedroom.
'I'll get Mum,' she said, leaving Esther alone. 'Mum? You
here?' Nin went down the hall.
Esther looked around her bedroom, overwhelmed. It was
the same mess it had been when she'd left. She wasn't sure
what she'd expected, maybe for it to have become a new
therapy room for her dad or tattoo ink supply cupboard for
her mum. But it was eerily untouched; clothes still spilled
from the open doors of her cupboard, where she'd yanked
whatever was clean and stuffed it into her bag. Her planetary
fairy lights. The glow-in-the-dark constellation stickers on
the ceiling. Maria Mitchell poster on the wall. Her bookshelf

crammed with old school science books and her desk drawers concealing incomplete applications for astronomy courses. Her desk stacked with the pile of blank journals Jack had gone through a phase of giving her as gifts in her early twenties, full of unwritten dreams. Then she saw it. On her windowsill. The potted violet she'd bought for Aura, a 'welcome home from Denmark' gift, was lush and tended.

Her legs began to tremble from the strain of carrying the swan. She looked around, considering her options. There was space under her bed. She crouched and put the dead swan on the floor. Gently slid it under her mattress, out of view. She sat and shook out the tension from her arms. In the stillness, she noticed for the first time that her room was filled with tiny squares of light, sweeping across the walls and floor. Esther watched them for a moment, then stood and followed them to her window.

Outside, the wind had died down and the garden was still and glowing, transformed into a neon-lit wonderland. A marquee had been set up with hanging, slow-turning mirror balls that scattered glittering light over a large photo of Aura, propped on an easel. Esther stared at her sister's face. Her pulse pounded behind the tightening lump on her forehead.

'How is she?'

Esther pricked up her ears at the sound of Nin and Queenie's approaching conversation.

'Maybe in shock? Nasty lump on her forehead. She flat-out refused the hospital.'

Their voices dropped to whispers for a moment. Then an intake of breath.

'Ya, Starry? Nina nayri?'

Esther turned to see Evonne Goolagong come into her bedroom, carrying a medical bag. A hand-drawn cardboard tennis racket was pinned to the front of her iconic white tennis dress with blue floral trim, and an oversized replica of the 1980 Wimbledon women's singles trophy was pinned to her back, like a shield. Queenie had been tennis-mad for as long as Esther could remember; she'd often joked that watching replays of Evonne's matches had saved her life, never mind chemo. Seeing Esther, Queenie had the same look on her face she'd always had when the girls used to come barrelling through the front door crusted in salt, wearing seaweed bracelets and banksia-leaf necklaces, their pockets full of gumnut stars, sea glass and shells. It was an expression that was equal parts suspicion and endearment.

'Hi, Queenie,' Esther answered. 'I'm okay.'

'Glad I didn't leave this at home.' Queenie set her medical bag down. 'Tell me what happened?' Her brow furrowed as she looked Esther over.

Nin told Queenie about driving behind Esther and seeing her crash, coming around the bend to find Esther hurt and confused. When she mentioned the dead black swan, Esther didn't miss the look Queenie exchanged with Nin. *Eala,* witnesses had told police Aura had been calling to the sea by the stargazing shack. *Eala. Eala.*

Everything had a watery nonsensical quality to it. Esther wanted to jolt herself awake and be back in her staff house on the west coast, surrounded by ancient tree ferns and fairy wrens chittering to each other on her veranda between collected shells and river rocks. Where her past wasn't embedded in the sky, the sea, the land.

'Ninny, I was in the process of making myself a cuppa while the French onion dip sets. Would you finish fixing it for me, love?'

Nin left the room. Esther listened to the kitchen pipes groan as Nin filled the kettle. The squeak of the crockery cupboard opening. The clack of cups and saucers.

Queenie took out her flashlight and stethoscope from her doctor's bag. Indicated for Esther to turn towards her.

'Esther, I'm checking you for concussion. Tell me when and how you got this injury?'

'I was driving, driving … home' – Esther stumbled over her words – 'and it just seemed to happen. I mean there was no warning, something hit my ute, slammed into my ute, it sounded like a bomb going off, and I tried to brake, but it felt like I kind of just ran off the road, into the grove, by the seven boulders. I don't remember hitting my head. I got out of the car, saw the swan. Next thing I remember was hearing Nin say my name.'

Queenie shone her flashlight between Esther's eyes, making her squint.

'Any dizziness? Nausea?'

'No.'

'Any sudden sleepiness?'

'No.'

'Sudden mood swings?'

'Reckon my mood's pretty consistent with killing a black swan on the day of my dead sister's memorial.'

Queenie suppressed a sad smile. 'Glad to see your sense of humour's intact.' She took her stethoscope from around her neck and moved behind Esther, who sat up straight for Queenie to listen to her breathing. 'Tell me your full name?'

'Esther Svane Wilding.'

'Where are you and why are you here?'

'I'm at home, in the Shell House. Getting checked for concussion by Dr Queenie Robertson, in Salt Bay, Lutruwita.'

'And why are you in Salt Bay?' Queenie came to sit in front of Esther.

'I'm not sure this is still a concussion exam?'

Queenie waited.

'Because,' Esther sighed, 'twelve months after my sister went missing, my parents have decided it's time to have a funeral, or memorial, whatever, for Aura. In eighties fancy dress because it was her favourite.' Esther's voice ran dry.

'Your coordination and reflexes are good. Memory and concentration seem okay.' Queenie reached for Esther's hand.

'You did the right thing coming home.' She rubbed a thumb over the back of Esther's knuckles. 'It's good for all of us. To see you again.' Queenie nodded towards the kitchen where Nin could be heard moving around. Esther squeezed Queenie's hand.

'So, kylarunya just flew into your windscreen?' Queenie stood. Put her stethoscope and flashlight away.

Esther shrugged. 'It happened too fast. It sounds silly but she seemed to just fall out of the sky.'

'It doesn't sound silly. New council measures are trying to re-wild the black swans by banning everyone from feeding them. They've been found dead around the place the last few weeks. It's been in the news. There's every chance your swan died of starvation and did actually fall out of the sky, exhausted.' Queenie shook her head. 'They're starving our ancestors.'

Esther's mouth puckered, imagining the majestic bird, one of Nin and Queenie's ancestors, giving up, mid-flight, plummeting to her death. 'I'll bury her,' she said quietly, though Queenie didn't seem to hear. Her attention was on Nin, walking into the room with three cups of tea.

'I think the French onion dip's good to go, Mum. I got the Jatz, cheese and cabanossi started. Seafood cocktail in the fridge looks great. And I've checked on the ham and pineapple pizzas and mini sausage rolls in the oven, nearly done.'

'Thanks, Ninny. Maybe you could give me a hand with the fairy bread? It's the biggest job; I've got a dozen trays to make.'

'I can help,' Esther offered.

Queenie reached out to rub her shoulder. 'Why don't you rest? We'll keep an eye on that bump overnight. If you feel dizzy or sick, you let me know immediately. In the meantime, leave the food to me and Nin. Drink your tea. And have a hot shower. I could smell the booze on you from the hallway. Maybe stay off the plonk tonight, hey?'

Esther's face burned. Nin and Queenie turned to leave.

'Can I ask you a favour?' Esther hurried to ask.

They turned back.

'Don't tell Mum and Dad about this? I don't want to worry them tonight.'

Queenie and Nin both nodded.

'I'll help you get ready once you've showered,' Nin offered as she followed Queenie, closing the bedroom door behind her.

Esther let her full weight fall to her bed. Pressed her eyes shut with her fingertips. Tried to press away the image of the swan, wrapped in the dark, beneath her bed. *We can immerse ourselves in the sea and float our bodies between what's above and below, Starry. This is when the veil between worlds is thin and everything you can dream of is possible.*

Around this time four years ago, Aura had left Salt Bay bound for Copenhagen, months from turning twenty-seven years old, feverish with excitement about the prospect of studying in Denmark, a master's in Humanities, specialising in Scandinavian myths and fairytales. Aura had left Salt Bay and Esther behind; the longer she was away, the less frequent her emails, texts and calls became. When she suddenly came back, three years after she'd left, Aura wasn't the same. Shrunken, hollow, withdrawn. Somewhere between islands, above and below, Esther's dreamy, beautiful big sister had lost her way.

Esther curled her knees to her chest and tucked in her chin. Opened her eyes and watched the confetti of mirror ball light drift around her bedroom.

3

Drawn back to her window by the sounds of voices, Esther watched as people started to arrive outside and mill in the garden. Parked cars lined the street for as far as she could see.

She turned away from them. Took a deep breath and crossed her room, glancing once at the blanketed heap under her bed. Shut her eyes against a vision of black wings falling lifeless, Falling

Esther faced herself in the mirror. Scrutinised her appearance. Black jeans, boots and jumper. If anyone asked, she'd blag something about *The Addams Family*. Coming home had taken all her effort. Besides, she had tried, one night on her laptop with a bottle of vodka in hand, to search the internet for ideas. But the sight of leg warmers and hair crimpers, of fishnets and glitter, had cut a path of panic through her so cleanly it had taken half the bottle of Smirnoff to close the gaping memory of being twelve and watching Aura, fifteen, get ready for her first big high school party. She and Nin had been in year ten and got an invite to a year twelve house party. Aura had gone through three different Cher costumes before Freya and Jack agreed on one that she was allowed to leave the house in.

In front of the mirror Esther looked at the reflection of her face this way and that. Picked at invisible things clinging to her black clothes. It had taken a few attempts, but she'd managed to cover the bruise on her swollen forehead with make-up. If she stayed out of direct light, her side-swept hair and the shadows would conceal her injured face.

A soft knock at her bedroom door.

'Come in.'

'How are you—' Nin halted as she walked in. A wall of fragrant hairspray followed. Her wig was freshly teased, make-up retouched, all blue and coral shimmer and gloss, but her eyes had fallen flat. 'What are you wearing? Why aren't you in fancy dress?'

Esther pulled her sleeves over her hands. Her previous bravado about being Morticia or Wednesday withered under Nin's scrutiny. 'There's not exactly a plethora of fancy dress shops on the west coast.' She tried to keep her voice strong but inwardly cringed at how feeble she sounded.

'Fuck's sake,' Nin said under her breath.

'I just couldn't—'

'Starry, listen.' Nin took a deep breath and softened her expression. 'I know this isn't easy for you. I'll tell you right now, it's not easy for anyone here tonight. You've been gone. And you've had your reasons for going. But for everyone here, who hasn't been able to escape every place and part of themselves that Aura left behind ...' Nin's voice cracked. She tipped her head back and blinked. Tears rolled down her temples in fine blue, shimmery streams and disappeared into the hairline of her wig. Esther wanted to comfort her but, startled by Nin's tears, she froze, unsure of what to do.

'What I mean is,' Nin went on to say, dabbing at her eyes with a tissue tugged from her pocket, 'even though it's hard, I guarantee that no one out there has shown up tonight not bothering to fancy dress. So, in the age of this little thing called internet shopping, make sure I'm the only one you give that excuse to about how you're fronting up for your sister's memorial.'

All the words Esther wanted to say caught at the back of her throat. Stars of silent mirror ball light danced over their skin, between their bodies. The hum of hushed conversations drifted inside from those gathering outside in the garden. Queenie's voice rose occasionally, welcoming people.

Nin went to the window. Esther joined her. She'd been listening for her parents, but still no sign. Aura smiled at them from her luminous photo on the easel. It had been taken the morning before they'd all gone to the airport. For Aura's long journey that would eventually land her in Copenhagen. Hugging her goodbye had felt like water slipping through Esther's fingers.

After a moment Esther realised Nin was no longer at her side. She was walking in semi-circles, looking Esther up and down from different angles. Came to stop directly in front of her, tapping her chin with a pressed-on red fingernail.

'What are you doing?' Esther asked.

'Figuring out what I have to work with. How to make this' – Nin gestured up and down at Esther – 'complement the things I brought you.' She took her phone from the pocket of her denim jacket and started tapping the screen.

'You brought a costume for me?' Esther's chest tightened; Nin had known she'd come home with nothing but excuses. 'Nin,' Esther started to try to explain again.

'Be quiet, Starry.' Nin waved her hand in the air, her brow furrowed. 'I'm drowning in an abundance of search results for *white girl eighties costumes*.'

Twenty minutes later, Esther was still in black clothes but had endured a wincing, scalp-stinging session of frizzing and teasing until her hair was a nest of fluffed-out curls. Pulled through a black sun visor Nin had brought and piled on her head, held in place by nearly a whole can of hairspray and countless bobby pins. Esther caught a glimpse of her reflection in the mirror, now a foot taller. She groaned.

'I don't want to hear it,' Nin admonished her from behind, continuing to tease out random sections of curl fluff. 'Face me. And hold up my phone so I can see the photo again.'

Esther did as she was told. Nin narrowed her eyes as she studied the photo on her phone screen, then turned and rummaged through her bag until she retrieved two identical brooches. She pinned them to Esther's black top, over her heart. Reached into her bag again. Popped the lid off a tube of pink lipstick.

'No.' Esther pressed her lips together in refusal.

Nin waited. Waited.

Esther rolled her eyes. Huffed surrender.

Nin applied Esther's lipstick, then stepped back, tilting her head to one side.

'I think we're done here.' She looked Esther over. 'You can see now.'

Esther turned to the mirror to find herself at the centre of the 1988 cover of Kylie Minogue's debut album. As if she'd stuck her head through the hole of a comic foreground, the kind at carnivals, and emerged as Australia's Princess of Pop. She and Aura were kids when 'The Loco-Motion' came out; they'd shimmied around the Shell House singing it repeatedly until their dad begged them to stop. Esther poked a sprayed-stiff curl that didn't dent. Ran her fingers over the two brooches of identical cat's-eye sunglasses pinned to her jumper.

She took a step towards the mirror. 'I look just like her,' she marvelled.

'You should be so lucky.' Nin winked. Esther almost laughed.

A surge of music outside interrupted them, the end of Bowie's 'Ashes to Ashes'. Nin and Esther gathered at the window. Clusters of people moved to make way for someone coming through the crowd, approaching Aura's photo. Bowie finished. The marquee fell quiet. Esther's face prickled as she recognised the tinkling opening bars of Fleetwood Mac's 'Everywhere'. The drums kicked in.

Esther, sitting in the back of their old Kingswood, folds her arms, sullen. Aura has unfairly claimed the bench seat, prized for its proximity to Freya on road trips. They're on their way home from

Nipaluna, Hobart; Aura rode in the front on the drive down. It's Esther's turn for the drive home. Despite Esther's protests, Freya has let Aura get away with it. Another reason it hasn't been a fun trip: Freya didn't get the artist job she interviewed for at yet another tattoo parlour in the city. *But why?* Aura asked, incensed, her fists clenched, outside The Drunken Sailor, glaring at the tattooists inside. Freya grabbed both girls by their hands and dragged them back to the Kingswood. *Because the world is a boys' club*, she sighed. *Get in, girls; we'll go and get fish and chips. With chicken salt.* Freya unlocked the car and Aura dived into the front before Esther had a chance. She whined in complaint, and Freya shouted at them, a rarity that left a sting in Esther's skin.

It's during their second hour of silence on the drive home that the radio crackles from static to song as they come over the range. The latest hit from Freya's favourite band fills the car with tinkles and drums. Freya turns the volume up and leans her head back, the tension visibly disappearing from her shoulders. Esther and Aura don't speak; they've grown up learning there's no point talking to Freya when Fleetwood Mac is playing. Especially if Freya is in her studio, drawing. As the music swells and fills the Kingswood, Aura looks across at Freya, and over the seat at Esther, to whom she offers the tiniest smile. Esther sulks against the smile tugging at her mouth, but joy eventually wins, wide and warm. Thawing. Knees bouncing. Heads bopping. And Freya sings, louder and louder, reaching across for Aura's hand. But when the chorus starts, it's Esther that Freya seeks out with her eyes in the rear-view mirror while she sings. Aura spins the volume dial up as far as it will go before distorting and joins Freya, turning to sing to her little sister. Years later, when Esther gets drunk for the first time, she recognises the light, limbless feeling from that afternoon in the Kingswood, Fleetwood Mac playing loud and her mother and big sister singing and howling to her like she is the moon.

~

Outside, in the marquee, someone turned the volume up. A silhouetted figure walked through the crowd. Nearest to Aura's photo, a group of women stepped aside, making room. Esther recognised them from her early teenage years spent in her mother's tattoo studio; some Freya had tattooed, others she had taught to tattoo. Their faces were heavy with sorrow, but their arms opened wide, holding space for the approaching figure. One woman's arm caught the light, wrapped in fresh cling film. *Freya's in her studio with an appointment running over time.* As Esther stood inside pressed to the window, watching, the tinkling riff of the song went through her blood. The drums beat painfully in her chest. She watched. Waited.

Dancing in the glitter of mirror ball light, long, blonde shaggy hair falling over her shoulders and layered silk dress floating around her body, Freya Wilding swayed towards her disappeared daughter's photo. Arms outstretched. Singing 'Everywhere'.

Esther felt Nin take her hand. She looked at Nin's face, sombre beneath Tina Turner's likeness. Tried to rally her body despite how she was shaking, and followed Nin out of her bedroom. Down the hallway hung with family photos.

Out of the Shell House. Into Aura's last party.

4

The low-lit marquee gleamed against the night sky. Strung along low branches of the surrounding gum trees was an abundance of glow sticks in neon pink, green, orange and yellow. Between them clung curls of rainbow-coloured Slinkies. Streamers drifted freely over the grass, stuck in some places by dew. Tethered around the garden were oversized, inflatable eighties icons: a boombox, a pair of roller skates, a trio of EPs. They bobbed in the slight breeze, which carried the fragrance of Freya's night-blooming lilies, a delicate scent Esther had loved once. Tonight it gathered at the back of her throat, cloying.

Esther dragged her feet behind Nin. She could no longer see her mum. No sign yet of her dad. The music had faded to a background beat. Esther kept her head down, grateful for Nin all over again; her visor and bouffant hair concealed her face enough to prevent her from having to make eye contact with anyone. From having to be the little sister. The surviving daughter.

As they approached, Esther and Nin were enveloped by the general momentum of the gathering, moving towards the marquee. Her palms were sweating. She squeezed Nin's hand. Nin squeezed back and didn't let go.

Inside the marquee, a chandelier of black cassette tapes hung over tables set to one side, laden with fluorescent purple punch, tiered platters of fairy bread and the rest of Queenie's eighties smorgasbord. Esther turned to the other side, where a small stage was set up with what looked like a DJ booth, though no one was behind it. A smartphone screen glowed where it sat, plugged into speakers on tall stands either side of the stage. A fog machine beside the speakers emitted occasional clouds of fruity-scented vapour, over which hung the relentlessly glittering mirror balls.

Again, the poster-sized photo of Aura smiled at Esther from the large easel embracing it. She stared at her sister's frozen-in-time face from four years ago. The moment after the photo; the hope in Aura's eyes as she'd hugged Esther goodbye. *I'll find Agnete for you, Starry.* A promise to visit the sculpture depicting a Danish folktale they'd grown up with, and then Aura was gone, walking towards the departure gate for her flight to Copenhagen. The next time Esther had seen her, returned unannounced from Denmark nearly three years later, there was no hope in her eyes.

Esther looked over the crowd, through the marquee and out to the night sky, searching for a constellation to anchor herself with. The distant stars were dulled by the glow of the party.

The music cut. A hush fell over everyone.

Freya, resplendent as her beloved Stevie Nicks, walked onto the stage from the collective embrace of her tattooed women, Queenie among them. A few seconds after, she was followed by Doc Brown, in his plutonium radiation suit from *Back to the Future*.

Esther's eyes welled at the sight of her father. She flushed with grief and love to see his choice of costume. Freya cleared her throat. Esther braced herself.

'Friends,' Freya began, her voice starting strong and clear, 'tonight has been a long time coming.'

Murmurs of support rippled through the crowd.

'It's been a year since our daughter, our firstborn, Aurora Sæl Wilding, was last seen. Walking to the sea.' Freya swallowed. 'We all know where we were that day. We've been asked enough times. Larry ...' Freya nodded at Larry Thompson in the crowd, their local sergeant who had led the investigation into Aura's disappearance. He'd been the one to tell them her dress and shoes had been found on the sand. And later was the one to break the news that her search party was being called off; Aura's case was closed and given to the coroner, who ruled an open finding. Larry had weathered their anguish and rage over the ambiguity, the lack of answers. Catching her eye, the sergeant returned Freya's nod, his sorrowful expression in stark contrast to his *Knight Rider* quiff and black leather jacket.

Freya held his gaze for another moment before looking out at everyone gathered before her. Esther held her breath, waiting for her mother to spot her. But Freya's eyes were unfocused, glassy with memories.

'When she was a baby and I was teaching her how to say her name, she decided at some point that Aurora was too hard. In the end, Aura informed us what her name was. As if we'd almost got her name right, but just needed her help to settle it.'

At her side, Esther felt Nin take deep breaths. Freya paused and looked at Jack, his face pained by emotion, his eyes magnified by his Doc Brown goggles.

'We wanted to name her after the lights our ancestors saw dance over their northern island, and the sister lights we see here in our southern home,' Freya went on. 'But in the end, whether by mispronunciation or not, Aura named herself better than we ever could. She wasn't the sky. She was everything in between. We were lucky to have her for thirty beautiful years. She is the energy that surrounds us all here tonight. I mean, look at us,' Freya said, sweeping an arm over the crowd in fancy dress. 'After we lost her—' Freya sucked in her breath. 'After we ...' she tried again. 'You showed up. All of you. To help us look for Aura. To try to find her. My girl. I thank you for that. For coming. Tonight. This ...' Her voice cracked, and she shook her head.

The first phone calls and emails about a memorial had started three months earlier. Esther hadn't ever warmed to the idea, no matter how much her mother had talked about the power of grieving, or even when her father had cried once on the phone, explaining *ambiguous loss* and *how important ritual is, even if we don't have a body*. That phrase had shut Esther down to the idea completely. She could not think of her sister that way. In those terms. Eventually Freya had stopped emailing to share ideas about how they might create an evening fit for remembering Aura, and Jack had ceased leaving any mention of a memorial on Esther's voicemail. Weeks had passed. One day, mail came to Calliope with an envelope addressed to Esther. Inside was a *Back to the 80s* party invitation:

> *Please gather with us at the Shell House, to bring joy to a memorial honouring the life of our daughter, Aura Wilding, who loved 80s fancy dress.*
>
> *Dress code essential: come as your favourite memory of being with Aura in the 80s, or as your favourite 80s experience.*

On the back, a handwritten note.

> *We love you so much, Starry. Love, Dad.*

She'd been tempted to rip it up and put it straight in the bin but couldn't bring herself to do it. The invitation sat under a magnet on her fridge, following her like the eyes in a painting, until that very morning, when she'd woken at dawn, called in sick, and started the drive east.

'There are a few ways we invite you to remember and celebrate Aura tonight.' Freya had regained strength in her voice. 'She loved View-Masters; thanks to Erin, my sister, we've had slides made up especially, which you can find on the tables at the back.'

At the mention of Erin, Esther peeked from beneath her black visor but couldn't find her beloved aunt's face in the crowd.

'Tonight's music is Aura's own playlist, so please dance. We want to revel in the joy of our love for our darling girl.' Freya took a moment. 'Finally, when you came in you might have seen at the far end of the garden the fairy lights in the silver birch tree – we have a little table set up there with a memoriam book. Please feel free to write anything you'd like to share with us in it. This wouldn't have been possible without so many of you. Thank you for joining us in such fine form. Special thanks to Queenie for her impressive eighties catering. Please, eat, drink ...' Freya's speech ended to impassioned applause. The crowd surged forward, engulfing her and Jack as they stepped off the stage. A squeal of interference between speakers crackled to clarity; Aura's eighties playlist resumed. The Church, 'Almost With You'. Esther ducked her head and left Nin's side to make her way to the back of the marquee. She ladled purple punch into a neon yellow plastic tumbler and glugged it back, wincing at the indistinguishable taste it left in her mouth. Ladled another cup. Set her jaw against the sickening sweetness and downed it.

People hugged and mingled. Some cleared a space and started dancing. Watching pairs form, Esther studied one couple: Aura's high school English teacher, Mr Verona, dressed as Madonna in her *Desperately Seeking Susan* fishnet era, had his arms wrapped around his husband, Marco, a perfect linen and pearl replica of Rosanna Arquette's Roberta. Aura had loved them both; after she finished high school, Mr Verona and Marco had come to the Shell House for dinner to celebrate Aura's acceptance into a Bachelor of Arts degree at university in Nipaluna, Hobart. *When Mr Verona and I talk about stories, it feels like everything is still possible,* Aura had said to Esther as they got ready for the celebratory dinner. Esther had smiled but at fourteen, only in year nine, she was confused; what did Aura mean, *still*? Was high school ending that dramatic? When Aura had dropped out of university after her first year and come back home, Mr Verona had helped her get work at Marco's restaurant. *Uni just wasn't what I thought it would be, okay Starry?*

Drop it, she'd said to Esther, her face blank as she buttoned up her waitress uniform. It was the same job she'd kept right up until she was nearly twenty-seven and left for Denmark.

Track change. 'I Should Be So Lucky'.

A waving fishnet-gloved hand caught Esther's attention. Mr Verona and Marco indicated for her to join them on the dance floor. Esther lifted an awkward hand in polite refusal. When Mr Verona adjusted his head scarf and began to move through the crowd towards her, crucifix and shiny plastic bead necklaces swaying, Esther panicked at the prospect of small talk. She sidestepped and ducked, hiding in the dim light on the edge of the crowd until, through the clusters of bodies, she saw Mr Verona's fishnets return to Marco's pumps and pressed chinos.

When Esther stood, she found herself behind the wings and tail of Falkor from *The NeverEnding Story*. He was drinking punch with Bastian, Atreyu and Tina Turner; Nin was chatting with some of Aura's friends she'd waitressed with after university hadn't worked out. They'd worn the same *NeverEnding Story* costumes to Aura's twenty-first fancy dress party, gathered at her feet as Aura had clutched a karaoke microphone with one hand, a wine cooler stubby with the other. Alcohol had made Aura magnetic. That night she'd glowed in ivory sequins and tulle, a four-strand pearl headpiece draped over her pale, pulled-back hair. *Say my name*, she'd bellowed raucously at her friends, mimicking the Childlike Empress in the film instead of singing along with Limahl's lyrics. *Save Fantasia*, and she'd raised her arms, eliciting a roaring cheer from her party, all the light in the garden drawn to her and reflected in her joy. Esther, months away from turning eighteen, had stood on the edge of Aura's party where she'd promised she'd stay. *Say my name*, Aura had cajoled her friends again. From the shadows Esther had watched, her skin prickling with awe and envy as Aura's friends bellowed back to her: *Moon Child*. When Aura had re-watched the film to prepare her costume, she'd rewound that moment in the film

a dozen times, to watch Bastian scream his grief aloud and, in
doing so, save himself and everyone he loved.

'You okay?' Nin asked, coming to stand beside Esther.

'Peachy.'

'Spoken to them yet?'

Esther looked to the crowd still gathered around Freya and
Jack, and back at Nin, rolling her eyes.

'You could just go to them,' Nin urged.

'Hounds of Love' started playing.

'Who does this?' Esther gestured around them, to the
memorial. 'Who the fuck does this?' She smiled maniacally at
Nin. 'More punch?' She raised her empty cup as she turned to
walk away. Kate Bush cried out across the marquee.

'No thanks,' Nin said warily. 'Starry ...'

Esther waved Nin's concern away. She drank two more cups
of punch in quick succession and, with her third, idled to the
table Freya had mentioned in her speech, with an arrangement
of red View-Masters and an album of reels. The thunderous
drumbeats of John Farnham's 'You're the Voice' reverberated
through Esther's body. *Sing it, Famsy.* Aura jumping around her
bedroom, holding both arms over her head, fingers in hand-
horns.

She picked one of the View-Masters and chose a reel
from the album, labelled *Childhood*. Slotted it in and lifted
the viewer to her eyes. Through the dark red viewing tunnel,
in vivid, three-dimensional colour, Aura stared back at her
with a wide, gummy grin; she held a newborn Esther in her
arms. Esther's eyes smarted with tears. She pressed the lever,
clicked the reel onwards. Aura and Esther stood in matching
hooded windcheaters, drawn tight around their faces, as they
clutched each other in the bracing wind atop Kunanyi, Mount
Wellington, laughing at the puffs of clouds gathered around
their feet. She clicked. The two of them with their She-Ra
swords at the stargazing shack, arms raised in the air, their faces
distorted by their battle cries, Jack between them laughing.

Cold Chisel's 'Flame Trees' started as Esther clicked through more memories until she reached the end of the reel. Took it out and replaced it with the next one from the album, labelled *The Teens*. The first slide: Aura, a freckled teenager, her face lit by the glow of the candles on her thirteenth-birthday cake. Her summer-bleached hair. Her open, joyous face beaming at the camera. Next, Aura and Nin dressed as Cher and Tina Turner before leaving for their first big high school party, fifteen years old and radiant with their excitement. Esther clicked again. Aura stood far away at the edge of the grey sea on a colourless day, her back to the camera, the light outlining her in silver. *Click.* Aura had her arms wrapped around her knees; her face was turned away from the camera as she sat in the shadows on the veranda of the stargazing shack. *Click.* Aura stood at the base of the silver birch tree, looking straight at the camera, as if she'd just heard the photo being taken, her eyes piercing. Jimmy Barnes screamed through his chorus. Esther clicked until she came back to the photo of Aura's birthday, shocked by the difference in her sister's demeanour in one reel.

She glanced briefly through the album for another reel of Aura's teen years, unable to find one. She picked a reel labelled *The Graduates* and clicked through it to see photos of Aura and Nin when they were seventeen, holding their high school certificates, with Queenie and Freya, all wearing marina shell necklaces; Queenie and Nin's aunts had made them especially. There was no matching iridescence in Aura's eyes. Esther had been standing beside Jack when he took the photo. He'd asked Aura three times to smile.

Esther put the View-Master down and turned back to look at the crowd milling around the empty stage. She avoided the possibility of making eye contact with anyone but her dad, who was standing behind Freya while she spoke to people gathered around her.

Huey Lewis and the News belted out of the speakers. 'The Power of Love'.

Finally, Esther's dad looked in her direction. A latch opened in Esther's chest.

Jack smiled. She gave him a small wave.

He pulled his goggles down to hang around his neck, and, in a way that only Esther would understand, pressed his thumb and index finger together for a few seconds at arm's length in front of his body. Overwhelmed, Esther returned the gesture. Her father smiled again, this time his face distorted by emotion.

The nausea she'd been fighting all day rushed, urgent and merciless, from her gut.

As she ran from the marquee, Esther didn't notice she was followed.

5

The chill in the night air pinched Esther's skin. She ran to the fairy-lit copse of trees at the far end of the garden and doubled over, vomiting onto the grass. Sucked in big lungfuls of air, trying to breathe slowly. Trying to slow her heart down. When her body had nothing left, she sat, exhausted.

Her head ached; the swelling on her forehead pulsed against the band of the visor. She pulled at the bobby pins holding it in place and yanked the visor off, exhaling with relief. She ran her fingers up the lengths of her hair, sprayed into vertical place yet drooping without the visor to hold it all together. Every part of her was starting to hurt. Fatigue, shock, grief. The absurdity of it all.

Esther wiped her eyes. The body of the dead swan under her bed, neck limp. Not flying. Not breathing.

Synthesiser beats filled the air. 'Tainted Love'.

She hung her head. Didn't see him coming. Didn't hear him approach.

'Esther-san.'

She startled. Aged by talcum powder, Mr Miyagi stood over her in his button-down beige shirt and trousers. Tied around his forehead was his signature lotus flower hachimaki. Esther almost laughed. Tom Matsumoto. There he suddenly was. They were together on the edge of a party again. As if they were teenagers at one of their high school house parties, him finding her in a dark corner reeking of vomit, offering her a glass of water, his face filled with love and concern.

'Tommy-san,' she said. 'You followed me?'

He shrugged, smiling. It was a year since she'd last seen him, after Aura's search party was closed. Not that they'd spoken much then, or in the preceding few years: things had grown awkward between them in their early twenties after the wedding of a couple they'd both known in high school. The ease between them, from a friendship formed in childhood, turned out to be more potent than the champagne they drank together with black Sambuca chasers at the wedding bar. It was the first time Esther had ever seen him drink; it had been a messy fumbling. They'd woken up in a bougainvillea bush on the golf course green, wedding guests gone and early-morning staff starting to arrive. Afterwards, neither had been able to bridge the gulf that bad sex had created between them; they'd grown apart into total silence.

Tom shoved his hands in his pockets, a sad smile on his face. 'I saw you.' He glanced towards the marquee. 'Couldn't catch your eye.'

Esther took the glass of water from Tom, drank it, then stood. They hugged. Esther held on for too long; a sharp pang when Tom stepped away first. After a year on the west coast where everyone she met was new and transient – tourists came and went within a week, average staff turnover was three months – Esther was struck by the power of seeing Tom again, remembering how intimately he knew her stories, how much of her life he carried tucked within the folds of his own. How inseparable they'd been as kids.

'How have you been?' she asked.

'Good, yeah.'

'Still down in Nipaluna? At uni? Kelp, right?'

'Yep. Marine and Antarctic studies. Our giant kelp reforestation project is amazing; we've had some exciting breakthroughs with seedlings and propagation—' Tom cut himself off. 'Sorry.' He looked down at his feet and rocked back on his heels. 'Not the time for kelp talk.'

'I'm glad you're doing well,' Esther said. She looked to the edges of the gathering under the marquee. Freya and Jack were moving from group to group. Her father craned his neck, searching over the crowd.

'And you? Astronomy?' Tom asked.

Esther chewed on her bottom lip. Looked away.

Tom cleared his throat. 'I've been thinking about your dad with all the news lately about the Space Shuttle Program ending in a couple of months. NASA says when the *Atlantis* comes home in July, that's it. The final voyage.'

Esther kicked at a patch of grass with her boot. When they were kids in the eighties and nineties, daydreaming in the stargazing shack, the Space Shuttle Program set their minds on fire with awe. Imagining where they would be in their lives beyond the year 2000, when they would be adults in their twenties, was as exhilarating to them as space exploration. If it was possible to build an International Space Station, who might they each become? Tom had stayed true to his marine biology dreams. *I'm going to become a scientist and invent new ways to study the stars*, Esther had declared throughout her childhood. She frowned as her stomach cramped again. What a let-down she was to her kid-self, a twenty-seven-year-old drop out. She swallowed another wave of nausea. Her life as an adult in 2011 was nothing like the future she'd envisioned for herself when she was young.

'Almost lost my shit in there when Jack gave you the Space Club signal.' Tom looked at her.

'You noticed that?' Esther's voice was thin.

Tom nodded.

'Remember the day he taught us?' Esther asked, blotting her nose on her sleeve.

'Of course.' Tom half-smiled. 'Jack said, "Today, space is going to teach us about perspective." And you swore at him.'

'No, I didn't.'

'Yes, you did. Even though you loved space, you were such a pain in your dad's arse. And mine.'

'Only until Dad came up with a secret Space Club signal. Then it was cool to be in a club with him. Then I got on board.'

'True. Before that, he couldn't even win you over with the t-shirts he had made.'

'That's right.' Esther remembered. 'Those fucking t-shirts.'

'I still have mine.'

'No, you do not.'

'I do. How could I have thrown out the motto?'

They smiled at each other, slipping into their old rapport. '*De Profundis ad Astra*,' they recited in unison. '"From the depths to the stars."'

'Don't You Forget About Me'. Simple Minds blared across the garden from the marquee.

'Did you ever confess that we found Jack's sci-fi subscription magazines and figured out he didn't come up with the motto on his own?'

Esther snorted. 'And break his heart?'

Tom chuckled. 'Sometimes I catch myself looking at the night sky and can't resist.' He held his hand up at arm's length and pressed his thumb and index finger together at his eyeline. Raised an eyebrow at Esther, an invitation.

She bit on her smile. Lifted her arm. They stood with their hands raised towards the stars.

'An area of the sky the size of a grain of sand held at arm's length contains ten thousand galaxies. Each galaxy contains billions of stars,' Esther recited, remembering Jack's lessons in Space Club. Her arm brushed against Tom's.

'Still blows my mind,' Tom said.

They stood together watching the sky. Kenny and Dolly started singing 'Islands in the Stream'.

'Man, I loved Space Club,' Tom went on. 'Especially when Jack used to take us to the stargazing shack.'

'Yeah,' Esther agreed. 'We loved the shack.'

Growing up, Esther and Aura hadn't had a treehouse or a secret cubby, they'd had the stargazing shack. Built and used by nineteenth century sealers and swanners, the small wooden shack had fallen into disrepair over time. Until Jack Wilding approached the town council about fundraising for restorations, with plans to become its caretaker.

What followed became a fireside-story favourite in their family: through the summer that Freya was pregnant with Aura and local fur-seal mothers readied to birth their pups, Jack restored the shack, plank by beam by nail. Three years later, the winter Freya carried Esther, as black-swan mothers hatched cygnets in wetland nests nearby, Jack had the shack set up for use as an all-weather stargazing shelter. Though it was basic – one room with two neat windows and a small, open veranda – it had a clear view of the night sky and a sweeping outlook across the sea and wetlands.

'Esther?'

She looked at Tom blankly.

'I was just saying, the shack, do you spend much time there?'

Esther shook her head. 'Not lately. I've been on the west coast for the last year. Since ...' She let the sentence go.

'Yeah,' Tom said, his voice soft. 'I would have taken off too.'

Though they hadn't spoken since their friends' wedding, during Aura's search party Tom was one of the people who'd shown up early and stayed late at the Shell House. Esther remembered so little of that fortnight with clarity; Tom's presence during that time was one thing she could clearly recall. He'd been there, morning and night, making flasks of hot tea and cheese and tomato toasties. He'd been there when the police told the Wildings they had closed the search for Aura and were giving her case to the coroner; when Jack held Freya in her hysteria, and Queenie arrived with her doctor's bag. Tom had stayed late into that night when Esther slipped outside, thinking she'd gone unnoticed. Until she turned and saw him inside, at the window, bearing witness while she sat at the base of the silver birch, tearing at its bark.

Esther glanced at Tom, dressed as Mr Miyagi, wondering if he was remembering the same moment as she was. The birch tree's shimmering white bark, almost silver, was now coiled in fairy lights. A small table was set at its base, draped with a neon tablecloth. A large hardcover book was open, pen lying in its centre. 'Take on Me', sang A-ha.

'Have you written in it?' she asked Tom.

'No,' he said. 'But I will,' he rushed to add.

'I don't care either way.' She wondered if there might still be punch left in the marquee.

'I take that to mean you haven't written in it either?'

Esther scoffed, 'No.' She pushed one of the sagging sections of her sprayed-stiff hair out of her face. 'There aren't enough pages. Not enough empty books in the world for my stories of her.'

Tom studied her face. 'Tell me one,' he said softly.

Esther scratched the tender scarred skin on the inside of her arm.

'Only if you want to,' he said.

She remembered how their friendship felt. The way he made space for her. As he'd always done.

'Aura loved this fucking tree,' she whispered. 'But you know this story already,' she continued, self-conscious.

'Tell me again.' Tom's eyes watered. 'I'd love to hear it.' From the marquee, The Church strummed guitars. 'Under the Milky Way'.

Esther took a breath. 'We were teenagers – I think I was about thirteen, which means Aura would have been sixteen – and Mum was thinking about expanding her tattoo studio, remember?'

'I do.'

'Mum had her eye on this corner for a possible remodel, but the prospect of this tree being cut down made Aura go apeshit. We all knew she loved it, but she was extreme about this tree. She started making this list of facts in protest.'

Tom smiled. 'It was impressive.'

'Right.' Esther remembered Aura following Freya around the Shell House, reciting silver birch tree facts; how her voice shook with passion, rage and conviction. *A silver birch tree sheds its bark like humans shed their skin. In the wild, silver birches are rarely found alone because of how easily they seed, so essentially they grow up in groves with their kin. They provide food and habitat for hundreds of animals.* 'Aura went on and on for days. It seemed to become this battle between Mum's tattoos and Aura's stories.'

'I know who I would have bet on.' Tom looked up at the silver birch.

Esther smiled. 'Then came the clincher that night at dinner when Aura finally explained that the year before, when she was in hospital to have her appendix out, she was really scared of her surgery and Erin told her that when it was over, the silver birch trees were here waiting for her. Erin told her this story about how the silver birch is revered in eastern European cultures as a curative for sadness: you tell your heartache to the tree, wrap your arms around it, give it all your pain and the tree takes it from you. Then sheds your pain in its bark, like an unneeded skin. Everything is transformed. You, your pain, the tree.' Esther looked at the silver birch, its pale bark luminous in the night. 'Aura told us, that night at dinner, that ever since she'd got home from the hospital it had become her ritual to tell her stories to this silver birch. That's why she loved it so much. It took her sadness and fear and shed it in its bark, silver like a seal skin. That's when Aura named it her Selkie Tree. I remember Mum's face went white.'

'Aura loved her selkie stories,' Tom mused.

'She did,' Esther whispered. 'She was obsessed with them for as far back as I can remember.'

~

Esther huddling beside Aura on bean bags at their primary school library, a large storybook open across both of their laps. Their lunchboxes open beside them. Aura holds half a Vegemite sandwich in one hand and reads slowly, running a finger across the words on the pages so Esther can follow.

'In stories from islands in the North Atlantic Ocean, selkies are seals able to shed their skin and take human form. The most well-known selkie tales are about seals coming to shore on a full moon, slipping off their skins and stepping on land as women. That's when a curious fisherman steals one of the selkie's seal skins and hides it from her, forcing her to stay with him for seven years. He promises he'll return her seal skin to her. But he never does. Most often, the woman finds it herself, slips it back on and returns to the sea as a seal.' Aura finishes reading, breathless. When she turns to Esther, her eyes are wide with awe.

Esther looked up at the stars shining over the silver birch, its gentle boughs moving in the night breeze. 'She was always the seal, I was always the swan.'

'What stories did Aura tell the Selkie Tree?' Tom asked.
'Sorry.' He shook his head. 'Don't say. Of course.'
'It's okay.' Esther shrugged. 'Normal teenage shit, I guess. Her conviction was contagious. A few days after she'd told us the silver birch was her Selkie Tree, Mum was coming in from her studio for the night and saw us. Aura had me and Dad down here at the tree, telling our stories to its bark. Aura mentioned things like dickheads at school giving her a hard time. I did the same. I remember the way Dad smiled at Mum when he saw her, as if to say, we can't beat her … Next thing, Mum was hugging the silver birch tree and Aura and Dad were crying. It was intense. But that's my family.'

'And Freya's remodel?'
'Never mentioned again.'

Tom chuckled. 'It makes sense,' he said after a moment.

'What does?' Esther asked.

'The Selkie Tree being able to take your pain. You know, because, to some degree, trees can actually feel each other's pain.'

Esther frowned with scepticism.

'Seriously. If a tree is in danger, it can send a signal through its roots to warn other trees, which pick up the signal and respond. So, if the Selkie Tree's bark was, say, threatened by an insect, it would send a distress signal out to neighbouring trees, which might then begin to give off a chemical to make their own bark repellent. It's not crazy to think that the folklore Aura loved about this silver birch could have some science to it.'

Esther studied Tom's face, lined in shadows and empathy. He'd always done that, taken something Esther shared with him, carefully looked it over because it was important to her and handed it back to her a little shinier than before. He was unbearably good to her. Still. She gave him a playful nudge.

'What was that for?' he asked.

'Nothing,' she said.

They watched the night sky together in silence.

'Your dad's always been so good like that,' Tom said after a while. 'Right?'

Esther looked at him.

'I'm just thinking about Jack sitting here, having a blub, with his arms around his daughter's seal woman tree,' Tom elaborated. 'That's just what he does: brings a bit of softness and magic to everything, just through kindness. I mean, teaching us as ten-year-olds how to find perspective in the stars.' Tom shook his head.

Esther smiled at the memory of Jack in his Space Club t-shirt walking down to the stargazing shack with Esther and Tom trailing behind him as he pointed out areas in the sky where they could expect to see constellations.

'I still use it, you know.'

'What's that?' Esther asked.

'The Space Club signal,' Tom said. 'When things get on top of me, I remember ten thousand galaxies in a grain of sand. No one else I know learned that kind of stuff when they were ten.' He caught Esther's eye. 'So often I've thought to myself that Jack's been the closest thing I had to a dad when I was a kid.' He cleared his throat. 'What made him think to teach us that? About perspective?'

'You were getting bullied at school,' Esther reminded him.

'That's right.' Tom glanced at her. 'And you were jealous because Aura was growing up faster than you. I remember you being so outraged you couldn't speed up time to keep up with her. To be exactly like her.'

They both smiled, but Esther's resolve crumpled fast. She covered her face with her hands.

'Oh, Esther.' Tom reached out to steady her. 'I'm so sorry. Oh mate, I'm sorry. This is so rough. Tonight. I'm struggling with all this; I don't know how you can bear it.'

The synthesiser bass of Bananarama pounded in her chest. 'Cruel Summer'.

She took in his costume, his hair tied back, streaked with talcum powder. Recalled the invitation: *Come as your favourite memory of being with Aura in the 80s, or as your favourite 80s experience.*

She remembered that night when they were nine years old, after their inaugural Space Club meeting, Jack's new weekly initiative to try to distract Esther from the pain of Aura turning twelve and pulling away from her. As Esther's best friend, Tom had been invited to join. Afterwards they'd put Esther's prized *Karate Kid* VHS on, eaten the plate of homemade vegetable gyozas Tom had brought from his mum, and then, somewhere between Tom pretending to be Mr Miyagi and Esther pretending to be Daniel, he'd leaned forward and kissed her. His lips, closed, pressed softly to hers.

It was a few seconds, but it was a first, an experience all her own. Just hers. And his.

'You came as Mr Miyagi,' she said, staring into the tallest branches of the silver birch, remembering him as a boy, his love of Space Club, his gentle nature and earnest face. How her lips had tingled after he'd kissed her. How wet and strange it was. How warm it had made her belly.

Tom said, 'I didn't know Aura that well. I don't have a favourite memory of her. Watching *Karate Kid* with you was my favourite eighties experience.'

Desperation clawed at the back of Esther's throat. For a year she'd savoured feeling unmoored and adrift. It was all coming undone; he was so beautifully familiar.

'I'm so sorry, Tom. For—'

'You've got nothing to apologise for. Or, if you do, then so do I,' he said, resting a hand on her arm. 'We learned the hard way what happens to friendship after shots of black Sambuca.' He smiled. 'God, it could make me dry-retch, just the memory.' A quick colouring in his face. 'The memory of the shots could make me retch, I mean. Not, well, anything else.'

Esther rolled her eyes and shook her head at their shared awkwardness. From the marquee came the opening chords of Paul Kelly's 'To Her Door'.

Warmth spread through her body from where Tom's hand was still resting on her arm. She put her hand on his.

He smiled. 'You okay?' he asked.

'Yep.' She kept her hand on his. Took a step towards him. Ignored the flicker of uncertainty in his face. Touched one of the buttons on his beige shirt. And lunged forward to press her mouth to his.

Tom leaped back. 'Oh, jeez, Esther, no. Sorry, sorry, I'm sorry.' Covered his mouth with his hands.

The glint of something on his hand caught the light. Caught her eye. A wedding ring.

Somewhere in the distance someone howled in anguish.

Hot with humiliation, Esther started to run. Away from Tom, from his calls, through the garden, far from the marquee, her parents, her life.

She ran until she'd outrun the reach of Aura's playlist. Until she got to the old stargazing shack by the sea where all she could hear was the blood rush in her ears, the wind in the blue gums and the waves. But the howling had followed her.

It took a few beats for Esther to realise her face was wet. The howls were her own.

6

Sunlight rippled across her face, drawing her through shallow sleep into the morning. She opened her eyes, unsure of where she was, felt the sickening feeling she'd forgotten something. Looked around. Her childhood bedroom. Her bed. Flashes of the night before: Nin had brought her home. Tucked her in.

Esther relaxed onto her pillows. Pulled the covers to her chin. Soft shadows of trees outside in the wind swayed through her window, across the wall, violet and gold. For the last year mornings had been the same, a few seconds of forgetting before remembering. Aura was gone. That morning, also, a barrage of shrieking tyres and exploding glass, the metallic smell of blood and the rigid weight of a dead swan in her arms. Aura's photo smiling in mirror ball light. Her mother, singing, radiant in grief, and her father, offering galaxies to her between the pinch of his fingers. The sour aftertaste of vomit. Tom. The look on his face when he rejected her. Esther groaned. Crossed her arms over her ears and eyes until everything was muted and dark.

After she'd run from Tom, away from Aura's memorial to the shelter of the shack, Esther had sat on the small veranda, searching the night sky in vain. It wasn't the right time of year; the Cygnus constellation was under the horizon. Aura sitting beside her, nudging Esther's shoulder with her own. *Dad used to tell me that, before you were born, he'd bring me here … Said he pointed up at Cygnus and told me my little sister was coming from the brightest star in the swan's spine, down her wings, into my arms on Earth. When they brought you home from hospital, I apparently cried and demanded you be sent back; story goes I'd expected my little sister to be a starry baby swan, not an oddly shaped, pinch-faced little screamer.*

In the early hours Nin had shown up at the shack, Tina Turner wig in hand and face lined with worry. Esther had clung to her. Of course, she'd known where Esther would flee to – the shack was where she'd always sought solace when she was overwhelmed. The last day Aura was seen alive she'd been near the shack, calling to the sea. *Eala, Eala.* Calling for Esther. Nin had stayed with Esther and watched the stars, until she was ready to leave.

She rolled over in bed, trying to roll away from memories but dived further into them. Aura's face hiding behind a Princess She-Ra mask, only her eyes visible, twinkling with mischief and mischief. *Sisters of Seal and Swan Skins! Séala and Eala! Raise your swords and your voices!* Her shrieks echoing off the granite boulders as she runs from the shack down to the sand, through vines and shells. Esther running to catch up, roaring behind her big sister, both girls brandishing their gold plastic She-Ra swords in the air.

Esther sat up and kicked her legs free of the sheets. Slid an idle foot under her bed, toeing the soft edge of the blanket holding the dead black swan. Her heart pounded fast.

'Are you okay?' she whispered.

Beyond her closed door, a ribbon of Nin's laughter floated down the hallway. Esther shook herself into her senses. Left her bedroom and went to the kitchen.

Sizzling frying pans cooled on the stove. The lingering smell of fried eggs, toast and coffee made hunger growl through her body.

'Ya, Starry,' Nin said around her last mouthful of yolky toast.

'Ya, Starry. Nina nayri?' Queenie sat by Nin, nursing a cup of tea. Raised her eyebrows in question of Esther's wellbeing.

'Morning,' Esther answered them. 'I'm good,' she replied to Queenie before turning to Nin. 'Thanks for bringing me—' She stopped when she noticed Nin smile at something over Esther's shoulder. Goosebumps shivered across her neck; she sensed someone behind her.

'Is the flux capacitor playing tricks on me?' Her father's voice. Esther turned to see Jack, his arms outstretched. 'Or is this our girl, come home?'

Esther stepped into his hug. 'Hi, Dad.' She softened her body into the reliability of his worn flannel shirt and the smell of the same sandalwood soap on his skin. The hard edge of his collarbone was unyielding against her cheek; there was so little of him for her to bury herself in. Hidden in costume the night before, she hadn't realised how much of a physical toll the last year had taken on him. 'Where's—'

'We're going to head off,' Queenie intercepted. 'Let you two catch up.' Nin took her cue and started gathering their overnight bags and the small tower of Queenie's serving platters.

'Thank you so much for last night and for … everything, Queenie. We're so grateful,' Jack said.

'You're welcome, Jack. Wulika.'

'Bye, Queenie.'

'I'll walk you both out,' Esther offered. Nin started to protest but stopped as she caught the look on Esther's face.

'What's up?' Nin asked when she and Esther were alone by the front door.

Esther fidgeted with the hem of her shirt. All her words came out at once. 'I have to go. I can't stay here, Nin. Have you seen Mum this morning? What, she can't pull herself away from the studio long enough to have breakfast with us? With me? I haven't had a conversation with her since I got back. And Dad. His sadness. He's so thin. Fuck, he's so thin.'

'Breathe.' Nin braced her by the arms. 'I'm guessing you haven't exactly made an effort either, to go to your mum and talk to her?'

Esther hesitated. 'No.'

'Things take the time they take.' Nin gave Esther an affectionate squeeze. 'This isn't just about you. You're not the only one this is hard for. Right?'

'Right.'

'Okay. First things first,' Nin said, 'I'll get your ute sorted today. I've still got your keys. I'll ring Nifty's and get it booked in and I'll let you know how long it's going to take.'

Esther's shoulders sagged in relief. 'You're wonderful. Thank you. For last night, and for this, and for looking out for me, Nincompoop.' Aura's old nickname for her best friend rolled off her tongue. 'Sorry,' she mumbled. 'Old habit.'

Nin clenched her jaw. 'No one's called me that in a while.' She breathed deeply. Took a moment. 'I know this: when we lose people we love, they go back to our ancestors, back to the stars. All that love doesn't just vanish. It's absorbed by country and sun and sky, by everything, and it lives on. I know this,' Nin said. 'But it still hurts, every single day that she's not here with us.'

Esther's eyes welled. 'It feels good to talk about it. Missing her.'

'Listen,' Nin said, after a moment. 'Mum's on call today, but we need to put ourselves back together a bit after last night, so we're going out later to collect shells. If it all gets too much here, take a break and come with us, like old times?'

Esther sitting next to Aura, two teenagers on the white sand. At their backs, towering blue gums and coastal heath bushes. The sea rolls out in front of them like a jeweller's velvet mat. In gentle breeze and warm sun they sit, holding shell jars, minding flasks of tea and packets of biscuits, all the while watching the women on the shore. Nin, Queenie and others in their family stand in calf-deep saltwater, bent at the waist, trousers rolled up, sweeping their hands through fronds of golden bull kelp. Every now and then pausing to pluck an inconspicuous brown shell off a frond and drop it into a clear, small jar. Later the shells will be taken home, cleaned out and, by an ancient practice unknown to Esther and Aura, become piles of iridescent gems on Queenie's shell-stringing table. Glowing in captivating purples, blues, greens, pinks, silver and gold, the colours of an Aurora sky. As if the shells were lit from within.

'I'd love that,' Esther said. 'I'll see what happens here, if Mum can separate herself from her tattoo gun. Text me later?' She opened the front door.

'Will do.' Nin started to walk out to her car where Queenie was waiting. 'Starry?'

'Yeah?'

'Tell him. Now. About kylarunya. Get it off your mind. Start yarning.'

Esther waved Nin and Queenie off. Shut the front door and leaned against it.

'Starry?' Jack called. 'Cuppa?'

Esther walked back into the kitchen, nerves shooting through her stomach. She didn't know how to be at home, alone with her dad. How to pick up from where she'd stormed out over a year ago on that still, silent afternoon. How was she meant to begin, to unpick the knot of all the things they'd never said to each other since Aura came home from Denmark, and then disappeared. Let alone how to broach the subject of her accident with the swan the day before.

'Hey. You're shaking, love. Come, sit down.' Her dad drew a chair at the kitchen table.

Esther sat. Jack went to the kettle and poured hot water over a tea bag.

'So. Where's Mum?' Esther asked.

Jack kept his back to her.

'Gone for a dive,' he said. 'Went early this morning.'

Of course. If Freya wasn't in her tattoo studio, she was in the sea. It was an obsession she and Aura had shared, craving the depths off the coast, through the kelp curtain, where underwater forests grew tall, and bobs of seals swam.

When Jack turned, he couldn't meet Esther's eye. He set her cup of lemon and ginger tea down and sat beside her. 'Didn't see you much last night. All I could get out of Nin was that you two ended up at the shack. Are you okay?'

Esther took sips of her hot tea, craving its warmth. 'Got anything stronger?' she joked.

'Sure,' Jack replied and stood.

'Dad, I was kidding.'

'I've got whiskey, sloe gin, some mulled wine. What's it gonna take to get you to tell me how you are?' This time he met her gaze.

'Whiskey, please.'

He took a bottle off the shelf over the stove and eased the cork from the top. Poured a nip into her steaming cup. Sat back down and looked at Esther expectantly.

She sighed. 'It was just rough, coming home, Dad.'

'I get that, love.'

'No, Dad. I mean. Fuck.' Esther put her head in her hands.

'Swearing, Starry.'

'I killed a swan.' Esther sat back and lifted the hair from her brow to show Jack her forehead.

'You what?'

'Queenie checked me out last night before the party, I'm fine. It happened down at the grove near the boulders. I drove into it. The swan. Or it fell onto my ute. I don't fucking know, Dad ...'

'Swearing, Starry,' her father murmured, holding her face as he looked over her bruised forehead. 'Tell me what happened?'

Esther recounted her homecoming.

'And the swan?' Jack asked.

'It's under my bed.'

'Pardon?'

'I have to bury her,' Esther said quietly.

'I can do that for you.'

'I have to bury her, Dad.' Esther's voice broke.

Jack nodded, processing. 'Okay. You'll need a shovel. I'll get you one from the shed.'

'Thanks.' Esther took another sip.

'Your ute?'

'Windscreen's smashed, bonnet's banged up. Nin's taking care of it for me.' The whiskey had started softening her jaw and the tension around her eyes.

'You'll be staying home for a bit, then.'

'A few days, yeah.'

The mantel clock that sat on the top shelf in their kitchen, a gift from a Danish relative, chimed a quarter past the hour. It stuttered on the last chime, as it had always done.

'How's work going?' Jack asked. 'Running Calliope must be full on.'

'Yeah, great. Busy.'

'I'm proud of you, doing so well in a management role. It takes courage to dedicate yourself like that in the kind of year we've had. Can't have been easy.'

Esther's face went hot. 'Well.' She forced herself to smile. 'I've got a great team. Plus, it's only Calliope. It's not like I'm running The Ritz.'

'No, just a protected historical settlement, staff and tourists.'

'You're biased, Dad.'

'Happily.' Jack winked at her. Hesitated. Took a breath. 'You haven't said anything about last night.'

Esther swilled the lukewarm tea in her cup.

'I'm so glad you came. I'm sorry it's been so hard.' Jack put an arm around her.

Recalling the emotion on her father's face the night before, as he spotted her in the crowd, caused a pain in Esther's chest. She rested her head on Jack's shoulder.

'Do you want to share how you're feeling today?' he asked into her hair.

Esther went rigid. Willed herself not to react to Jack's therapy voice. Remembered what she'd yelled once before. *I'm not one of your clients.*

The clock ticked. Her silence stretched out.

'Erin was looking for you last night; did you see her?' He changed subject in a bright voice.

Esther shook her head. 'I want to, though.'

'You'll have time to catch up with her while your ute's in the shop.'

She knocked back her laced tea. 'Listen, Dad,' Esther said, standing, 'I'd better get going, I'm shell collecting this arv with Nin and Queenie.'

'Starry.' Jack reached for her. 'I want to say …' Desperation pinched his face. 'The accident, the swan. It isn't a sign of anything, you know that, right? This is not about you being there to save her. You know that. Right?'

Esther rubbed a hand over her chest. 'Don't think you've got me all figured out,' she said with a sniff.

'Afraid, I do, love.' Jack smiled. 'Sorry about that.'

Esther wiped her nose on the back of her hand. Her head ached, weary and overwhelmed. She again made to leave.

'Hey.' Jack let out a long breath. 'Can we start again? I'm just so happy to see you. We don't have to talk about anything you don't want to. We do have to eat though. Right? I can make eggs? With that hot sauce you love?'

All the pent-up resistance Esther had been carrying rushed from her body in a sigh. She sat, exhausted. 'Eggs would be really fucking great, Dad.'

'Swearing, Starry.'

The coastal road was dappled in warm light. Esther drove southwards, through forests of gums and drooping she-oaks. The sea air was thick and heady with a mixture of kelp, salt and tea-tree oil from the surrounding shrubbery. When she spotted Nin's car alongside a few others, Esther pulled over. After they'd eaten eggs on toast, Jack had offered Esther the use of his 1968 Neptune blue Kombi, the one and only vehicle he'd ever had. It had taken her a moment to respond; as a teen she'd been ready to trade vital organs to borrow Jack's Kombi, on nights Aura had taken their ute even though it wasn't her turn. Back then, nothing had made Jack yield. *I'd give you girls the stars. Just not my Kombi.* And yet. *See you this arv,* Jack had said, freely handing over his keys, grinning as he heard his own words. *See you this arv,* he'd repeated. *I'll make cheesy potato pie for dinner,* he called as she'd driven away. Esther's favourite. She'd looked back once before she turned out of the driveway. Couldn't be sure if she'd seen or imagined a shadow in the window of her mother's tattoo studio, behind the house.

She gathered her bag and hot flask, swung out of the Kombi and closed the door, relishing its satisfying clunk. Made her way beneath an understorey of pines and silver banksia onto the path that wound through broom heath and wattle into sagg grass. She brushed her fingers along the tops of white iris, thinking of the woven baskets Queenie had made Freya over the years. Each new basket adorning the mantel, or a windowsill, desk edge or bookshelf, after every visit Queenie made to Freya's tattoo studio. A constant non-verbal exchange of stories between them.

Emerging from the canopy, Esther held a hand over her brow to shield her eyes from the high sun. The women were at the foreshore, heads bent and bodies curved. Hands sweeping across the sand to gather shells. Some went into their jars, others were discarded. The movement, a ritual, was repeated, again and again.

Esther kicked her thongs off to walk barefoot onto the white sand. Curled her toes in the softness.

'Ya, Starry,' Nin called to Esther, waving from the shore. Queenie looked up, held a hand over squinting eyes and waved.

Esther waved back, raising her flask of hot tea. 'I brought Iced VoVos,' she sang out, taking a seat on the sand, a distance from where the women were collecting.

'Smoko,' Nin shrieked over her shoulder to the others and broke into a run.

7

After cheese and salad sandwiches, Esther uncapped the flask and poured tea into the six upheld cups of Queenie, Nin and family sitting together in camp chairs. She opened the packets of biscuits and passed the Iced VoVos around.

'Hi, Coral,' Esther greeted one of Nin's younger cousins as she filled her teacup.

'Ya, Starry,' Coral replied, with a shy smile.

'How's your apprenticeship going?' Esther asked lightly, her eyes darting to the gum-leaf tattoo on Coral's lower leg. Freya's work.

'Good,' Coral said, her cheeks colouring. 'Your mum's amazing, hey.'

Esther tried to smile in a way that was neutral enough to mask her interior collision of pride and envy.

'Ya pulingina, young Starry,' Romy, an Elder in Nin's family, interrupted. 'Welcome.' She bit into an Iced VoVo and licked desiccated coconut from her fingers, wiggling her eyebrows with joy. 'Good to see you.'

'And you, Aunty Ro,' Esther answered, grateful for the diversion.

'You going in?' Aunty Ro asked, looking Esther up and down.

Esther held herself steady. 'I don't swim in the sea anymore, Aunty Ro. Remember?' After Aura was gone, Esther had sworn she wouldn't step into the ocean again.

Aunty Ro regarded Esther, her face impassive. 'You've been gone a long time,' she stated.

'I have.' Esther poured herself a cuppa. 'How's it going today?' she asked, eager to change the subject. Though she'd been coming since she was a girl to sit with Nin and Queenie while they were shell gathering, Esther didn't join them. Queenie had taught her young: kanalaritja, the practice and art of shell stringing, was a story that wasn't hers to know.

'Good. Worrying, but. Never as many marina anymore as when I was younger. When Mum was gathering. Or her mum. Or Pilunimina.' Aunty Ro tutted. 'Ocean's too hot. That rikawa's dying.'

Esther dug her hands into the sand and made fists, desperate for something to hold on to as she took in Aunty Ro's words. Fewer rainbow kelp shells. Dying kelp.

'You remember Pilunimina's story?' Aunty Ro asked her.

'Yes, Aunty Ro.'

Esther walking behind Nin and Aura down a quiet hallway into the art gallery, all three jittering with excitement as they follow Freya, Queenie, Aunty Ro and Queenie's cousin Zoe, who is in gallery uniform. Zoe leads them all into a cool, dry room with various drawers, shelves and lamps. Esther admires the king marina on a black cord Zoe is wearing around her neck. Zoe gives them pairs of soft gloves to put on and takes them to a cabinet of drawers. Queenie and Aunty Ro hold hands. Zoe slowly opens a drawer. Everyone seems to stop breathing as the oldest shell necklace in the gallery's kanalaritja collection is revealed: Pilunimina's long strand of dazzling, iridescent blue marina shells.

On the drive down from Salt Bay, Aunty Ro shared stories about Pakana women. Like Pilunimina, who was abducted as a girl by European sealers, and who survived over twenty brutal years living with various sealing men on different islands in eastern Bass Strait. Who in later life rebelled against the church forced upon her and, despite punishment for doing so, continued her cultural practices and rituals, like kanalaritja.

Esther leans towards Pilunimina's necklace, strung in a pattern using small to large shells. Zoe tells them that Pilunimina made the necklace in 1854, when she was in her fifties, living in destitute conditions. Esther tries to understand how such glowing, powerful, everlasting beauty could have been made during a time of such suffering. Yet there it is, iridescent in the lamplight, the handmade shell necklace a hundred and fifty years old, holding women's knowledge, shimmering all the colours of the sea, the stars and the moon.

Queenie kneels by Nin, Aura and Esther. 'Kanalaritja is our unbroken story that connects our past, present and future,' she says.

Esther opened her hands to grab more sand. Looked at Nin and her family. After everything their people had survived during colonisation, and continued to endure, now their sea country was too hot. The kelp forests were dying. No kelp, no shells. Her stomach tensed.

'It's going to be a very special exhibition that we're gathering these shells for,' Queenie announced, her voice strong. 'Has Nin told you, Starry? She's working with Zoe to organise the whole thing.' Her face shone with pride. 'There are plans for a national tour of our necklaces. Nin and Zoe are in the final stages of consultation between the gallery and the community, and our Ninny is going to include some of her own designs. She's got some fancy clout now, after her own first collection of kanalaritja and a few of her sculptures sold out on exhibition at that gallery in Salamanca Markets.' Queenie winked.

Awed, Esther turned to Nin. 'You had an exhibition? When?'

'About six months ago.' Nin beamed. 'I'm working on a sculpture for the national tour now.'

'Nin,' Esther gasped. 'You're a working artist? I had no idea.'

'I emailed you to let you know. Sent an invite to my exhibition,' Nin said, her tone clipped.

'Well, ladies.' Queenie stood abruptly from her camp chair. Esther caught a glimpse of one of Freya's tattoos peeking out from under her shirtsleeve. Blue-grey tail fins. 'Shall we?'

Nin hung back with Esther. They watched the women resume on shore.

'I'm sorry, Nin,' Esther said, wringing a sandwich wrapper between her hands. 'I'm sorry I wasn't at your exhibition. I stopped checking emails, social media, all that stuff after she was gone. I figured if anything was ever important enough someone would ring me at work.'

'Pretty awful way to be, locking out everyone who loves you.'

'I've been so shit,' Esther said. Let her words breathe. Couldn't look at Nin. She watched Nin's family in the sea. 'It's still the most special thing to me,' she said. 'To be able to be here, thank you. Thank you for inviting me again.'

'You're always welcome, Starry,' Nin sighed. 'No matter how shit you are.'

They watched the women together, left hands lifting fronds of kelp, right hands sweeping over them, searching. 'Being with them, here, is my medicine,' Nin said. 'The greatest relationships I have in my life are with these women.'

'I can only imagine,' Esther replied, watching Nin's family, thinking of their stories she considered herself lucky to have grown up learning. 'So how are things with this exhibition going? A national tour? That's incredible.'

'Good, actually. We're starting to get some private donations. That fundraiser your mum did at that Melbourne tattoo convention she headlined really helped too, you know?'

'Sure.' Esther took a deep breath. She didn't know. She didn't know anything about what life had entailed for her parents over the last year.

'It was amazing, Starry. Right? I mean all her slots for the whole convention being booked out in twenty minutes, and still women queued asking for cancellations, or to go on her books here. Freya donated money from every tattoo she did to support our funding. It really helped to spread the word.'

Esther forced a smile. 'She's pretty unstoppable when she puts her heart into something.'

'Sure is.'

'Queenie said you're including your own necklaces?' Esther added.

In a rare show of shyness, Nin blushed. 'I'm working on a little collection of my own and helping a few women from the community who are just starting out and learning.'

Esther gaped at Nin. Shook her head in wonder. 'Remember when you and Aura let me go with you on our road trip to Wupatipa's grave—'

'Let you?' Nin kicked a playful spray of sand at Esther. 'You hid in the tray of the ute. Took ten years off my life.'

'As I was saying,' Esther said smiling, 'you let me go with you.'

Nin scoffed.

'Remember when we were standing there, at Wupatipa's grave?' Esther asked, her expression turning serious. 'You said then you'd make this happen one day.'

It had been springtime. Nin was seventeen years old and had just got her licence. In the lead-up to her driving test, all she'd talked to Aura about, meaning all Esther had overheard when she was eavesdropping through their bedroom wall, was Nin and Aura's first road trip. Down the east coast, to the hill where Wupatipa's empty grave overlooked the sea. To see Wupatipa's snowdrops in bloom. *Let's take her some shells*, Esther heard Nin tell Aura, muffled through the wall.

Thinking of Wupatipa's story, as she'd learned it from Aunty Ro, Esther had decided then and there that Nin and Aura would not be going on their road trip to see Wupatipa alone. Wupatipa, who had been stolen as a teenager to become a European sealer's slave. Wupatipa, the expert swimmer, as Pakana women and girls were, who dived into the icy sea to rescue the very man who had enslaved her. Wupatipa, who no one came to rescue when she needed saving. She'd escaped enslavement, along with other abducted Pakana women, but a group was sent to find them. A note in the newspaper of the day speculated on the cause of her death. *Possibly died of injuries sustained in the capture, which no doubt was not done very tenderly.* After Wupatipa's murder, a gravestone was put in place to mark where she'd been buried at the time of her death. The inscription read, *This stone is erected by a few of her white friends.* It was still the only known gravestone erected to a Pakana person during the nineteenth century. Decades after her death and burial, in the late eighteen hundreds, Wupatipa's grave was exhumed by the Tasmanian Museum, for 'scientific investigations'. Her remains were put into a box, labelled *Native Currants* and sent to Nipaluna, Hobart. No one was consulted on the exhumation. It took almost another century before Wupatipa's remains were returned to the Pakana community. Her empty European-style grave remained standing. Snowdrops were said to bloom around the headstone every spring.

Do you really think snowdrops will be blooming for her? Aura had asked Nin. Listening through the wall, Esther made her plan.

The day Nin and Aura left, she hid in the tray of the ute and for the whole drive lay watching the sky change. Until the ute finally came to a stop, and Esther gave Nin and Aura a screaming fright when she popped her head up through the back window.

Later, Aura and Esther hung back to let Nin go first to Wupatipa's empty grave. Around which bloomed clusters of snowdrops. After a while the sisters joined Nin and sat at what had once been Wupatipa's resting place. Nin scattered dove shells around her headstone. Laid a few thick fronds of dried kelp at its base. She'd not said very much since they'd arrived. As the shadows grew long, she stood. Fists clenched by her side. *I'm going to make sure people know about luna rrala. Our women, our strength. Our beauty. Our culture.*

Esther drifted over memories, coming to refocus on the women at the shore. 'Not many people say they're going to do something and stay committed like you have. You blow me away, Nin.'

Nin batted away the praise, but looked at Esther in gratitude. She turned to the beach where Queenie and her family were collecting shells. 'I have powerful inspiration,' she said.

Esther followed her gaze. Aura sitting on the beach, watching Queenie at the shore, teaching others which shells to look for, which to discard. Turning to look at Esther, smiling. *It's like a secret language*, Aura saying, her voice full of quiet awe.

'She'd be so proud of you.' Esther's voice cracked. 'Aura would just be out of her skin with excitement for you.'

Nin wrapped her arms around herself. Nodded.

'She was so lucky to have you, Nin. I've never had a friend like she had you.' Esther picked up a handful of sand and let it trickle from one hand to the other. 'I just had Aura.'

'Hey.' Nin nudged her, wiping her eyes.

'You know what I mean. I had you too, of course. And Dad, Aunt Erin and sometimes Mum. I guess Tom when I was a kid. Ugh.' Esther cringed, thinking of leaning into him the night before. 'I never had a best friend the way you and Aura had each other.'

'What about on the west coast, though? Aren't you the mayor of a whole town or something? You haven't found your women there?'

Esther snorted. 'Hardly. It's an old copper mining settlement on the river, converted into tourist cottages. It's not exactly a mecca of the sisterhood.'

'Yeah,' Nin said. 'I get it. No one wants to be friends with the boss.'

Esther was saved by Nin's phone ringing. She answered. Listened for a moment. Gave Esther the thumbs-up. Ended the call.

'Your ute's not a write-off,' she announced, triumphant. 'Needs a new windscreen and panel beating, mostly. They're closed tomorrow but Nifty said to ring him Monday and he'll run through his quote.'

Esther's pulse quickened. She'd overdrawn her account on her last petrol stop the day before.

'Your ute's going to be okay,' Nin reassured her, misreading the worry on Esther's face. 'You're okay.'

She felt anything but. 'You doing anything later?'

'Meeting with the gallery mob. You?'

Her answer came as clear as a tolling bell. 'I have to bury her.'

Nin looked at her for a long moment. 'Kylarunya,' she said. Esther nodded.

'You sure you're okay doing that alone?' Nin asked.

Esther watched bodies of golden kelp curl in the shallow, rhythmic waves on shore. Nodded again.

'Any idea where?' Nin asked.

Esther looked sidelong at Nin.

'Ah,' said Nin, reading Esther's face. 'You're going to bury her there.'

Esther scanned the softening sky. 'Before the first star comes out,' she said, beginning to gather her things.

The light was purpling when Esther got back to the Shell House. In the dusky garden the white marquee used for Aura's memorial was still standing, a ghost ship.

Esther idled the Kombi along the driveway to a stop. She sat, staring in the beam of the headlights at the shovel with a folded piece of paper taped to its handle, propped against the side of the house. Beside it on the dirt lay a posy of pink paper daisies.

Esther got out and read her dad's note in the fading light.

Starry,
> *We didn't talk about where you're going to bury her.*
> *Wrap her in something biodegradable like cotton or wool, okay?*
> *With her grave, the most important thing is to dig deep. At*
> *least three feet down. And keep it wide so it doesn't collapse in*
> *on itself. You must make the grave big enough to easily fit the*
> *swan. Lay her body in the hole and cover it with dirt, tamping*
> *it down periodically. When you fill the hole in, mound the dirt*
> *up just a little so it will level out when the dirt settles.*
>   *Starry, this might be very hard to do. I'm going out for*
> *a quick run now but will be back and making dinner soon.*
> *Come and get me anytime. You don't have to do this alone.*
>   *Love, Dad.*
>   *PS I picked these daisies earlier. Thought you might like*
> *them for her burial.*

She read the note twice, folded it until it was a tiny chunk of
paper, and put it into her pocket. A year on and Jack was still
running at night. Keeping up the pretence it was a quick dash
for exercise, and not the same ritual scouring he did of the
shoreline that he'd taken up from the day Aura had disappeared.

'Dad?' Esther called as she went into the house.

No answer.

'Mum?' she tried.

Just the clock in the kitchen, stuttering as it chimed the
hour, answered her.

Esther walked down the hallway, not looking at Aura's
closed bedroom door. Not allowing her mind to open it. She
rifled through the linen closet and grabbed the first woollen
blanket. Caught herself thinking the swan needed wool, not
cotton; she wanted her to be warm.

In her room she gathered a pair of gloves and a headlamp
and put them, along with her woollen blanket, into a bag. Took
a slow breath to steady her heart-rate.

After another moment, Esther reached under her bed.

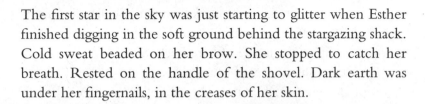

The first star in the sky was just starting to glitter when Esther finished digging in the soft ground behind the stargazing shack. Cold sweat beaded on her brow. She stopped to catch her breath. Rested on the handle of the shovel. Dark earth was under her fingernails, in the creases of her skin.

Aura facing the sun, her face stricken, her long hair dancing in the wind. Nin, solemn beside her, reaching for her hand. Esther standing back, at a distance.

'What is it, girls?' Freya calls, walking up the sand behind them. They're on a beach picnic together; Freya has taken a rare day off from her tattoo studio. Aura was the one to spot the tiny seal pup, on its side, tangled in kelp. Unmoving.

'Is she dead, Mum?' Aura asks in a shaky voice as Freya approaches. The look on Freya's face makes Esther cold all over. Their mother drops to her knees, cradles the pup in her arms. 'Mum,' Aura says in a small voice. Esther runs and hides her face in Nin's arms.

Later, behind the shack, Freya digs a grave and gathers the paper daisies she's asked the girls to pick. Grips them in her fist until her knuckles turn pale, then throws them into the pup's grave. Takes up her shovel and begins filling in the dirt.

'My love will not leave you,' Freya whispers. 'My love will not leave you.' Her voice breaks into a sob.

Esther stands very still, watching the dirt fall and cover the soft pink bundle in the ground; Freya wrapped the seal in one of their baby blankets from the back of the linen closet. It gives Esther a strange feeling to think of it being under all that cold dirt.

Once the pup is buried, Esther goes to Freya and tries to snuggle into the curve of her body. Her mother looks at her with eyes like empty rooms.

~

Esther searched through her bag for her headlamp. Tried to adjust it in a way that didn't sit painfully on her swollen forehead. Switched it on. The swan lay wrapped in Nin's blanket at her feet. Esther bit on the inside of her cheek. Stalled.

'Fuck this,' she muttered to no one.

After a few quick, short breaths for courage, Esther unwrapped the black swan. Her dead eye. Her parted red beak. The shattering explosion of windscreen glass.

She trembled as she laid out her woollen blanket and, being careful to support the swan's head, hefted her across from one blanket to the other. Rewrapped the swan and lifted her, wrapping two corners of the woollen blanket around each hand for leverage to lower her into the grave.

Esther dropped the pink paper daisies into the darkness of the earth. They seemed to hold the light and glow. Esther stared down, into the ground. 'My love will not leave you,' she whispered.

As she picked up the blanket, something fell from within its folds. Two small black feathers. And another. Another. Esther unwrapped the blanket. Four more feathers. She gathered all eight. Tucked them carefully into her back pocket.

Esther breathed hard, shovelling dirt into the grave. She and Aura, they'd been children of sea and sky from the moment they each took their first breaths in the world: Aura born at the same time as seal pups in the summer, and Esther with the hatching cygnets in winter. Freya's stories and their names had told them this. Aurora Sæl. Esther Svane.

As she shovelled, her shoulders ached. Forming blisters stung her hands. She tried not to think about swan bones, seal bones and a baby blanket three feet under the ground where Aura was last seen alive. About the feathers in her pocket burning a hole through her conscience. Tried to bury her worries about her empty bank account, the mess she'd left behind in Calliope.

And the ever-creeping of fear of what else might come undone because she'd made the mistake of coming home. Esther kept shovelling.

My swan sister. Aura smiling at her in the low light of an overcast day, sitting on the white sand together, their backs against one of the seven granite boulders. Watching black swans fly over the sea, the white undersides of their wings flashing quicksilver.

The second skin: Reckoning

He will give you flowers to forget.
You plant seeds, to remember.

8

She drove back under a marbled black sky powdered with stars. Ahead, the Shell House shone. Its own island, its own star.

Esther turned into the driveway. Someone, she presumed Jack, had left the veranda light on for her. It wasn't until she got out of the Kombi that Esther saw a candle burning in the kitchen window. To have one lit in any space she occupied night or day, was Freya's tribute to their dead. *The ancestors don't sleep.* Esther's heart fluttered at the sight of the small, single flame. She ambled along the path through the garden and up to the veranda. Her muscles had cooled from the digging; everything was stiff. As she was about to reach the front door, it flung open.

'Mum.' Surprise closed Esther's throat.

Freya stood in the doorway, eyes brimming, silver-blonde fishtail braid hanging long over her shoulder.

'Min guldklump,' she whispered her nickname for Esther from childhood. *My gold nugget.* Opened her arms wide.

Caught off guard, Esther couldn't stop herself from falling into her mother's arms, closing her eyes and breathing Freya in – saltwater, sage shampoo and the faint lemony fragrance of tattoo wash. For a second or two, Esther thought her mother was shaking. They parted before she could tell.

Freya stood rigid, her face tense. 'I looked for you at the memorial last night.'

'Oh?' Esther clenched her jaw.

Freya seemed about to speak, then changed her mind. She took a breath. 'Well. It's good you're here.'

Esther nodded, looking anywhere but into her mother's eyes.

'Come in,' Freya said, dusting her hands of unsaid words. 'I made dinner.'

The dining table was set for three, with four candles lit in the centre. Jack sat at the table in a fresh flannel shirt, his hair still damp from a shower.

'Hi Dad,' Esther greeted Jack, a hint of caution in her voice. 'What happened to cheesy potato pie?' she asked under her breath.

Jack winked at her but said nothing. Pulled out the chair beside him. Esther sat.

'Everything's warm in the oven,' Freya said.

'Do you want help?' Esther asked.

'No,' Freya said sharply. 'No, thank you.' She softened. 'Won't be a minute.' Freya went into the kitchen.

Esther waited until her mother was out of earshot. 'What's going on?' she hissed at Jack. 'I don't remember the last time Mum cooked anything.'

'Just go with it.' Jack gave her an encouraging smile. 'How'd you go with the swan? You okay?' He placed his hand on Esther's.

She shrugged in response.

'Here we are,' Freya said, as she ferried dishes from the kitchen to the table. A steaming bowl of potatoes with parsley cream sauce. Pots of pickles and marinated beetroot. A platter of shallow-fried salt-and-pepper tofu patties. A loaf of rugbrød and a dish of butter.

Jack patted Esther's hand. Her eyes widened as she looked over the dining table.

Freya sat, poured them each a glass of red wine and raised hers. 'Skål,' she said, her face slightly flushed.

Jack joined her toast, his free arm around Freya's chair.

'Skál.' Esther raised her glass, trying to keep her growing sense of dread from showing in her face.

Freya took a long sip of wine. Offered Esther the potatoes. 'Jack, would you slice us some rugbrød, please?'

Esther spooned a few potatoes onto her plate. A tofu patty. Esther couldn't remember the last time Freya had cooked vegetarian for her. *Just go with it.* 'This looks great, Mum.' It wasn't a lie.

Freya paused, the pain in her eyes momentarily lightened by cautious relief. 'I'm glad. I wanted this to be special.'

They held brief eye contact. Esther forced a polite smile. The three of them started eating.

'So, Starry,' Jack said after a few moments. 'Tell us how things are going in Calliope?'

The bite of buttered rugbrød Esther had taken turned to ashes in her mouth. She swallowed it down with wine, finished her glass, and refilled it. 'It's fine,' she said, her tone clipped. 'It's good. Going good.' Glugged more wine. 'I love it.' She couldn't resist throwing a defiant look in her mother's direction, which Freya caught.

'You love it,' Freya repeated. Jack shot Freya a look of warning, which went ignored. 'So, you're finding it fulfilling then, going from a science degree to working in hospitality?' Freya's tone was wry.

Stung, Esther glared at her mother.

'Now Starry, she didn't mean—' Jack started, stopped. 'Frey,' he said, turning from Esther to his wife.

'What? I'm not being provocative, Jack. Esther said she loves her job. I'm just trying to show an interest, learn more about the rewards of hotel management. I'm just trying to understand.' Freya sipped her wine.

'Understand what?' Esther retorted. 'That I could be happy, living my own life? Away from you? From here?' Blood pounded in her ears.

'Enough,' Jack said quietly. 'Can we just enjoy our meal, please?' He looked from Esther to Freya. 'Can we just enjoy this, our first dinner together again after so long?'

Esther had to force herself to swallow her words. *I would never have left if either of you had shown up when you said you would, had chosen our family over your own grief.*

They resumed eating. Avoided each other's eye contact. A request for salt or more bread occasionally broke the strained silence.

Towards the end of the meal, Jack cleared his throat. 'This rugbrød is delicious, Frey.'

Freya gave him a tight smile. Jack turned to Esther.

'Remember the first time you tried baking it, Starry, for one of our Space Club meetings with Tom? It came out all misshapen and soggy in the middle.' Her father's smile couldn't mask the desperate plea in his eyes when he looked at Esther. A classic therapist move: anchor the present to a happy memory in the past.

'It turned out soggy,' Esther said slowly, swallowing another mouthful of wine, 'because Mum promised me that we'd spend an afternoon together so she could teach me how to bake it.' She levelled her gaze at Freya. 'But Mum forgot and went diving with Aura instead. So, I made rugbrød alone.'

Freya threw down her napkin. Scraped her chair back, gathered some of the dishes and began clearing the table.

Esther dug her fingertips into the soft skin on the underside of her wrist. Kept her eyes down.

The presence of Aura's absence sat quietly at the table, in every passing moment and mouthful. The fourth flickering candle flame.

9

When the table was cleared and Freya had returned from the kitchen, Esther reached for more wine. It was as she emptied the bottle into her glass that she caught the almost imperceptible look her parents exchanged.

'What was that?'

'What was what, love?' Jack asked.

'That look.' Esther made a point of taking a long drink of wine. Put her glass down. 'What was that look that you just gave each other?'

Freya chewed on the inside of her cheek, her eyes lingering on Esther's wine glass.

'Something you want to say, Mum?' Esther asked, her face flaming.

Jack closed his eyes as he took a deep breath. Her father tried to wave the tension from the air. 'Shall we have some dessert? Mum made risalamande, with cherry sauce.' Jack looked at Freya, imploring.

Freya held Jack's eye. 'That's right. Cherry sauce.'

'None for me, I'm done.' Esther revelled in the churlish satisfaction of rejecting her mother's homemade dessert, before descending into self-loathing over such behaviour.

Freya didn't seem to notice; she was looking at Jack, locked in their silent exchange. She broke their eye contact. Turned to Esther. 'There's something we need—'

'Frey, I don't know if it's—' Jack interjected.

'—to tell you, Esther,' Freya finished.

Esther's stomach did a slow, dreadful flip-flop. 'What?'

Freya's eyes were brimming. 'I've found something. Of Aura's.'

Jack pressed his hands to his mouth, as if in prayer, as he watched Freya stand and go to the bookshelf. She clutched a book to her chest, brought it back to the table. Didn't take her eyes off Esther as she sat.

'I was cleaning Aura's room,' Freya started. 'After she was gone …'

Esther winced at the image: her mother tending Aura's things.

'This was on her desk.' Freya's voice held, almost didn't quiver. She pushed the book across the table towards Esther. 'Do you recognise it?'

Caught off guard, Esther stared at Aura's teenage journal. On the cover She-Ra held the Sword of Protection aloft, its bejewelled hilt sparkling, surrounded by wafts of gold stars against a black background. The journal had a gold ribbon page marker. A gold elastic band to hold the covers closed. Aura had won the She-Ra journal in a showbag raffle on a family trip to the Royal Hobart Show. It was the only showbag Esther had wanted, with She-Ra's gold face mask and sword, complete with holographic gem sticker and a She-Ra journal. Esther had saved her pocket money for weeks to buy one. Aura won hers on a fifty-cent ticket in a raffle.

At the dinner table, Esther tried to even her breathing. She studied the edges of Aura's journal where it was worn, on the corners and spine.

'Open it,' Freya urged.

Esther sat forward. She slid the gold elastic from the cover. Eased it open with a finger. Pages of her sister's loopy handwriting stared up at her.

She slammed the book shut, breathing hard. Deep in her bag, hanging from her chair, her mobile phone started ringing.

'Starry,' Jack said.

'Esther,' Freya spoke over him, her face tense, 'it's Aura's journal. Or something like a journal. From when she was a teenager. But it must have been important to her – she took it with her to Denmark.' Freya reached for the book and opened it in front of Esther. Turned slowly through the first few blank pages, to the inscription.

This journal belongs to Aura Wilding. If you're reading this and you're not me, a curse will be upon you for seven years!!!

The points in the exclamation marks were in the shape of small hearts. Esther smarted at the sight, a tiny detail from her sister's teenage world when Aura had gone through a phase of dotting her i's, j's and exclamations with hearts. Naturally, Esther had secretly copied her in her homework, but couldn't ever do the hearts neatly enough to look like anything other than tiny kidney beans.

Freya flicked beyond where Aura's teenage writing stopped. Angled the journal to face Esther again. In black ink, in the centre of a page, a line was written by Aura's adult hand.

The Seven Skins

Esther looked from her sister's handwriting to her parents' faces. Freya motioned for her to turn the page, which she did.

The Binalong Bay Girl sculpture stared up at Esther, smiling from a cut-out photocopy pasted onto the page. Above the photocopy of the sculpture, Aura had written cryptic words.

The first skin: Death

On the opposing page, Aura had written a line.

If you want change, raise your sword, raise your voice.

A shudder went down Esther's spine. 'What is this?' she asked her parents, shrinking from the book.

'We don't know,' Freya said. She turned to a new page. It was set out the same, with a different photocopied image pasted under more enigmatic lines.

The second skin: Reckoning

The image was an illustration, an underwater scene: a naked young man, his face obscured by a frightening swathe of dark hair, laid a wreath of flowers on the head of a demure, fully clothed woman. Silver fish swam around them.

On the opposing page, more lines.

He will give you flowers to forget. You plant seeds, to remember.

Esther had a visceral reaction as she read Aura's words, though she didn't understand their meaning. She flicked forward through the pages. Aura had pasted an image of a sculpture or an illustration with a numbered title on one page and cryptic lines on the other, seven times.

'Do they make any sense to you?' Freya asked, her voice strained.

Esther flicked back and forth. Her head filled with increasing pressure. 'No.' She shut the journal. Pushed it away.

Watching her, Freya rubbed her temples in exasperation. 'This is your sister's journal, how can you just shrug?'

'Easy,' Jack said quietly, reaching for Freya.

Freya tried to collect herself. 'These images and words mattered to Aura. Don't you want to know what they mean?'

'Whatever. I don't get why it's such a big deal. Aura always had a notebook on her.' Indignant, Esther ignored the urge to draw the journal back to her, to touch each loop and scrawl of Aura's handwriting. Feigning ambivalence was easier than admitting the truth: her sister's journal frightened her, taunted her with the painful reminder of how little Esther knew about Aura's life in the end.

'Actually,' Freya said, visibly shaking, 'we think it's a huge deal. Enough to make us ask you' – Freya searched Esther's face, her eyes wild – 'if you'd read through it, and take it with you.'

Esther looked back and forth between her parents. 'Take it with me where?'

Freya glanced at Jack, but he kept his focus on Esther. She folded her hands, took a sharp breath. 'We want you to go to Denmark,' she said.

Esther snorted. 'Yeah, right.'

'We've talked about it a lot this past year, whether we should go to find out more about Aura's life there and what happened to her before she came home. Since I found her journal, going there just feels   ' Freya trailed off.

'What?' Esther asked. 'Meant to be?' she jeered. 'Are you joking?' Esther stared in disbelief at her parents. Through the View-Master she sees Aura facing the sea. Her arms at her sides, her back to the camera. In the depths of Esther's bag, her phone rang again, sending vibrations up her spine. 'Are you joking?' she repeated to her parents. 'You seriously want me to go all the way to the other side of the world because you found a book of Aura's scribbles?'

'Esther,' Freya shouted and stood.

Esther jumped at her mother's outburst.

'Frey,' Jack cautioned.

Freya ignored him. She leaned against the dining table and gripped it with both hands, struggling to keep her composure. 'Esther, you don't know. These things that Aura wrote. They're not just random scribbles.' She jabbed a trembling finger at the journal. '"If you want change, raise your sword, raise your voice." This meant something to Aura. And something else you don't know.' Her mouth twisted. 'She had all seven verses tattooed on her body before she disappeared.'

Esther laughed in her mother's face. 'No, she didn't. Aura didn't have tattoos. She was terrified of needles.' The heat of indignation crawled up her neck.

Freya sat. 'Esther, listen to me,' she demanded. 'Aura was private about her tattoos. She kept them hidden.'

Esther stared. 'No.' Her mind snapped shut. 'No way. I would have known if she'd had tattoos. She would have told me. I would have seen them.' A counterargument occurred to her. 'Besides, if she was so private about her tattoos, how do you know about them?'

Freya looked to Jack. The slight shrug he gave Freya, confirming he knew something that Esther didn't and that he'd kept it from her, kicked Esther in the chest.

'Dad?' she whimpered. 'You know about this?'

Jack looked at her, his eyes watering.

Freya looked coolly at Esther. 'I know about Aura's tattoos because I did some of them myself.'

Esther looked at her mother, unblinking.

'She had some of them done while she was overseas. I tattooed the others after she came home. Before she died.' Freya swallowed. Exasperated, she looked at Jack. 'Some input? Please?' she pleaded.

Jack cleared his throat. 'Starry,' he said, his voice hoarse. 'It's … we need you. We need you to go to Copenhagen and see if you can find out what happened to her there. Before she came back. You know how different she was when she got home. She was so … distant.' He stopped for a moment, pressing his hand over his mouth, before starting again. 'We've tried contacting people who knew her in Denmark but … we just don't know what happened to her there.'

'That's right,' Freya said, conviction returning. 'But something must have happened. We brought you home so we could show you – so you could see for yourself how extraordinary Aura's journal is.' Freya's face was feverish with desperation. 'Answers must be in there somewhere.'

Esther glared at her parents. 'If you want to know so badly, if you're so worked up about going to Denmark, why don't you go yourselves?' she snapped.

Freya sat back. Jack avoided Esther's eye.

'Well?' Esther looked at each of them.

'You were the closest to her.' Freya's voice was pinched. 'That's why we're asking you to go. You knew her best. You'll be able to find out. Whatever she couldn't bring herself to tell us.' Freya pressed her hand over She-Ra on the cover of the journal. Jack said nothing.

Esther sat, unmoving, watching how protectively her mother held Aura's journal. Her mind reeled with imagined scenes of her sister being tattooed by Freya, of Aura making the effort to hide her tattoos from everyone, including Esther. The images gave her the same feeling as the day Jack had called her, strangeness in his voice. *Sunny, Aura's home. She's home.*

Esther speeding north from Nipaluna, Hobart, to Salt Bay, nearly popping out of her skin with excitement to be reunited with her sister after nearly three years. It happens, she tells herself as she drives. Sisters grow apart sometimes, especially when one moves overseas. On a whim Esther stops at a roadside stall and buys Aura a potted blue African Violet; ever since she was a teen Aura preferred something alive and growing to cut flowers.

When Esther arrives at the Shell House she rushes inside, violets trembling in her hand, expecting to find the same woman she'd farewelled at the airport with glittering eyes, jangly bangles and a radiant grin. But the woman sitting on the couch in the living room is a spectral, brittle version of the spirited sister Esther knows and loves.

In the weeks that follow, while Aura stays behind her closed bedroom door, mostly ignoring Esther's knocks, fear begins to spread through Esther's body, a sickness. Aura is home. But she's not the sister Esther knows at all.

~

At the dinner table with Jack and Freya, the same sickening fear seeped through Esther's body. Again, the muffled sound of her phone rang from her bag. She picked at the skin around her fingernails. Freya's words echoed over and again in her ears. *We brought you home so we could show you – so you could see for yourself how extraordinary Aura's journal is.* She looked slowly from Freya to Jack.

'What do you mean,' she asked, 'that you brought me home?' She looked at her parents. Narrowed her eyes. 'What did you mean, Mum, by "brought you home"?'

Neither Freya nor Jack answered.

'Oh my god.' Esther tried to shake away her realisation. 'Is that what last night was? The reason for her memorial? To trick me into coming home?'

'It wasn't like that, Starry,' Jack said quietly. 'It wasn't the only reason.'

Esther pushed her chair back hard and stood. 'This family is fucking batshit.'

'Swearing, Starry.'

'Dad, are you kidding me? I jeopardised—' She caught herself, barely. Started again. 'I left work, drove for seven hours, killed a fucking swan. That's right, Mum, did Dad tell you? A fucking black swan fell to her death, onto the windscreen of my ute. Nin pulled me together and brought me home. Nin did that. Then dressed me up as Kylie fucking Minogue, because what kind of person wouldn't bring home a costume to honour her dead sister?' Esther shook her head. 'It was just a bullshit excuse to get me back here. Because you knew I couldn't stay away. You knew I'd come home for her. I'd always ...' Esther's voice broke. 'Neither of you can bear admitting why I left in the first place. Can't you see how fucked up we are? Your grief has always come before mine.'

Again, Esther's mobile phone rang. She finally wrenched it from her bag and checked the screen.

'I have to take this,' she mumbled. Turned her back on her parents and walked as far from their earshot as she could. Tapped the green icon on her phone screen with a trembling finger.

'Ms Wilding,' an unmistakably caustic voice said. Esther's stomach dropped. 'This is Simon McGrath, General Manager of Calliope Lodge. It's come to my attention that you left work yesterday without leave approval and didn't show for your shift today.'

Esther scrambled for composure. 'It was a family emergency,' she murmured into the handset, cupping her hand around the mouthpiece. 'I let my duty manager in the kitchen know.' She'd texted him before she left: *Kane, family emergency, driving home east, back ASAP, cover for me.*

'Kane said he has no record of any such thing.'

She cursed her boss under her breath; they'd spent enough drunken nights together for her to reasonably expect his solidarity.

'Be back for your next shift tomorrow night or pack your things, Ms Wilding.'

The line went dead. Esther slid her phone into her pocket. Turned to face her parents.

Freya had her head in her hands. Jack was ashen-faced. Pins and needles started in Esther's limbs. An urge to run.

'I knew there was something to all of this,' she said, walking back to her seat at the table. She picked up Aura's journal. 'Why couldn't we just have had dinner together?' Her voice was small.

'Starry, why don't I put on some coffee, and we'll talk more about this.' Jack stood, opening his arms to her.

'Yes, coffee,' Freya urged. 'I can talk you through Aura's seven tattoos, explain what I know about them, and share some of our ideas about your trip to Denmark. My cousin, Abelone, is so looking forward to meeting you.'

'Fuck,' Esther exploded. 'I'm not going to Denmark,' she said, incredulous. 'This isn't about me.' She waved Aura's journal in the air. 'This is about you not being able to accept what haunts us all. She's fucking gone. She's gone.' Esther took a deep breath. Closed her eyes to breathe for a few beats.

When she opened her eyes, her shoulders sagged. She looked from Jack to Freya.

'Going to Denmark isn't going to bring her home,' Esther said quietly. She slid her bag off the back of her chair, took Aura's journal and walked out of the house. Into the silver cold night.

10

Esther sat on the top step of the stargazing shack with Aura's journal open in her lap, lit by the flashlight on her phone. As she turned slowly through the pages, the hairs on the back of her neck stood on end.

The first half of the journal was full of Aura's life, in the summer holidays at the beginning of 1995, when she'd just turned fifteen. Photographs of her and Nin had been cut out and glued in, their edges traced with varying colours of sparkling ink from glitter pens. Smiling faces behind oversized sunglasses, gumball machine candy lockets hanging around their necks, the ends of their hair bleached blonde from summer days in the sea, wearing their latest haul from the local op shop: vintage chiffon night gowns as day dresses with combat boots. Aura had written captions underneath each one. *Shell Girl and Seal Girl, Best Friends 4 Eva.* The odd note in Nin's handwriting. *Best friends until the rain bows, the kitchen sinks, the butter flies, and the water falls.* Esther shook her head, as much in amusement as endearment, at Aura and Nin's teenage language. Who had she ever talked with like that when she was fifteen, fuelled by the heady joy of friendship? No one. Only Tom, and even then their talk was filled mostly with facts about space. Esther turned the page, and another. Dozens of pages, warped from the glue of clippings from *TV Hits*, *Smash Hits* and *Dolly*, all of River Phoenix, surrounded by the repeated declaration, *Aura loves River Tru Luv 4 Eva.*

'Ah,' Esther whispered, remembering her sister's infatuation with him.

Nin and Aura's conversations on the nights Queenie was on call and Nin slept over were all about him. River. How he was older, but that didn't matter. It just meant Aura would be able to have meaningful talks with him, unlike with the boys in their grade. Esther had pressed her face into her pillow to suppress her guffaw over the embarrassing way Aura talked, as if River Phoenix was still alive and lived in Salt Bay, and it was only a matter of time before he, like the rest of the world, was in love with her.

Esther wedged her phone's flashlight under her chin to better go through Aura's journal with both hands. She flicked past River Phoenix and came across a double-page spread that was devoted to a list. The title made Esther's eyes well.

1995: Things I Want To Do This Summer And In My Life
— by Aura Wilding

Esther read through Aura's bullet points.

- *Learn macrame*
- *Bake Erin's painted cake recipe*
- *Have a garage sale to sell my kid stuff to start saving $$$ for a car*
- *Volunteer at TAC with Nin*
- *Learn how to play the bass guitar*
- *End world hunger*
- *Memorise the names of the lunar seas*
- *See Fleetwood Mac live*
- *Swim with seals at St Helens*
- *Become a diving instructor*
- *Protect the kelp forests*
- *Become a world-renowned fairytale expert*

- *Build Nin a sculpture studio and gallery for all her family's kanalaritja*
- *Cast a selkie spell to meet my sisters from the sea*

Drawing had never been one of Aura's strengths; in the margin of the list was her sister's attempt at what Esther assumed was a seal in the sea, though it looked more like the love child of a sausage dog and a dolphin. It almost made Esther laugh out loud. She read the last item again, surprised at how easily her childhood envy still flared.

Cast a selkie spell to meet my sisters from the sea

Their personal mythologies had been foretold, sisters of sea and sky. Sisters of seal and swan stories. Which Esther had mostly loved, until Aura became a teenager and started obsessing over finding selkie kin in the sea. Her single-minded desire to be with her seal sisters was what led Aura to start diving with Freya. Esther never learned to dive. Going deeper than her waist, beyond where her feet could touch the sand, terrified her. *Why am I not enough for her, Dad?* Esther had cried to Jack, sitting on the top step at the stargazing shack one morning, after Freya and Aura had gone diving together. *She loves you so much, Starry,* Jack had said soothingly. Esther realised much later that neither of them had specified who they were talking about.

There was one last item in Aura's list, written in red ink.

Put Starry through star school and support her dreams of becoming a scientist so that the whole world knows her name, like Carl Sagan

Esther ran the heel of her hand over her chest as she reread the words over and again. It shocked her somehow, to imagine Aura at fifteen, caring so much about Esther's kid dreams. She'd been approaching twelve at the time Aura had written the list.

Esther didn't remember her sister paying much attention to her dreams of becoming a scientist, specifically an astronomer. Yet there it was. The yearning of her soul. Written by Aura's hand.

The next page was filled with heart doodles. Aura's words were giddy; it was the night of her first big party, just before she and Nin left the house. A musk-vanilla-scented memory: Esther lingering in the hallway watching Aura and Nin disappear into a cloud of fragrant aerosol smoke as they douse each other with Impulse body spray before they leave the Shell House for the party.

9 April 1995
Today at school, Nin and I had our paper chatterboxes confiscated for using them during assembly, but I didn't really care, because I'd already got my fortune told. I kiss River!!! Which I'm going to do at his 80s party tonight. Nin's going to be here any minute. She's going to the party as Tina Turner, obviously because she's Simply the Best. I'm going as Cher, obviously because I'd do anything to turn back time to that day at the corner shop when River first talked to me, and I froze!!!

Esther read Aura's words again. Was there actually a boy in Aura's life called River? She couldn't remember anyone in town by that name. She flicked the pages. Back. Forward. Something unwelcome stirred in Esther's mind. After that last entry about the party, there was nothing else, no other teenage entries. Just a few blank pages before the words that marked the beginning of Aura's time in Denmark.

The Seven Skins

She whispered them aloud, tasting their cold and shivery edges in her mouth. She thumbed through the seven images of the sculptures and illustrations that Aura had taped into the journal. She paused on Aura's seven titles, and corresponding lines.

The first skin: Death. If you want change, raise your sword, raise your voice. The second skin: Reckoning. He will give you flowers to forget. You plant seeds, to remember. Esther's heart began to drum loudly. To have something of Aura's that she hadn't seen before filled her with a slippery, dreadful sense of hope. The kind that was dangerous, made Aura present. It was the sort of hope that caused Esther's skin to prickle, as if Aura might walk up the path to the shack at any moment, moonlight on her shoulders and iridescent shells around her neck. *So, Starry, you found my journal.*

'Starry.'

Esther gasped in fright, holding her feeble phone light up to the darkness.

'Hey, hey, it's just me.' Her aunt's face came into view.

'Erin?'

'Sorry, I didn't mean to scare you.' Erin raised a bejewelled, tattooed hand. 'I knew I'd find you here.'

Esther got up to wrap her arms around her aunt. 'You're a sight for sore' − she drew back to look at Erin in the bright moonlight − 'everything.'

Erin stroked a hand over Esther's hair and face. 'Nice shiner,' she said, looking over the bump on Esther's forehead. 'Jack told me. You hit a swan?'

'I buried her over there.' Esther pointed to the fresh mound, dirt still under her fingernails.

Erin shook her head. 'Never one to do things by halves, are you, Starry? Let's get you home. There's a cold front coming in overnight.'

'I'm staying here.'

'I meant my home. There's painted cake cooling as we speak.'

Esther raised an eyebrow at her aunt. 'Oh really?'

'Don't give me that face.' Erin chuckled. 'Let's go.'

Esther tucked Aura's book under her arm and followed her aunt on the path to the road. She lifted her eyes to the stars, her mind spinning, grateful to be reminded of the few still points in her life that hadn't changed.

11

After a year living away on the west coast, nothing about Erin's weatherboard cottage overlooking the bay seemed different to Esther except that it had become home to more stories: books, artworks, cabinets of curiosities – bones, shells, dried kelp, raw gemstones. While Freya was revered as a trailblazing tattooist on the island, her sister, Erin, was an academic, specialising in women's roles in myths, folklore and fairytales. She freelanced for the university in Nipaluna, Hobart, and was sought after for her lectures and workshops in women's storytelling. She was the first person Aura had told about her intention to move to Denmark and study in Copenhagen.

Esther settled herself at the kitchen counter. Erin picked a handful of mint leaves from the plant on her windowsill and boiled the kettle to make tea. The air was thick and smelled of honey, spices … and sex.

'Are we' – Esther looked around the tiny studio – 'alone?' Raised an eyebrow at her aunt.

Erin bit on her smile as she sliced two thick wedges of warm painted cake and slid them onto vintage saucers with scoops of honey ice cream. Pushed one saucer across the counter in Esther's direction with a silver fork. Esther appraised the dessert with a low whistle of admiration. Thick icing oozed down the side of the golden cake, which was decorated with rose petals, crushed pistachio and pieces of candied ginger. As with most things in Erin's life, her dabbling in baking revolved around old stories; she'd discovered painted cake after reading a seventeenth-century Italian fairytale about a lost bridegroom and the woman who conjured him back to her by baking a cake in his likeness. Since she was a teenager, Esther had known Erin to bake painted cake to conjure love.

'So?' Esther asked, grinning around her first mouthful. The flavours of cardamom, almond, rose and ginger melted on her tongue. She was lightheaded with relief to be away from her parents. From that threat-laden work phone call. The addition of the honey ice cream made her eyes roll back in her head in pleasure. 'I'll say it again.' Esther sectioned another wedge of cake with her fork. 'So?'

Erin chuckled, leaning against the counter, legs crossed neatly, eating her cake and ice cream. Her face remained deadpan as the bedroom door opened behind her. A familiar face emerged. Frankie, a local fisherman Esther doubted she'd ever heard say more than a handful of words at once, smiled sheepishly at her. Walked to Erin, kissed her cheek and whispered something in her ear.

Esther sat agape.

'Your painted cake conjured Frankie?' she screeched after he closed the front door behind him.

'Don't ever underestimate the shy ones.' Erin sighed, blissful as she lifted her fork, laden with cake, to her lips. 'Or the magic of an old fairytale recipe.'

Esther snorted. 'I don't mean to be a naysayer, but it might just be about more than your cake.' She pointed her fork at her aunt: her mess of curls, beguiling tattoos that started at her fingertips and wound up her arms, silver jewellery and the bright sharpness of her pale eyes. 'I can tell you right now, if I baked a cake from a fairytale recipe to conjure a lover, I'd get' – Esther paused, her stomach tightened, thinking of her work mates in Calliope – 'fish dregs.'

'Ha,' Erin retorted. 'Many great stories begin with fish dregs.' She licked her fork clean and put her empty saucer in the sink. 'Besides, when did you forget, my eastern star, that the whole point is never the cake, it's the power of the ritual.' Erin rinsed her hands under the tap. Dried her hands on a tea towel and strained their mint tea. She turned to Esther. Her playful expression had become serious. 'It's been an intense couple of days. The swan. The memorial. Tonight sounds like it was ... a lot,' Erin said.

Esther searched her aunt's face. 'Which one of them called you?'

'Freya. Soon as you'd left the house. Want to talk about it?'

Esther shrugged. Erin went to the cupboard above her fridge. Opened it, took down a bottle of Danish akvavit and two glasses. Jiggled them in offering. 'Shall we ditch the tea and bring Johanna and Gull in on it?'

Esther gave her aunt a reluctant smile. The ritual to evoke their distant Danish ancestors had always been Erin and Aura's thing, not hers.

Erin brought the glasses and akvavit to the counter, poured a nip in each. She crossed the room to a cabinet and took out a jar of sea water, a pot of black ink, a candle and a box of matches. Turned and raised an eyebrow at Esther. Exhaling her resistance, Esther made space, clearing the counter of books, papers, pens, shells and pumice stones from the beach. Erin brought her things from the cabinet and arranged them on the countertop. Struck a match and lit the candle. Esther watched the wick catch and burn. Aura's favourite moment. She waited for her aunt to speak.

'Old People. Ancestors. Johanna and Gull. Women of our line, from sea to stars, we ask you for courage.' Erin opened the jar of sea water, dipped a fingertip into it and drew a clear, wet line on one of her wrists. Esther did the same. Erin opened the pot, dipped a fingertip in the ink and drew a black, wet line on her other wrist. Again, Esther did the same. Erin handed her the tea towel to dry her fingertip. Esther knotted it in her hands, watching the sea water and ink glisten on her skin, one line clear and one line black.

When their wrists were dry, Esther and Erin raised their shot glasses. Knocked them back.

'Water of life,' Erin coughed as she swallowed.

'Liquid fire,' Esther rasped as the liquor went down. 'So, what now? Chill down the spine? Glass falls off a shelf? Lights will flicker? Should we be expecting Johanna and Gull to pipe up any time soon?'

Erin leaned on the counter to face Esther. 'When we were teenagers, your mum and I, we learned this ritual in Denmark from our cousin Abelone, and the first thing we understood is that the point of the ritual is to connect you to everything bigger than you and your life. To acknowledge the stories we come from and the stories we pass on. The point is to open your mind and heart. Which, by the sounds of how dinner played out tonight, you could use some help with.' Erin's scrutiny made Esther flush with shame.

'You know about her journal!' she asked her aunt, already knowing the answer.

'Freya's shown it to me.'

Esther gave herself a moment to suppress the whine that tried to rise from her belly. Why was she the last to know? She reached into her bag and put Aura's journal on the counter. She-Ra gazed up at them.

'Mum and Dad are so convinced that the second part in it, the *Seven Skins* part, is full of symbolism and "clues" that they want me to go to Denmark to, I don't know, decode or something equally batshit. Which you already know, obviously.'

'Obviously.' Erin eyed the journal. 'It's not that far-fetched though, is it? Your parents' theory?' She drew the journal close, opened it to the sculpture of the Binalong Bay Girl. 'The way any story is understood reveals both the nature of the person telling it, and the person who reads it or hears it. Stories are living things because we make them so, right? A story only dies when it is forgotten. My feeling is there could be truth in how your mum and dad are feeling about this journal, in terms of the stories Aura left behind. Stories she valued, for whatever reason.'

Esther scrunched up her face. 'That's very beautiful, but could we have less lecturer Erin and more my aunt Erin? I want specifics. About Aura's life. Mum said Aura had all seven verses tattooed on her body. So, whatever the seven images and her cryptic little words in there all add up to, they must have meant a shitload to her.' Esther couldn't help her voice rising. 'And she didn't tell me about one of them.'

Her bedroom door slamming behind her harder than Esther intends as she walks into the hallway. Esther storms to the front door but turns to glance back. Their eyes lock: Aura lingers in the doorway to her bedroom. Esther's words hang unanswered in the air. *Just tell me what's going on with you, Aura. Tell me what's been going on with you since you got home from Denmark, and I'll stay, I won't go back to Nipaluna. I'll stay with you. But you have to tell me. Just tell me.*

Erin reached for Aura's journal, ran her hand over the cover. 'Hmm. I remember the appalling shock of realising our sisters don't tell us everything.'

Esther rubbed the knots of tension in her neck. 'Can you just help me, please, Erin? I came home for Aura's memorial only to find out the whole thing was a set-up because Mum really wanted to show me that' – she pointed to the journal – 'and then tells me they want me to uproot my life and go to the other side of the world to follow Aura's footsteps, for what? To bring home answers that they think will fix us all? As if going to another country I don't know, where I know no one and can't speak the language is going to be anything other than a total disaster? I'm not going. Whatever is in that journal, whatever the *Seven Skins* stuff means, none of it brings Aura home. None of it will tell us what happened to her that day. Did you know Dad's still running at night? In case he finds her. In case he—' Her voice broke.

A beat passed between them.

'Where should we start?' Erin asked.

Esther exhaled. 'I don't know. You've had more time than I've had to sit with her journal, so ...'

'Have you seen all the seven verses and images?'

'Flicked through them, yeah.'

'Any you recognise?'

'Binalong Bay Girl. Of course. And her line, her first tattoo. "If you want change, raise your sword, raise your voice". That's a take on the thing we used to do when we were younger, every time we went by that fucked-up sculpture. Seeing it made me feel bad until ... Aura ... she made me see it in a different way; she had an ability to make me feel powerful and joyous instead of trapped and claustrophobic every time we went past it.'

Erin raised a brow. 'Maybe Aura's done something similar here.' She looked to the journal. 'Maybe Aura's first line, which became her first tattoo, was her way of reimagining how she related to the sculpture? Rewriting the story of her sculpture and what it meant to her?'

An image of the Binalong Bay Girl played in Esther's mind – not as she was, but free, stepping out of the stone rubble that had once entrapped her, one hand on her hip and the other raised, holding her sword. A look on her face, of self-knowing and freedom.

'Is that what Aura's done? Is that what her words are?' Esther asked. 'What her tattoos were about?'

'Look at the second image.' Erin turned to the next page. The illustration of the man and maiden underwater, him laying a wreath of flowers on her head. Esther studied it. Drew blank.

'Agnete ...' Erin hinted.

'Oh my god, is it?' Esther leaned forward, studied the illustration again. 'I don't know this artwork though. But yes, it is, isn't it?'

Esther and Aura had grown up being reminded of a Danish folktale, 'Agnete og havmanden' – 'Agnete and the Merman' –

every time their kitchen clock chimed and stuttered on its last bell. On either side of the clock face the merman and his seven sons held time, waiting for an absent Agnete to return. The clock had arrived in a tightly packaged box covered in postage stamps, all the way from Copenhagen, when Esther and Aura were young. Freya and Erin's Danish cousin, Abelone, had sent it as a gift. The same Abelone that Freya and Erin had stayed with in Copenhagen when they were all teenagers, and who'd taught them their ancestral ritual. Esther and Aura only knew of Abelone through the sporadic letters she and Freya had been sending each other since they were young. They imagined her to be of Hans Christian Andersen's ilk; the stories of snow and ice, the sea and the Aurora Borealis that Abelone shared in her letters from her northern island were familiar yet strangely spellbinding reflections of Esther and Aura's southern island home.

Sitting by their new ticking clock in the kitchen, Esther listens as Aura reads Abelone's letter to Freya aloud. A new sculpture inspired by the ballad of 'Agnete og havmanden' has been installed in Copenhagen and a range of commemorative wares has been made, of which the clock is one. Abelone has also sent photos.

"'*Agnete and Her Merman* is one of the newest sculptures in Copenhagen but it's one of our oldest and most beloved stories,'" Aura reads, eyes flashing. "'Did your mother ever tell it to you, Freya? A young woman, Agnete, was passing by the sea one day when a merman emerged from the waters and invited her to live with him beneath the waves. She was adventurous and spirited, so she said yes. He laid enchanted sea flowers on her hair in their underwater kingdom, which made her forget everything she'd left in her earthly world. Agnete and the merman had seven sons in the deep and all was well, until one day Agnete swam close enough to the surface to hear bells on land ringing. She remembered her home, all she loved there, and left her life in the sea, promising her family she would return.'" Aura pauses, presses her lips together.

'And?' Esther asks, leaning forward, hands splayed on the kitchen table. Aura pauses for dramatic effect.

'And?' Esther pleads.

Aura relishes the suspense. Lowers her voice to keep reading. '"Some say Agnete returned to the home she had chosen in the sea. To others though, like Suste Bonnen, the sculptor, Agnete refused her watery loves and the spell that drew her under, and stayed with her family on land, never to return to the sea again."'

Esther grips the photos, studies the sculpture. Eight figures, the merman and his seven sons, cast in bronze and positioned on a bronze platform, sit below the surface of shallow green water. She glances between the photos of the sculpture and the clock. Motions to Aura for Abelone's letter.

'"People walk by it in Frederiksholms Kanal every day,"' Esther reads aloud, '"unaware that the sculpture is there, because the water is either too choppy or the day too overcast and glary. But when the water is smooth and the sun falls just right, you can see the figures in the water there. Waiting for Agnete to come home."'

Across the table Aura sighs dreamily. 'The merman must have been so enchanting,' she says.

Looking at the sculptures of the merman and his children among the reeds and waving mosses, captured in palpable anguish and longing, Esther has a pain in her stomach. Some bury their faces in the crooks of their arms or their hands, while others reach towards the surface of the water, pleading for Agnete, who is missing from the sculpture altogether.

Erin stroked Esther's arm. 'Starry?'

She looked at her aunt. 'I was just remembering our clock and how much Aura loved Agnete's story.' Aura smiling at the airport departure gate, leaving for Copenhagen. *I'll find Agnete for you, Starry.* Then she was gone. And, in a sense, had never come home again.

Esther took the journal in her hand and ran her fingertips over Aura's verse on the page opposite the illustration of Agnete and the merman. *He will give you flowers to forget. You plant seeds, to remember.*

'Do you think that these words of Aura's are a way to ... retell ... the story that goes with each image?' she asked.

'You tell me,' Erin said, her eyes reflecting candlelight.

Esther turned to the third image. Another sculpture. On a plinth against a background of trees stood a young girl, bare footed, in a peasant dress with a kerchief around her hair. Shoulders thin and arms bracing her chest, she had one hand at her waist, one hand at her throat. Her vulnerability was clear. Above the image, Aura's writing.

The third skin: Invitation.

And on the opposite page, her third line.

Maybe she chose the depths. Maybe she's free.

'No.' Esther pushed the journal away. Shut her eyes against the intrusive thought of Aura's lifeless body in the sea. 'I need a break.' She shook her head. 'I need a break.'

'Okay, Starry,' Erin said, taking Esther's hands in her own and squeezing them. She let go and went to the coat rack. Lifted a woollen scarf. 'Let's get some sea air.'

12

Under the light of the full moon, the shoreline was silver, laced with foam left by the night-inked sea. The waves rolled from the horizon in small, calm sets, looking to Esther like torn white curls of paper, little boats in the path of the moon. She took deep lungfuls of salt, kelp and eucalyptus, walking in time with Ciin.

Ahead, the violet-edged silhouettes of the seven boulders stood silent and backlit by the sea, stalwarts of the Wilding sisters' lives. Esther glanced behind her, watching her footprints in the wet sand fill with moonlight in the wake of each step. They'd been much smaller the night she'd sneaked out of her bedroom window and run down the same shore to follow Aura. All the way to the seven boulders. She thought she'd stayed well hidden until they reached the cold sand.

Aura looking back over her shoulder. 'You might as well join me.'

Esther scurries to her sister's side. Reaches out a timid hand, which Aura clasps. Esther is almost ten. Aura, thirteen, has a bag slung over her shoulder.

'Are you leaving?' Esther whimpers.

Aura stops and bends down to level her eyes with Esther's. 'I'd never leave you, Starry. No matter how annoying you are.'

Esther's insides feel brighter than the moon. 'If you're not leaving,' she asks, 'then where are you going?'

Aura points at the seven boulders ahead. 'To the hidden lagoon. I'm going to cast a spell for selkie love.'

Esther chortles. 'Ew.' She waits for Aura to agree, or to say she's joking, love is gross. But her sister says nothing. Instead, there's a look in Aura's eyes that Esther has noticed more and more since Aura's recent thirteenth birthday. As·if she understands something about the world Esther doesn't.

'How are you feeling now?' Erin asked, hooking her arm through Esther's.

'Bit better,' she said. 'The air helps.'

'Want to sit?' Erin pointed to the large trunk of a fallen gum upshore.

Esther settled herself on the tree trunk. 'You haven't said yet.'

'Said what?' Erin asked.

'What you think of Aura's journal.'

Erin took a deep breath. Folded her hands in her lap and faced the sea. 'I think it's very deliberate. The *Seven Skins* part, I mean.'

'Deliberate, how?'

'That Aura chose the number seven for a reason. Chose "skins" as a fairytale way of describing stories. And chose every image in her journal, and the words she wrote in response to them, very carefully. I know it's a lot for you to take in, Starry, but I'm with your parents on this. I think the journal is Aura telling her story.'

Esther shook her head, trying to keep up. 'One thing at a time. Seven. Why seven?'

'You know what she was like,' Erin answered steadily. 'Aura became besotted with any story that helped her make sense of herself. That's what took her to Copenhagen in the first place, the idea that studying the myths and fairytales she'd always loved would bring meaning and purpose to her life, after, what, eight years of being stuck in that same waitressing job since she was eighteen and quit uni? Stories became her passion. She lived in them and through them. In some ways she lost herself in them.' Erin paused. 'Which is why I said she chose seven for a reason. In the worlds of myth, folklore and fairytale, seven is a charmed number.'

Esther indicated for Erin to say more.

'Well, it can be pragmatic, right? Like seven days of the week. Or religious: seven deadly sins, seven sacred sorrows. Seven chakras. It's in the natural world too: seven colours of the rainbow, seven continents. The myth of seven seas,' Erin explained. 'Celestial, even: cultures all over the world have been telling stories about the seven sisters of the Pleiades since ancient times. As you'd know.'

'And the seven ages of starlight,' Esther added.

Erin looked at her, inquisitive.

'Birth, adulthood, red giants, white dwarfs, supernovae, neutron stars and black holes,' Esther recited. 'Stars form, burn, explode and die.'

'So, they transform,' Erin said, eyeing Esther carefully. 'Through seven stages?'

'Yes.' Esther's skin tingled with the same awe she'd felt in the darkened uni theatre the first time she'd learned about the lifecycle of a star.

'There are innumerable places that take their names and stories from the number seven too,' Erin went on. 'The House of Seven Gables in Salem, Massachusetts, that inspired the classic Nathaniel Hawthorne novel. The Forest of Seven Lucky Gods in Japan, rendered in thousand-year-old wood. The Seven Sacred Pools in Hawaii, Lake of Seven Colours in Mexico, Seven Coloured Earths in Mauritius. The Seven Sisters Cliffs in England. I could go on.'

'The Seven Sisters waterfalls in Norway,' Esther said. 'Aura used to have a photo of those waterfalls on her bedroom wall when she was a teenager.' She could see it, the page Aura had torn from Jack's *National Geographic*, pinned to Aura's corkboard.

'She did?' Erin asked.

Esther nodded, seeing in her mind's eye the waterfalls in lush green fjords, remembering the story Aura used to tell her about them. 'The long waterfall on the other side of the fjord is known as "The Suitor",' she recited, 'banished, in solitude, after several unsuccessful attempt to court the sisters.'

'That mirrors the story of the sisters in the stars. Unrequited love is another common theme in myths and fairytales,' Erin said pointedly.

'You think it's connected to Aura's journal too?'

'"He will give you flowers to forget. You plant seeds, to remember,"' Erin quoted.

'Someone in Denmark?' Esther asked.

'We don't know.'

Esther plucked a strand of dried Neptune's pearls from the sand and fidgeted with them. 'So, you think Aura chose seven because it's charmed in all the stories she loved, about love?'

'I do,' Erin said, 'but more than that is my hunch that she chose seven because it's the number of transformation, the very nature of story itself.'

'For the laywoman, please?'

'In narratology—'

'Laywoman,' Esther repeated with a groan.

'Okay, okay,' Erin said, chuckling. 'There's a theory in academic writing circles that, just like starlight, every story has seven points to it.'

'Not just a beginning, middle and end?' Esther asked.

Erin shook her head. 'Think of the points like events, seven things that happen to the main character that change her in little ways, that move her through her, well, skins, if we use Aura's term. So that who she becomes by the end of her story when she's shed seven skins, or seven stories, is a result of what she's gone through in all of them.'

Esther frowned, concentrating. 'The number of transformation,' she mused.

'"The first skin: Death"; "The second skin: Reckoning",' Erin said.

Realisation made Esther shiver. 'That's what you think her numbered titles in the journal are?' Esther asked. 'You think they're events that happened in Aura's life?'

'It makes sense,' Erin said.

Esther thought of the sculpture of the vulnerable young girl. *The third skin: Invitation.* Aura's handwriting. *Maybe she chose the depths. Maybe she's free.* Her eyes filled.

'That third one though …' Esther swallowed. 'That really hit me.' She rubbed her chest.

'It hit me hard too, the first time I saw it.' Erin fixed her eyes on the sea. 'I get sucked in, down a rabbit hole of wanting. Wanting to know, wanting to think I understand. Was she telling us something? "Maybe she chose the depths. Maybe she's free." Was that her goodbye?' Erin took a shaky breath. 'But then, I remind myself: Aura wrote those words when she was overseas, more than a year ago. We can't know what they meant to her at the time, or if they have anything to do with what happened later …' Erin waited until she could continue. 'I think the only thing we can take comfort in is that Aura's words are about what each image and its story meant to her.'

'Which is?' Esther asked.

'I don't know.' Erin smiled sadly. 'Searching the internet for "sculpture of girl near trees" hasn't been very helpful so far.'

Esther dug her heels in the sand. 'I know you and Mum and Dad are geared up about this big discovery of her journal, but it does me in,' she said quietly. 'I don't get it. I mean, there's the Binalong Bay Girl, and Agnete, I know those stories, but I don't know why Aura's put them in a shitty old teenage journal, then written words about each of them that she had tattooed on her body.' Esther tried to rub the tension from her brow. 'Mum and Dad want her journal to be this huge deal that makes me fly off to Denmark, on a quest for my dead sister like I'm fucking Frodo, but it doesn't do that for me.' She hung her head. 'They said they want me to go because I knew her best, but Aura's journal just makes me feel like it's been a really long time since I've known anything true at all about her.'

'Oh, Starry.' Erin wrapped her arms around Esther and gave her a strong, assuring hug. 'It's so hard.'

Esther leaned into Erin's embrace and began to soften, until a thought niggled. She sat back, faced her aunt. 'You haven't said how long you've known about her journal. You seem to know it back to front.'

Erin straightened her posture. 'Not long. Freya found it in Aura's room a couple of months after she disappeared, after you left for the west coast. But I've only known about it for a couple of weeks. It's like an earworm though. I haven't been able to stop thinking about it.'

'Two weeks? You've known about it for two weeks?' Esther leaped off the tree trunk in agitation and started pacing.

'Freya only showed me first, before you, because she just wanted to know what I thought of it, what my professional opinion was of the images and their stories, and how Aura connected to them through her words. And tattoos. When Freya showed you the journal, she wanted to be able to give you answers, not just questions.'

'There are still plenty of questions though, aren't there,' Esther said, coming to stand in front of Erin, the moon and ocean at her back. 'Like why I didn't know Aura had seven tattoos. Why would she tell Mum but hide that from me?'

Something flickered across Erin's face. 'Another way of thinking about it might be, when were you around enough to see something so intimate of Aura's?'

Esther took a step backwards, as if Erin's words had struck her with a physical force. 'She went overseas and shut us all out, Erin. She shut me out. I wrote and called and texted her for months while she was in Copenhagen. And what, she came home out of the blue and I was supposed to keep hanging around here in case she said more than a few words to me? What should I have done?' Esther threw her arms in the air. 'Decided not to go back to uni? Just because Aura suddenly decided to return without any explanation of where she'd been or why she'd cut us off? And then made me sit around all day waiting for the moment she might have opened up to me? To tell me what happened to her over there? I extended my deferral for a whole term. I was here. Begging her. She kept me shut out. And then I left ...' Esther heaved for breath. Nearly mentioned the note Aura had left her, on the last day, but kept the words at the back of her throat, unspoken.

'Listen,' Erin said firmly, 'you're trying to understand why you didn't know about Aura's tattoos. I'm only trying to help. I mean, maybe if you'd just spent more time with each other—'

'No,' Esther snapped. 'Don't put that on me. Erin I was here.

Silence stretched taut between them. Esther clenched her jaw, thinking how her life had changed in such a short space of time. A little over a year ago, she'd been at uni, had friends and a share house she loved in Nipaluna, Hobart. Then Aura had come home and upturned everything. Esther's jaw ached. Her old life felt like a dream. One she couldn't have again.

After a while, Erin stood from where she was sitting on the tree trunk. 'I'm sorry,' she said, stepping towards Esther.

Anger held Esther rigid.

'I'm sorry,' Erin said again. 'I can only imagine how shut out of Aura's life you've felt and are feeling right now.' Erin reached for Esther's hands. 'What I said wasn't helpful, I'm sorry. Grief sneaks up on me too, sometimes.'

Esther squeezed Erin's hands once in acknowledgement before letting them go. Turned to face the wind, which had picked up. The cold, salty air cooled her anger.

'I'm not going to do it again. Walk away from my life elsewhere for Aura. Just because Mum and Dad think she hid her life in seven old stories and a bunch of tattoos. They won't tell us where she is now. Nothing brings her back.'

Esther changed the subject. 'It was one of your things with her, wasn't it? Teaching her Irish?' she asked Erin.

'For a time. After Aura did her family tree assignment at school, remember? That's when she became interested in the Celtic side of our ancestry,' Erin said. 'Why do you ask?'

Esther shrugged. '"Sisters of Seal and Swan Skins!"' She raised an imaginary sword in the air. 'She was so proud to teach me Irish: Séala and Eala. Seal and swan.' Esther sighed. 'That's the last thing we know she said that day: Eala. Eala. She was calling for me, and I wasn't there.'

'Don't punish yourself with what you can't possibly know for sure. We don't know who she was calling for. Or the context. No matter how likely it seems.'

How could it be anything different? Esther was too exhausted to argue.

Erin began to walk back the way they'd come. Esther fell in step beside her. Nearby the beating swoop of wings and nocturnal cry of a tawny frogmouth.

'I never had the heart to tell you girls.' Erin looked ahead in the moonlight, a sad smile on her face.

'Tell us what?'

'When you were kids and I was babysitting you both one day, Aura came pestering me about the Irish words for seal and swan. I was trying to work and was only half-paying attention. She wouldn't let up. I sat her down with my Irish dictionary, trying to buy myself some peace from her nagging. Later, when I heard and saw you two playing on the beach, how overjoyed you both were about her discovery, I couldn't bring myself to burst your bubble.'

'What do you mean?' Esther asked.

'In Irish,' Erin explained, 'the word for seal, the animal, as Aura was asking me for, is "rón". You should have been, "Sisters of Seal and Swan Skins, Rón and Eala". But Aura first

found a different context and meaning for seal in the dictionary.'
Erin chuckled. 'To seal a letter, to seal a window, to give your
seal of approval. Seal as in a fixative.'

'What?' A sharp snort of laughter took Esther by surprise.
She shook her head. 'You mean we were running around
town declaring ourselves warriors of sealed windows and
swans?'

'Or a sealed pipe, or sealed puncture.' Erin pressed her lips
together in a grin. 'She was so mind-blown by how similar the
words were for your sister symbols that when I realised, I just
couldn't correct her; I couldn't do it.' Erin chuckled. Esther
laughed, a hollow sound cut short by sorrow.

They walked together, watching the moonlight catch a ride
on every wave curling to shore.

'I guess in some ways, it kind of makes sense,' Erin said.

'What's that?' Esther blotted her damp cheeks with her
palms.

'When Aura found the translation in the dictionary, and
declared your names Séala and Eala, I remember how radiantly
she announced, "It's meant to be."' Erin wrapped an arm
around Esther's waist. 'And, if you think about it, she was right.
"Meant to be" is another use for seal. As in "to seal your fate".
Her fate was sealed. As was yours. You are and will always be
seal and swan sisters. Aura Sæl. Esther Svane.'

A sharp pain, a quick intake of breath. Esther's mouth
puckered.

'Just take your time,' Erin suggested. 'Read the journal.
Read Aura's words, her tattoos. Absorb from them what you
can. Then you might be able to start to figure out how you feel
and what you think about Denmark.' Erin rubbed her hand
across Esther's back.

When they got back to Erin's house, she went into the living
room to pull out the sofa bed for Esther. 'I've got an early class
in the morning. Let's get some sleep.'

After they'd readied themselves for bed and said goodnight, Esther sat in the shadows with Aura's journal open in the moonlight at the third image of the young girl in the journal. *An invitation.*

Esther stayed there, watching the waves roll into the bay under the guiding light of the moon, long after Erin had gone to bed.

13

Esther made her decision in the darkest hour before dawn. Without her life on the west coast, she had nothing but loss. She had to get back, had to keep her job. That's what she told herself this time. When she'd dropped out of university after Aura disappeared, Esther told herself it was because she'd lost interest, antropology was irrelevant. When she left her family and the east coast, she told herself it was because she didn't belong there, she'd be better off alone. When her life on the west coast started to fall apart, when she started to party too hard in Calliope and got warnings at work, it was because of the staff culture at the resort. Running away from self-reckoning was what Esther knew how to do. Anything to avoid admitting that she found it easier to abandon what mattered to her, instead of facing what she could not bear. Living, without Aura.

From Erin's couch Esther watched the rosy ball of the sun rise over the black and turquoise sea. Rays of light illuminated the algae on the boulders, from brown to red, to blazing orange.

She left her blankets folded in a neat pile, a repeatedly apologetic note under a magnet on the fridge and Aura's journal on the counter. There was nothing in its pages for Esther. Nothing but things she didn't want to feel.

Esther crept to the key peg by the front door. Lifted Erin's car keys and slipped out into the cool blue morning.

The living room filled with morning sunlight. In Esther's wake, dust motes tumbled, luminous, in the air. Behind Erin's closed bedroom door, a clock radio alarm beeped. A few moments later, the shower started running.

The front door eased open a crack. Esther inched her head around it. Seeing Erin's bedroom door still closed, she rushed for the counter, grabbed Aura's journal and ran out again, easing the door shut with a soft click behind her.

She was driving westward on the highway before the sun had finished rising. Over the ranges, through gum forest, into the brightness of early afternoon. Esther got back to Calliope, the dark green river country she loved, with just enough time to shower, drink a double-shot coffee and be on time in the kitchen.

An hour into her dinner shift, after the general manager had walked by and registered Esther's presence, the kitchen phone rang.

'Grab that,' Kane ordered.

Esther scowled at him, wiped her hands on her apron and answered.

'Call for you,' the receptionist said.

Esther's stomach dropped. She'd told her family never to ring her on the work landline unless it was an emergency.

'Esther.'

'Erin.' Esther balked. Steadied her voice. 'Erin, I'm so sorry I took your car. Like I said in my note, I had to get back to work for a management emergency, but on my next days off, in a couple of days, I'll drive it back to you, pick up my ute. I had no choice, and I know you use your bike to ride to work, so I thought you wouldn't mind—'

'Esther.' The sternness in Erin's voice made her stop and listen. 'We can talk about all of that and why you've been lying about being a dishy later.' She sighed. 'The receptionist just corrected me when I asked for you, the manager.'

Esther hung her head, squeezing her eyes shut.

'Why would you lie to us? You don't need to prove anything to anyone, least of all your family.'

Esther held the phone receiver away from her ear then pressed it hard into her forehead.

'What's going on with you? You should have asked before you took my car; you don't know what my schedule is like. What if I'd needed it to get to a conference in Launceston or something?'

Esther didn't respond.

'I'm worried about you. Your behaviour. I'm worried about how much you're carrying. You need help; you need—'

'Erin, this is really sweet of you, and I appreciate you calling.'

'Esther, I—'

'I love you. I'm sorry. I have to go.' Esther pressed the phone quietly back into its cradle, her heart racing. There was a tightness forming in her chest that she'd learned to recognise as panic.

'Kane,' she snapped across the kitchen at her boss. He hadn't apologised for not covering for her when she'd gone home for Aura's memorial. 'Tea break.'

'Ten minutes,' he replied, pausing his chopping to point his knife tip at the clock on the wall. He looked at her for a moment too long, as he always did. She took in the intensity of his pale eyes, his thick, dark hair and his broad shoulders. On any other night Esther would have enjoyed her body's response to him, but in that moment she hated how the invitation in his gaze made her palms clammy, her thighs warm.

She swiped an open bottle of merlot from the counter beside a braising pan and hurried out the back of the kitchen to the staff smoking pit. Sat in one of the plastic chairs. Sculled from the bottle and took deep lungfuls of air. When the wine started softening her muscles and the tightness in her chest had passed, she slid down to rest her head on the back of the chair. Looked up, searching the night sky.

~

Jack knocking on her bedroom door. She's ten years old, at her desk, reading *Cosmos*. Jack opens the door, hand behind his back, eyes full of mischief. With a flourish, he unrolls a new poster for her wall. It's a painted portrait of a woman in a black Victorian dress, standing at a telescope, looking upwards. Down one side of the poster in typeface is a quote. Esther reads it aloud.

'"We have a hunger of the mind which asks for knowledge of all around us, and the more we gain, the more is our desire."'

And beneath the quote: *Trailblazing nineteenth-century astronomer Maria Mitchell.*

Jack grins at Esther. 'One day there'll be a poster just like this one, but with a different portrait and equally profound words on it from trailblazing astronomer Esther Wilding.'

'Alright, chick.'

Esther startled. Hid the wine bottle under her seat and turned. 'Deidre.'

As Calliope's longest-serving staff member, Deidre was a waitress in the restaurant at night and head housecleaner during the day. No one knew her age. She wore her hair in a perfect Dolly Parton blonde quiff, chain-smoked, split her tips evenly but was feared by the youngest staff for being a terrible gossip who'd started countless rumours that travelled through the staff like wildfire. Esther avoided her at every opportunity.

'All good?' Deidre asked, scraping a plastic chair across the concrete to sit beside Esther. She took a packet of Winfield Blues and a lighter out of her apron and lit up.

'Fine, thanks,' Esther replied.

Deidre exhaled a plume of smoke upwards into the night, picking flecks of tobacco off her tongue with candy pink fingernails. 'Your one-year contract must be coming up for renewal soon,' she said, dragging on her smoke.

'Yep,' Esther said, staring up at the stars, resenting every minute of her precious ten away from the kitchen that was ticking by lost to small talk.

'You'll be up for promotion from dish pig to kitchen hand then,' Deidre said with a wink. 'Chopping veggies is a whole new world. Plus, the extra moolah is nice. That's how I got my break here too.' When Esther didn't give more than a polite nod in answer, Deidre tutted. 'If I'm honest, I didn't think you'd last more than a month here, girly. Not your type. But you've surprised me, staying on this long.'

'And what's my type?'

'Smart.' Deidre tapped a pink fingernail at her temple. 'Someone with something to say. Kane's type, actually,' she offered.

Esther stilled. She and Kane had been careful to be discreet. Inter-kitchen relationships were frowned upon.

'He's always drawn to the deep thinkers,' Deidre continued, a hint of mockery in her tone. 'But,' and she laughed huskily, 'his looks only get him so far before he realises he's out of his depth then trades in the brains for the next bimbo in retail or reception. Ah, the stories I could tell, chick.'

Esther kept her face impassive. Deidre's eyes were sharp, a fox on the hunt for a tasty morsel.

'Guess I've just got what life here takes,' Esther said breezily as she stood. 'Like you, Deidre.'

Flattered, Deidre smiled, frosty pink lipstick on her teeth. 'What's our secret, do you reckon?' She tapped the ash from her cigarette.

Esther summoned her sweetest smile. 'Knowing when to mind our own fucking business.' She pushed the plastic chair out of her way, tucked the wine under her arm, out of Deidre's view, and walked off.

Around the corner, at the kitchen screen door, Esther paused. Tried to gather herself, to stop her hands shaking. Did everyone just think of her as Kane's latest disposable fling? She took a few deep breaths, which only made space for Erin's phone call to replay through her mind. The hurt, disappointment and concern in her aunt's voice.

In Esther's pocket, her mobile vibrated.

A text from Nin. *Starry, Freya's just been over. Told me and Queenie about Aura's journal. About your dinner. Are you okay?*

Esther clicked her phone screen to black. Put it back in her pocket.

She opened the screen door. Sneaked the wine back onto the counter, next to the braising pan. Righted her posture but dragged her feet back to her sink, stacked with a new tower of dirty dishes.

After she'd finished her shift and was back in her room in her staff share house, Esther tossed and turned in bed, her head full of chaos. Lines written by Aura's teenage and adult selves jostled for space. *Cast a selkie spell to meet my sisters from the sea. Put Starry through star school … Maybe she chose the depths. Maybe she's free.*

Esther sat up, exasperated. Pressed a pillow to her mouth and screamed from her belly into its downy softness. She dropped the pillow, panting for breath. Her throat stung from strain.

A tap came at her window. She startled.

'Wilding? You awake?'

Esther got out of bed and peeked around the corner of her curtain. Then drew it back. Kane stood on the grass, holding up a bottle of whiskey. She opened the window.

'Peace offering?' He gave her the smile that made her knees soften with wanting.

'Peace offering,' Esther repeated, folding her arms across her chest, trying to be indifferent. 'You know you fucked me right up, not covering for me?' She tried to conceal her desire to mean something to him. To matter.

'I told you when this started, Wilding, no special treatment in my kitchen,' Kane said. 'No matter how good you are in bed.' He gave her another half-smile. Esther smiled back to hide the sickening thud of disappointment in her stomach.

Kane raised a brow in question. Wiggled the bottle of whiskey.

She regarded him for a moment, almost resisted. Then nodded him towards her front door.

14

Esther stumbled into the restaurant kitchen for her breakfast shift with a violent hangover and very little memory of the night before. She'd woken in bed naked with an empty whiskey bottle. Kane was gone. No note.

Throughout the morning, clearing the grease and congealed fat of sausages and bacon from breakfast plates, she had to regularly abandon her sink and run for the staff toilets, where she retched into the toilet bowl until she saw black spots in her vision.

At a point near the end of her shift, when Esther was again in the toilets and didn't have the strength to get up off the cool, tiled cubicle floor, the entry door swung open. Two of the morning waitresses chatted loudly.

'Sooooo. Have you seen him this morning?'

'Who?'

'Don't give me that smile, you know who.'

'I might have.'

'Oooh, what does that mean?'

'We bumped into each other at the servo on his way to work. He was all charm and swagger.'

'Look at your face. You're a goner.'

'So, what if I am?'

'What about Esther?'

Behind the closed door of her toilet stall, curled in a ball on the floor, Esther pricked her ears.

'You've heard about her and Kane.'

Nausea gripped Esther's body. She clamped a hand over her mouth, willing herself not to retch.

'Ugh, I don't get what he or anyone sees in her. The way she barely speaks to anyone around here, but the minute you add a drop of booze to her, she turns into everyone's party favour. She's fucked up.'

'Right? But guys love her. She was with Mark in Landscaping first, remember? Then Ryan in Maintenance. Ben, her housemate is obsessed with her, always going on about how hot he thinks she is. And now she's got her claws into Kane. Deidre was telling everyone at the pub the other night they're definitely fucking. Said she's seen him coming out of Esther's share house more than once.'

'Ew. Whatever. I'm not worried. Esther's no threat. Guys will look after-... like her because they can. She's easy play.' A pause. 'I'm not like her. That's the thing with Kane and me: I'm not just giving him what he wants. What he really, really wants.'

'Okay, Baby Spice.' The two women giggled. 'Can I borrow your lipstick?'

Shame made Esther's skin crawl. She wiped cold sweat from her upper lip, silently begging her stomach not to convulse.

After what felt like hours, the two waitresses left, just before Esther vomited another stream of bile into the toilet. She collapsed, trying to breathe, to settle. When the entry door to the toilets swung open again, she couldn't stop herself groaning. One of the taps over the sink turned on, then off. The hand dryer blew. Then silence. Esther put her head in her hands and waited for whoever had come in to wash their hands to leave again.

'Esther,' Deidre said, her shadow at the door.

Esther lowered her hands. Didn't answer.

'Kane sent me to look for you. Big night, eh?'

Esther bit on the inside of her cheek, temples pounding.

'Are you alright in there, girly?'

'Just fuck off, Deidre,' Esther flared. 'I don't need your help.' She pressed her hands to her temples, willing her raging headache to subside. Esther heard the bathroom door swing open and slam closed. She dragged herself to her feet, wiped her mouth. Flushed the toilet.

At the basin, Esther splashed water on her face. Took a few deep breaths. Checked the time on her phone. Twenty minutes of her shift left. She could do it; she didn't need that old gossipmonger or anyone to help her. She could look after herself.

After another splash, another few deep breaths, Esther walked shakily out of the bathroom. Didn't once meet her own eye in the mirror.

When she woke in her bed it was late afternoon and the shadows were purpling along the river. She'd gone straight home from her shift, showered, drunk two dissolved Beroccas, swallowed two paracetamol and fallen into a deep sleep.

Esther stretched her arms overhead, relishing the absence of a headache. But, without the pounding in her temples, memories came crashing in. She pulled her doona over her head and squeezed her eyes shut. *I don't get what he or anyone sees in her. She's fucked up.* Esther groaned. It was true, wasn't it? She remembered the way she'd abandoned her studies after Aura disappeared – all the formal letters from the university advising her of the cut-off dates for deferring her course that she'd ignored and left unanswered. Her unpaid student debt. Her academic advisor's emails, some she'd never bothered to open. Her flatmates that she'd found through Tom, whom she'd abandoned and left to cover her share of the rent. Had Tom known at the memorial that she'd done that? Realisation buffeted her: of course, he would have known. Yet he was still kind to her, despite his kindness being the very last thing she deserved. Then she'd tried to throw herself at him. The horror on his face. It was just another thing Esther had ruined.

She kicked the doona back. Stared at the ceiling. A sharp pain went through her stomach. She couldn't remember the last thing she'd eaten.

Esther sat up, swung her legs over the edge of the bed. She didn't know what she felt like to eat. Couldn't think of a thing she wanted.

'As if you deserve anything,' she whispered. Hunger persisted. She sighed, stood, and shuffled out of her room into the kitchen.

Later, Esther sat in the armchair by her bedroom window, half of her cheese and tomato toastie left on her plate. She sipped her cup of tea as she watched the sky darken and the storm rise. Autumn equinox was days away, bringing with it nights that would last longer than the days. Cygnus was still under the horizon. It wouldn't rise until dawn, and, even then, it would be hidden from view by the light of the sun. To the northwest, the Seven Sisters sat low in the sky, just beneath the waxing crescent moon. By the end of the month, they would slip below the horizon.

Esther looked at the ephemeral objects she'd gathered on her windowsill from walks during her year living on the west coast: river rocks, dried fern fronds, periwinkle shells worn down by water to their green and purple iridescent skins, and dried kelp from the estuary sands. Tiny talismans. Proof she'd survived her first year without Aura. But to what end? As she was, Esther would be nothing but a disappointment to her sister. To the version of Aura that she knew best, the woman Aura was before she went to Copenhagen.

'How do I make things right, Ra-Ra?' Esther murmured.

As the moon rose its pale light bounced off the bonnet of Erin's car outside. Esther studied the glint of it, recalling walking the shoreline with her aunt. *Just take your time. Read the journal. Think about it.*

Aura's journal was where Esther had left it, in the darkness of the glove box. She hadn't wanted to look at it since she'd returned to Calliope. But now she remembered it, the journal had the same magnetic pull to it that had made Esther sneak back into Erin's to get it. Esther put her cup of tea down, went out to the car, got the journal and hurried back inside.

'Esther, come party with us,' one of her housemates, Ben, called from out the back. *Ben, her housemate is obsessed with her, always going on about how hot he thinks she is.* Reggae music and the smell of barbecue wafted past her.

'Maybe later,' she called back. Shut her bedroom door behind her and switched a lamp on. Nestled herself in her chair by the window, with her curtains open and her room filled with the thin light of the moon.

Esther took another sip of tea and a steadying breath. Ran her hands over the cover showing She-Ra with her sword held aloft, then opened Aura's journal. Thumbed through everything she'd read before, to browse the four remaining images and Aura's verses.

She ran her fingertips over Aura's handwriting, imagining words inked into her sister's skin. A swell of anger; Freya had seen Aura's tattoos. But not Esther. Aura didn't share them with her. Why? Despite how often she'd texted and written to Aura while she was overseas, Esther never got much response. Aura was the one who'd shut Esther out, the one who'd severed their connection.

Esther waiting by Aura's closed bedroom door. Clutching the tray of breakfast that she's prepared for her sister: a plate of Vegemite on buttered toast, a cup of tea, and her potted blue violet. She rushed home as soon as Jack called her, only to be met by a baffling change in Aura's demeanour. Esther tells herself to be patient.

But day after day Aura's bedroom door remains closed. Jack and Freya hover around the house, whispering to each other in the hallway, huddling with the coffee cups around the kettle in the kitchen. When Esther tries to join their conversations, they change the subject. To the weather. Tides. The sky. Esther becomes so frustrated with feeling shut out, first by Aura and then her parents, that she starts going out at night, drinking in the local pub, as if whiskey and strangers can cure the hurt of being left behind.

Her tipping point comes the day Aura leaves Esther her note. It is too little, too late. She gets into her car and speeds back to Nipaluna, Hobart. It is a choice Esther will regret for the rest of her life.

She wiped her eyes and turned back to the third image and verse in Aura's Seven Skins. Studied the sculpture, of the young fisher girl with her hair in a kerchief and her feet bare. The vulnerable set of her shoulders and the way she held her arms over her chest, one hand bracing her waist, the other at her throat. Though it was a black and white photocopy, as all seven images were, it was still striking, particularly the light and shade of the trees behind the sculpture and the details of the young girl's face, some of which was hidden by dark patches of tarnish. Esther guessed she would once have been golden-hued in her original bronze form, her dreamy, melancholic expression catching the light.

Esther was about to flick over the page when something she hadn't noticed before at the bottom of the image caught her eye. She frowned, looked closer. The light of her lamp didn't help. She put Aura's journal down and got up to turn the main bedroom light on. Came back to it and checked the image again.

There, beneath the photograph, was a watermark. Half-concealed by the piece of clear tape Aura had used and the fuzzy resolution of the black and white printing.

Esther dug a flashlight out of her drawer and pointed its beam on the watermark for further clarity. Printed in tiny font was a name: *Klara Jørgensen.*

She rummaged through her bed and the clothes on her floor until she found her laptop. Stabbed at the keys. Nothing. Plugged it in to the charger and cursed every deity she could think of waiting for it to charge enough battery power to switch on.

'Phone,' she said to herself, casting her laptop aside and looking for her mobile, which she finally found behind her bedside table. Also flat.

She lay face down on the floor until the thought of what might be in her carpet repulsed her enough to move. As she sat up, her laptop hummed cheerily as its screen came to life. Esther pounced on it. Opened an internet search window. Her hands were shaking as she typed *klara jorgensen photographer.*

Her index finger hovered over the enter key. She held her breath. Pressed the key. Search results appeared on her screen: *Danish photographer based in London.*

Esther slouched in disappointment. She didn't know what she was expecting but it felt like an anticlimax.

'Maybe you just loved her work,' Esther said as she looked through the menu on Klara's website. Her pulse started to slow.

She went through the gallery of Klara's photographs. Her landscape photography was richly toned, capturing dramatic mountains and strange, vast seascapes that looked like somewhere from a dark, salt-glittering fairytale. Somewhere Scandinavian, Esther figured. She clicked on a link to 'Portraits'. Scrolled through the thumbnail images on Klara Jørgensen's site. A sense of knowing dawned on her. Copenhagen was the backdrop to a series of Klara's portraits; Esther recognised places and landmarks she'd pored over with Aura, on the internet, in books and in vintage photographs glimpsed through the dark red tunnel in Aura's View-Master. After Aura had moved to Denmark, Esther had spent countless nights exploring the city in two dimensions on her laptop screen, imagining her sister's new life set among the multicoloured buildings of Nyhavn or the fairy-lit glow of Tivoli Gardens. Klara Jørgensen's portraits, taken in the city that had drawn her sister so powerfully with its stories and light, were evocative and luminous. In one, a couple of elderly women held each other's hands bound in seaweed beside the fountain of Gefion, the Norse goddess of fertility, agriculture and abundance. In another, two men knotted together in sea nets sat on the rocks beside the famous Little Mermaid sculpture. Esther's body twitched with compulsion. Had Aura scrolled through these photographs too? She took a shaky breath. It was strange, painful and more beautiful than she dared to let herself imagine, to feel a closeness to Aura's life again.

Esther came to the end of the gallery. Clicked. The last portrait began to load.

Adrenaline thundered through Esther's body. She leaned forward.

The unfocused background of the photograph was a flaming pink sky, ornamented by silhouettes of leafless trees. In the midground stood the sculpture of the young girl, the one in the third image in Aura's journal.

In the foreground a young man laughed as he turned his face away from the camera. He had collar-length hair, a deep-dimpled smile and beard. The rest of his face was obscured by low light.

She was the heart of the photo.

Resplendent in a sea-green coat, she looked straight at the camera.

Wrapped in the man's arms, her face flushed with joy, stood Aura.

The third skin:
Invitation

Maybe she chose the depths.
Maybe she's free.

15

Esther faked a stomach bug and called in sick for the next couple of days. She retreated to her bedroom, only emerging for food and showers after she'd heard her housemates leave.

Hiding in bed, she spent hours poring over Klara Jørgensen's photo of Aura. What did it mean? Esther studied every visible detail about the young man with Aura. His dimple. His beard. The angles of his smile and his gaze. The shadows that fell across his face, obscuring his eyes from view. Who was he? Was he the reason Aura had come home without any light in her eyes?

Esther scoured Klara's website, clicking between Aura's photo and Klara's contact page, which offered a blank form and message from Klara: *Please fill out the information below and get in touch. I'd love to hear from you.*

Back and forward Esther went, between the photo of Aura and Klara's contact page. She chickened out every time.

On her second night off, when she should have been on dinner shift, there was a knock on her bedroom door. Ben came in with a cup of tea and paracetamol.

'Heard you were sick,' he said as he put the tea and pills on Esther's bedside table.

Esther stared at the tea, wary of Ben's kindness.

'Give us a yell if you need anything. The boys and I are just playing video games out here.'

She saw how his eyes drifted over her face and body, how his cheeks reddened in response. *She's easy play.*

'Thanks,' she said stiffly.

He left her room, pulled the door shut behind him.

Esther stared at the back of her bedroom door. Pulled her blankets to her chin. She looked again at the photocopy of the sculpture of the young girl pasted in Aura's journal, and then to her laptop screen. Aura and her man standing in front of the same sculpture. A question: had the photo been taken in Copenhagen?

She reached for her laptop and opened a new tab in her search engine; *young girl sculpture copenhagen* only brought up pages and pages of photos of the Little Mermaid sculpture. She tried varying her search terms – *young girl statue copenhagen, sculpture of girl copenhagen* – but still, nothing. Esther studied the sculpture, the trees behind her. Thought for a moment. Tried again: *young girl sculpture in garden copenhagen.*

She bolted upright as an image of the sculpture appeared in the first line of search results. Clicked the link.

'Liden Gunver,' Esther read aloud as she scrolled through pages of information and images about the sculpture of the young girl. She clicked on another link.

*Liden Gunver was a character in an eighteenth-century
Danish folk song that premiered as part of a theatre
performance in Copenhagen but became hugely popular.
The song tells the story of a fisher girl, Liden Gunver, who
followed the alluring calls of a deceitful merman into the sea.*

Esther clicked on an English translation of the Danish lyrics.

*A merman rose from the depths and appeared, in seaweed clad,
His eyes glowed with warmth and his words sounded as sweet
    as harps,
Oh, young girl, beware of false-hearted menfolk,
Oh, young girl, beware, oh beware.*

Esther shuddered. Continued reading. At the end of the song, fishermen find Liden Gunver's corpse washed up on the rocks after the merman has done with her.

'Fucker,' she muttered.

After she'd finished reading, Esther leaned back against her pillows. Rubbed her eyes as she thought through Liden Gunver's story: a young woman accepts an invitation from a merman to go on an adventure, to explore her temptation, curiosity and desires, only to lose her life to his betrayal. Esther reached for Aura's journal, open at Liden Gunver's image. Ran her fingers over Aura's words. *Maybe she chose the depths. Maybe she's free.* Were Aura's words prophetic? Had she chosen freedom in the depths of the sea? Or was her sister flipping the power dynamic in Liden Gunver's story, to go from a girl being punished in the worst way for following her curiosity, sexuality, desires, to giving her power through choice? Esther clicked to the tab on her laptop with Klara's photo of Aura. Her smiling, radiant, beautiful face.

She pushed the journal and her laptop away, her eyes bleary and watering. 'I don't know what any of this means, Ra-Ra.' Why did her sister tattoo herself with words she'd written in her teenage journal that reimagined stories of disempowered women? Esther's conversation with Freya at dinner echoed in her mind. *You were the closest to her, you knew her best. You'll be able to find out. Whatever she couldn't bring herself to tell us.*

On her next shift in the kitchen, Esther kept her head down. She didn't make small talk with any of the other staff and said little more than the bare minimum to her kitchen colleagues. Towards the end of her shift, she tried to catch Kane's eye a couple of times, but he was avoiding her. She yearned to get out of her head, to lose herself in his arms.

When Esther was finished for the night, Kane was nowhere to be seen. Not in the restaurant talking to guests. Not in the kitchen or reception. Esther lingered by the staff toilets for a bit, but he didn't emerge. As she did last checks and left the kitchen, she realised she hadn't checked the smoking pit. If he wasn't there, then she'd give up and go home alone.

As Esther walked in the shadows to the smoking pit behind the kitchen, her ears pricked at the sounds of soft moans and an occasional giggle. Her pulse hammered in her solar plexus, sickening. She peeked around the corner. Kane was sitting on a crate, facing her, his back against the wall. Kim, one of the waitresses, had her back to Esther and was straddling him, her skirt hoisted up, her blouse open. Esther didn't know whether to make a scene and shout or cry. She just stood there. Staring. Feeling as if all the blood was leaving her body. When Kim leaned closer to Kane, Esther had a clear view of him. His face twisted in pleasure. He looked up, directly at her. Esther stared. Kane tightened his grip on Kim's hips and held Esther's eye contact.

She bolted. Away from the smoking pit, fighting back her tears. In the dark, on the dirt road that led to staff housing, she tripped and fell. Scraped the skin off her hands and knees. She sat on the gravel, picking stones from her skin and wiping her cheeks. Ahead, loud reggae music and the sounds of a partying crowd blared from her share house.

Esther got up, took a few deep breaths, dusted herself off. At the path leading to her front door, she fixed a life-of-the-party smile on her face. Then walked inside.

She'd lost count of how many Smirnoff cans she'd sneaked from someone's Esky by the blazing firepit in the backyard. The world was spinning, and her body hurt after her fall. The image of Kane's face as he locked eyes with her, Kim writhing on his lap, wouldn't stop replaying in Esther's mind. She slipped into the house, scurried to her bedroom and locked the door behind her. Turned in circles, wishing she had someone to call. Nin and Jack had been texting her almost every day since she'd left Salt Bay, but Esther hadn't known how to reply, what to say. Freya's silence since Esther walked out on their dinner had been deafening. She took another long glug of the citrus vodka mixer, insatiable for the burn it sent through her body. Glanced at her closed laptop on her bed. Opened the screen. Stared at Klara's website. Aura's face. Esther pressed her face to it. Enlarged the photo until Aura was life size. Another long glug from her can of vodka. Turned her stereo on. Speaker volume at max. Fleetwood Mac.

'Where are you?' Esther shouted at her sister's photo. 'I need you. Where are you?' she shouted again. More vodka. Finished her Smirnoff can and chucked it to the floor. Clicked on the contact page of Klara's website. She typed a brief message and tried to reread it, tried to focus through the blurry haze of her vision. A loud knock at her door distracted her. Later, the last thing she would remember of the night was opening the door to find Ben swaying there, with bloodshot eyes, two vodka cans in hand and a nervous smile.

She woke the next morning in her bra but no knickers. Ben was beside her in bed. The anvil of another hangover hammered through her body.

Esther sat up, winced; her hands and knees were bruised and tender from her fall. She tried to gather her thoughts. Checked the time. Swore out loud and scrambled from bed.

She was twenty minutes late for her breakfast shift.

Esther sneaked through the back door and went to the sink, then worked as fast as she could to clear the pile of dirty dishes.

'Boss wants to see you in his office.'

She turned to face Kane, who was leaning against his station, wiping his knife on a tea towel. He looked her up and down with a slow head-shake of disapproval.

'Now,' he said to her. Then turned his back and kept working.

Numb, Esther walked from the kitchen through the restaurant to Simon McGrath's office. Deidre and Kim and a couple of other waitresses murmured under their breaths to each other as she walked by.

'Ms Wilding,' Simon said when he saw her in the doorway to his office. 'It's come to my attention that you were late for your shift, again, this morning. That's your second chance, done and dusted. I want you cleared out and your swipe card handed in by close of day.'

It took the hour-and-a-half drive from Calliope to Queenstown for Esther to stop shaking from humiliation and shame after she'd realised that Kane must have been the one who'd dobbed her in to the boss. Her job, and her life in Calliope, had been on the line; he could have covered for her, saved her skin, and didn't. He'd got rid of her instead.

As she drove down the main street through town, Esther's stomach was in knots. After she'd left Simon McGrath's office, she'd fled to her share house and packed up. None of her housemates were home. She left only her dirty uniforms and keys behind. All she had to show for her life on the west coast was shoved into her duffel and garbage bags piled in the back of Erin's car. Esther gripped the wheel.

She pulled over at the first chemist she spotted. Sat in Erin's car and washed down the morning-after pill with a Berocca dissolved in her water bottle; she couldn't be sure she and Ben had had sex. She'd blacked out.

Esther nibbled at a stale salad sandwich with slices of rubbery packet cheese from a nearby takeaway shop. Stayed parked on the side of the road with no idea where to go. Took her phone out of her pocket and scrolled through her contacts, considering her options. Erin – no, not after she'd essentially stolen her car. Nin – a possibility, although staying with her would make lying low and away from Freya too complicated if Queenie got involved. She kept scrolling. Stopped on Tom's name. Esther looked at the road leading out of town to the point where it became an intersection. One way north. The other way south. Where Tom was. She could go there. Her behaviour with him at the memorial had been ghastly, but he'd never said no to her before.

She mulled over the idea as she prised the lid off her takeaway coffee. What other option did she have? An image of the Shell House flashed in her mind.

Esther took a sip of coffee and cringed. It was cold and bitter. She opened her car door, emptied the coffee into the gutter and tossed her takeaway cup onto the floor of the passenger side. Picked up her phone again, and aimlessly started scrolling, hungry for distraction. She opened her texts, saw the unanswered messages from her dad and Nin and closed them again. Opened her emails, scrolled through spam and bills. She stopped. Had she imagined it?

She scrolled back up, slowly, until she found it. There was an unread email she had no recollection of receiving. From Klara Jørgensen. Replying to the email Esther had typed in her room and had no memory of sending. As she read Klara's words, Esther's eyes filled.

Dearest Esther,
    It was so good, and a terrible shock, to get your email today. I had to take a long walk before I could reply. It's complicated: I've hoped to hear from someone like you in a long time. I mean, someone in Aura's life outside of Denmark.

From her life or family in Australia. At the same time, for the last couple of years, I've been dreading that an email like yours would come one day: I've been worried about Aura ever since she left and stopped answering my calls and emails.

I'm heartbroken to learn what has happened. I am so very sorry for you and your family. I don't know how you found me or have connected me to Aura's life. I'm so glad you did. Thank you for reaching out.

You said you're thinking about coming overseas. If your trip to Copenhagen happens, please, let's meet. The timing couldn't be better, I'm leaving London soon to go home for the summer. And, yes, of course, in answer to your question, I'd be happy to tell you about Aura's life in Denmark.

If this makes it an easier decision to make, please know, you have friends here you just haven't met yet, Esther. All you have to do is get on the plane. Copenhagen and I will take care of the rest. Just come.

Kærlig hilsen,

Klara

Esther dropped her phone in her lap and put her face in her hands. She fought against the wave of emotion rising inside her. *Starry.* Esther's ears pricked at the sound of Aura's voice. She lifted her face, looked around. Down at her phone. Picked it up, trembling as she reread Klara's email. *You have friends here.*

She looked again at the road leading out of town. Jammed her seatbelt on and the key in the ignition. Sped to the intersection where signs pointed north and south. She idled until the car behind her beeped its horn. *Starry.*

'Okay,' she said aloud. 'Okay.'

Esther flicked on her indicator and turned north. Towards Salt Bay.

16

Esther drove eastward through the afternoon, eyes bleary, head spinning. Didn't stop for rest, or to eat, or drink. The shadows were long when she reached the coast road and followed it all the way to Erin's driveway.

The front door of the cottage swung open. Her aunt strode out in the blue light to meet her.

'About bloody time,' Erin said, her arms folded. 'You've been totally out of line, you know that, don't you?'

Esther took the keys out of the ignition and got out of the car. Lightheaded and dizzy, she leaned against the driver's door to steady herself. Held her hands up in weak surrender. 'I'm sorry,' she said, her voice flat. 'I don't know what else to say. I'm a piece of shit.' She offered the keys.

Erin took a step towards Esther. The anger in her face turned to concern. 'Are you alright? You're not a good colour.'

'I'm fine,' Esther said, waving Erin's inquiry away with one hand, still steadying herself against the car with the other.

Erin came closer. 'Holy hell,' she muttered, holding a hand to her nose. 'You smell like a brewery.'

Esther shrugged.

'When was the last time you ate? Showered? Slept?'

Esther shrugged again.

Erin looked over Esther's shoulder into the back of her car. When she spotted Esther's duffel and the rest of her belongings

in garbage bags, realisation dawned on Erin's face. 'Come on.'
Her voice was resolute. 'I've got dinner on the stove.'

Esther searched her aunt's eyes, wanting, but unsure.

Erin sighed. 'Got a better plan? You haven't answered Nin's
texts since you left. Or your dad's. And I gather neither you or
Freya have reached out to each other.'

Esther didn't respond.

'I'm it, kiddo.' Erin put her hand on Esther's shoulder.
'Come in, eat something. And take a damn shower.'

Esther laid low at Erin's for a few days. While Erin was at work
on campus, Esther slept. She unpacked her belongings from
Erin's car then gave it a wash, polish and vacuum. Put loads
through the washing machine. Hung them out to dry. Watered
Erin's veggie garden. Sat outside under the gums with a cup of
tea and a view of the rolling waves in the distance. Wished it
was all enough for redemption.

Countless times a day, Esther checked her phone. No one
messaged. No one called.

Over dinner on their third night together, Erin held her wine
glass and gazed thoughtfully at Esther across the dining table. A
cheesy basil pizza they'd ordered in sat between them.

'What?' Esther asked, pulling a string of mozzarella from
her pizza and popping it in her mouth before washing it down
with her red wine.

'We haven't talked about Aura's journal since you got back.'

Esther drank more wine.

'How are you feeling about it after a bit of time? About
Denmark?'

Klara's photograph filled Esther's mind: Aura grinning,
standing in front of Liden Gunver, in the arms of a man she
clearly loved. Esther hadn't told Erin, or anyone, about her

discovery. Of the photo, or Liden Gunver. Or about her email from Klara.

Esther looked into Erin's face, grappling with how good – right – it felt to finally know something about Aura that no one else knew.

'I haven't thought about it,' she lied to Erin. 'Not really. Things have been pretty hectic.'

Erin reached for another slice of pizza, her silver bangles clinking. 'When are you going to see Jack and Freya?'

The directness of the question made Esther's skin turn cold.

'You can't avoid her forever,' Erin said.

'Mum knows I'm here?' Esther asked.

Erin gave Esther a pointed look.

'Of course she does,' Esther mumbled, pushing her plate away.

'What did you think? That you could storm out of dinner with them after they'd shown you Aura's journal, and that would be the end of it?'

'You don't get it,' Esther said quietly. 'You don't know how hard Mum is to talk to.'

'I've known her a lot longer than you have; I think I might.'

'Yeah, but not like me. Not as her daughter.'

Erin seemed to take in Esther's words. After a while she reached across the table for Esther's hand. 'Bottom line, there's an unfinished conversation you all need to have together. Avoiding that isn't going to change it. Grieving for Aura is hard enough. You need to go home to your folks. Go to your mum.'

The next afternoon, Esther dragged her feet down the side of the Shell House towards Freya's tattoo studio. The curtains to Jack's office window were drawn. After her pizza with Erin, Esther had texted her parents to say she was back in town and could they meet. Jack had replied straight away. He was at a conference for a few days but couldn't wait to see her.

Freya took a few hours to reply. *Hi Esther. Come to the studio tomorrow afternoon. I'll be finished with clients by then. We can talk.*

Esther tried to shake out her nerves as she walked the path to the studio. Though it was only late afternoon, not yet dusk, a candle burned in the window. *The ancestors don't sleep.* Music came from inside; the strains of Christine Anu's voice singing 'My Island Home', soothing as a river. There was the watery murmur of women's conversation: Freya with others. An occasional laugh. Wafts of eucalyptus smoke. Esther straightened her shoulders, tried to take even breaths.

At the closed door to Freya's studio, the air grew close with a familiar, heady scent. Bushes of Casa Blanca lilies grew thick on either side of the studio door. Some had started to unfold; by nightfall their glistening white flowers would open into large, fragrant stars. Their perfume reminded Esther of afternoons she'd spent as a girl, loitering around the threshold of her mother's sacred space. She pressed a hand lightly to one of the lilies, as she'd done countless times as a kid. Made sure to splay her fingers as if the flowers might read her palm, her heart, and grant or deny her entry. When she was young, it'd been so thrilling when the door seemingly swung open by magic.

Esther took her hand away from the lily. Adjusted her backpack slung over one shoulder and knocked hard on the closed door.

'Mum?' Her voice was thin in the cool air.

Her knock went unanswered. She tried the knob. The door opened.

She went inside and closed the door behind her. Walked into the studio, around the partition screen set to the side. Freya was bent over her client, long silver-blonde braid hanging over her shoulder as she spoke to someone out of Esther's view. Then, the cicada–like buzz of the tattoo gun.

Freya was expecting Esther, had told her when to show up. And yet. There she was, being made to wait. Esther pinched the soft skin of her wrist between her fingernails. Why was she disappointed? When would she learn? The scent of the lilies distracted her. It clung to her hair, her clothes.

Aura at fifteen, coming down the hallway carrying an armful of the starry flowers, her face as white as each petal.
'Who are they from?' Esther begs. Aura is unyielding. 'Mum, Aura won't tell me who sent her flowers,' Esther whines through the house.
'Shut up, Starry; they're a prank. They're from no one,' Aura hisses at her.

Esther twitched with impatience. 'Mum.' She raised her voice over the tattoo gun.
Freya turned. The coolness of her gaze hit Esther in the chest. She held up a hand, fingers splayed. *Five more minutes.*
Esther took in the studio, remembering. The pink velvet chaise longue Freya bought on eBay; Esther's school play that she'd missed to drive to Launceston to pick it up. The antique gold-leaf partition screen Freya was behind, with the hand-painted dance of seven white cranes in flight across it. As a child, Esther used to stare at the cranes, willing them to move, to show her how to fly.
Bitterness weighed heavily on Esther's shoulders as she surveyed Freya's space, her mother's self-made success. After she'd been repeatedly rejected by tattoo parlours in Nipaluna, Hobart, Freya had decided to restore and convert the shed behind the Shell House into her own tattoo studio.
Esther ran her fingers along the back of the light caramel-coloured leather couch set in the middle of the room. It was covered with names; every woman who had come to Freya as an apprentice had tattooed their name on the couch after completing their first professional tattoo. Esther traced the

curls and sharp edges in some of the lettering. She and Aura lying drooped across it, collars of their high school uniforms unbuttoned, sharing a bag of hot chips from the corner shop after school. They lick the chicken salt from their fingers before tracing the names of the women who flocked to learn from Freya until they could tattoo on their own. All the names spiral outwards from one Freya tattooed at the centre of the couch. *Queenie*. Freya's first client.

When Freya had first opened her studio, she'd struggled to get more than a few clients a month. Things had continued that way until Doctor Queenie Robertson, healed from her preventative double mastectomy, found Freya through the recommendation of one of her patients. She spent two full day sessions on the tattoo bed in Freya's studio. After that, word of mouth made it known that Freya was skilled with scar cover-up work. From surgery. Or abuse. Self-harm. Freya began to make a name for herself for specialising in turning pain and loss into beauty and solace. Women in the community who'd been tattooed by Freya began talking about how she made them feel. Seen, heard, tended to. Freya began offering apprenticeships. Social media was the bird that carried the ember in its beak and spread the wildfire: women started coming from all over Lutruwita, Tasmania, first, then the mainland. Some to get tattooed, others to learn how to tattoo. Freya started a waitlist. The women continued to come.

Esther checked the time on her phone. Freya's five minutes had so far been twenty-five. Behind the painted partition screen, the tattoo gun stopped and started, stopped and started. Esther stared at the cranes dancing across the screen until one of them flapped their wings for her. She glimpsed the pale pink skin underwing. Remembered the black swan crashing into her windscreen, its feathers bloodied, the explosion ricocheting through her body. Esther squeezed her eyes shut against the sounds and visions in her head, but they only shifted to thoughts of Aura. Aura had been there, Esther realised. In Freya's studio.

Behind the screen, lying on the tattoo bed, under Freya's gun. The two of them together in their own secret world of transformation. Without her.

'We're done,' Freya announced. She emerged triumphant from behind the screen, followed by Coral, Nin's cousin whom Esther had seen at the beach the day after the memorial.

They were joined by the woman Esther realised Coral had been tattooing, who, oblivious to Esther's presence, stepped gingerly in front of the mirror with her eyes closed. When she opened them and saw her reflection, she gasped. On one of her arms, from her shoulder downwards, Coral had tattooed richly toned yellows, golden browns and olive greens: the stipes and blades of giant kelp. Coral had given the kelp an edge of aqua and turquoise, a hint of the sea. The effect was mesmerising. Esther couldn't help but stare at how the kelp seemed to dance over the woman's skin, reaching down her arm. On the underside of her elbow was tattooed one pink-tipped green marina shell, almost hidden like a secret by the kelp.

'Is it normal to feel this amazing after sitting in pain for so many hours?' the woman asked, staring at her arm. 'I feel like I can do anything.' She laughed tearily, gazing in adoration at her new skin.

'Adrenaline and endorphins are a winning combo,' Freya said to the woman, her voice warm.

Esther studied her mother, envy and resentment cutting through her. After Aura had disappeared, Freya had taken to living in her studio. Slept on the couch. Used the kitchenette and cold shower. She didn't come back into the house unless it was for something essential. Sometimes Esther had stood outside Freya's studio at night, in the dark with the lilies, picking at the skin on her arm, listening to her mother's voice break inside as she sang with Stevie Nicks on the stereo.

'I love it so much, bub,' the woman in front of the mirror was saying to Coral, her voice breaking. 'I belong to myself again,' she whispered.

'Let's get you wrapped up.' Coral walked the woman back to the tattoo bed behind the partition screen.

Freya watched them go. When she looked at Esther, her smile faded. 'I hear you've left the west coast,' she said.

Esther gave a nod.

'What are your plans now?' Freya folded her arms.

Esther eyed her mother. 'How many of her tattoos did you do?' she countered. *Which line did she ask you to tattoo first? Did it hurt her? Did you listen to music while you tattooed her? Burn gum leaves for cleansing, with her too? What did her face look like when she saw her new skin in the mirror? Why didn't she ask me to be there with her? Why didn't you?*

'We're done here, Freya,' Coral interrupted. Freya plastered a smile on her face and saw Coral and the freshly tattooed woman out of her studio. When she came back, her expression was unreadable.

They stood together in awkward silence.

'Do you want a cup of tea?' Freya asked.

'No,' Esther said. 'I want to know how many of Aura's tattoos you did in here.'

Freya leaned against the wall. Regarded Esther. 'Four. I did the last four of the lines from *Seven Skins*. The first three she had done overseas.'

Esther took her backpack off her shoulder, unzipped it and lifted out Aura's journal. Freya's eyes flickered at the sight of it. Esther handed it to her mother. Freya thumbed through the pages. Stopped, and handed the book back to Esther. 'This was the first one that I tattooed on her.'

Esther ran her fingertips over the image taped to the page. It was an illustration, in a similar style to Agnete and the merman, of a woman dressed in elegant finery, standing on a grassy knoll, looking in sorrow and yearning at three swans flying in the sky, away from her. Above the image, Aura had written:

The fourth skin: Threshold

On the facing page, her line:

Who would you be if you'd never strayed to the shore?

Esther looked at Freya, so tempted to tell her mother about finding the photo online of Aura and her mystery man in front of Liden Gunver. About Klara Jørgensen and their email exchange. Years of built-up stubbornness stopped her. 'Where were the tattoos on Aura's body?' she asked Freya instead.

Freya hesitated, then motioned for Esther to turn around. She turned. Behind her, Freya swept Esther's hair over her shoulder and pressed her fingertips to a point between Esther's shoulder blades.

'Her first tattoo, the first line in *Seven Skins*, started about here,' Freya said. Then she traced a finger down Esther's spine. 'Each line followed. Downwards. Black ink. Fine needle. Aura's own handwriting.'

A shiver went through Esther's body as she felt her mother's hands on her back, felt on her own body where Aura had been tattooed on hers. She imagined her sister's spine lined with ink, her own handwriting, her own words. A ladder. A constellation. A map.

Esther turned to face Freya. 'What did she tell you about them? Her tattoos?'

'Just that she'd had the first three tattooed overseas, in the order that they appear in *Seven Skins*,' Freya said, her voice tender. 'I don't know why she didn't get all seven done in Denmark.'

Esther flicked back through the journal to reread the first three verses.

If you want change, raise your sword, raise your voice.
He will give you flowers to forget. You plant seeds, to remember.
Maybe she chose the depths. Maybe she's free.

'Aura told me that while she was in Denmark tattoos became her selkie trees,' Freya said.

Esther looked out of the studio window to the far end of the garden where the silver birch grew. 'But what sorrow was she giving them? What pain were the tattoos taking for her?'

Freya hesitated. 'She wouldn't say. And maybe it was the wrong thing to do, but I didn't push her to tell me. I was so grateful she'd come to me, that there was something practical I could do for her. We didn't talk much while I was working on her. But I got such a strong sense of how much these lines meant to her ...' Freya's eyes were distant. 'It felt significant. Like she wanted to tell me more,' she said. 'Us,' Freya quickly corrected herself. 'She wanted to tell *us* more. She just didn't know how.' Freya's eyes filled. 'It just felt good to be there for her somehow. To do that for her.'

Freya's words sent guilt and anger crashing together inside Esther. She could have been there for Aura, could have answered her plea for help. But Esther had ignored Aura's note. Esther shoved Aura's journal back into her backpack.

'Hey, careful,' Freya chided, watching her.

Something hardened in Esther's chest. 'I wouldn't know,' she said sharply.

Freya wiped her cheeks. 'Wouldn't know what?'

'I wouldn't know what it's like. For you to be there for me when I needed you.' Esther struggled to stay composed.

'I beg your pardon?' Freya clenched her jaw.

'It's great you were there for Aura, Mum. Here with her, in your own little secret tattoo sessions, because she'd let you know she needed you. It's great. Really. I'm just saying, I don't know how that feels. Because when I needed you most, you were nowhere to be found. Oh, no, that's right. Surprise, surprise: you were in here. Tattooing women. Supporting other women. Saving other women.' Esther knew she was lashing out but couldn't stop herself.

'Esther, watch it,' Freya warned.

'What, Mum? Truth hurt too much?'

'You're talking bullshit,' Freya said dismissively.

Her words slapped Esther in the face. 'That day, I was the one who booked us a family session with that shrink friend of Dad's and I was the one who waited inside for you both, waiting and waiting, like a fucking dog. You were out here. Being someone else's saviour. You couldn't even be bothered walking ten metres inside. Same with Dad. He was off saving a client from their own grief. Meanwhile I was here. In there,' Esther seethed, jabbing a finger in the direction of the Shell House. 'I showed up for our family. Unlike either of you.'

Freya glared at Esther but stayed silent.

'You've really got nothing to say?' Esther shouted. 'You're just going to stand there, in silence? And you wonder why I won't go to Denmark?' She scowled at her mother.

Freya's eyes glittered with anger and pain. Still she said nothing.

Esther turned and stormed out of the studio, slamming the door behind her. Leaned back against the door, chest heaving. Her body ached with hurt and rage.

A few moments later, muffled strains of Fleetwood Mac blared from Freya's studio. 'Everywhere'. Esther clenched her fists. 'That fucking song,' she shouted. Inside, the volume went up.

She looked down at her mother's lilies, her vision heated and watery. Before she knew what she was doing, Esther had snapped the heads off their stems, tossed them into the garden bed and strode away.

17

A few days later, Esther walked the path winding between moonshine bushes and shivering sea grass. Ahead, the stargazing shack was illuminated by afternoon sun. Its windows caught the light and reflected gold.

When she got to the veranda, Esther swept the top step clean of blue gum leaves and sat. Watched the sea roll from the shore to the horizon. She scanned the lines and edges of the island – all she'd ever known. Glanced at the grave of the black swan. Her dirt was drying out. *My love will not leave you.*

Esther rubbed her hands together, trying to rid herself of the prickling nerves she'd felt ever since she and Jack had agreed to meet. Checked the time on her phone. Jack was late.

While she waited for her dad, Esther took her phone from her pocket and opened Klara Jørgensen's email. She'd read it so many times since she'd left Calliope that she nearly knew it by heart. *You have friends here.*

The soft whir of little beating wings broke Esther's concentration. She looked up from her phone. Behind her in the corner of the veranda fluttered a mass of shimmering brown with occasional flashes of blue and purple. Esther waited until her eyes adjusted to the shadows. They fluttered, an eclipse of moths, like women shaking out jewel-hemmed shawls before rewrapping themselves and settling.

'Here she is.'

Esther turned to see Jack approaching, bag slung over his shoulder.

'Sorry I'm late.'

'Hi Dad,' she whispered and pointed behind her, smiling.

'Ah,' Jack said, easing himself onto the top step beside Esther. 'The old ladies have gathered with you.'

'Old ladies?'

'Southern old lady moths.'

'That's right,' Esther said. 'I remember them from when we hung out here when I was a kid. I haven't seen them like this – so many, I mean – in, well, longer than I can remember.'

'That's their spot. They're always there, in that cool, dark corner,' Jack said. 'They can sit motionless, sometimes for months at a time, right in plain view.' He nudged her. 'Maybe you just weren't seeing what was right in front of you, Starry.' Jack smiled, well intentioned,

Esther looked away. Ever the clear-eyed therapist. Except when it came to his own grief.

'You used to love them,' Jack went on. 'Their blue eye spots on their wings, and the jagged line markings beneath.'

She frowned as a memory surfaced, one she couldn't clearly recall. 'Their wing markings look like heartbeats,' she murmured. The rhythmic sound of a machine beeping. A bright, sharp line peaking and falling on a monitor screen. 'You brought me here to see them, Dad, after we visited Aura in hospital that time, when I was a kid. When she had her appendix out. Right?'

Jack busied himself with his bag.

'Dad?'

He glanced at Esther, then up at the moths. 'Right.' The sound of little wings continued to beat in the shadows.

Her mind skittered over the vague hospital memory from childhood: the garish light, the beeping heart monitor and its green, jagged line. Aura lying in bed, sleeping. Freya curled around her; a second skin, a shell.

Esther's thoughts flurried, until they settled. Flinging open the front door of the Shell House and running down the hallway calling for her sister. Careering into the living room and coming to a halt. The dull stone of Aura's eyes. The inward curl of her shoulders. The enormity of her spirit seemingly shrunken to the spectral woman who bears no resemblance to her wild, spirited sister. In those weeks before Aura disappeared, what had been in plain sight? What had Esther missed?

'So,' Jack started.

Esther came back to herself, sitting beside her dad, southern old lady moths at their backs. She swallowed the lump in her throat. Pressed her hands together.

'I wanted to meet up today to apologise, Dad,' Esther said. Jack looked at her, eyes flooded with empathy and forgiveness. 'I'm sure you've heard all about the fight Mum and I had and I'm sorry about that.' Blue gums tapped the roof of the shack, whispering to each other overhead.

'I'm not sure I'm the one you should be apologising to, Starry,' Jack said softly.

Esther turned away. Thick ribbons of kelp shone bronze, black, green in the clear, rolling shallows. 'I don't owe her anything.'

Jack let Esther's words settle. After a moment, he took her hand. 'Your mum told me some of the things you … talked about.' He rubbed a circle on her hand with his thumb. 'I'm sorry we weren't there for you that day, love. For our family.' He swallowed. 'I'm sorry we let you down.'

Esther looked at her father. Willed herself not to crumble inside. 'Thanks, Dad.'

Jack continued to hold her hand. 'You said in your text that you had something to talk to me about?'

After her blazing row with Freya, Esther had texted Jack, asking him to meet at the shack after he got back from his conference. 'I do,' she said, taking a breath. 'It's going to put you in an uncomfortable position, Dad, and I'm sorry about that. It's the way it has to be, though.'

'My god, what is it, love?' Jack's brow furrowed.

Esther took her laptop out of her bag and showed him Klara Jørgensen's photo of Aura and her mystery man in front of Liden Gunver. She held Jack's hand tightly as he sucked in his breath at the sight of Aura. Esther pointed to Liden Gunver in the background, which Jack recognised from Aura's journal, and told him the story of the sculpture, the folklore song, and how Aura's corresponding line in her journal seemed to be rewriting Liden Gunver's fate. She told him how she'd been fired from Calliope and, lastly, mentioned her emails with Klara. Jack sat blinking furiously as he tried to absorb all the information.

'There's one more thing,' Esther said, taking a deep, slow breath. Jack looked at her, braced. Before she'd arrived at the shack, she hadn't known if she'd go through with it, but after telling Jack about Klara's email, and with the black swan's grave in her peripheral vision, Esther's decision was spontaneously made. She took another deep breath.

'Dad,' she said slowly. 'I will go to Denmark.'

Jack stared at her. 'Oh, Starry,' he said, his voice thin.

'On one condition,' she said firmly. 'I don't want Mum to know I'm going.'

Dread filled Jack's face.

'I'm sorry, Dad, I know it's a lot to ask, but it's my one condition.'

Jack looked towards the sea. 'How will that work?'

'It means Erin can't know. Nin can't know either. Not at first, anyway. You'll have to tell everyone I've gone down south, for work. It'll just be you and me who know. And whoever I'm going to stay with in Copenhagen. Mum and Erin's cousin? Abelone?'

Jack nodded, distracted.

'You'll have to ask her to keep it to herself too.'

'That shouldn't be a problem; she's not in regular contact with Freya and Erin,' Jack said, his voice sounding far away.

'Right,' Esther said. 'So, we'll just take it as it comes, Dad. But I'll go. This is how I can go.'

With the words spoken and outside of her body, Copenhagen suddenly became Esther's future reality. It loomed in its strangeness, an unknown two-dimensional pop-up place of spires and stone Esther knew only from childhood storybooks, View-Master reels, and screens. She looked around at the familiarity of the bay, gum trees, sea, the seven boulders and the shells that held her life within them. Let go of Jack's hand and swallowed the lump in her throat. Pins and needles travelled up her legs.

'Love?' Jack asked.

A swift tug of panic drew tight across her chest. She shook her head. 'Ugh,' she said, her tongue swelling with nausea. 'I don't know how to do this, Dad. Fuck. I don't know if I can go.'

'Swearing, Starry.'

Esther shot a withering look at Jack. In apology, he opened his arms. She shuffled across into the alcove of his body. He kissed her head.

'Listen,' he said, finding his words, 'this is scary, what you're doing. But I'll help with whatever you need. Flights, money, information.' He sat back, met Esther's eye.

'You won't tell her?' Esther asked, searching his eyes.

'I won't tell her,' he promised.

Esther leaned back into him. 'Okay,' she whispered. 'I'm going to Denmark.'

They sat together watching the waves.

'This is going to ask a lot of you, love,' Jack said into her hair. 'It's bound to feel uncomfortable and bring up all sorts of fears. Going into any situation that is as unknown as what you're facing going to Copenhagen is hugely challenging. But ... I know you're strong.' He rested his chin on her head. 'Maybe it would help to remember that what you're feeling is what every great questing story is about. To reach the treasure she seeks, our hero must first get past the dragon.' With her fingertip, Esther traced the blue line of a vein under the thin skin on the back of Jack's hand.

The sun had nearly sunk under the glowering line between sky and sea. Esther half-closed her eyes in the light, a trick Aura had taught her when they were kids. *Catch the gold in your eyelashes so we have light for later, Starry, so it won't be dark in our dreams.*

'You know, love,' Jack said, 'you could have told us you were a dishy in Calliope. No shame in that. You didn't have to lie about being a manager to validate your life there.'

Esther bristled. 'Can we not do therapy right now, Dad?'

'I'm not trying to give you therapy.'

'Sure you're not,' Esther said.

'It's not a bad idea though, have I have many trusted colleagues that I think you'd—'

'Dad!'

Jack let the conversation go. They sat together watching the sky change.

'What now?' Esther asked after a while.

'Well, tomorrow, we'll look at booking your flights. And I can get in touch with Abelone if you'd like.'

'That'd be good,' Esther agreed. She clenched her fists.

'And then …'

'And then,' Esther said, unable to keep the tremor of nerves from her voice, 'I go to Denmark.'

The next day Esther met Jack in a café with her laptop and notebook. Heads bent together over coffees, they planned Esther's departure for the following week, to coincide with Freya being in Nipaluna, Hobart, on a guest artist residency at a popular tattoo parlour.

'It'll just keep things simple this way,' Jack said to Esther. She nodded.

Jack took his credit card out of his wallet and placed it beside her laptop. Esther eyed it. He nudged the card towards her. Slowly, she began to type in the numbers. When it came to confirming the booking, her fingers hovered over the mousepad.

'Am I doing this?' she asked shakily.

Jack's face was serious. 'Are you?'

Aura stands in front of Liden Gunver, in the arms of a mysterious man. Light in her eyes, her face, falling over her shoulders. *Maybe she chose the depths. Maybe she's free.*

Esther took a deep breath. And clicked.

The day before she flew out, Erin drove Esther, with her packed bags, to the smash repair shop to pick up her ute.

'Make sure you check with them that the ute's in good enough nick for the drive to Bruny,' Erin said. She wrapped her arms around Esther. 'Stay in touch, okay? And answer your bloody mobile when I text or call.'

'I will,' Esther whispered into Erin's curls. She'd stuck to the plan. As far as Erin knew, Esther was going south for more hospitality work. While they hugged, Esther was seized by the temptation to tell Erin the truth. Not only about where she was really going, but what she'd done before she'd left Erin's house. *While you were in the shower, I stole your painted cake recipe from your cookbook. To take you with me.* Lying to her aunt made Esther's stomach burn, but the alternative – Erin, and then, inevitably, Freya knowing she'd gone to Copenhagen – kept her quiet. Esther was too angry with her mother to give Freya that kind of satisfaction.

When they parted, Erin had tears in her eyes. Esther swallowed back her own as Erin drove off and she waved goodbye.

After she'd collected her ute, Esther drove to the storage facility where Jack had arranged to have it kept while she was gone. He met her there, and after her ute was safely locked away, they went home to the Shell House together. Jack made toasties for dinner. They put on extra jumpers, ate outside and watched the stars with a few glasses of wine. Esther spent her last night on the island sleeping fitfully in her old bedroom, filled with old dreams.

The moments before dawn were raw with the cold promise of winter. Esther's breath puffed in icy little clouds as she watched the stars and moon begin to fade. The sky started to lighten to a thick oyster-shell grey. Through a carpet of low mist, Esther paced in the garden, back and forth in front of the silver birch tree. Some of its autumn bark had begun to shed. She looked across the garden to Freya's studio; the windows were dark. From lofty heights in the surrounding gum trees, kookaburras began to laugh. A line of rosy light pierced the bank of grey cloud on the horizon.

Esther shook out her limbs as she paced; her body was heavy with fear. She eyed the silver birch. After a while, walked to its trunk. Laid her bare hands on its bark, cold, rough and almost silver in first light. Aura stood at its base with her arms wrapped around it. *You tell your heartache to the tree, wrap your arms around it, give it all your pain and the tree takes it from you. Then sheds your pain in its bark.*

Esther stepped closer. Wrapped her arms around her sister's Selkie Tree. Held on as tightly as she could.

At the airport, three hours head of her flight time, Esther and Jack checked her baggage and sat in the waiting lounge. Jack bought their drinks. Esther's half-serious request for a morning whiskey was ignored. She tried to drink the peppermint tea he brought her, but it tasted like soap. Jack kept an arm around her, didn't say much. Esther kept checking the departures information board, bit a nail down to blood; time seemed to lose all traction in the transience of the airport. She went to the bathroom for something to do. Afterwards, she browsed in a souvenir shop. On a whim she bought a packet of Iced VoVos and tucked them into her bag. Re-joined Jack at their table. Sat. Continued to wait.

After a while, Jack reached into his pocket and took out his keys. He slid a keyring off the main loop. Esther watched, curious.

'To take with you,' Jack said and pressed the keyring into her hand. It was silver, a hand with thumb and index finger pressed together.

'Space Club.' Esther snorted. 'Did you have this made?' she asked, incredulous. Flipped the keyring over. A sequence of numbers was stamped into the silver. 299 792 458. She looked at Jack quizzically.

'The speed of light,' he explained. 'More specifically, how many metres per second light travels. I had it made after Aura was … gone. After you left for the west coast. I wanted something tangible I could hold on to. To remember. That I wasn't alone. I want you to take it. So that you remember. While you're away. You're never alone.' Jack leaned forward and ran a fingertip over the number sequence. 'The light in the stars that you'll look up and see in Denmark is travelling from the past. Some of that light started its journey when she was—' He looked to the dimming sky. Waited out the emotion. 'I want you to remember that some of the starlight you'll see every night in Denmark started its journey when Aura was still with us,' he finished.

Esther clutched the keyring in her palm.

'It's made from recycled Lutruwita silver. You're taking this island, and those of us on it who love you, to the island that awaits you.'

'Dad.' Esther tried to find words.

'"De Profundis ad Astra",' he said, his voice wobbling.

'I really fucking love it, Dad.'

'Swearing, Starry.' Jack smiled.

'Thank you,' Esther said, 'for all of this. For everything you've done to help me. For not telling Mum. For understanding my reasons.'

They sat together as the airport bustled around them. Jack cleared his throat. 'Did you know,' he said, 'that southern old lady moths have been found thriving as far from their home habitat in the southern states of Australia as Macquarie Island in Antarctica?'

Esther eyed him sidelong. A suspicious smile pulled at the corners of her mouth. 'I suppose in this analogy I am a southern old lady moth. And my Macquarie Island is Copenhagen, where, far from home, I'm going to find myself thriving or some such shit?'

Jack made a face as if about to protest, but changed his mind. After a moment he put his arm back around Esther. Exhaled deeply. 'Fuck knows, love.'

'Dad,' Esther shrieked. 'Swearing.'

'Don't get used to it.' Jack's voice was strained. 'It's just fucking called for the day your youngest leaves home for the wide world.'

She squeezed his hand in hers. 'Fuck yes, Dad ... it is.'

An announcement came over the airport speakers, calling Esther's flight to board. It was suddenly happening too fast. She wasn't ready to go.

'Okay, you've got everything, right?' Jack fretted. 'I've sorted Abelone; she's picking you up in Copenhagen. And you've emailed Klara, you'll meet her soon?'

'Yes, Dad. And yes.'

They walked to her gate. Jack kept his arm around her. A Saturday morning, Esther and Aura dive-bombing their parents in bed. Snuggling and nagging until Jack relents and lets the girls watch *Rage* and *She-Ra* cartoons.

Esther leaned into Jack's warmth. Looked down. Focused on her feet, one step after another.

'I don't want to drag this out,' she said at the boarding queue. She gave her dad a short, tight hug.

'Call me, anytime. Text. Let me know if you need money. Or help. Anything.' Jack held on to her hands, until she pulled away.

At the front of the queue to board, Esther handed her boarding pass to the airline staff, who scanned it and waved her forward. She took a few steps but came to an abrupt stop. Her hands and feet prickled with panic. She turned. Jack was where she'd left him, watching her go.

'Miss?' The staff urged her forward. 'Please. It's a full flight.'

Esther moved towards the boarding bridge. 'I can't,' she said to unhearing passengers stepping around her, passing her by.

She looked back at her dad, standing, arms folded, cast in ripples of shallow morning light, as if he were underwater. Esther strained to see his face. Jack murmured something. He raised his hand. Thumb and index finger pressed together at eye level. Jack nodded at her.

'Miss, please,' the staff addressed Esther.

Esther forced herself to walk. To move towards the plane. Aura running ahead into the sea, beckoning as she dives under the waves.

When she entered the boarding bridge, Esther thrust her arm in the air. Thumb and index finger pressed together in the Space Club signal, until she was out of view.

18

Esther stumbled off the plane and into Copenhagen airport, crumpled and nursing a headache after too many vodka and sodas, her attempt to quell her fear of flying and leaving everything she knew behind. The terminal windows looked out into darkness. After twenty-four hours, she'd stopped counting how much time had passed since she'd left home or trying to figure out where she'd lost or gained time while she was flying. How surreal and ridiculous that idea seemed. As she followed the people walking towards customs, her mind skidded along the edge of delirium.

In the queue at the passport checkpoint, she recalled advice Jack had given her. *When you get to customs, just give the information you're asked for. Keep it brief. Keep it calm.*

'What is the purpose of your visit today?' an officer asked, reaching for Esther's passport.

'I, uh,' Esther cleared her throat. *Keep it brief. Keep it calm.* 'My purpose is to find out what happened to my sister when she came to study here in Copenhagen.'

'What do you mean by that?' the woman demanded.

'She came here, my sister. Aura. Then she left and went back home to Australia. And disappeared. Or drowned. They think she drowned in the sea. They don't know if it was on purpose, or not. So, my parents asked me to come, to Denmark, to meet friends and family who knew her. Who loved her. My big sister. This is my first time away from

Australia. Lutruwita. Tasmania. Where I'm from. I have a relative picking me up, who I'm staying with while I'm here. She's Mum's cousin. This is my first time overseas. Did I say that? I've never been so tired. Long-haul overseas flights really don't fuck around, do they.' Esther ran out of breath and sucked in oxygen as heat rose to her face. She pushed her fists deep into her pockets.

The officer scrutinised her. Looked her up and down.

Unable to trust herself to do anything else, Esther held her nerve and stared back.

After an interminable wait, the officer flicked back and forth through Esther's passport, stamped two pages with a force that made Esther flinch, and handed it back to her.

'I hope you find what you're looking for,' she said, a flicker of warmth in her eyes. 'Welcome to Denmark.'

Clusters of people flowed around her at the arrivals area, arms outreached, hugging and smiling. Esther searched the crowd for Abelone. Jack had shown her a photo; Esther looked for a head of white hair. No luck. She scanned the faces around her again. Out of the corner of her eye she saw a waving flash; a woman with a thick knot of white hair speared in place with a thin black paintbrush waved as she approached.

'Esther?'

'Abelone,' Esther said with an awkward wave. She could taste the alcohol on her breath. It was too late to buy mints.

Abelone stepped forward to give her a brusque hug. Her black coat smelled faintly of tobacco, salt and aniseed. When they parted, Abelone held Esther at arm's length and looked her over. Esther tried to hold her breath but, after she caught the flicker of disapproval in Abelone's eyes, knew she'd smelled the booze on her. Esther tried to smooth some of the wrinkles out of her clothes.

'You are so much like Freya,' Abelone said. Over her heart, a brooch: a bright, warm, honey-coloured chunk of raw amber.

Esther stiffened. Jack had said he'd told Abelone that her travels were sensitive for their family, and that Freya didn't know about Esther's trip.

'People have always told me how much I'm like my dad,' Esther replied coolly.

'Well.' Abelone took Esther's heavy suitcase from her. 'Let's get you home.' She turned towards the terminal exit. Esther followed. 'The flight from Australia is for Satan,' Abelone said over her shoulder. 'You must feel plum fucked.'

'Sorry?' Esther balked, thinking she must have heard wrong. She hurried to keep up with Abelone's pace.

'Have I got it wrong?' Abelone stopped. 'How do you say it? Plum fuckered?'

Esther thought for a moment and, despite their bumpy meeting, started to laugh. 'Do you mean plumb tuckered?'

Abelone snapped her fingers. 'Yes, she said. 'Plumb tuckered. That's it. You must be plumb tuckered out.' She carried on, leading the way.

Esther followed, trying to reconcile the gruff and abrupt woman in front of her with the one Aura had described in some of her first emails from Copenhagen, when she was still writing to Esther.

I feel immediately at home here, Starry. Abelone has a heart the size of the sea, swears all the time in Danish, smokes a tobacco pipe, and has long white hair that she always wears up, held in place by any random thing. A pen, a stick from the park, a paintbrush, a fork. Undone, I think it might be down to her knees. You would love her too.

'Keep up,' Abelone called to Esther as she dragged behind. 'The car's not far, and it's only a twenty-minute drive until you're in bed.'

They walked together out of the airport terminal. Into the cold northern hemisphere air.

Aura's View-Master reels came to life in front of Esther's eyes
as Copenhagen streamed by the passenger window in Abelone's
car. An enchanting blur of streetlights, cobblestones and
shadows.

Through a lattice of trees, the lights of Tivoli Gardens
glowed. Esther pressed her fingers to the window.

Aura saying, 'Tivoli is the second oldest amusement park in
the world, Starry; it opened in 1843,' as her face pops up from
behind her View-Master. Her eyes dilate with wonder. 'You
know what that means, right?' She hands Esther her View-
Master for a look.

Esther shakes her head; she doesn't know. She looks
through the viewfinder to see a magical place of hanging
flowering gardens, trees strung with lights, an exotic aquarium,
a rollercoaster, a palace with swans.

'Our ancestors, Johanna and Gull, might have been there.
When they were girls, like us. We could go one day; we could
walk where they walked, together. Can you imagine what that
would be like?'

Abelone braked. People on bicycles whooshed by. At slower
speed, Esther was able to read a passing street sign.

'We're seriously on Hans Christian Andersens Boulevard?
That's really the name of this street?' she asked.

Abelone nodded. 'There's a sculpture of him just up here.
A castle in Tivoli is named after him. His house in Odense is a
museum. And, of course, everyone comes to Copenhagen for
his Den Lille Havfrue at the water.'

'The Little Mermaid?' Esther clarified.

'Ja.'

~

Esther lying on Aura's bed. 'Why Copenhagen, though?' She flicks through the brochures Aura has brought home from the travel agent. 'Why not just go to Sydney or Melbourne?'

Aura recoils in faux-disgust. 'Starry, it's in our blood, a northern island made of myth and fairytales. It's a city built on stories. They're by the sea, in the earth, written in stone. Hans Christian Andersen is revered like a king there because he wrote them down. But I want to know who his contemporaries were. Where were the women writers and their fairytales? Where else could, or would, I go to study them?'

Esther sat straighter in the passenger seat as she recognised an imposing red brick building with an ornate façade and a spire reaching to the night sky. 'City Hall,' she murmured.

'Københavns Rådhus.' Abelone pointed. 'Did you know inside is Jens Olsen's World Clock? A very boring name for an advanced astronomical clock that has a perpetual calendar and can tell lunar and solar eclipses, positions of the stars, and the time.'

Esther thought of Jack, holding the Space Club signal for her as she boarded the plane. 'You really love clocks,' she said, looking across at Abelone 'We still have your Agnete clock in our kitchen at home.'

'Ja.' Abelone nodded. 'I have the same clock too in my kitchen.'

'My sister loved it so much.'

Abelone's smile faded. She glanced at Esther then back to the road. 'She told me, when she was here. Asked me to change the time on my clock from Copenhagen to Salt Bay, her two worlds above and below. Hey, I could take you,' Abelone said.

'Sorry?'

'Now. To the sculpture, in the canal. Agnete's sculpture. Of her havmanden and their children, waiting for her. It's lit up at night, the time when Aura most loved to visit it. It's haunting, ja, but so beautiful.'

'I, um,' Esther started to say.

'No problem. Sleep is what you need.' Abelone changed her mind. 'Let's get you home.'

Esther gripped the edges of the passenger seat as they careered around a corner, shadows chasing them in her passenger mirror.

'Nearly there.' Abelone flicked open a compartment in the console of her car and rummaged within. Took out a confectionery tin and popped it open with her thumb. 'Salmiaklakrids?' She offered the tin of glittering black pastilles to Esther. When she saw the look on Esther's face, Abelone erupted in husky laughter. 'Salt liquorice?'

'Uh, sure,' Esther said, compelled by politeness. She took a pastille and popped it into her mouth, only to spit it out again seconds later. 'What ... is that?' she gagged, all politeness gone. The pastilles were encrusted in glittering salt, not sugar.

'Aj, you don't know these? I thought you must have. I should have warned you. It's not like liquorice you might know. It's truly salty, not at all sweet. Like the sea.'

'Like tar,' Esther choked.

'You'll know better for when you try again next time,' Abelone said, smiling.

Esther wrapped her uneaten liquorice piece in a tissue from her pocket. There would be no next time.

As they drove through the city, waves of fatigue and dizziness began to roll over Esther. She grew restless. Her eyes were too bleary. The new world inside and outside Abelone's car was too blurry. She looked up through the window, searching for familiar constellations, for an anchor. Studied the upturned bowl of night, yearning for stars she knew, but all Esther saw was a spill of unfamiliar silver. For just a moment, Esther let herself close her eyes.

'Hjem, kære hjem.' Abelone's voice startled her. 'Home, sweet home.'

Esther sat up straight, wiped the corner of her mouth and tried to roll the kink out of her neck. 'Did I sleep?' she asked, disorientated.

'Only for moments.'

They unloaded Esther's bags from the car onto the footpath. As they turned to go through a gate in a walled garden by the street, Esther stopped. Across the road was a lake, on the inky surface of which floated two white lanterns.

'Our local lake, Sortedams Sø. It's one of three. The bridge there' — Abelone pointed — 'separates it from the other two. And they,' she said with a smile, 'are our local swans. In bed for the night.'

Eala. That's what they said Aura was calling by the sea, where she was last seen. *Eala.*

'Did Aura see them? Those swans?' Esther narrowed her eyes to try to focus. To try to make sense of her understanding that everything she was seeing, her sister had seen. She wanted to wrap her arms around everything, draw it all close.

'Well, yes,' Abelone replied. 'I'd guess so. I mean, maybe not those exact swans. But you are staying here where she stayed with me. Your apartment up there' — Abelone pointed at the dormer windows in the house that were lit with a soft glow — 'was her apartment. Her neighbourhood. Her lake. What you see is what she saw.' Abelone unlocked the gate in the garden wall with an old, thick key. 'Come in.'

Esther followed Abelone along a short path through a garden of blooming hydrangeas. Somewhere in her mind she registered that it was spring in the north, not autumn as she'd left behind.

At the threshold to the house, Abelone unlocked the front door and pushed it open; a wedge of golden light spilled into the garden. They wrestled Esther's suitcase and bags inside. Abelone shut the door after them.

'Welcome.' She shrugged off her coat, hung it by the door and stepped out of her wooden clogs into hot-pink felt slippers.

Rolled up the cuffs of her long sleeve shirt, revealing the waves of a fine-line black tattoo swirling around one of her wrists. Between each wave, a line of tiny writing.

'Tak,' Esther replied, pausing to catch her breath. She tried not to eyeball Abelone's tattoo.

'Very good,' Abelone praised Esther's pronunciation.

'Don't be impressed. That's pretty much the full extent of my Danish.' Esther looked around the narrow entryway to Abelone's home. It had a high ceiling and pale blue walls. Drifting across them were hand-painted clouds, lined with cream, peach and gold. A bewilderingly steep spiral staircase ascended beyond view. Esther craned her neck. From the ceiling hung various lengths of small, star-shaped lights, an illuminated waterfall falling through the stairwell, all the way to the deep blue rug on the entryway floor. Among the strings of lights flew meticulously detailed papier-mâché white swans.

'Wow,' Esther breathed.

Abelone reached towards the swan nearest to her and gently pulled on a string hanging from its belly; the swan's wings moved up and down, as if flying. 'Hans Christian Andersen wrote, "Between the Baltic and the North Sea there lies an old swan's nest, and it is called Denmark. In it have been born, and will be born hereafter, swans whose names shall never die." He was also responsible for our love of swans and why it's the national bird of Denmark. We're a country obsessed with The Ugly Duckling.' Abelone smiled.

'I've never seen a house like this,' Esther said in bleary wonder. 'It's' – she reached for words – 'magical.'

'I hadn't either. Which is why I made this installation.' Abelone gestured to the lights and swans. 'It's my contribution. Our ancestors have all left the mark of their lives here in one way or another. I inherited this house, down through the women in our family line. From my fifth great-grandmother, Gull, who bought it outright with her own money.'

Goosebumps rushed over Esther's skin. Johanna and Gull had only ever been two-dimensional characters in stories, objects of Aura's dreamy affection. Until now.

'I didn't know that. Aura never mentioned that in her emails when she was here. When she was still writing to me.' Esther looked down at her boots, standing on the threshold that her ancestors, and Aura, had crossed.

'Leave your bags here. We will have dinner now,' Abelone said, walking down the hallway.

'Sorry,' Esther called after her, overwhelmed by her growing desperation to lie down.

Abelone turned.

'I've never had jet lag before and it's really – what did you say at the airport about flying?'

'For Satan.'

Father smiled, 'Yes. That's it I think jet lag is also for Satan. So ...'

'You'll have a shower now and go to bed. Let me show you your room.' Abelone pushed Esther's heaviest suitcase towards the stairs.

'Oh, it's okay,' Esther insisted. 'I can take that one.'

Abelone waved her concern away, lifted the suitcase and started ascending the near-vertical spiral stairs.

Left with her two lighter bags, Esther followed. At first, she was puzzled by the thick piece of rope strung through metal loops in the wall up the full height of the stairs, until her quad muscles started to burn and vertigo kicked in. Her arms shook under the weight of her luggage. She gripped the rope, hauling herself along. Looked up to see Abelone nearly at a violet door on a narrow landing at the top of the stairs.

'What kind of fresh hell,' Esther panted, 'is this?'

By the time she reached the landing where Abelone had opened the door and was waiting, Esther was covered in a fine sheen of sweat and huffing for breath. She shoved her suitcase and bags through the door.

'I didn't know,' she gasped at Abelone, 'that mountaineering skills were required to scale staircases here.'

For the first time since Esther had arrived, Abelone grinned. 'They are good for the heart and the muscles. You go up a staircase in Denmark, you know you're alive.' Abelone looked around. 'Now, let me show you this place.'

Esther stumbled around her luggage as Abelone switched on more lamps. Every dormer window looked on to Sortedams Sø. The couch, dining table and two armchairs reminded Esther of the Scandinavian catalogues Freya got in the mail from Melbourne, except Abelone's furniture had the charm of being worn and threadbare in places from decades of beloved use. Esther ran her fingers over the low-hanging, three-shade lamps and the books with cracked spines and yellowed pages stacked on a mint-green bookshelf. She poked her head into the tiny kitchen with forest-green tiles, an assortment of pink crockery and a window that looked across surrounding chimneys and rooftops into the deep sky.

'This is your room,' Abelone said, taking Esther into the only bedroom. She flicked the low-hanging lamp on. The ceilings were slanted, A-frame. One wall was taken up by a heavyset, ornate wardrobe and, against the other wall, a double bed was made with crisp-looking white sheets and a fluffy doona. Esther's body hurt with wanting at the sight of it. Off the bedroom was the bathroom: a handheld showerhead extension fixed to the basin taps, and a toilet, in a narrow, tiled space the size of a closet.

'It's not full of space, but it has everything you will need for your stay.'

'It's perfect,' Esther said. 'Thank you.'

'You just need to get your stair legs. Like a sailor, but different, ja?' Abelone smiled.

'Stair legs. Got it.'

'When you come down in the morning, make sure you use the rope again. Believe it or not, coming down can be harder than going up. Until then, I'm downstairs if you need anything.' Abelone handed Esther the key to the violet door. 'See you tomorrow.'

'Goodnight,' Esther said.

She waited for Abelone's footsteps to descend the stairs before she let herself fall face-first onto the bed. Then she rolled over and rummaged through her pockets for her mobile phone. Sent a text to Jack. She swivelled her head around to look through the bedroom doorway into the apartment that Abelone had made of the attic. Once Gull's home. Once Aura's.

Esther got up. Took off her coat, her scarf and went into the living room where she'd left her luggage. She unpacked only what she needed to brush her teeth and shower.

After spending what felt like an age trying to figure out how to use the showerhead without it becoming a force of its own and soaking everything in the bathroom, Esther gripped it between her knees and did her best to wash in the confined space. As she tried to run conditioner through her hair, she relaxed the grip of her knees for a second, only for the showerhead to rear back and spray her in the face.

Later, body stinging from hot water and fatigue, Esther pulled back the doona and got into bed. She groaned as she rested her head on the pillow, closed her eyes and pulled the doona to her chin, relishing being able to stretch out after so many hours in the confines of the planes. Exhaustion and relief dragged her under. She'd made it to Denmark.

'Stair legs,' she murmured before her breathing deepened.

Outside the window beside her, the sleeping swans floated on the dark lake. Two fallen stars in an inverted sky.

19

Jack Wilding sat on the top step of the stargazing shack, with his mobile phone in hand. He looked into the distance, where the bay curved around the shallow lagoon hidden by the line of seven boulders. Where visions of his daughters lingered. Two were running between the boulders and the sea, kicking up spray. One remained in the shadows of the blue gums, in the glint of the sea.

He rubbed his brow, easing fatigue and tension. The autumn sea, opalescent, reached for the edge of the world. From somewhere beyond, Esther had texted him before sleeping under spring Copenhagen stars. When Esther was younger, they'd go swimming in the bay together, paddling about in the shallows, while Freya and Aura were usually further out, in the deep. Esther hadn't set foot in the sea since Aura disappeared; in those awful, early days of the search party she vowed that she never would again.

Jack sighed. If was it up to him, the morning after his youngest daughter had flown beyond his reach would have had an emotionally reflective sky: low, thick and rolling with heavyset cloud. But it had dawned crystalline. A clear, vivid morning in Salt Bay. The air was cool; the sun was hot; the sand was cold. The sea was still and clear. Perfect diving conditions.

He'd stirred at first light when Freya had slipped from the knot of their bodies, their skin still salty; she'd returned from Nipaluna, Hobart, and reached for him in the middle of the night. A remembering. A reckoning. In the early silver shadows, through the blur of half-awake vision, Jack watched her leave the warmth of their bed, pull on the grey skin of her wetsuit, and go. To the sea. It was one of the few rhythms in their marriage that never changed. Jack had a session first thing; after it ended, he'd seen his client out of his office and, passing the bathroom, found Freya's wetsuit hanging in the shower. Wet and shimmering. Lifeless but vital. Across the tiles, out of the bathroom and down the hallway, was a trail of little saltwater puddles. Jack had stood alone in the empty house, hands in his pockets, staring at the dots and dashes of water Freya had left behind her.

In Jack's final year at UTAS, he'd been offered a place in Introduction to Myth and Philosophy, a highly coveted elective among Psychology and Arts majors. The first lecture for the now school year happened on a day of anomalies. Jack slept through his alarm. Missed the bus. Arrived late and anxious, halfway through the lecture. He sneaked through the theatre doors, praying for a free seat to sink into, but all the seats nearest the aisle were taken. As he clung to the shadows, his skin turned feverish and tender. Panic rash. When he glanced down at his feet, to focus, to breathe, he saw it: a sporadic trail of dark droplets on the light blue carpet. Jack followed it with his eyes. The trail led to a couple of empty seats at the back of the lecture theatre. Lightheaded with relief, he took a seat where the trail in the carpet ended, behind a woman with wet, silver-blonde hair. It was braided in a long rope down her back and water dripped from the ends, leaving a blooming dark blue circle on the carpet. Jack unpacked his books. Tried to focus on the image the lecturer put up on the screen and talked the class through. *Zeus banished Atlas to stand at the western edge of the Earth and hold the world on his shoulders ...*

Jack couldn't focus. The woman in front of him wasn't watching the lecture screen or taking notes. She was concentrating on something in front of her, something out of

Jack's view. He moved to better see; the woman was drawing on her own arm. The lecturer changed the image on the screen again to a painting of the sea, wild and reaching for the stars, which cast the lecture theatre in muted shades of blue light. *Atlas married Pleione, a sea nymph. Together they had children, seven of which were sisters. Also known as The Pleiades.* Jack watched as the woman used a fine-line black ink pen to sketch on her skin. A burdened man standing on the edge of the world, his arms laden with stars. While, in the sea at his feet, a woman beckoned.

The lights came up and the lecture theatre began to empty. The woman kept sketching. Jack fumbled to get his books and bag together, taking as long as he could. Delaying until they were the last two left in the theatre. That's when she turned. Looked him in the eye. On a day when everything had gone wrong, Jack Wilding met a woman with the sea in her hair and stories on her skin. He'd loved Freya every day, through everything, since.

Standing in the hallway of their home, staring at Freya's saltwater droplets on the floor, Jack had thought about following them. As if they were gingerbread crumbs. Out the back door and down the sandstone path to the threshold of Freya's studio. Where her tattoo gun had been buzzing all morning.

He'd thought about it. Instead, he'd gone to the shack.

Jack brushed gum leaves from the top step. The wind had picked up; he pulled the collar of his padded vest up, around his neck. Glanced at the grave of Esther's swan. Opened Esther's text again. A tremor went through his body as he reread it.

I'm here. I'm safe. If you don't hear from me for a week, it's because I'm asleep. Jet lag is fucked. Or, in cleaner terms for you, Dad: jet lag is for Satan. PS I'm kidding. I'll text you tomorrow. And the day after that. And the day after that. Goodnight x

After a year of almost having to beg Esther to engage in any kind of communication when she'd only been a few hundred kilometres away on the west coast, it had seemed impossible before she left for Denmark that she wouldn't relapse into a similar silence once she was on the other side of the Earth. It had seemed impossible that they wouldn't lose her too. And yet. There she was. Maybe it was going to work. Maybe his idea to have the memorial, to bring her home, was going to work. *It could bring her back to us, Frey, but more than that, it could bring her back to herself. She's sleepwalking through her own life.* Freya had been reluctant at first. But then, as Jack started planning, it became real for her. She got involved. Asked Nin and Queenie for help. The memorial became more than a reason to lure Esther home so that they could show her Aura's journal. The memorial became a ritual for Freya. It took on the gravity of the funeral she'd refused to ever have and gave her the chance to acknowledge, celebrate and mourn their firstborn.

Jack looked at his phone again. Freya hadn't mentioned Esther since she'd told him about their fight in her studio. How was he going to lie to her about Esther being in Denmark? He would have to tell Freya at some point. When would that be?

To console himself, Jack read Esther's text again. There she was. Keeping her promise. Saying without saying, *I'm not going to disappear from you too.*

He tapped out a reply and sent it. Slid his phone into his pocket and stood. Leaned against the railing and watched the sea as he took a few deep breaths to slow his racing heart. Esther was safe, with Abelone. His daughter was safe.

As Jack stood to head home, he cast a backward glance at the seven boulders. His daughters' keepers.

At the Shell House, Jack set the kettle to boil and made a cup of tea. Went into his office and began going over his notes for his next client. He'd taken a sabbatical after Aura's disappearance, but getting back to work once he was deemed fit to do so had kept Jack going. The rhythms of working around loss with his clients gave him a sense of purpose. Explaining the seven stages of grief to his clients often felt like reciting a prayer.

> *Shock and denial.*
> *Pain and guilt.*
> *Anger and bargaining.*
> *Reflection, loneliness, potential depression.*
> *The shift.*
> *Reconstruction.*
> *Acceptance and hope.*

Jack caught himself regularly hoping that if he went through the process enough, if he helped enough people to survive each stage, then surely he'd find his own way through. Every week, he glimpsed in his clients how to live beyond grief. Every week his own therapist, Will, reminded him that no model of grief was linear. *Are you still running at night, Jack?* Will had recently asked.

A reflection from his office wall caused Jack to frown, break concentration. He put down his papers and pen and looked to where the flare came from on the wall. The mid-morning light fell through the window, reflecting off glass photo frames. One, of Esther and Aura, just months before everything changed. Wildness in their eyes, unbridled adoration for each other mirrored in their vibrant faces. The photo had been taken on the beach, only weeks before Aura had gone into hospital. Jack's chest tightened.

Esther gripping his hand; the two of them stand in the doorway of Aura's hospital room. Aura is asleep in bed, hooked up to the heart monitor. Freya is with her, as she's been all night since the call came from Emergency. Her body fits snugly around Aura's in her hospital bed. It all happened so fast; Jack and Freya haven't talked about what to tell Esther.

'Let's leave them to sleep,' Jack suggests. 'We'll come back tonight.'

Later that afternoon, when Jack takes Esther to the stargazing shack to show her the eclipse of southern old lady moths, she studies them intently, her face solemn.

'Are they the moths' heartbeats?' She points at the markings on their wings. 'Like Aura's heartbeat on that little box in hospital?'

'I can see why you'd think so, Starry.' Jack smiles. 'A very observant insight. But no, they're not the moths' heartbeats.'

'What's wrong with her, Dad?' Esther asks in a small voice, her skinny shoulders curling inwards. Jack is reminded in a palpable, crushing way, that in Esther's eyes Aura is invincible. Magic. Untouchable.

In that moment at the shack, at a loss for what to tell his daughter, Jack opens his mouth and hears himself lie.

'She's just had her appendix out, Starry. Routine procedure. Nothing to worry about.'

The lie gathers its own momentum once Jack tells Freya and Aura about it.

'Don't ever tell her the truth. I don't ever want her to know,' Aura begs her parents, her eyes wet and dark. 'Promise me. Mum. Dad. Please,' she cries.

Jack leaned forward at his desk and put his head in his hands. Nearly two decades on, he and Freya had kept their promise. They'd never told Esther what had happened to Aura, that night by the seven boulders down at the sea. He recalled the pained determination in Esther's face as she had boarded the plane. Her hand held high in the Space Club signal as she walked out of view.

'Starry,' he whispered.

Jack reminded himself of his steps. *Give a name to what you're experiencing. Celebrate what remains. Imagine new sources of courage and connection.* He tried. Nevertheless, as Jack readied his office for the arrival of his next client, his movements were burdened with his panic and his hope that he'd done the right thing.

20

Esther woke, warm and cocooned. Took in the slanted ceiling, the heavy wooden wardrobe, remembered where she was. Her arrival in darkness the night before seemed like it had happened long ago; Salt Bay felt impossibly far away. She stretched out her limbs. Somewhere outside, a cheerful bicycle bell rang. Birdsong close by. Pieces of rainbowed morning light danced over the wall. She reached behind her and drew the curtain a fraction. The little rainbows disappeared in sunlight. Closed the curtain. The rainbows reappeared, dancing in the muted shadows.

An acute sense of knowing settled: she was in Aura's bed, in Aura's lakeside loft, in Aura's beloved northern city made of salt and fairytales. Their ancestors' home.

Esther sat up. Rubbed her eyes.

She padded through the loft to the kitchen. Made a cup of coffee and took it to stand at the windows overlooking the lake. The muffled sound of her mobile phone chirped from her bag on the couch. She dug it out, along with Aura's journal. A text message waited for her from Jack.

So happy to hear you're there and you're okay, Starry. All is fine here. Careful with swearing; as a mark of respect, maybe learn to swear in Danish? If you must. Cygnus is on the rise this week here. Have you seen her in your new sky yet? Love, Dad xo

Esther smiled at Jack's message. Sipped her coffee. Took a seat by a window and scrolled through her phone.

She opened Karla Jørgensen's photo. Again. If it had been made of paper, Esther would have dog-eared and thumbed it bare in places. As she zoomed in on Aura's face, Esther thought of science class in high school, when she learned that the word *photography* came from the Greek words *photos*, meaning light, and *graphia*, meaning writing. In Klara's photo, Aura was written in light. Her eyes were sparks. Her open-mouthed smile looked how belly-laughter sounded, unrestrained and free. Esther zoomed in again. Closer. The colour in her sister's face, the rush of blood to her cheeks. Life. Aliveness. Aura's hands were on her stomach. Esther breathed through the ache; how she loved Aura's hands. She zoomed in further, to Aura's fingers. They were hooked through the fingers of the man holding her. The intimacy and familiarity of their embrace was alienating. As was the deep-dimpled smile of this stranger Aura had clearly loved. Esther zoomed out. Liden Gunvor stood over them. Her story, of being seduced into the depths and death by a man from the sea, was tragic. Yet standing with her sculpture, Aura wasn't burdened by sorrow. She, and her companion, were radiant.

What had Esther been doing at home on their southern island in the moment Klara Jørgensen had taken the photograph of her sister? Held by the arms of a man she'd met and loved on the other side of the world? Who was he? Had he broken Aura's heart? How had Aura gone from being in such a happy photo with him to the spectral woman who had greeted Esther in the living room of the Shell House?

Esther put her phone down. Curled her knees to her chest.

Outside, a skein of white swans flew low over the lake, gliding to land on the dark surface. Her heart lurched at the sight of their grace and beauty, at the memory of the black swan hitting her windscreen; her weight between Esther's arms as she'd lowered the swan into the dirt. The shimmering black feathers she'd tucked into her travel wallet and brought with her. Esther thought of the fourth image in Aura's *Seven Skins*. The woman mournfully watching the sky in her finery, yearning for her own flight. As if she was earthbound or trapped. As if she'd been left behind.

The fourth skin: Threshold. Who would you be if you'd never strayed to the shore?

Restless and agitated, Esther finished her coffee and looked around the loft. Her unpacked luggage beckoned.

Twenty minutes later, she had her clothes hung in the wardrobe, and belongings set out around the loft. In the kitchen she made another coffee. Took it and the packet of Iced VoVos she'd bought at the airport into the living room. Her bag was on the arm of the couch; she reached inside and clasped the Space Club keyring Jack had given her. Held it in her palm, moved it in the light. Jack's voice. *You're never alone.*

But she was. On the other side of the world. In a foreign country.

A sudden bout of dizziness made Esther lurch sideways. Keyring in hand, she staggered for the couch. Rested her head. Her hands and feet turned numb. She tried to make fists, panic rising in the back of her throat. Her breath was short, her stomach cramped with nausea. Cold sweat formed on her top lip. She started to shake. Esther squeezed her eyes shut in terror. After a few moments that felt like hours, the sensations in her body passed. She lay on the couch, depleted, frightened. Her hands were still shaking. She tried to steady her breathing.

'Esther?' Abelone's faint voice called from downstairs.

Esther shook her head. What had she been thinking? It was all a mistake: she couldn't be there. She couldn't be in Denmark.

Abelone's calls rose to the loft a few more times. Esther ignored them. She took her phone, coffee and Iced VoVos into her bedroom. Set them on her bedside table and got back under the doona. Rolled towards the wall, pulled the doona over her head and shut her eyes.

Esther stirred in her bed at the sound of the loft door opening. Her room was full of softening afternoon light; Abelone's footsteps approached. Esther lay still, feigning sleep. Abelone tiptoed into her room, paused and retreated. There was the sound of something being set on the table in the living room. A drawer being opened. The rustle of paper. The drawer closing. A few moments of quiet. Then the sound of the door opening and closing. Abelone's footsteps descending the stairs.

An aroma wafted through the loft that lured Esther from her bed. She waited until she couldn't hear anything, then threw back her doona. Her mouth was furry from sugar; she'd eaten most of the Iced VoVos throughout the day. When she walked into the living room and saw a tray set for her with a bowl of steaming aromatic soup and a side plate of thick bread glistening with cold slices of butter, she made a small squawking noise. The last proper meal she'd had was on her flight. She read the note Abelone had left.

I'm going out tonight so won't see you if you come down.
This fiske suppe was Kristina's answer to everything: jet lag,
heartbreak, exhaustion. You will eat it and feel better. See
you in the morning.

Esther did as she was told. Lifted the spoon and stirred the bowl of white fish, potatoes, leeks, celery, carrots. Dunked the buttered bread in it and ate, leaving the fish to one side. Then she laid the fish pieces on the windowsill for the gulls to eat, and went back to bed.

The next morning, standing under the shower, Esther let her thoughts run. Maybe she'd take Aura's journal and venture out, into Copenhagen. Maybe to places Aura had gone? Or to Aura's university? Or, where? Where would be best? Once she decided where she was going, what was she meant to do then? Just follow her instinct? To what end? Esther watched her thoughts go down the drain with her soapy water. She didn't know anyone, or speak Danish, or have any understanding of how to get around Copenhagen. The thought of a bike was charming, but she didn't know the road rules. What if she fell off? She scratched at the tender skin on the underside of her wrist. Held the scalding water from the shower rose against it.

After her shower, Esther stood in front of her open wardrobe wrapped in her towel. Overwhelmed, she let her towel drop and got back into bed. Pulled the doona once again over her head. Remembered the morning after she'd woken with Tom in a bougainvillea bush at their friends' wedding.

Aura bringing a glass of water and two paracetamols into her room. She sits on the edge of Esther's bed and tugs the covers from her face.

'How am I ever going to face him again?' Esther demands of her big sister. 'My lip is actually swollen from when we mashed teeth. Also, a bougainvillea thorn stuck into my boob. It drew blood, Aura. Blood. From my boob. I think he may have even passed out at some point when I was on top. He threw up afterwards.' She buries herself in Aura's arms. 'Some of his sick got on me.'

Aura does so well not to laugh. Or gag. 'I mean, take your oldest friend from childhood and all those decades of sexual frustration and curiosity, then add champagne and Sambuca chasers, at a wedding, no less … Go easy on yourself, Starry. Horrendous outdoor shagging was kind of the only way this could have gone.'

Despite her misery, Esther can't help but laugh.

'I know this isn't a specific answer,' Aura offers.

Esther groans in anticipation. 'Go on.'

'You need to get up. Go for a walk.'

'What?'

'I'm serious. Sometimes the simplest way to face something you don't know how to face is to start by going for a walk. Remind yourself how the look of something changes once you're moving, step by step by step.'

Esther studies Aura's face. There were countless days when they were teenagers, after school, when she glimpsed Aura, alone, walking back and forth along the sea.

'Step by step,' Esther repeats.

Aura's eyes catch the light. 'Step by step by step.'

Esther pushed the doona back. 'Fine,' she grumbled. Got up. Yanked her black jeans and a black knit jumper from the wardrobe. Laced up her boots. Tucked Aura's journal into her bag. Took the tray and Abelone's clean dishes in hand.

'Fine,' she muttered again as she opened the loft door.

At the bottom of the staircase Esther let go of her white-knuckled one-handed grip on the guide rope. Relaxed her grip on the tray. She took in the morning light filling the entryway. Abelone's papier mâché swans hung in suspended, quiet flight.

Esther followed the hallway and pushed through the swing door at the end of it, squinting as she walked into a bright living room. It was open-plan with floor-to-ceiling windows on one side, full of light. Eggshell-white walls, and built-in bookshelves, crammed with books and papers. Tall, potted fig trees and glossy monstera plants. A mix of mustard and green velvet couches. Pink rug patterned with Danish folk art; Freya had mixing bowls with a similar pattern at home. Mid-century wooden coffee table. Three-shade lamps hung low and glowing from the ceiling.

In the centre of the room, an accent wall. Painted a pale metallic gold, the colour of memory. It seemed to absorb the light. Esther stilled. On the golden wall, hanging in a large, square frame was a painting of two swans. She moved closer, drawn by its mystery. Through the middle of the painting was a horizon line, on either side of which the beaks of the two swans met, one white, one black. They were mirrored negative reflections of each other, in their positioning and colouring. Duality. Light and dark. Above and below. Esther studied the only other point where they met: the tip of one of their wings touched at the horizon line, the wing of the black swan ever so slightly overreaching into the white swan's half of the painting. Esther was sure she'd never seen it before, but something about the painting felt deeply known to her.

'Esther?' Abelone's voice called from somewhere beyond the living room.

Esther took a breath to ready herself then turned from the painting and followed Abelone's voice. 'Good morning,' she replied, venturing through a doorway and around a corner into a lemon-yellow kitchen. Aromas of cinnamon, sweet milk and tobacco filled the room. On the kitchen countertop a bowl of icing sugar glistened. She set down the tray and dishes.

'God morgen.' Abelone tapped the ash from her smoking pipe into a dish on the sill of the open window.

'God morgen.' Esther attempted. 'Thank you. For the soup and bread yesterday.'

Abelone studied her face. 'It worked. You look better.' Her sleeves were rolled up and her hands were covered in a fine dusting of flour. Atop her head, her hair was fastened in a pile with a thin basting brush.

Esther took in the sugary warmth of the kitchen, the cheering green vase of blooming pink irises, the black and white checked floor.

'Breakfast?' Abelone gestured to a loaf of bread still in brown paper wrapping and a small wedge of speckled cheese. 'Nothing fancy, but the bread is fresh this morning and the danbo has caraway seeds in it, which means your first breakfast here will be a very Danish one.'

'Yes please.' Esther helped herself to the bread and cheese. As she finished her last mouthful, the rhythm of a ticking clock caught her attention. She looked around. On a shelf behind her the merman and his seven children, frozen in grief, held time waiting for Agnete to return. The familiarity of the clock hit Esther square in the chest. Compounded by her quick-to-follow realisation that it was on Salt Bay time, as Abelone had said in the car the night before.

'I've never been able to change it back,' Abelone said, dusting her hands of breadcrumbs. Esther looked away. Gave herself a moment. Abelone filled a coffee cup with warm water from the kettle, took a lemon from her fruit bowl, cut a slice and popped it in the cup. Offered it to Esther, who took it without question. Abelone refilled her pipe. Esther sipped her lemon water, noticing for the first time Abelone's paint-splattered apron.

'I can't tell, are you baking or painting?' Esther pushed away the image that kept circling back to her, of Aura standing where she stood, asking Abelone to change Agnete's clock to keep Tasmanian time.

'Ha. It's a good question. I use the same apron. For painting and baking. Now, I'm baking. An old family recipe. Sosterkage. Or Seven Sisters Cake. For us. Later.' She pointed to the oven, lit and humming, inside which sat a brimming cake tin.

Not knowing how to respond to Abelone's kindness, Esther said nothing.

'Three centuries ago,' Abelone went on, 'if I'd been a sailor's wife – åh gud,' she groaned, crossing herself, 'then every winter, I'd be baking this for my husband before he went to sea. Vikings navigated by the stars, so to bake this cake any time of year was to honour powers above, below and beyond the visible at sea. But to bake Sosterkage in November especially was to honour the Seven Sisters. That's when they shine from sunset to sunrise. We're far from November darkness today but it is still April, the month of all seasons at once. Very bad weather is forecast later. So, I'm baking seven stars for us to honour all that is unseen. I'll light a fire and we'll eat dinner, then cake, and you can tell me everything.'

Esther pressed her lips together, already dreading how she might fail Abelone's expectations; Aura was the storyteller. Not her.

Abelone looked Esther over. 'You're all buttoned up. You're going out?'

'I thought a walk would be good.'

'Absolut.' Abelone lit her pipe and took a few short, sharp inhalations until smoke curled from the end of it. She exhaled a thin plume out of the window. Seemed to be deciding on whether she wanted to say something. She cleared her throat. 'Your father said your mother doesn't know you are here.'

Esther bristled. Shook her head.

Abelone regarded her for a moment. 'That's how family is sometimes, ja?'

Esther gave a half-shrug.

'Where are you going to walk today?' Abelone changed the subject. 'Do you need directions?'

'I'm fine,' Esther said. 'There's a sculpture I might go to Rosenborg Castle Gardens to see.'

'An easy walk from here,' Abelone said. 'Give me a moment, I'll draw you a map.' Before Esther could protest, Abelone reached for a spiral-bound notepad and pencil on the counter. When she was done, she tore off the page and handed it to Esther.

'Thanks,' she said, shoving the map into her pocket.

Abelone took another drag on her pipe. Held her breath for a moment before she turned her face to the window to exhale. She looked over her shoulder at Esther. 'Liden Gunver's story is an old, sad one that began as a Danish song. My mormor, or, uh, grandmother, yes, she used to take roses to Liden Gunver, leave them at her feet. She used to say stories can be like mirrors, ja? They show us what we don't always want to see. Like Liden Gunver, my mormor once believed a man she shouldn't have. Aura loved it when I told her that.'

'Which part?'

'Just, I think, that my mormor related to Liden Gunver so much. Like Aura did too.'

'She did?'

'Ja,' Abelone said. 'But you know that too, since Aura had Liden Gunver in her book. Jack told me about it. Said you've brought it with you.'

Esther nodded. Abelone seemed to be waiting for her to elaborate. She moved her weight from one foot to the other. How was she meant to explain Aura's journal? Or how it had led her to Copenhagen. At a loss for words, Esther glanced at the tattoo on Abelone's arm and said the first thing that came to mind. 'Aura had words she wrote in her journal tattooed down her spine.'

Abelone raised an eyebrow.

'She gathered seven images in her journal and for each of them she wrote a line,' Esther continued. 'She had all seven of them tattooed on her body.'

'Seven?' Abelone asked.

'You seem surprised,' Esther said.

'I only knew about one,' Abelone answered. Shook her head. 'I often think about this.'

'Aura's tattoos?'

'Nej. I mean I sometimes wonder if the desire to be tattooed is something we inherit. Like trauma. Or love.'

Esther took in Abelone's words. Woman after woman stepped in front of the mirror in Freya's studio, the same look of revelation in their faces. 'I've never thought of it that way,' she said.

'You know about Gull. Our ancestor.'

'A bit,' Esther said. 'Aura was more into family history than me.'

Abelone began clearing up her baking bowls and spoons. 'Gull was the first in our family to own her skin. She was defiant. Dressed as a man, she sailed east in the nineteenth century. Came home to her quiet sister, Johanna, with a collection of tattoos she'd had done on her travels, hidden under her clothes. The stories of her tattoos became the kitchen-table stories in our family. Surely your mother told you all this.'

Throughout her youth Esther vaguely remembered stories of Gull and her tattoos being mentioned in Freya's studio, but she'd never really paid much attention. It was Aura who had hung on every word about Johanna and Gull. Esther's brow furrowed with realisation: since they'd been teenagers, Aura had treasured a story about their ancestor who left home, marked her skin by choice on her adventures and returned home, tattoos hidden from the world.

Abelone washed her hands and dried them on her apron. Again, Esther noticed the waves of her tattoo ebbing around her wrist and up her forearm. Catching her eye, Abelone offered her arm to Esther. Shyly, Esther moved closer, to read the fine text within the waves inked into Abelone's skin.

'*A cure for everything ... saltwater ... sweat ... tears ... the salt sea*,' Esther read aloud, a swelling in her chest.

'It comes from a story by Karen Blixen,' Abelone said. 'Or Isak Dinesen, as she was known.'

Sweat, tears, the salt sea. All three had been true for Esther once, until she had stopped swimming. After Aura.

'My Kristina loved these words,' Abelone murmured. 'They were part of our ceremonial vows. Saltwater is how we met, swimming in the sea basins. We were the only two there in winter. She said it was her cure. Cancer didn't agree.'

'I remember Mum telling us when we were teenagers. She lit candles down at the beach for seven nights after Kristina died,' Esther said quietly. 'I'm sorry.'

'Tusind tak.'

Outside, blackbirds carolled over their nest in a magnolia tree, heavy with new spring buds.

'Do you only have the one tattoo?' Esther tried to keep her voice steady. The spill of Abelone's grief threatened to upend her own.

'Only one. So far. But' – Abelone rubbed her hands together – 'I'd like to fill both arms. With all the words I've read and loved. Words Kristina wrote to me. Lines from stories she cherished.' She shrugged. 'Who knows. I'll do as I please. When you find the love of your life in your fifties only to lose her a year later, if you're lucky enough to survive the loss, you realise you've got nought fucks to give.'

It took Esther a second to figure it out. Her mouth twitched. 'Do you mean zero?' she asked. 'You've got zero fucks to give?'

'Ah ha. Zero fucks. Precis.'

'Where are you hearing all of these phrases?' Esther snorted.

'I teach at the city art school. My students all speak two, three, four languages. They keep me up to date in my English.' Abelone rolled her wrists as she spoke, just as Aura had done. Lines of blue waves rolled into a gathering of beautiful words then back to waves on her skin.

'The design is just beautiful,' Esther murmured, gazing at Abelone's skin. 'The way the writing is part of the waves. There's no separation between the two.'

'My artist is wonderful. Lille Heks. She owns one of the oldest operating tattoo parlours in Europe. Right here in Copenhagen.'

'Really?'

'Ja. Tattoo Stjerne. It's at Nyhavn. Ten minutes by bicycle from here. Over the lake, through Rosenborg Castle Gardens that you want to go to and, poof, you're there.'

A small shiver ran down Esther's neck. Liden Gunver was within her reach.

'It's been a tattoo parlour since the nineteenth century, when Nyhavn was a rough part of town. Someone from every kind of life you can imagine has since sat in the parlour and been tattooed. Sailors, sex workers, circus folk. Rumour has it even some royals. We think our Gull was tattooed there too. So, I figured, why not me?' Abelone smiled. 'I went to meet Lille Heks, and I told her about Kristina and the words I wanted. She came back to me with this design. It was love at once sight. Once?'

'First.'

'First sight,' Abelone corrected herself.

'I love it all,' Esther said. 'Your tattoo, the story of the parlour, your tattooist.'

'So did your sister.'

Of course, Aura had known of and loved Abelone's tattoo. Esther picked at the soft skin around her thumb nail.

'She especially loved it when I told her your mother, aunt and I visited Tattoo Stjerne when we were teenagers. The summer Freya and Erin came to stay with our family from Australia. It was the first time any of us had stepped into a tattoo parlour, but none of us dared to get in the chair. We didn't know then that our bodies belonged to us.' Abelone opened a drawer by the counter and took out a soft, leather tobacco pouch. 'But we've learned. Your mother, in particular. And Erin. I know she wears her own stories on her skin.' Abelone tapped the ash from her pipe and refilled it. 'For me, it took a little longer. Not for Aura though.'

Esther stopped fidgeting. 'What do you mean?'

'Tattoo Stjerne.' Abelone repeated the parlour's name, as if it should mean something to Esther. She shook her head, clueless.

'Where Aura got her first tattoo. I don't know about the others. Like I said, I didn't know she had seven.'

Esther jiggled a knee. 'Mum said Aura told her that she'd got her first three done overseas but not where she had them done. Do you know who tattooed her at Tattoo Stjerne?'

Abelone leaned against the counter, arms open. 'Yes. She and Aura became very close during Aura's studies. She's there, right now. Today. You can go and meet her.'

'Who, Abelone?'

'Lille Heks, Esther. Lille Heks was Aura's tattoo artist too.'

21

She walked along the lake, taking in the pearly quality of the blue midday sky, as she twirled the keys to Abelone's house around her index finger. Caught them and closed her fist around Jack's Space Club keyring she'd attached the keys to. Released and twirled them again.

Jack sitting on the veranda of the stargazing shack with Esther and Tom under a blue sky. It's their weekly Space Club quiz.

'Light travels in a straight line,' Jack says as he grips his quiz cards, 'unless something gets in its way, which is usually one of three things. One is when light is reflected, by a mirror. The second is when light is bent by?'

'A prism,' Tom bellows. Jack gives an officious nod: Tom punches the air.

'Suck-up,' Esther whispers at him, grinning.

'The third way the travelling direction of light is altered is when?' Jack asks.

'It's scattered,' Tom shouts.

Jack's eyes twinkle. 'By?'

'Gases and particles in the air,' Esther roars, beating Tom to the answer. He pinches his mouth in concentration.

'Correct. Why is a blue sky an example of scattered light?' Jack asks.

'Because blue …' Tom starts then trails off, his face drawing blank. His eyes dart to Esther. She wracks her brain, then folds her arms with a scowl. Tom squeezes his eyes shut. He opens them, eyes wide. 'Blue scatters more than other colours,' he yells, leaping to his feet, 'because it travels in smaller, shorter waves.' He throws his arms in the air, relishing his quiz victory. Resigned to defeat, Esther stands and offers her hand to shake Tom's. With great ceremony, Jack presents a Milky Way and a copy of the latest *National Geographic* to Tom. He tears open the Milky Way. Esther tries to pretend she isn't watching him closely. He takes a bite of the chocolate bar and looks for a second like he's going to keep it all to himself. Then he splits it in two and gives half to her. His smile is its own sun.

Esther walked along the lake, pushing her way through a frenzy of images in her head. The look on Tom's face as she'd leaned in to kiss him at Aura's memorial, the flash of his wedding ring. The twist of pleasure in Kane's mouth; the unflinching way he'd held Esther's eye contact. A fragment: Ben's face over hers, close and unfocused. Esther frowned, willing it all away. Almost subconsciously, she lifted thumb and index finger to her eyeline. Between her fingertips, beyond the blue, she pinched the woven black yarn of countless galaxies, burning with silver and gold. For a few seconds, she was calm. *Some of the starlight you'll see every night in Denmark started its journey when Aura was still with us.* Esther dropped her hand. Twirled her keys. Twirl. Catch. Release. Twirl. Catch. Release. She pushed on, following her sister's invisible footfalls.

'Follow the map I drew you and you'll find Tattoo Stjerne is almost a straight line from here,' Abelone had said at the front door before Esther left. She handed her a set of house keys. 'As the swan flies.' Abelone winked. 'I'll come out and get my bike for you.'

'No, thanks,' Esther said lightly, trying to mask her overwhelming sense of intimidation at the thought of trying to navigate Copenhagen cyclists. 'I feel like walking.'

Abelone's gaze didn't leave her anywhere to hide. 'Walking's also a good idea,' she said. 'You see more by foot. It will take you less than thirty minutes from here. Aura preferred to walk too. You'll be fine with the map I gave you. I also marked where to find some of my favourite local places to get the best pastries and good coffee. Oh, also my favourite bookshop. They have a good stock of English titles.'

'Thanks, but I've got GPS on my phone too, so ...' Esther couldn't stop herself from saying.

Abelone snorted. 'Where's your Norse spirit, to navigate by your senses and the stars?' She went to the coat rack and took down an umbrella. Offered it to Esther. 'They said it's going to rain cats and frogs this afternoon.'

'Dogs.' Esther smiled.

'Cats and dogs.' Abelone returned her smile.

Esther glanced at the clear sky. 'I'll be right, thanks,' she said.

'Suit yourself.' Abelone tucked the umbrella under her arm.

'See you later, then.' Esther gave a polite smile as she turned to leave through the garden.

'Don't forget dinner and Sosterkage tonight,' Abelone called after her with a wave. 'Seven o'clock sharp.'

Deep in thought, Esther walked up steps from the lakeside path onto a bridge. Streams of bicycles ridden by effortlessly stylish people broke around her, water to rock. She lunged to the side, wedging herself against the bridge railing, as far out of the way as she could get. Suddenly disoriented, she wanted to turn around, crawl beneath the bridge and hide. She reached for her phone. Looked up Tattoo Stjerne at Nyhavn on her GPS map. The route took her through Rosenborg Castle Gardens in a straight line from Abelone's.

Esther looked ahead to the intersection on the other side of the bridge where inner-city Copenhagen awaited. Dared to imagine standing beside her sister there, at the traffic lights, waiting to cross the street, headed for Nyhavn. Together. Aura on her way to get her first tattoo. Skittish and shaky. Excited. Her pale eyes firing with determination. *Raise your sword, raise your voice.*

Esther crossed the bridge and stood at the intersection alone. An impossible wish. *Wait for me, sister. Wait for me.*

The route on Esther's GPS took her down Sølvgade, a main one-way street lined with ornate stone buildings and busy with traffic and cyclists. At street level the buildings seemed mostly occupied by businesses: a bicycle shop, a hair salon, the occasional restaurant, closed until dinner service. Gazing through one window of an Italian restaurant made Esther's mouth water. *I also marked where to find some of my favourite local places to get the best pastries and good coffee.* She ignored Abelone's map in her pocket and kept walking. She'd find something herself.

Ahead, Sølvgade opened to a four-way intersection, across which Esther spotted a canopy of green. She quickly glanced at her location on her GPS map and, in a rush of confidence, tucked her phone away in her pocket. She'd found Rosenborg Castle Gardens. On her own.

When the pedestrian lights turned green, Esther smiled to herself, smug, as she crossed the road.

Forty-five minutes later, after she'd walked her third circle around the gardens only to arrive again at the gates she'd first entered through, Esther sagged on a park bench under a cherry blossom tree, cranky with hunger and defeated. Took out her phone and tried to orientate herself with GPS. She struggled to focus through jet lag and a hunger headache. She hadn't found Liden Gunver. She hadn't managed to get anything to eat – she'd spied a food cart earlier across a quadrant in the garden, but when she'd looped back it was gone.

Esther rubbed the tension and hunger headache from her temples. The soft blue sky that she'd admired when she first set out was now covered by rough wool clouds. The wind had picked up; a cold finger reached through a crack in Esther's scarf. She pulled her jacket closed around her throat. Dizziness plagued her. Anxiety prickled the pale pink skin on the undersides of her arms.

 A clicking and the flapping of wings; a raven settled in the boughs of the cherry blossom tree overhead. It walked along a branch, hopped around the fluffy pink flowers, and tilted its head as it inspected her. Esther knew ravens at home, knew their distinct, guttural call: *korr-korr-korrrr*. While she'd lived on the west coast, a pair of forest ravens had been some of her most reliable company on her days off by the river. She'd started reading about them. They mated in pairs, and together defended their territory for life. After learning that, she always trod a little more wildly when she walked by the river, when she sat among the ferns.

Esther watched the raven as it watched her. She was comforted by its familiarity. The gloss of its feathers, its pale, piercing eyes.

'Where's your mate?' she asked the raven. 'She should be here.' The raven's pale eyes twitched and darted. Petals of cherry blossoms fell from the branch as it leaped and flew away, a black scarf caught on the wind in a darkening sky.

The air brewed around her, close with rain. Esther glared at the clouds, cursing herself for not taking Abelone's umbrella. She groaned. If she could just make something of her first day out in Denmark, if she could just not fail at the first thing that she'd said she would do.

Esther took out her phone and re-opened her map. Maybe there'd been something she'd missed. She focused on her screen. After a few moments, she stilled. It couldn't be right. She tapped refresh on the map. Zoomed out of the green space the blue dot of her location was in. Looked up and around her, confused. Again, looked at her map.

'Excuse me,' she called to an animated group of women engaged in conversation, passing by. 'What's the name of this park?' she asked them.

'Østre Anlæg,' one answered, then gave a wave and kept walking with her friends.

'Oh my fucking god,' Esther said through her clenched jaw. She looked again at her map. She'd been doing laps looking for Liden Gunver in the wrong place: Rosenborg Castle Gardens was still ahead of her, a block away. She gripped her phone in frustration, stifling an urge to throw it, to yell at herself.

Esther stood and pulled her coat tight around her body again. An anvil of a thought: not one person in the world knew exactly where she was in that moment. She could evaporate on the spot, disappear into thin air, and no one would know.

By the time Esther found Rosenborg Castle Gardens, light rain had started to fall. She quickened her step as she strode through entrance gates to the walled gardens. What she'd do once she found Liden Gunver, she didn't know. She just had to find her.

As she hurried through the gardens, Esther vaguely noticed the spires of the king's red brick castle and rose gardens in red bloom. She passed a café and followed the path that took her to a playground. Broke into a half-run, frantic as she looked through rows of thick-leaved trees for the sculpture Aura would forever stand in front of in Klara's photograph. With the man she'd kept a secret.

Esther continued down the path through the gardens, which constantly split in varying directions. She aimlessly chose her way, second-guessing all her steps. Ahead she caught sight of the tell-tale blue-green hue of verdigris. A sculpture. Esther's heart raced. She rushed into a clearing; her shoulders fell. The sculpture wasn't Liden Gunver. It was at the centre of a round fountain surrounded by park benches and trees.

As she drew closer, Esther examined the sculpture: a child
of similar appearance to a Renaissance cherub straddled the back
of a swan, as if trying to ride it, gripping the swan by its neck.
A tightness closed around Esther's throat. The swan's wings and
feathers were unsettled, as if it was flapping, trying to escape.
Its head reared back, strangled by the hold of the child's hand.
Around the swan's neck appeared to be a fallen crown. From its
mouth a fountain of water shot upwards.

Esther was gripped by the horror of the sculpture. Her eyes
welled as she tried to catch her breath. Her coat was too tight.
She untied and unzipped it, flapping it open for air, trying to
throw off the weight pressing on her throat, her back, her chest.

She turned her back on the sculpture. In her mind, the
screech of brakes. Shattering glass. Guilt wrenched at her gut.

The rain kept falling. Esther tried to make sense of the paths
ahead of her. Which way? There was no one to ask; the gardens
had emptied in the turning weather. Her pulse pounded in her
temples. She checked her phone. The screen was black. She
prodded it, pressed the side buttons. Remembered: she hadn't
thought to charge it the night before.

Esther clenched her fists to her mouth and screamed. She
started to shake. Tried to retrace her steps, to remember how
to get back to Abelone's. She glanced at the sculpture in the
fountain. The terror in the swan's face. Her mind fogged with
panic. The rain grew heavier. She covered her head with her
arms and began to run down any path that took her away from
the fountain.

Finally, she exited the gardens and emerged onto a street
with traffic lights. Esther looked around, hopelessly searching
for anything she might recognise, anything that might take her
back to her bed and doona in Abelone's loft. Then she spotted
a sign. *Nyhavn*, it read. With arrows. The traffic lights turned
green.

Esther followed the signs that led her a few blocks away,
to Nyhavn. The streets were wet and grey, thick with tourists

and the blur of heavy rain. She hurried down one side of the harbour, looking for Tattoo Stjerne, panicked and desperate. Pushing through the damp crowds, she couldn't clearly tell where she was, nor, she realised, did she know what she was looking for. She didn't have an image of Tattoo Stjerne in her mind; she hadn't thought to look it up on the internet before she'd left Abelone's.

Thunder growled through the sky; the rain started to belt down. Tourists scattered for shelter. Despairing, Esther ducked into the nearest bar.

An hour later, she was still sitting at the bar. Aura's journal was open in front of her. Rain and sleet needled the windows; grey dusk light spilled on the floor. She'd only picked at the hot chips she'd ordered but was on her third tulip glass of akvavit. It was served ice-cold but burned through her chest. Her body loosened. Her heart slowed.

She locked eyes with the young guy behind the bar who'd been serving her. Tapped her empty tulip glass with a slight smile. He walked the length of the bar to where she was sitting.

'Alright, love? Same again, yeah?' A northern English accent. Sleeves rolled up to his elbows, forearms bearing tattoos, all dark blue ink. His eyes were the same colour as the ink in his skin. Esther didn't flinch, didn't break their eye contact. She tapped the tulip glass again. Her thighs tingled; her body recognised the energy.

He brought her drink, placed it on a fresh coaster in front of her. Held her eye as he walked away to serve. She ignored the other singles at the bar. Ignored everyone else around her. Watched him lean forward to take an order, watched the muscles in his forearms move under his tattooed skin as he pulled beers, poured shots. Dark blue swirls. Clouds. He glanced at her again, and again, between orders. She openly stared at him, finally feeling some sense of control. This, she knew. This was steady ground beneath her feet.

Esther ran a hand over the image and words on the pages she'd opened Aura's journal to. The black and white photocopy quality of the illustration was grainy: a woman in a dark gown with a yearning expression on her face watched the sky, where three white swans with crowns on their heads flew away from her. The woman was holding something that looked like it might have been a silk handkerchief, but it reminded Esther of something else, draped as it was between the woman's hands. There were leaves swirling in the air, some of which looked like floating hearts. Esther wished she could see the details of the illustration in fine lines and full colour. She traced a fingertip over her sister's handwriting.

The fourth skin: Threshold.
Who would you be if you'd never strayed to the shore?

Aura's enigmatic words tolled in Esther's mind. Freya's voice quickly followed. *You know her best.* But she didn't, Esther didn't understand Aura's words at all. She was in the city her sister loved but hadn't managed in a whole day to find even one place that had mattered to Aura. So far, from the moment Esther had walked off the plane to meet Abelone, reeking of vodka, to staying in bed all her first day, to ending up in a local bar alone, Esther's experience of Copenhagen was one she knew well: failure. She knocked back the akvavit.

'Another, love?' Dark Blue asked.

'Please.' Esther snapped Aura's journal shut and put it in her bag. 'When's your break?' She looked him directly in the eye.

He studied her face. 'Soon,' he said. Poured her another akvavit and walked to the other end of the bar, leaning in with a smile to say something close to the ear of one of his colleagues. Esther picked at her cold chips, a scavenging gull.

The weather worsened; gusts of ice needles tinkled and chimed as they broke against the windows. Couples and groups started to fill the bar, laughing together on their travels as they shook off the sleet and rain. Getting caught in a storm in a foreign country was apparently hilarious. They drew chairs for each other, shared menus, took selfies, wrapped in each other's arms with radiant smiles. Some of the bar staff lit candles in jars on the tables, casting everything in a cosy glow. Esther took a long sip from her glass, willing the cold spirit to burn through the bitter pit in her stomach, the image of the swan in the sculpture, the fear in its face.

A couple settled at the table next to where Esther sat at the bar. The familiarity of their accents made her ears prick up in a strange false recognition, as if she knew them, as if friends from home she was waiting for had finally arrived.

'So, where are we going this weekend?' the woman asked excitedly.

The rustle and scrape of paper, something being unfolded. 'You're going to love this,' the man replied, warmth in tone. 'Lars was telling me about it at the clinic. There's a place, about three hours' drive from here, called the Seven Years' Lakes. We can stay in a bed and breakfast in one of the little villages nearby. Walk the trail. Eat some more smørrebrød.' They laughed at his terrible pronunciation. 'The sea's not far either.'

She murmured something. He murmured something back.

Esther sneaked a look at the couple. The woman had her back to her, dark hair and a flower behind her ear, but the man was in clear view. His eyes were focused only on the woman.

'Why's it called the Seven Years' Lakes?' she asked.

'You knew I wanted you to ask.'

'I did.'

'This is what you'll love most and why you'll want to go: locals say the lakes get their name because of how they mysteriously appear every seven years, then vanish.'

'Shut up,' she said, joyous.

'I won't,' he said, equally joyous. More laughter.

'The lakes rise and fall because of the groundwater, which determines their visibility. So, the lakes are always there, what changes is when they can be seen,' he said.

Goosebumps swept over Esther's body.

'Reminds me a bit of rain in the desert back home,' the woman said, her voice changing. 'The land waits until the rain returns.'

'And all the dormant seeds burst into bloom. Wildflowers.' There was a smile in his voice. A beat. Two.

'It's what you did for me, and Pip. Waited for us. Until we returned.'

Esther accidentally knocked her phone off the bar, sending it clattering to the floor. She fumbled to pick it up, her face flaming, as if she'd been caught eavesdropping. But when she looked up, the couple were oblivious to everything but each other and the map on the table between them.

A movement, out of focus, caught her attention. Dark Blue stood at the end of the bar, staring at her.

Esther put her phone away. Downed the last of the cold akvavit, wincing as she swallowed, and gathered her things.

She followed Dark Blue through a door marked *Staff Only* behind the bar. Glanced back once, looking around, as if she had someone to say goodbye to.

The fourth skin: Threshold

Who would you be if you'd never
strayed to the shore?

22

Esther fumbled the latch of the front door open and sighed with relief as the howling wind masked the sound of her clumsy entry. She closed the door behind her, leaned against it, listening for any signs of Abelone still being awake. The house was quiet. Dark. Esther reached out a hand to steady herself against the wall and tried to step on one of her boot heels to tug her foot free. A tiny rivulet of rain trickled from the ends of her hair down her spine; she'd been caught in the ongoing downpour while she waited at Nyhavn for a taxi. She hadn't been able to give the driver an address; she didn't know Abelone's, and her phone was flat. All she could ask was to be taken to the bridge over the lake. She'd been dropped at the wrong bridge of the three over Sortedams Sø and had walked in the rain the rest of the way. It wasn't until her key had worked in the door that Esther was certain she'd picked the right house to come home to.

Leaning against the wall, with one foot free of one boot, Esther tried her other boot. She bent forward to tug her foot free but as she yanked on her sock, she lost her balance and fell into something hard and sharp in the hall. The sound of her yelp was followed by something smashing to pieces on the floor.

Over the roar of blood rushing to her head, Esther listened for any movement in Abelone's room above. After a few moments without any sounds in the house, she staggered to her feet, ran her hands down the walls for a light switch. Flicked it on. A green ceramic vase of fresh pink tulips had shattered across the floor.

Head spinning, Esther did her best to clean up the mess. She gathered the pieces of the vase, and the tulips, and swayed down the hall. Stumbled through the swing door to the kitchen. Pale light from a streetlamp outside fell through the window; Esther spotted the bin. As she dropped the pieces of broken vase and flowers into it, she sliced her finger on a jagged piece of ceramic. Winced and stuck her fingertip in her mouth.

It was when she turned that she saw it. Sitting on the counter. Under a glass bell jar glistened a cake of seven scrolls. The cake Abelone had been baking that morning. To welcome Esther to Copenhagen.

Esther blinked at the cake, shame engulfing her. Abelone had told her to be home by seven o'clock, which Esther had completely forgotten. She looked at the digital clock on the oven. It was two in the morning.

Back in the entryway, Esther used her already wet coat to try and mop up the water from the vase. It did very little to help. She took off her jumper and tried using it instead. It absorbed most of the water.

Esther shivered in her bra, carrying her wet coat, jumper and boots in her arms, as she climbed the spiral staircase to the violet loft door. She could smell him on her skin.

The next morning the vice of a hangover tightening around her head awoke her. Esther groaned. Rolled over. She was on top of her doona. Still in her bra and jeans. She sat up. Gagged. Ran for the bathroom and made it to the toilet bowl just as she retched. Her stomach was empty, she had nothing to purge, but her body wouldn't stop convulsing.

Once the nausea had stopped, she got out of her clothes and crawled under the showerhead. Sat on the floor letting the shower beat down on her body. Letting it wash him off her. Moments flashed through her head, as if she'd been outside her body, watching herself with him. Jeans down around her ankles. Hands gripping the edge of a table. The sound of his moans. She lifted her face to the shower water. Raised her knees to her chest. Her finger was throbbing. She looked at the cut on her fingertip, trying to remember how it had happened. The sound of the vase smashing in the hall when she'd come in; the pale light in the kitchen; Abelone's cake. It all came back to her. The swan sculpture in the gardens. The panic thundering through her body. The burn of akvavit in the back of her throat. The couple behind her at the bar with their weekend plans and joy. Esther opened her knees and doubled over, retching again. Gasped for breath until the convulsions stopped. She leaned her arms on her knees and hung her head back, letting the hot water fall on her, willing it into someone else.

When her skin was pruned, she got out of the shower. Pulled on a pair of trackies and a jumper. Searched through her bags for paracetamol. Took two with a shaking hand and drank down a glass of water that hit her stomach, cold. Hung her wet coat and jumper over a radiator to dry. Plugged in her phone to recharge. Went into the kitchen and put the kettle on. Searched through the empty cupboards. She'd been in Copenhagen for two days and hadn't bought anything to stock her own kitchen. She didn't even have milk for a cup of tea and the only thing she had to eat was what remained of her stale Iced VoVos. Riled by shame, she poured herself a mug of hot water and took it with the biscuits to the couch.

In the bedroom, her phone began to beep repeatedly as it came back to life. Esther went to check it and brought it back to the couch. Scrolled through her notifications.

Voicemails from Jack. A voicemail and text from Nin.

Ya, Starry, I just got back from the Shell House. Went to see you. Your dad told me where you are. He swore me to secrecy. Don't worry,

I won't say anything to Mum. Starry, I can't believe you've gone to Copenhagen. I wish you'd said goodbye. But I can understand why it might have been easier not to. I just can't imagine what you're going through being there. Nina nayri? You haven't answered any of my messages in a while. Please don't leave and be a stranger to me again.

Esther's finger hovered over the screen to reply. Instead, she closed her texts. Unable to bring herself to listen to Nin's or Jack's voicemails – to hear in their voices how she'd let them down – she threw her phone to the other end of the couch.

She clenched her fists. Looked around the loft.

Jiggled a knee. Bit a nail. Then began picking at the soft, scarred skin on her wrist.

At the point when she usually stopped herself, Esther allowed her thoughts to run through a mental checklist of the contents in her toiletries bag and consider the edges inside. Her razor. Her tweezers. Her nail scissors. She allowed herself to remember the relief each one had brought her after Aura was gone. After she'd left her note for Esther the day she'd disappeared. And Esther had ignored it.

She touched the raw, tender skin of her wrist. Considered the edges.

A tremor went through Esther's body. And another. She curled up in a ball on the couch, her stomach cramping. Was she going to throw up again? She tried to take deep breaths through an onslaught of lightheadedness. As the cramping eased a little, Esther recognised the pain in her gut. Hunger. She'd barely touched her hot chips at the bar. Before that, had only eaten bread and cheese with Abelone for breakfast.

Trembling, she sat up and reached for the stale Iced VoVos. Forced one into her mouth. Chewed and took a mouthful of hot water to help swallow it down. Had another. Waited. Worried for a minute that she might bring them both back up. But the biscuits stayed down. The tremors started to ease.

Esther curled back up on the couch. Covered her face with her hands. Begged tears to come. Almost considered praying.

Anything to feel any sense of release. Her eyes stayed dry. Prayers did not come.

She stared at the ceiling, berating herself. Why was she even there? Because a stranger who'd taken a photo of Aura once told Esther that she had friends in Copenhagen? Pathetic. She should just leave. Go back home. To where she at least knew how to be the useless fuck-up that she was.

Esther rolled to her side. Stared at the bookshelf against the wall.

Most of the spines had titles in Danish but the few that were English caught her eye. *Understanding the Nude*. *Impressionism*. *Ways of Seeing*.

She ran her eyes further over the shelves. Noticed more English titles. *Art in Nature*. *Painting With Light*. *Fire in the Sea*.

A memory agitated. Stirred from the depths to the surface in her mind. Night time. Winter.

Esther following the beam of her torch, crunching through gum leaves; their sharp scent rises in the cold air. She breathes deeply. The night is still around her. Ahead, the sound of the sea. It's her thirteenth birthday.

She's left Jack, Freya and Aura in their tents. They've been away from Salt Bay, camping for the last week in a campsite at The Neck, the natural isthmus connecting the north and south of Bruny Island. The trip is her birthday present; the bay on the side of The Neck open to the ocean is known to come aglow at night with bioluminescence. Esther has been obsessed with it since she first learned about it in science class, besotted by the thought of seeing the ocean glowing and glittering at night, as if brimming with blue stars. Even more so when she learned that the blue glow was caused by living things in the sea that responded to disturbance by making light in their bodies. When her science teacher told her one of the best places to see bioluminescence was their very own island, Esther started begging Jack to take her to see stars in the ocean.

Finally, the trip of her dreams is happening for her thirteenth birthday. But every night since their arrival, Jack, Freya, Aura and Esther have gone to the shore and watched the sea in the darkness. Waited. Only to return to their tents disappointed. Esther's pining to see the glow is permeating her dreams; she's woken every morning in her tent looking for stars on her skin. Not everyone shares her fever for bioluminescence. During the days while they've been out as a family exploring Bruny Island, Freya has been distracted and searching for internet cafés. Aura has been sullen and distant.

On this last night at their campsite, Jack made Esther's birthday dinner around their campfire: tinned spaghetti and toast. Despite wearing party hats, Freya was grumpy; Aura was withdrawn.

Sensing the flat mood, Esther put as much brightness into her voice as she could. 'Make sure everybody eats enough for later. We'll need our energy. I've got a good feeling about tonight.' She adjusted the elastic strap of her party hat. It was cutting into her chin.

Aura groaned and Freya shot Jack a look.

Jack looked at Esther, torn. 'Starry, we've gone out every night this week and not seen anything. Maybe your mum and Aura will give it a rest tonight, hey, love? I'll still come with you, though.' Shadows of exhaustion hung beneath Jack's eyes. He tried to smile for her, to show her his enthusiasm.

'It's fine, Dad.' Esther took off her party hat. 'We don't need to go tonight.'

Jack's shoulders sagged with relief. 'I promise we'll come back another time. In the warmer months. Maybe we'll have better luck then.'

Esther looked at her mother's and sister's reluctant faces around the campfire; Aura's was the worst. Lately it seemed like their family revolved around whatever Aura wanted. It had been a battle to get her to agree to come camping in the first place.

When they all went to bed, Esther left her tent unzipped. After the rustling in the others' tents stopped and she heard soft snores, Esther sneaked from her tent with her torch.

Now she follows the beam of it along the path through the gum trees. Breathes deeply. Soon the bush opens to the sand. She switches her torch off. She's reached the sea.

Esther looks up at the sky, thick with stars but no moon. The sea is gentle, lapping the shore of the bay. Perfect conditions. She sits on the fallen log where the path ends and takes off her shoes and socks. Leaves them there with her torch. She read in *Oceanic Digest* that when searching for bioluminescence it's best to let your eyes adjust to whatever natural light is available. She recites the other tips. "'Never go night-swimming in the open sea. If there are no waves, stick to the shoreline and kick some water around instead. And be patient.'"

She walks to the shore. Wanders the wet sand. Walks and walks.

The length of the bay stretches almost out of sight. She kicks tentatively through the shallows. Nothing. She walks.

Esther reaches the end of the bay and turns to head back. Kicks again through the shallows. Nothing.

'At least you tried,' she says to herself.

A breeze ruffles Esther's hair. She looks up. Ahead.

At first, she thinks she wants to see it so much that she's imagining the electric blue glow on the shoreline. She stops. Stares. Starts to run and kick through the water.

Esther gasps as the sea lights up around her, neon blue, glowing, like a thousand stars are glittering at her feet. She runs through the shallows, shrieking with delight. Kicks up the waves. Squeals as she sees her footprints on the sand are filled with the magical blue glow. She runs into the sea, causing blue light to scatter and glow around her. Runs out of the waves. Runs back in. The stars are in her hair and on her skin. She slows down. Pants for breaths. Notices the seaweed and shells washed up on shore are glowing, lit up. She turns them over in

her hands. Drapes glowing seaweed over her shoulders. Holds
luminous shells between her fingers like blue jewels. While she's
clowning about, she glimpses something gleaming nearby on
the sea. Esther splashes towards it. Realises it's a black feather.
She scoops a hand through the water, all aglow, and pinches the
black feather between her fingers. Its edging is white. Maybe
a magpie? Esther thinks of the reference in her bird book and
shakes her head. She feels certain it's a black swan feather. She
holds it aloft and flaps her arms as she runs through the sea.
Her body is fizzing with wonder and awe. She wants to shout
something, to express her joy, but doesn't know what to say.
Sisters of Seal and Swan Skins? She remembers Aura's scowl and
groan at dinner. No.

'I am Esther Wilding,' she howls to the stars above, and
below. Then runs, giggling, a thirteen-year-old girl in a neon-
blue world, all her own.

Esther sat up on the couch. Wiped her eyes. Stared at the wall.
The scent of crushed gum leaves, the glow of the sea, lingered
in her senses.

After a while she reached for her phone and checked
the time. It was midday. Abelone would be at work, she
guessed.

She went into her bedroom. Took her travel wallet from
her bedside table. Lifted out the eight feathers. Ran her fingers
over their black vanes and sometimes–white edges. Held them
in her hand.

'I am Esther Wilding,' she whispered.

Esther put the feathers back into her travel wallet. Tucked
it into her bag to take with her.

She looked around her room. Plucked off the floor the
black jeans that she'd worn the day before. Checked the
pockets. Found the map Abelone had drawn her. She unfolded
it. Looked it over. Almost smiled at one of Abelone's markings,
for a nearby local bakery. *The pastries here are finger-sucking-good!*

Esther went to the loft windows and looked down on Sortedams Sø. White swans dabbled and swam; one opened its wings to their full span and stretched.

The sky was cloudless. Esther checked the weather forecast on her phone for the rest of the day. Fine.

She went to her wardrobe and took out fresh clothes.

Downstairs, the house was quiet and empty. Esther found a notepad in a drawer of the side table she'd knocked into the night before. There was no sign of the smashed vase. She scribbled a note of apology to Abelone and a promise to bring home dinner for them both. Esther locked the front door behind her and tucked her keys on Jack's Space Club keyring into her pocket.

As she crossed Fredens Bro with Abelone's map in hand, Esther opened her arms in the pale sunshine and stretched. Breathed. Resettled.

When she reached the other side of the bridge, she glanced at the map, crossed at the intersection and continued past Østre Anlæg Park to Rosenborg Castle Gardens.

Through the entrance gates, Esther followed the lines of Abelone's map, drawn with a felt-tip marker. Bright and clear. Neon blue.

23

Esther took the path on Abelone's map that led down an alley of leafy trees and cut between a tall, trimmed hedge. A pair of ravens cawed overhead. When Esther looked up, she was stopped in her tracks.

Liden Gunver, the fisher girl, stood on a plinth, her gaze downcast. The contrast between her vulnerability and helplessness and the image of Aura standing right there, glowing with joy, was dizzying.

Esther studied the uncertainty in the curl of Liden Gunver's narrow shoulders, her bare feet and the hopeful, curious look on her face. The presence of the merman's absence in the sculpture was what made it profound. His omniscience.

A sense of suspicion made Esther dig her fingernails into her palms. What had Aura loved so much about Liden Gunver and her story? Had she been standing there in the arms of her own merman?

Esther tried to shake the images in her mind from Aura's journal into some sort of meaning. The Binalong Bay Girl was trapped in a frozen sea. Agnete had been drawn to the depths by the enchantment of the Sea King. Liden Gunver was lured into the water by a man from the sea and never returned. The common themes between them were clear, but what did they have to do with Aura?

As she brushed away stray leaves gathered around Liden

Gunver's feet, Esther wondered if Aura had once done the same. Standing where she stood.

There was a bench beside the sculpture. Esther sat. Stayed a while. Watched people walk by. Looked again at Liden Gunver.

She reached into her bag for her travel wallet. Stood, slung her bag over her shoulder. Walked to the sculpture. Took a moment, a few slow breaths, as she tucked a black swan feather into a crack beneath one of Liden Gunver's feet.

After Esther left Rosenborg Castle Gardens, she continued with Abelone's map and discovered colourful, cobbled streets, where medieval spires and romantic Renaissance architecture sat alongside the neat and angular edges of modernist buildings. She took another bite of the kanelsnegl she'd bought at the bakery Abelone had recommended. Finger-sucking-good. Her limbs hummed with warmth, cinnamon and sugar.

'You have to try kanelsnegl,' the baker had told her, taking a tray of flaky, gooey pastries from the glass cabinet she stood behind. 'Of course, too,' the baker said, 'you should choose this one because it's Wednesday.'

'Of course,' Esther had said, feigning understanding.

The baker smiled. 'We eat kanelsnegl on Wednesdays,' she explained, then pointed out the snail-shell shape and swirl of the iced-cinnamon delicacy. 'We call it Onsdagssnegle.'

Esther tried to repeat the Danish word.

'That's right. Wednesday snails,' the baker said, sliding the pastry into a paper bag. Esther had smiled at the strange delight of translation.

She looked up as she walked, taking in buildings painted in varying ochre, honey and mustard hues, colours that reminded her so vividly of home: sandstone, resin, volcanic soil. As she ventured further down Gothersgade, Nyhavn opened ahead of her.

It might as well have been a totally different place from the one she'd seen the night before in a haze of panic and fear. Nyhavn was lined with moored sailing boats. On either side of the harbour, rows of townhouses were painted in cheerful colours, vibrant in the light: pale blue, pink, yellow, orange, navy and green. Most had been converted into restaurants and bars. The cobbled streets were thick with people, queuing for tickets to a canal cruise, or sitting at one of the countless restaurants with outdoor seating under giant umbrellas.

Esther took Abelone's map from her pocket. *Walk down what we call the sunny side of the harbour.* She looked from one side of the harbour to the other. *Tattoo Stjerne is in the basement of the first blue townhouse. Look for the pots of flowers on the street.* Esther walked along the sunny side, scanning the outdoor restaurant awnings until she spotted a blue townhouse. Blooming white and pink flowerpots led around the corner of the building into a laneway. Esther did a double-take: the bar she'd found Dark Blue in yesterday was above the tattoo parlour. She'd been right there but, in her state, hadn't realised.

'At least you tried,' she murmured, tucking the map into her pocket. Her hands shook from the rush of sugar, caffeine and adrenaline; she'd made it.

It wasn't until she turned down the laneway that the basement tattoo parlour was visible. From cobblestones, a few steps descended to the parlour's heavy wooden door. Over which hung a sign painted in a traditional tattoo font: a pin-up-style woman sprinkled a handful of stars over the words, *Tattoo Stjerne.* On either side of the door, street-level windows offered flash designs and views into the small parlour. Pillar candles burned inside glass bell jars next to more pots of white flowers. Esther's mind played tricks on her. For a moment she almost thought she could smell lilies in bloom.

Tourists flowed around Esther as she stood unmoving at the entrance to the tattoo parlour. The hairs on the back of her neck rose as she thought of who else had stood where she was.

Sailors, sex workers, circus folk. Rumour has it even some royals. We think our Gull was tattooed there too. Gull, who had dressed as a man, sailed the Atlantic and come home secretly tattooed, had stood where Esther was, well versed in the power of marking herself by choice. As teenagers, Freya, Erin and Abelone had been there, each daring the other to go first through the door. Esther reluctantly imagined her mother, young, carrying the image of Tattoo Stjerne in her mind as inspiration, dreaming of one day opening her own tattoo studio. Decades later, Abelone, grieving the love of her life, had stood where Esther was, before she transformed her skin with Kristina's wedding vows. Aura, alone, half the world away from home, had stood where Esther was, had faced the same door, stencil for her first tattoo in hand. Esther gripped the small banister by the steps.

'Undskyld,' a voice said behind her.

A young woman brushed past Esther, went down the steps and pushed through the wooden door into the parlour. Esther hurried to follow before the door closed behind her.

Inside, the noisy bustle of the crowded harbour faded away. A sea-blue vase of coral-pink roses sat on a reception desk, behind which the woman had settled herself. On the white walls, dozens of framed certificates. Some photos. A pink neon sign, in English. Esther read it, struck by the words. To the side, shelves of ink, arranged by colour. In every spare space near the windows, potted plants. The light was tinged green. A giant monstera pressed its leaves to the ceiling. Esther looked up. The leaves wavered in her vision, as if she was underwater, gazing up at lily pads.

'Can I help you?' the woman behind the reception counter asked, glancing up at Esther from beneath her glossy, black fringe. The rest of her long hair was tied up in a midnight-blue scarf, the same colour as her eyes. She had a delicate gold septum piercing, and double gold hoops in each of her ears that chimed when she moved. Fine line tattoos were inked on the top of both of her hands and every finger, accented by gold nail polish.

Esther cleared her throat. 'Are you Lille Heks?' she asked.

The woman shook her head. 'Tala.' She took off her coat, revealing a series of black geometric patterns and symbols tattooed on her décolletage and both of her arms. 'Do you have an appointment?'

The familiar buzzing of a tattoo gun started behind Esther. She glanced over her shoulder at another woman leaning over someone lying on their side on a tattoo bed, their shirt lifted and ribs exposed.

'I'm not here for an appointment.' Esther stared at the pink neon sign on the wall.

Tala turned. 'Sylvia Plath,' she said.

Esther looked at her, not understanding but desperately wanting to be the kind of woman, like Tala, who did.

'It's a quote. Sylvia Plath.'

'Oh.' Esther nodded. 'It's beautiful.'

Tala pressed her red-tinted lips together in a polite smile.

'I'm here to talk to Lille Heks,' Esther said.

Tala eyed Esther warily. 'Are you from upstairs, because Lille Heks made it really clear that without her lawyer present—'

'What? No, no I'm not from … upstairs? I'm …' Esther paused. Noticed an alcove behind Tala, and, tacked to its main wall, countless tattoo stencils. Moons, arrows, flowers, mountains. A mermaid. A towering, curling Hokusai wave. 'My sister came here.' Esther returned her attention to Tala. 'She was tattooed by Lille Heks. I wanted to ask if she had any time to talk with me about her.'

'And your sister is …?'

'Aura Wilding.'

Tala studied Esther's face. 'Ufattelight,' she murmured.

'Sorry?' Esther frowned.

'You must be Starry,' Tala said. 'The one Aura got tattooed for.'

Esther sucked in her breath. 'What do you mean?'

'Oh no, nothing bad,' Tala rushed to say, misreading Esther's reaction. 'I just mean Aura spent a lot of time here. We all liked her, and she liked Lille Heks, so she'd come and hang out. Most of her stories were about her little sister. There was this thing she used to say about the two of you, this phrase, every time before she got tattooed: something like ... what was it, something about ... raising your sword?'

Sisters of Seal and Swan Skins! Séala and Eala! Raise your swords and your voices. Esther swallowed the words in her throat.

'Every time?' she asked. The strain of keeping her composure made a muscle in her cheek tic. 'She got more than one tattoo here?'

Tala seemed to consider her answer. 'Have you asked Aura?'

Esther waited until her voice was steady. 'I would ask her if I could,' she said slowly. 'Aura died, just over a year ago. I'm trying to put her life here together so my family and we can understand what happened to her before we lost her.' She answered questions before Tala could ask them. 'We don't know exactly how she died. Presumed drowned. She was last seen by the sea in our hometown. They found her things – her dress, her shoes – on the shore. It sounds like you were fond of her; I'm sorry to have to tell you.'

'Oh my god,' Tala said, her face turning pale. 'I'm so sorry.'

Esther looked away. She didn't want to see the tears or shock in Tala's eyes. Didn't want to risk seeing the flicker in her face that Esther had come to expect when people glimpsed the depths of her grief and silently processed relief it wasn't their own.

After a few moments, she turned back to Tala. 'What did you mean, before,' Esther asked, 'when you said I'm who Aura got tattooed for?'

'Oh.' Tala's face had softened. 'Aura had—' She started again. 'Are you tattooed?'

Esther shook her head. 'Our mum is a tattooist; we grew up around her studio.'

'That's right, I remember Aura saying.' Tala leaned over the reception desk, dropping her voice. 'Aura was one of us, you know? Tattoos were meaningful for her. She used to call them skin spells; her stories that lived.'

The geometric patterns tattooed on Tala's arms were hypnotic, shimmering, almost an optical illusion.

'And the way Aura talked about you when she was getting tattooed … well.' Tala's smile turned into a slight frown as she drew back. 'But she didn't tell you about her tattoos here?'

The back of Esther's throat pinched. 'I'm staying with one of our relatives, Abelone. She told me Lille Heks did her tattoo, and that she also tattooed Aura. That's why I'm here. I'd love a bit of time with Lille Heks if she could spare it. If she could tell me anything about Aura or her tattoos, anything at all.'

'Of course.' Tala looked at Esther kindly, accepting her diversion. 'She's not in this week though. We're going through a tenancy disagreement with the landlord. This place is an icon of local history and culture but they want to turn it into a restaurant kitchen.' Tala flicked through the diary on the desk. 'Lille Heks will be back the week after next. Do you want to book some time with her so it's in her diary and she knows to expect you?'

Esther nodded, unable to speak around disappointment. A two-week wait seemed interminable.

'I'll let Lille Heks know,' Tala said after taking down Esther's details. 'She'll be so happy to meet you. Like I am.'

'Thanks.' Esther gave a small smile. 'Me too.'

'Anything else I can help with?' Tala asked.

Esther thought about it. 'There is actually.' She told Tala what she was after.

Tala's eyes glittered. She reached for paper and pen. Wrote down some details and handed it to Esther. 'These two places have never let me down.' She smiled. 'Good luck.'

Esther took the paper, said her thanks and turned to leave.

'Hey,' Tala called after her. 'I don't know your name. Aura only ever called you Starry.'

'Esther,' she replied. 'I'm Esther Wilding.'

'Pas på dig selv,' Tala said. 'Take care of yourself, Esther Wilding.'

24

Esther walked down row after row of fresh-cut flowers in the market, her eyes glazed over. An empty shopping basket dangled from her arm as she went, distracted, thinking through her conversation with Tala. She stopped in front of a bucket of bouquets of tight pink buds. Stared vacantly at them. She'd set out from Abelone's daring to hope she'd do better than the day before, and she'd found Liden Gunver and Tattoo Stjerne – she wanted to feel good about her day. But her conversation with Tala and the reality of all that she didn't know about Aura's life had hit her like a wave she hadn't seen coming and reminded her just how out of place and adrift she was in the wash of all Aura had left behind.

A woman approached the same flower bucket Esther was standing in front of and reached for one of the bouquets of pink buds. She was about Abelone's age, dressed in all black, with red lipstick and solid silver jewellery. Said something to Esther in Danish.

'Sorry, I don't speak Danish.' Esther gave an apologetic shrug. Started to walk away.

'I was just saying,' the woman switched to English, 'don't you love peony season.' She smiled and picked a bouquet.

Esther watched her walk away. Looked back at the clusters of tight pink buds in front of her. 'Peonies it is,' she said to herself.

On a shelf near the check-outs, Esther found a green glass vase. She put it in her shopping basket with the peonies. Clicked her phone screen to life. The takeaway order she'd placed at the Indian restaurant on her way to the flower market would be ready.

Esther had told Tala she needed a florist and restaurant that sold flowers and food that were beautiful and flavoursome enough to earn someone's forgiveness. So far, Tala's recommendations hadn't let her down. But the real test was yet to come.

Esther unlocked the front door to Abelone's house and took her bags inside. Shut the door behind her.

'Esther?' Abelone's voice echoed through the house to greet her.

'It's me,' she called back.

At the end of the hallway the swing door was propped open. She carried her bags into the living room. The three-shade lamps hung like low rising moons. A log fire crackled in the fireplace. Against the pale wall, the print of the swan painting shimmered; the black and white swans both reached for the horizon line between them, mirroring each other.

'In here,' Abelone called from the kitchen.

Esther went through. 'Hi,' she said, overcome by sudden shyness as she lifted her bags to the counter.

'Hi,' Abelone answered. She was sitting at the small dining table in the corner, window open, smoking her pipe. Her white hair was piled atop her head, fastened in place by chopsticks.

'These are for you,' Esther said, lifting the bouquet of peonies from her bag. 'And this.' She took out the vase wrapped in tissue paper. Gave both to Abelone, who set them on the dining table and looked evenly at Esther.

'I, uh, I'm really sorry for missing dinner last night.' Esther fidgeted with the zipper on her coat. 'I knew you went to a lot of effort to welcome me … and' – she searched for the right words – 'I'm very sorry for breaking your vase when I got in late. I made a mess of everything. I'm … sorry.'

There was the slightest softening in Abelone's face. She put down her pipe and stood. Carried the peonies and vase to the sink. 'Thank you,' she said to Esther.

'I also brought dinner home for us. Like I said I would in my note. It comes recommended by a local. I hope you like Indian?'

Abelone opened a cupboard to her side, full of crockery, and gestured for Esther to take out some plates. 'I like it,' she replied.

On their second helpings of coconut chickpea curry, mushroom palak and cumin potatoes, Abelone tore off another piece of soft, buttery naan bread and offered it to Esther. Her face was flushed from the spicy heat of their meal. A couple of times while they'd been eating, Esther caught Abelone admiring her peonies in their green glass vase that she'd set on the counter.

'You had a bad day yesterday,' Abelone stated.

Esther paused. Swallowed. Nodded.

'You got home late. It was for Satan outside.' Abelone arched a brow.

More than you could know, Esther wanted to say. 'It was,' she said instead.

Abelone watched her closely. 'But today?'

'Better,' Esther answered. 'All thanks to your map.'

There was a flicker in Abelone's eyes. 'Did you try a kanelsnegl from my favourite bakery? Find Liden Gunver? Meet Lille Heks?'

'Yes, so delicious, tak. Yes, I found her,' Esther said, 'and no. But I met Tala?'

'Lille Heks' daughter.'

'She didn't say.'

'It's not the first thing Tala shares about herself. She's trying to make her own way as a tattooist.'

Esther bit into a papadum. 'I left my details; Tala said she'd get Lille Heks to contact me.' She chewed and swallowed. 'Apparently, Aura was tattooed more than once by Lille Heks. It seemed like she'd spent a lot of time at Tattoo Stjerne.'

'Aura was always in and out, always busy, at campus, or out with friends. We didn't keep watch on each other. She worked hard, always studying, reading.'

Esther shifted in her seat. 'You said you only knew about her first tattoo?'

'As I say, we didn't know each other that way, confessing every detail of our days. She kept much of her life here to herself and her friends. It wasn't my place to intrude. When we spent time together, we talked about all sorts of things, but, from the day she arrived, Aura was private. I sensed there was always a part of her that she held back. That she kept unspoken.'

'What do you think it was?' Esther asked. Aura lingering in the doorway to her bedroom, staring at Esther in the hallway. Silent.

'If I knew, you would already know.' Abelone ate the last mouthful on her plate. 'You'll show me her journal tomorrow. I might be able to help.'

'That would be great,' Esther said.

'Precis.' Abelone pushed her plate away. 'Ooof.' She held her hands to her stomach. 'Would you like some tea?'

Esther glanced across at the counter where she remembered seeing Abelone's cake glistening under its bell jar the night before.

'Yes, please,' Esther said, eyes searching. Her mouth watered at the thought of biting into one of the glistening Seven Sisters scrolls. But the cake was nowhere to be seen.

They cleared the table and their dinner dishes. Abelone motioned towards the living room. 'Go through; the fire might need stoking. I'll bring the tea in when it's ready,' Abelone said.

Esther went into the living room and added a log from the basket by the hearth to the fireplace. She blew on the embers and used a poker to stoke the flames. Once the fire was blazing, she took a seat on one of the couches, among a pile of velvet cushions. Her whole body was floppy with relief; Abelone seemed to have accepted her apology.

She took in Abelone's living room, savouring the warmth
of her space: the potted plants, furniture, art, books, the fire,
lamps, colours and textures. Esther found herself wishing she
could inhabit a place like that. The image of her window ledge
in Calliope came immediately to mind. Her bedroom in her
staff house had remained as sparse as she'd found it the day
that she moved in. Except for her window ledge, where she'd
gathered shells worn to iridescence by the riverbank, fallen
feathers that flashed green and turquoise in the light, and dried
tangles of kelp.

'Hmph,' Esther said to herself. Stroked a green velvet cushion
in her lap. Smooth to touch one way, rough against the grain.

'Here we are.' Abelone carried a tray into the living room
and set it on the coffee table. She arranged an enamel teapot,
two mugs, a jug of milk and a dish of sugar cubes. Gestured for
Esther to help herself.

'Thank you,' Esther said, sitting forward. She took a mug.
Made herself a tea.

Across the coffee table, Abelone dipped a finger in her tea.
Drew a quick, wet line across each of her wrists.

Esther's heart hammered with recognition. Determined to
do right, she dipped a finger in her tea and copied Abelone.

Watching her, Abelone gave Esther a brief nod of approval.

'When did you learn?' Esther asked.

'My mother taught us this ritual when Freya and Erin came
to stay with us that summer in our teens. We did as you and I
are doing. Sitting and talking, welcoming our ancestors to join
us.' Abelone took a sip of her tea, closed her eyes in pleasure.
'After Freya and Erin took the ritual home with them, they
later told me that instead of smoky tea, they used saltwater and
ink to honour the letters Johanna and Gull wrote to each other
for the rest of their lives, after Johanna sailed to Australia.'

Esther blew the steam from her mug, moved to tears by
the thought of ink-written letters being the only connection
between sisters separated by the sea. 'I didn't know that,' she

said quietly. 'About Mum and Erin doing that to honour Johanna and Gull in their own way.'

'Aura didn't either. When she came to Copenhagen and we drank this tea together, she brought your generation of our ancestors' story full circle.'

Esther's face fell. It was all Aura's. Everything.

'Rituals are important,' Abelone said. 'They kept Johanna and Gull connected. They keep us connected.' She took a sip of her tea and sighed in satisfaction. 'Well?' Abelone asked. 'Are you going to try your tea?'

Esther forced herself to smile. To shake the weight pressing on her back. She sipped her tea. Sipped it again. 'This tea is weird. Weirdly good. The smoky flavour. With the sweetness of the sugar.'

'You haven't had it before?'

Esther shook her head.

'Ah. Russian Caravan. It's my favourite. The smokiness. The sweetness.'

The fire popped, a shimmer of embers spiralling golden, upwards, into the chimney throat. Esther's eyes were drawn back to the swan painting. After a while, she became aware Abelone was observing her.

'You know Hilma af Klint's work?' Abelone asked.

'No.' Esther shook her head. 'It's just, the two swans. They keep catching my eye. I find it hard to look away.'

'Oh, I envy you, discovering her for the first time.' Abelone turned to the painting. 'What makes Hilma extraordinary is her ability to paint beyond what we can understand or explain but can feel.' She stood and went to a bookshelf. Took down a thick book. The cover was a splash of swirling, abstract shapes and jubilant colours. She came back to the couch and handed it to Esther. 'She was a Swedish artist. In the nineteenth century.' Abelone paused. 'When she was eighteen, her sister died. She turned to art to survive grief.'

Esther stilled. 'Her sister died?' She opened the book.

Abelone nodded. 'I teach a course on her art.'.

Esther turned the pages, running her fingers over the glossy images.

'But I haven't always been an art teacher,' Abelone went on. 'I spent years keeping my dreams tucked away out of fear. But Kristina saw them. Saw me. She made me promise before she died that I would finally go to art school. On my first day, one of the first artists I learned about was Hilma. What I love about her story is how it seems grief cracked Hilma open and gave her a kind of sight, a way of painting what can only be felt. It's a way of seeing. Hard to look away from, as you say.'

Esther looked from the book to the print of the swans on the wall. 'What's it about? That painting.'

'Hmmm. What do you see when you look at the swans?' Abelone asked.

Esther pondered. 'I see home,' she said. 'Black swans remind me of home. Lutruwita. Tasmania. Beyond the obvious two swans, I don't know how to explain what I see, it's more a feeling, really.'

Abelone rolled her wrist, encouraging Esther to say more.

'I feel … unsure. Of whether the steadiness of that horizon line can be trusted. Of, I guess, whether anything is steady between the light and the dark parts of ourselves. Can we ever be whole?'

'Ha,' Abelone said, playfully swatting Esther on the shoulder. 'You could teach some of my students how it's done. They're zombies.'

Esther tried to laugh. The words she'd kept pushed down and silenced for years started to rise. She took a deep breath. Started. Stopped. Abelone looked at her, expectant.

'I've always wanted to be a scientist. An astronomer.' Esther winced as she heard herself say it. 'I started studying it at university. In Nipaluna. Hobart.'

Abelone's eyes sparked with interest. 'When did you finish?'

Esther shook her head. 'I dropped out, after only a year. When I finished high school, I didn't want to go to uni if it meant I had to leave home, so I hung around and lost a few years of my life working odd jobs. But then Aura left. And eventually I did too. I loved uni ... studying ... Then Aura came home ... and ... I threw it all away.'

Abelone reached for her tea. 'It mustn't have been the right time,' she said, simply. Her lack of judgement and willingness to listen, after Esther had behaved so badly, opened something in Esther's chest.

Instead of stuffing her feelings back down, she spoke them. 'My life is just mistake after mistake,' Esther revealed to Abelone. 'Like last night. Another big mistake.' She wiped her eyes. 'I just ...' Esther's voice broke. 'I just ... don't know what I'm doing. Here. Or, in my life.'

Abelone sat quietly, listening.

'All I know is how much I miss Aura. It's all I'm sure of. Not knowing what happened to her ... and not knowing anything about her life here ... it eats me alive.' Esther rubbed a hand over her chest. 'I just ... I was always running after her when we were kids, you know? Always begging her to wait for me. Wait for me. And now here I am, chasing after her in death, and it's fucking hard, it's all so fucking hard ...' Esther trailed off. 'Sorry, sorry, Abelone,' she said.

Abelone's eyes were kind. 'You think after everything you just shared, the thing I'd care most about is your language?'

Esther gave a shaky laugh.

Abelone topped up their mugs from the teapot.

'Can I ask you a question?' Esther added sugar and milk to her fresh tea.

'Ja.'

'I know you made a promise to Kristina. I know her love and spirit gave you the determination and courage to go to art school. And now you're teaching too, and that's all amazing.'

'But?'

'Don't you ever wonder what the point is? Why bother, when life can just crush you, just like that?' Esther snapped her fingers. 'People live, people die, so why love at all? When everything is so fragile? When the people you love can just … disappear?'

Abelone was pensive. She folded her hands in her lap. 'Esther, with six decades behind me, I am plum fucked if I know what the point is.'

Esther leaned her head back and laughed from her belly.

'Here's, I think, ja, a better question,' Abelone said, leaning forward. 'I am alive, Kristina is dead, and I will never understand it – but why are we all so obsessed with understanding everything? This is what Hilma af Klint tells me when I look at her swans, that she made from the inside, where things are felt, not known, not understood. She painted the mystery. Ja? There's a point between things where science and art connect, but, beyond that, everything is one big unknown mystery. Which none of us cope with. But it gives me hope. Because it means for better and worse anything is possible. That's beauty. That's joy. I will grieve for Kristina for the rest of my life. But, one day, I know I'm also going to laugh again until I pee a little bit. And I'm going to make art I cannot even dream of yet. And I am loving people. My friends. My students, even the zombie ones. And my family. Like the one who shows up at my door from the other side of the world with her heart in her mouth like a little bird, building her nest.'

'Thank you.' Esther smiled as she wiped her eyes.

'A few generations ago, the women we come from, two sisters, were separated by half the world and never saw each other again. Decades later, here we are sitting together in their house. How unlikely. How magical. That's the feeling I hold on to, skat. That's why I bother.'

Esther looked at Abelone, grateful.

'I think now, we sleep. Your eyes are sagging,' Abelone said.

As they began to gather their cups and plates, Esther's mobile pinged in her pocket.

'I've got this,' Abelone said, as she carried their things into the kitchen.

Esther wriggled her phone from her pocket and tapped the screen. An email. From Klara Jørgensen.

Dearest Esther,

I think you are here in my city now? Velkommen! I hope you aren't too jet lagged, and Copenhagen has been good to you so far. I am back too, just today, from London. Let me know when you'd like to meet up, and I'll make us a plan.

I'm very happy to see you soon.

Kærlig hilsen,

Klara

Esther read the email again and again. Klara's words collided with images in her mind. Of a woman painting from a place that she couldn't see but could feel. Of Aura tattooing seven stories on her skin, though she hid the words from sight. Of their ancestors, Johanna and Gull, who were separated by marriage and migration and lived out their lives in unrequited yearning for each other. Esther tapped out her email reply to Klara on her phone and hit send.

Outside, across the street, a skein of swans settled on the surface of the Sortedams Sø. Two kilometres away, shining bright through the window into the darkness, Sylvia Plath's neon words glowed on the wall of Tattoo Stjerne.

Wear your heart on your skin in this life.

25

Freya Wilding lowered the needle to the record and closed her eyes to listen to the crackle. A shiver of anticipation, waiting for Stevie's voice. 'Tango in the Night'. The drums. 'Big Love'.

She lit six candles; the reflection of flames shimmered in the windows of her studio. She glanced out, up at the tiny fires under the expanse of night. A waning moon was rising, mellow and golden. In Esther's northern sky it would be a bare wisp, a pale brushstroke in her afternoon blue.

Freya lit a seventh candle, shook out the match and stood, arms open, hands held towards the little flames. Then, a line of ink on one wrist, a line of saltwater on the other. She paced while she waited for them to dry.

The Shell House was dark; Jack hadn't stirred when she'd slipped from bed. Earlier in the evening Freya had sensed something was coming when Jack went running and stayed out longer than usual. When he walked back through the door, he still looked as tense as before he'd left.

'Good run?' she asked.

'Great,' he answered, frowning. 'Always run my best at night.' Everything he didn't say pressed to the corners and filled the cracks in the walls. A few weeks after Aura disappeared, Freya had followed Jack one night. Watched as he ran the shoreline back and forth, fretting the same path, an anxious dog along a fence line. Searching, searching.

As Freya readied herself to confront him it was that image of Jack along the shoreline that came back to her. She handed him a glass of water and looked him straight in the eye. 'What aren't you telling me?' she asked.

For the previous few days Jack had been unusually quiet, his face pinched with stress. He'd stayed out running longer each night; Freya had resisted making comment. It was their silent agreement. She gave him the nights to run. Jack gave her clear mornings to dive.

'What is it, Jack?' she asked him.

Jack took the glass of water but couldn't meet her eye. 'Esther's gone,' he said, his voice thin with exhaustion. 'She's in Copenhagen. With Abelone. I'm sorry, Frey. Her one condition was that I didn't tell you she was going.'

They stayed up late, Freya wanting to go over every detail about Esther's departure and journey until Jack's eyes were closing. In bed, Jack's breathing deepened moments after his head rested on his pillow. But Freya tossed and turned until the sheets were knotted and her body was feverish with agitation. Insomnia stalked her, a wild thing pulling at her hair. *Her one condition was that I didn't tell you she was going.* Guilt made her heart race and her head pound. The memory of her fight with Esther tormented Freya; she'd stayed silent when she could have told Esther what had happened to Aura. Her chance had been right there. But Freya hadn't spoken up. Was that right? Had she done wrong by her daughter? Which daughter? Questions looped without end through her mind.

Freya sat up in bed. It hurt to breathe.

She left the house. The night air was cool and welcome relief. She unlocked the studio door, locked it behind her and audibly exhaled. There were two places Freya breathed freely: the quiet green vale of the sea and the sanctuary of her studio.

The electric guitar hummed. 'Seven Wonders.' Freya stood before the candle flames.

'Old women, Lutruwita women, I honour you.' She held each of her wrists in a hand. 'Johanna. Gull. Granny. Mum.' Freya paused. 'My seal child. Aurora Sæl.' Her voice caught. 'Women of my line, I honour you. And I ask you for courage tonight.' She gazed through the flames to her studio door.

Aura's knock had come a couple of weeks after the taxi had pulled up at the kerb and delivered her back to them, after nearly three years away. At first, her knock had been so soft that Freya had ignored it, thinking it was a bird tapping at the window or the studio creaking and settling in the wind. Her second knock was stronger; Freya opened the door. Aura stood at the threshold, face haunted and pale. How unaware, how careless Freya had been at the time. *My wild wave of a daughter is disappearing right in front of me.* She wanted to go back and shake sense into herself. *Do something. Now.*

Aura had her She-Ra journal clutched to her chest. Freya had been playing *Tango in the Night*. There'd been a hint of a smile on Aura's face when she heard the opening bars of 'Everywhere'.

'How are you feeling?' Freya asked.

'Do you have clients today?' Aura avoided answering.

Freya shook her head.

'Will you help me, Mum?' Aura's eyes, dark and watery.

As she made a stencil copy from the page Aura had shown her in her journal, Freya heard Jack's advice in her mind. *It's important we let her speak in her own time,* he'd explained. Freya shook her head. *Fuck that.* When the stencil was ready, she handed the journal back to Aura.

'Isn't that from high school when you were going through your eighties retro phase?' Freya prompted.

Aura nodded. 'I wrote in it when I was fifteen. Up until that night.'

Her forthrightness hit Freya in the stomach. She kept her back to Aura as she lined up her pots of ink and readied her tattoo gun.

'I took it with me, so I didn't leave that part of me behind.

To make sure I remembered who I was there for, who I was trying to make good for.'

Freya kept her tone soft and quiet. 'Tell me about this tattoo.' She glanced over her shoulder at Aura.

'I wanted to get the whole series done in Copenhagen, but it didn't work out that way.'

'Series?'

'The seven verses that are in my journal.'

Freya's head spun as she tried to piece together the fragments that Aura was sharing. She wheeled her chair to the tattoo bed with stencil in hand and smiled warmly at Aura, hoping it was enough to mask her tempest of feelings.

Aura held eye contact for a moment before she sat up, swept her long hair to the side, and unbuttoned her tea dress, letting it fall to her waist. She rolled over to lie on her belly, leaving her back bare.

As Aura positioned herself on the tattoo bed, with such certainty and readiness, Freya's realisation was swift: it wasn't Aura's first time being tattooed. And then, she saw them.

Freya forced herself to keep her breathing even as she read the tattoos starting at the nape of Aura's neck, going down her spine: beautiful, fine black lines of Aura's handwriting.

If you want change, raise your sword, raise your voice.
He will give you flowers to forget. You plant seeds, to remember.
Maybe she chose the depths. Maybe she's free.

Freya stroked a gloved hand over Aura's skin.

'Do you like them?' Aura asked, quietly.

'They're beautifully done. And very powerful, min elskede.'

'They're my Selkie Trees, Mum.'

Freya held her breath as the meaning of Aura's words settled.

'I'm going to put your stencil on now,' she said, exhaling. 'You want this fourth verse in line with the previous ones? Same spacing?'

'Yes, please.'

Freya arranged her razor, rubbing alcohol and Vaseline. Began preparing Aura's skin for the stencil. Her elskede. Her beloved.

'Tell me more about the verses,' Freya ventured. 'What was that image I saw in your book with this verse? The one with the swans?'

Aura was silent. Freya tensed; she'd asked too much.

'It's an illustration from a Scandinavian fairytale I came across at uni.'

'A fairytale,' Freya said as she lined up the stencil on Aura's back. 'One I'd know?'

'It was written by a woman in the nineteenth century, not the Brothers Grimm or Hans Christian Andersen, so probably not.'

'Good point.' Freya kept her tone light. 'So, this is a series of seven fairytale illustrations paired with your own writing?'

'Only three images are illustrations from fairytales. The other four are sculptures.'

'Sculptures?'

'That are meaningful to me. From here, and while I was in Denmark, and in ... while I was overseas.'

Freya waited for Aura to elaborate on her omittance. When she didn't, Freya let the conversation lapse. She peeled the stencil paper off Aura's skin. Checked that the stencil aligned with the curve of Aura's shoulders and previous tattoos.

'I wrote them for courage,' Aura blurted out. 'The seven verses. To put strength and freedom back into the stories the illustrations and sculptures tell about girls and women. About their bodies. Their desires. And how the world punishes them.'

Freya stilled. She reread the words inked on her daughter's back, with the added stencil of the fourth verse she was about to tattoo.

Who would you be if you never strayed to the shore?

Freya's eyes smarted with tears as she looked over Aura's tattoos and understood. Aura was writing her story on her skin. She was done hiding.

'Seven stories. About seven women, whose lives were changed forever by water.' Aura's voice fell. 'Like mine was.'

Freya swallowed the lump in her throat. 'Oh Aura,' she whispered. 'There's so much I—'

'I got three verses tattooed in Copenhagen, Mum. I want you to do the last four. Then they'll be finished. Then it will happen.'

'What will?'

Aura looked at her. 'Transformation.'

Freya took a deep breath. Squeezed her daughter's leg with a gloved hand. Readjusted her grip on her tattoo gun. 'You ready?'

Aura settled. Nodded.

Freya touched the needle to Aura's skin, feeling the slight flinch of her muscle beneath. The buzz of the tattoo gun and Stevie Nicks' voice filled the silence between them.

'Why seven?' Freya asked after a while.

Aura looked over at her, smiled, almost serenely, the pain and adrenaline working their magic. 'Seven tattoos, seven truths, shed like a seal skin. They're my postscript, Mum. To that time in my life. How I've found my way. Ever since.'

Freya stopped her gun.

'Ever since,' she said, looking at her daughter.

Aura closed her eyes. Freya blinked back tears to focus on the fine black words she continued to needle into her daughter's skin.

The record player skipped and stuttered. Skipped and stuttered. Freya startled from the shallow sleep she'd fallen into on the couch. Aura's nearness faded. Through the window of her studio the sky was starting to lighten: the mottled grey skin of dawn before the spill of gold.

Freya sat up. The ink and saltwater on her wrists were long dry. She stood and blew out her candles.

'Esther,' Freya whispered through the smoke. At that moment, was she safe? And the next moment? And the next? Was she safe? At the window Freya watched the sun rise, turning the sea red with its deep, burning light. 'Min guldklump,' she murmured, staring at the horizon line.

Another daughter gone. Beyond her reach.

The sickening familiarity of it.

26

Esther woke to intense stomach cramps and lower back pain. She staggered from bed to the bathroom and rummaged through her toiletries bag for tampons and painkillers. Took two tablets with a glass of water and wished she'd thought to pack a hot water bottle or heat pillow. As she got back into bed and started to feel the edge of the pain in her body begin to melt away, her phone started ringing. She fumbled with the screen, realising too late she'd accidentally answered.

'Esther?'

'Hello?' Esther asked, disoriented. She threw her doona back. Focused on the screen. Cursed herself under her breath; she'd answered a video call. 'Erin,' Esther said, trying not to sound so surprised.

'Sorry to wake you. At midday there.'

'It's midday?' Esther asked blearily. Realisation sharpened her senses. She sat up. 'You know.'

'I know,' Erin said.

'Dad told you I'm here?'

'Freya did.'

'Mum knows?' Esther's voice rose.

'You didn't really think you could travel to the other side of the world and ask your dad to keep that kind of thing from your mum?' Erin's voice was firm, but kind. 'I would have liked to have known too, that day when I dropped you off to pick up your ute.'

Esther didn't reply. Didn't look at Erin on the screen.

'But,' Erin said, 'I can get my head around why you kept it to yourself.'

Esther picked at the skin around a fingernail. 'What's Mum said about it?' she couldn't stop herself asking.

'That's best for you and her to talk about, don't you reckon?'

Again, Esther didn't reply.

'So,' Erin said, pouring a cup of tea and taking it into her living room. 'How are you? What are you doing today?'

'Shit,' Esther said, remembering. 'I'm meeting Abelone for lunch at one-thirty.'

'I'll let you go.'

'No,' Esther said, surprising herself. 'I can talk for a bit.'

Erin took a sip from her cup. 'How's your first two weeks been?'

Esther thought of the glow of the green study lamps, the warm scent of the polished wooden desks, and the quiet she'd come to love in the Reading Room at the Black Diamond – the modern, waterfront extension of Copenhagen's Royal Danish Library. 'It's … okay. It's good,' she said. 'I don't know what I was expecting. I thought it would be …'

'Easy?' Erin asked, eyes softening.

'Maybe? Like all I had to do was just get here, and everything else would come together once I arrived. A huge shock to only me that that's not been the case.'

'You're being pretty harsh on yourself,' Erin said.

Esther sat up, propping herself against pillows. 'Being here just feels even more confusing somehow than it felt at home. She's everywhere here, Erin. Everywhere. And nowhere. It's … strange. Really strange. I think I also thought that I'd come and …'

'And …'

'It's so stupid,' Esther whispered.

'It's really not,' Erin whispered back. 'You thought you'd go and, somehow, find her? That she'd be there?'

Esther bit on her lip. 'I look for her in traffic. I'm sleeping where she slept. Living where she lived. But somehow, I feel like I'm the ghost. Does that make any sense?'

'Of course.'

'Everything I'm doing, she's already lived and done. I know that's the whole point, to follow her life here so we understand what happened to her, but, I dunno. Some days, it's really done my head in.'

'I can only imagine how strange it must be, balancing all these firsts that you're having – leaving home, travelling overseas, meeting Abelone, exploring Copenhagen – with the awareness that, in a sense, you're not doing anything for the first time either. Because Aura's already been there, done that. She had your firsts.'

'That's it.'

'That's tough, kiddo. And primal; the quintessential sibling experience.'

'You've felt this way with Mum?'

Erin snorted. 'Of course, but at both ends of the experience spectrum. I've been tormented and jealous when Freya did something before me, or I've been tormented and jealous when Freya did the opposite to me, and I missed out on doing whatever she was doing. You can't win.'

Esther shook her head. They sat together in silence for a beat.

'How's Abelone?' Erin asked.

Esther considered her answer. 'She's so much like ...'

'Us?'

'Yeah. And her hunger for life in her sixties, with the loss she's experienced and the grief she carries, just makes me feel ...'

'Inspired?' Erin ventured.

'I was going to say tired.'

Erin laughed. 'Careful, she might rub off on you.'

'I suspect that's her plan.' Esther stretched. 'How are you doing? Any painted cake cooling on the counter?' She shot her aunt a wicked smile.

Erin tried not to smile. 'I may need to go soon because Frankie is bringing me takeaway any minute.'

'I knew it.' Esther laughed. 'On this note though, I have a confession to make.'

'Okay?' Erin raised her eyebrows.

'I kind of nicked your painted cake recipe before I left. I took a photo of it. When you were in the shower.'

Erin cackled.

Esther laughed in surprise. 'I thought you might be angry?'

Erin shook her head. 'I don't think old recipes, like old fairytales, can really be stolen. They find you when you need them. Even if that means you pinch one from your aunt.' Erin raised a brow. 'So? Have you baked it yet?'

Dark blue clouds and waves on strong forearms embraced her as she gripped the edge of the desk in the back office of the Nyhavn bar, on that first stormy afternoon she'd sat drinking akvavit. Esther shook her head. 'Love isn't what I'm here for.'

'It'll keep.'

'The recipe, or love?'

Erin just smiled. 'Had any more contact with Klara?'

'We've been emailing. She's been busy with work, so I'm meeting her for the first time tomorrow.'

'That's exciting.'

Esther shrugged.

Erin narrowed her eyes at Esther, the way she did when she sniffed a lie. 'So, your time so far has been spent getting your bearings and finding your way around Copenhagen?'

'Pretty much.' Esther feigned confidence, her heart racing. 'I've been in a bit of a holding pattern, waiting for things to eventuate. Like meeting Klara. Also, I'm hoping soon to meet a woman from Aura's life named Lille Heks.'

'Lille Heks?' Erin's eyes were still narrowed.

'She's the owner of a tattoo parlour here. In Nyhavn. You've been there, Tattoo Stjerne, you know?' Esther's heart pounded.

'Where we went with Abelone as teenagers?'

Esther nodded. 'Where Abelone was tattooed after Kristina died. Where she says Gull was even tattooed once.'

'Wow.' Erin's eyes relaxed.

Her diversion had worked; Esther's heart began to slow.

'It's also where Aura was tattooed,' Esther went on. 'I don't know how many times. Lille Heks was her tattooist. She's been unavailable for the last two weeks; I'm waiting for her to call me. She and Aura were close, apparently.'

Erin's face changed. Turned serious. 'You're doing it.'

'Doing what?' Esther asked.

'Learning things about her we didn't know, and wouldn't know, without you. Being there. Proud aunty moment.' Erin smiled. 'Jack and Freya will be so grateful.'

At the mention of her parents, Esther stiffened.

'Your dad said he hasn't heard from you in a while.' Erin pressed.

Esther fought the panic rising in her chest. 'Erin,' she started.

Her aunt held up a hand. 'Whatever you share with me is yours to tell them in your own time.'

Esther relaxed. 'Thank you.'

'So, tell me more. What else have you been up to?'

Nerves fluttered in Esther's stomach. 'Actually,' she ventured to say, 'I've spent most of the last couple of weeks in the library.'

'Oh yeah?'

'I've been researching the illustrators of the images in Aura's journal.'

Erin paused, her cup of tea held midway to her mouth. 'And?'

'I've found her,' Esther said, fighting the urge to grin.

'Who?'

'The author. Who wrote all three of the fairytales that the illustrations in Aura's journal are taken from.'

Erin's brows shot up. 'And?'

Part of Esther wanted to keep the folder and stack of photocopied papers she'd been gathering at the library to herself. But only part of her. Esther reached for the folder on her bedside table. Opened it and held up the top sheet of paper.

'Meet Helena Nyblom.' Grinning, Esther held the image still for her aunt to see.

'Hello, Helena.' Erin leaned towards the screen, taking in the grainy black and white photo Esther had printed, of a young woman in Victorian dress, with dark hair swept off her face and fastened by flowers. She wore an unusual necklace with an abstractly shaped pendant, and her dress was pinned with a carved brooch. The expression on her face was passive. Unreadable.

'Do you know her writing?' Esther asked.

'No,' Erin said, 'but I'm sure some of my colleagues would.'

Esther put the photocopy down. 'Each of the three illustrations in Aura's journal comes from its own fairytale,' Esther said. She went through the folder. 'One of the illustrations, the one with the naked man laying the wreath of flowers on the maiden—'

'*Agnete and the Merman,*' Erin interjected.

'Yes,' Esther said, 'but that illustration, by Swedish fairytale artist John Bauer, was one of a series he drew for the publication of Helena Nyblom's retelling, which she called "Agneta and the Sea King". She spelled her Agneta with an *a.*'

'Oh my god,' Erin exclaimed. 'Aura actually found a written version of that story?'

Esther nodded. 'The next illustration that appears in Aura's journal was also by John Bauer, and again was part of a series he drew for what was Helena's most popular fairytale in Scandinavia, called "Svanhamnen". Or, in English, "The Swan Suit".'

Erin pressed her fingers to her temples.

'I know.' Esther revelled in her aunt's reaction. 'It's like a selkie story. Instead of a seal woman having her skin stolen by a fisherman, a swan princess gets her feather skin taken by an old woman, leaving the princess trapped in her mortal form with her only option being to seek refuge in the nearby castle as a beggar girl. Where—'

'A prince?' Erin interjected.

'A lord. Mr Olof. Falls in love with her and offers her every earthly thing she could ever want to stay with him. Which she does, but all she yearns for is something half-forgotten: her swan skin and her sisters in the sky.' Esther thought of the image in Aura's journal, of the lavishly dressed woman looking mournfully at crowned swans flying through the sky, and Aura's words. *The fourth skin: Threshold. Who would you be if you'd never strayed to the shore?*

'Does she get her swan suit back?' Erin asked.

'She does,' Esther said. Her heart had started to pound. 'She soars into the sky where she belongs and doesn't look back.'

'I think you got it right,' Erin said.

'She did, which is what makes her a fascinating writer of her time, and, I'd bet, why Aura loved her. I found this in the Reference stacks.' She read aloud from another piece of paper in her folder. '"Helena Nyblom was part of a movement in Scandinavian literature, when women writers subverted oppression and inequality by masking feminist messages with the narrative of their stories."'

Erin gave a low whistle. 'Women writers the world over have done this for hundreds of years; hidden themselves behind their writing to get their stories into readers' hands. Think of the Brontë sisters masking themselves behind men's names because that was the only way they'd get published.'

Esther nodded excitedly and held up a finger to indicate she had more to read. '"Helena Nyblom used accepted fairytale tropes, or retellings of well-known national myths, to subvert social standards. To rage, protest, speak out. It was, after all, 'just' fiction."' Esther looked at Erin on her phone screen. There was a gleeful shine to her aunt's eyes.

'Our Helena was a rebel,' Erin said.

'I don't get how she continued to get published though, if her stories were full of subversion. In the nineteenth century, publishing would have been the ultimate boys' club, right? No one cottoned on?' Esther asked.

'At best guess, I'd say she was probably smart about it. Maybe not all her stories had hidden messages. Many might have told familiar tales. Girl meets boy. Boy saves girl. Everyone lives happily ever after. But then in among those, there were stories like these that you've found. That Aura found. And loved.' Erin shook her head in amazement. 'Have you come across English translations?'

'Only for Agneta, and the Swan Princess,' Esther said. 'I can scan and email them to you.'

'Fantastic. And the third story?' Erin asked.

'I haven't found it yet. But I'll keep looking.'

'Great, let me know—' Erin was interrupted by a knock at the door. She called out for Frankie to let himself in. 'Starry, talk again soon. Okay?'

Esther said a rushed goodbye and hung up. Dropped her phone on the bed and, with it, her act. She rested the crook of her elbow over her eyes. Her heart pounded under the weight of everything she'd kept from Erin or outright lied about: her first two weeks in Copenhagen hadn't been spent waiting for pieces in Aura's life to align for her. Esther had been the one doing the stalling.

She'd delayed meeting up with Klara until it had become too awkward, and she'd had to commit. They were due to meet the following day, that much was true. Lille Heks had been calling Esther since the day after she'd gone to Tattoo Stjerne. She'd let her calls go to voicemail. Esther had been sending deliberately vague texts to Jack, avoiding most of his questions.

The truth was, Esther had spent the last two weeks researching in the library. But she'd also been using the library as a place to hide, a place that protected the fledgling sense of balance Esther had found within herself. A sense so seemingly fragile that Esther was terrified of anything that might tip her back into the undercurrent of grief and all its numbing habits. Going to the library had given Esther an excuse to be out of the house, to avoid sharing Aura's journal with Abelone, who she knew was growing increasingly wise to her procrastination.

In the last few days Abelone had taken to leaving notes under the violet loft door for Esther. Her latest had been waiting for Esther the night before, when she'd come in late from Nyhavn.

Esther, if I don't put my eyeballs on you soon, I'm calling in the police dogs. Meet me for coffee tomorrow afternoon at 1.30 pm. I'll be at the coffee cart opposite Rundetaarn. Directions below. Be there or be a box.

Esther reached for her phone and checked the time. Leaped from bed, texting with one hand and reaching for her jeans with the other. *I'm on my way for coffee with your eyeballs, Abelone. No need to call police dogs. I'll be there, so won't be square (not a box).*

27

Esther walked in long strides down the path by the lake, eyeing the swans gliding on the calm surface. Crossed Fredens Bro, the Bridge of Peace, and turned down Øster Farimagsgade, towards her coffee date with Abelone.

In her contact with Klara and Lille Heks, Esther had been able to feign politeness; Abelone was different. From the night they'd had their conversation about Hilma af Klint over mugs of Russian Caravan tea, the relationship they'd established was one of the first Esther had built since Aura disappeared that felt true. Abelone's note under the door the night before hadn't been unfounded: Esther had been avoiding her. But it wasn't personal. She just couldn't lie to Abelone. To face her meant facing questions about Aura's life, and her own life now in Copenhagen; she had no answers for either. But what was worse than facing Abelone was the thought of disappointing her. As she walked past Laurlaurs Bakery, Esther stopped, turned back and went to the counter.

'Hi. Two drømmekage snegls.' She pointed to the cinnamon-dusted pastries, glittering with sugar. Smiled to herself. Dream snails would go perfectly with their coffee. 'Tak.' Esther paid and tucked the paper parcel in her bag. She crossed the street, dodging bike traffic, and hurried on her way.

Ahead, the textured red and yellow bricks of Rundetaarn popped against the watercolour afternoon sky. Esther checked Abelone's directions and looked for a coffee cart on the street.

Spotted her signature white hair first, piled atop her head. As Esther walked closer, she smiled; Abelone's hair was held in place by a palette knife and a series of bulldog clips. She was holding two cups of takeaway coffee and had her back to Esther, talking to someone.

'Abelone,' Esther called.

She turned, smiled. 'Esther. Your coffee is nearly cold.'

'I know, I'm sorry, I was delayed by a video call from home. Aunt Erin.' Esther took the bakery parcel from her bag. 'I brought us dream snails,' she said brightly.

'Tak.' Abelone handed her one of the takeaway coffees. 'But I have to go.' She stepped back to include a third person in their conversation, the woman she'd been talking to while waiting. 'Esther,' Abelone said, 'this is Lille Heks.'

Her long, grey hair hung in thick waves to her elbows and her eyes were the green of the lagoons in Salt Bay. Across her décolletage was tattooed the black line of a horizon, the pink fire of sunset, and backlit against the skyscape, a murmuration of countless tiny black birds. The sum of their whole was the shape of one giant bird in flight.

Esther could not stop herself from staring.

'Hello Esther Wilding.' Lille Heks regarded her. 'I've been trying to call you for two weeks, ever since you came to my tattoo parlour.'

'Tala told Lille Heks you're staying with me, so she got in touch when she couldn't reach you. We decided to get coffee and I thought, why not bring us all together.' Abelone smiled.

Esther tried to smile. Her body stung with shame.

'I have to get back to work, so I'm going to leave you two to share coffee and dream snails,' Abelone announced. 'Will I see you at home tonight, Esther?'

Esther nodded.

'Fantastisk,' Abelone said. She winked at Esther, kissed Lille Heks on each cheek and waved to them both as she walked away.

Esther looked at the sky, the street, the people passing them by, her coffee cup, her boots, anywhere but at Lille Heks. 'I'm sorry I haven't returned your calls,' she said. Wordless space stretched between them. Esther was suddenly certain Aura had never kept a woman like Lille Heks waiting.

'So,' Lille Heks said, breaking the silence. Esther tensed. 'Abelone tells me you have an interest in the stars.'

Esther looked at her blankly. 'Um. Yeah.'

'Ja. So. I thought it would be nice for us to meet here, at this place, Rundetaarn. Or they call it in English, the Fairytale Tower.' Lille Heks gestured to the tower opposite. 'There's a planetarium and observatory. But also, one of the best views of the city and places to get an ice cream. Perfect on a sunny day for strangers to meet, no?'

Esther gave Lille Heks a small, grateful smile. 'Perfect,' she said.

As they crossed the street and walked together towards the tower, Esther was overcome with a yearning to share the moment with Aura. To squeeze her hand, to look into her eyes, to say, *These women you sought out, Aura; I feel why you loved them.*

They sat together on a bench at the top of Rundetaarn, in the shade of the observatory at the centre of the viewing platform. Paper coffee cups in hand and the sweet crumbs of their snegls on the bakery paper packet between them. People walked arm in arm around the platform, taking photographs, pointing at something in the distance, licking ice creams from the kiosk. Gulls cawed and pinwheeled by.

On their way to the top of Rundetaarn, Lille Heks had put Esther at ease with her warmth and conversation. As they'd walked, she'd told Esther that the spiral ramp winding around the tower's core had been commissioned by the king in the seventeenth century, who'd wanted a thoroughfare wide enough to ride his horses to the observatory at the top. To the stars.

'As one with a god complex does,' Esther scoffed.

Lille Heks smiled at her in appreciation. The nervous tension in Esther's body dissolved.

'I used to tell Tala that if a king could do it, so could she,' Lille Heks said. 'She had a hobby horse she used to bring when we'd visit, and she'd gallop on it all the way to the top, sometimes bellowing "To the stars!" as she went.'

Esther smiled at the thought, pairing the confident woman she'd met with Lille Heks' description of Tala as a child.

'That's who I named Tala after, goddess of the morning and evening stars in Tagalog culture. And why I bought the tattoo parlour in Nyhavn.'

'Because of its name?' Esther asked. 'Tattoo Stjerne?'

'Tattoo Star,' Lille Heks translated.

'And, sorry, whose culture?' Esther asked.

'Tagalog people. Of the Philippines. I met Tala's father many years ago under more stars than I'd ever seen in my life, on a beach there. It was the women in his family who first sparked my passion for tattooing. Both with the tattoos they had, rich in traditional symbolism and storytelling, and the tattoos some of them did. Tala's very passionate about it in her career.'

Esther recalled the power and grace Tala exuded the day they'd met. The mesmerising tattoos on her chest, arms and hands. Her red lipstick, gold fingernails, septum piercing. Her sense of self; Abelone's comment about how she was trying to make her own way as a tattooist. Esther sneaked a side-glance at Lille Heks and wondered what it was like to grow up with someone like her for a mother. She seemed to know herself with a certainty that was magnetic. Esther's eyes welled with sudden understanding: Lille Heks had the same kind of energy and allure as Freya.

They paused to peek in at the Library Hall, a bright, airy space bustling with tourists taking in small exhibitions of art and design. Shelves were lined with souvenirs of Hans Christian Andersen.

'This housed the university's book collection for two hundred years, until it outgrew this place. All those words of men, kept in a king's tower.' Lille Heks watched a couple take one of the Hans Christian Andersen souvenirs to the cashier. 'He used to come here when it was a library, for inspiration, then wrote about it. Makes you wonder, doesn't it?'

'What's that?'

'How many halls of kings you could fill with the untold, unwritten stories of women.' Lille Heks waved a hand dismissively through the air. 'Tattooing was the same when it started here in Nyhavn. Men were the artists; women's bodies were used for practice.'

Esther remembered black and white photographs on the walls of Tattoo Stjerne, tattooed women smiling at the camera, men sitting, tattoo guns in hand, cigarettes between pursed lips.

They continued spiralling upwards. At the top of the tower, Esther and Lille stood in front of a blue and gold planetarium hanging from the wall, showing the current alignments of the planets. Nearby a tour guide was explaining it to a huddle of visitors. 'The story of the Rundetaarn planetarium begins in Paris, where the Danish astronomer Ole Rømer made the ground-breaking discovery of the speed of light …'

Esther gripped Jack's keyring in her pocket, running her fingertips over the numbers engraved in the silver. *Some of the starlight you'll see every night in Denmark started its journey when Aura was still with us.*

'Let's go up?' Lille Heks suggested.

Esther followed Lille Heks from the planetarium up a short staircase to the viewing platform, which opened out under the vast blue velvet sky.

They'd eaten their pastries, finished their coffees, and fallen comfortably quiet in each other's company. Lille Heks basked in the warm sunlight, seemingly in no hurry to be anywhere else. Aura sat between them, unspoken.

After a while Lille Heks turned to Esther. 'So, Esther—'

'A murmuration, right?' Esther interjected. 'Your birds?' She pointed to Lille Heks' chest tattoo. Her palms were sweaty. All she wanted to talk about was Aura, yet the one thing she couldn't bring herself to talk about was Aura.

'Precis,' Lille Heks said, resting a hand on her chest. 'Starlings. You know about them?'

'Not a lot,' Esther said.

'Ja. Neither did I, until I saw Sort Sol with my own eyes.'

'What's that?'

'The Black Sun,' Lille Heks explained. 'It happens here in spring and autumn, hundreds of thousands of migrating starlings make a stop at wetlands on the west coast. There are so many birds that as they land, they block the sun.'

Esther tried to visualise what such a spectacle might be like. 'So, you got your tattoo after you saw the Black Sun yourself?'

'Nej,' Lille Heks said. 'I got my tattoo after I learned that a murmuration is a response to the threat of a predator. The flock transforms into one whole body, moving together, for protection. I raised Tala alone, bought Tattoo Stjerne alone, but couldn't have thrived as a mother or tattooist without accepting help. When I was younger, I was never very good at asking for support, or admitting I couldn't do it all.'

The hairs on Esther's arms stood up.

'My starlings' – Lille Heks rested an open hand over the tattoo on her chest – 'remind me of what I don't have if I don't reach out. Everything I've wanted most in life has been on the other side of finding the courage to ask for the help I need.'

Lille Heks' words sank into Esther's being, water to dry earth. A flood of faces, all the people she'd pushed away when they'd tried to help her: Tom, Nin, Jack, Abelone. Even – maybe – Aura?

'You tattooed my sister,' Esther stated, emboldened. 'Aura.' The relief of finally saying her sister's name.

'I did,' Lille Heks said. 'You want to know about her tattoos?'

Esther nodded. 'Aura had seven. Abelone told me you were her tattooist.'

'That's right. I was going to do all of them for her, but I only did three.'

'Why?'

'Aura never came back to see me again after her third tattoo. She was happy then, happier than I'd seen her. Like someone in love.'

Her third tattoo. *Maybe she chose the depths. Maybe she's free.* Esther's heart raced, thinking of the photo of Aura in front of Liden Gunver with the young man. 'Did she say she'd fallen in love?'

Lille Heks shook her head. 'I asked her if she'd met someone, but she wouldn't say. When she left, she said she'd see me soon. But that wasn't the case. I didn't know if she'd changed her mind or gone to another tattooist. I didn't know what had happened to her. Until two weeks ago, when Tala told me that you had come to our parlour asking for me.' Lille Heks pressed a hand to her heart. 'I've found it very hard to process. I'm so sorry for your loss, Esther.'

Esther kept her eyes down. 'Tala said the two of you were close. Did Aura tell you what her tattoos meant to her?'

Lille Heks shook her head. 'We were close, Aura talked with me a lot about tattooing. But she kept a part of herself hidden, like a closed room.'

'Abelone said something similar.'

'Ja. A lot of clients come to me because of what's happened to them in life – tattoos are their way of reclaiming their bodies, their story, their autonomy. But even when we grow close, I don't always know what meaning their tattoos hold. If they don't tell me, I don't ask. And Aura didn't tell me.'

Esther tore her napkin into tiny pieces. 'Are you saying Aura's tattoos were her way of reclaiming her body? Her story?'

'I don't know, Esther. That's all I'm trying to say,' Lille Heks said gently.

Esther shook her head in confusion. 'When did you meet her, do you remember?'

Lille Heks frowned. 'I could get Tala to check back through our books for you, but I think she'd been here for about six months. She was in the first year of her course at university, I remember that much. She came to our parlour initially, she said, for research. I'm used to that, people wanting interviews because we are one of the oldest tattoo parlours in Europe. But Aura asked great questions and I was intrigued by her spirit.'

Esther's eyes welled. In awe. In grief.

'Are you okay?' Lille Heks asked.

'Please,' Esther said, indicating for her to continue.

'Aura shared with me that she hoped to turn her tattooed words into a book one day.'

'A book?' Goosebumps prickled Esther's skin.

'Ja. Her studies at university here inspired her to create the seven verses; she wanted to write a book. A fairytale about women and water.'

'Aura wanted to write a book. Wow.' Tears rolled down Esther's face.

'This is painful and not very helpful,' Lille Heks said.

'It is, though. We've had nothing to help us try to understand. And this is something. It is helpful.' Esther looked to Lille Heks gratefully. 'Is there anything else you can think of? Anything at all?'

Lille Heks looked at Esther, intent. 'It's just a feeling.'

'Go on,' Esther said.

'Aura asked me a lot of questions about the history and ritual of women's tattoos. She told me about your mother, also a tattooist, who does a lot of scar cover-up work?'

Esther nodded.

'Aura was drawn to a different concept for her tattoos. Instead of having anything to cover up, she wanted the opposite. She talked about wanting to uncover, to reveal what was already within her.'

Esther looked over the rooftops of Copenhagen. Something Erin had said to her before she left swirled in her mind, about the seven points of a story. Overwhelmed, she leaned her head back against the wall of the observatory and looked up at the sky. 'I don't know how to do this.' Her voice broke. 'My family is counting on me to find answers about my sister, but I don't even know the right questions to ask.'

Lille Heks put her hand on Esther's arm. After a while, Esther forced a smile. She began to gather their rubbish, and her bag. Lille Heks stood and brushed down her coat.

'Where would you start, Lille Heks?' Esther asked as they started to leave. 'If you were trying to make meaning of someone like Aura and her tattoos, where would you start?'

Lille Heks frowned, thinking. 'After being a tattooist and getting tattooed for thirty years,' she said, 'there's one thing I know without any doubt: the decision to be tattooed starts with a desire for change. If I was trying to make sense of a tattoo's meaning, maybe that would be my starting point. Maybe I'd think about what desire Aura had inside for change that she mirrored on the outside with her seven tattoos. Maybe I'd wonder, before she was tattooed, was there something she wasn't saying? What story did she carry inside that her tattoos allowed her to tell?'

28

The next morning, Esther sat with Abelone in her living room, cradling a cup of Russian Caravan tea. Around them, the house ticked and settled in the spring morning sun. They'd caught up later on Esther's day with Lille Heks; Esther had sheepishly thanked Abelone for making it happen.

Abelone took a sip of her tea. Checked her wristwatch. 'What time are you meeting Klara?'

Esther checked her phone. 'In an hour.' She jiggled a knee.

'You're nervous.' Abelone turned through the pages of Aura's journal. She'd left a note under Esther's door that morning. *Come down for tea, Esther. Bring Aura's journal.*

Esther opened the photograph on her phone of Aura at the Liden Gunver statue with her mystery man and passed it to Abelone. 'Klara took this. I'm going to ask her about it.'

'Who's that?' Abelone frowned.

'That's what I'm hoping Klara can tell me.' Esther studied Abelone's face. 'You don't know him?'

'Nej,' Abelone said. 'But Klara must.'

Every time Esther looked at him in the photograph, since the night in Calliope when she'd first found it online, nerves cramped in her stomach. Was he the reason Esther was without her sister? Her fear that the answer was yes made her feel sick.

'It will be okay,' Abelone said, as she handed Esther's phone back. 'You will meet with Klara. Then you will know.' She returned her attention to Aura's journal.

Esther watched Abelone's face as she read. Every time she reacted – smiled, frowned – Esther interrupted to ask her which part she was up to. She'd avoided sharing the journal for fear of the discomfort and feelings it would bring up. What Esther hadn't expected was that sharing it with Abelone would give her such a strong, shared sense of connection. Abelone swept her hands over Aura's pages, whispering words here and there in Danish. She flicked through the blank pages separating Aura's teenage years from adulthood.

'"*The Seven Skins*",' she read aloud. 'Ooooft.' She sighed. Looked at Esther. 'Aura loved seal skin stories, ja?'

'Selkies. Yeah.' Esther fidgeted with her cup. 'Can you believe I used to get jealous? I just wanted her to think I was as cool as the idea of these mythical creatures in her beloved fairytales.'

'Ja, I can believe it,' Abelone said. 'You wanted to be everything to your sister.' She reached for her teacup. 'It's a story as old as time. Our ancestors were the same. All Gull wanted was to be enough to stop Johanna from getting married and sailing to Australia.'

The thought pulled painfully in Esther's chest. She looked around the living room, at the walls, the ceiling, the doorways. Gull's home.

'I think it started with Johanna,' Esther said, remembering. 'Aura's obsession with selkies; I think it started with our family mythology.'

'Ja?' Abelone offered more tea from the pot. Esther reached her cup across the coffee table for a top-up.

'Out of the two of us, Aura was always more interested when Mum and Erin pulled out old photos and family trees. I found it boring and stuffy. It was never real to me, like it was to her. But I do remember being struck by Johanna's story. Getting on the ship in Nyhavn, bound for Australia. Newly wed to a widowed husband, suddenly a replacement mother to his five children. Right?'

Abelone nodded, her eyes vivid and sparkling.

'And, on the voyage, it was the youngest of the five, a baby, that Johanna hid in the folds of her cloak. Right?'

Again, Abelone nodded. 'The family of the baby's mother wanted to raise the baby here in Denmark. Johanna's new husband agreed. But, I believe, only to keep the peace. Because when the day of their departure came, Johanna and her husband smuggled the baby on board, to avoid his name going on passenger lists. Sedated him with drops of diluted cognac in sugar water, hid him in Johanna's cloak.'

Esther snapped her fingers. 'When Aura heard that story, she decided on the spot that Johanna's cloak must have had the magic of a seal skin. That she was a selkie, bound to her mortal man and children. Forever longing for the family she left behind. She lived out her life pining for them. For Gull.'

There was a strange look on Abelone's face. 'It's a good story,' she said.

'Most family histories are, right? I think ours was the beginning of Aura wanting to come to Denmark. Mum's best friend, Queenie, taught us when we were young that stories and place go together – you can't take a selkie story from the North Sea and transplant it to sea country in the southern hemisphere, where we grew up. Lutruwita, Tasmania, has its own ancient stories of women, seals and the sea.'

'It's true. A selkie story in Denmark won't be the same as a selkie story from Ireland. Or Scotland. Stories belong to the place they come from. Absolut.' Abelone turned the page in Aura's journal, her breath catching in her throat. She held up the book, open to Aura's fifth image and verse.

Esther sat forward. 'You know that sculpture?'

'Ja.' Abelone's eyes were wide. 'Oh skat, ja. I do. *Kópakonan* is my favourite sculpture by my favourite Faroese sculptor.'

Esther studied the evocative image, of a sculpture so striking it still gave her a shivery feeling in her spine despite the countless times she'd already seen it. A woman rose naked from the sea, one leg stepping onto land, the other still in her half-shed seal skin. Her gaze was strong, her stance was powerful. Behind her, dramatic mountains of bare rock rose from dark water.

'Say her name again?' Esther asked.

'Kópakonan,' Abelone said. 'Seal Woman.'

Esther's heart hammered in her ears.

'"The fifth skin",' Abelone read aloud from Aura's journal. '"Discovery".' She paused. '"What was stolen can never really be taken."' She looked pointedly at Esther. 'Aura's talking about her own seal skin, saying it was stolen? But, also, that it couldn't be taken, the essence of who she was. Ja?'

Esther's head spun. 'Where is it? The sculpture? Can we go see her?'

'Oh, no, she's not in Copenhagen. She's in Mikladalur.'

'Where?' Esther shrugged.

Abelone looked at her. 'Kópakonan is in the Faroe Islands.'

Esther hurried down the block, towards the café where she'd agreed to meet Klara. Her head was still spinning from her conversation with Abelone about the seal woman sculpture. And what it, and the Faroe Islands, had to do with Aura. Esther's brow broke into a cold sweat as the café came into view. Her heart lurched when she spotted Klara waiting on the street; Esther recognised her pale hair and red lipstick from her website.

'Klara?' she called. Nerves pinwheeled through her core. Instinct made her want to turn around and run away from the questions she had to ask about the photograph of Aura, and every possible answer she was on the cusp of getting about her sister.

Klara turned and waved. 'Esther, hi.'

'Sorry I'm late. I got caught up with family stuff.' Esther tried to catch her breath.

'No problem,' Klara said. They shuffled awkwardly around each other, second-guessing whether to shake hands or hug, then settling on a brief hug and laughing in discomfort.

'It's so nice to meet you in person,' Klara said, bracing Esther by the arms and searching her face.

'You too.' Esther swallowed, straightening her jacket, smoothing her hair. Anything to try to soothe how tense with emotion she was.

Klara stared. 'You look so much like her, don't you?'

Esther subconsciously touched her face. 'I never thought so.'

'Really? Especially around the eyes. I'd do a double-take if I passed you in the street.'

Esther imagined it again. Passing her sister on a pedestrian crossing. Catching a glimpse of the colour in her cheeks, the wooden bangles on her arm.

'I must tell you, Esther, how sorry I am for your loss. For your family's loss. It was such a shock to get your first email. I can't pretend to know how you must be coping. I'm really so very sorry.'

Esther managed to meet Klara's eyes briefly. Tried to smile. 'One of the hardest habits to break when someone offers condolences is saying that it's fine. Or I'm fine.'

'Of course.' Klara dabbed her eyes with the back of her hand. 'Let's go in and get a coffee? This was one of Aura's favourite cafés.'

Esther followed Klara, into the next slipstream of life Aura had left behind.

They chose a table by the window.

'What can I get you, Esther?'

'Black coffee would be lovely, thanks.'

Klara smiled and walked to the counter to order.

Esther stared aimlessly through the café window, thinking of Klara's photograph. The love and radiance in her sister's face. The man holding Aura in his arms. She glanced back at Klara, waiting for their coffees. Nerves fluttered in Esther's stomach. An image of the stargazing shack came unbidden, a fluttering in the corner shadows. The rhythmic beeping in Aura's hospital room, her eyelids closed and twitching. Freya curled around her. Esther standing in the doorway watching her mother and sister sleep. Something is wrong. Something in her body knows it. In her throat, the queasy choke of fear.

'Here we are,' Klara said warmly as she returned with two coffees and a paper parcel. 'I got us a couple of hindbærsnitter. Or raspberry slices.'

'Tak,' Esther said, uneasy, taking her coffee and slice.

They talked about the weather and the sights Esther had seen in the city so far until she couldn't bear any more small talk.

'Can I ask you about my sister?' Esther gripped her coffee cup.

'Ask me anything at all,' Klara reassured her.

Everything I've wanted most in life has been on the other side of finding the courage to ask for the help I need. Lille Heks' birds flew in formation across her chest, a giant resplendent bird made of thousands of wings.

Esther let go of the breath she didn't realise she'd been holding. Took her phone from her pocket and unlocked the screen to reveal the photo of Aura standing in front of Liden Gunver.

'You took this photo.' She offered her phone to Klara. 'Can you tell me who this man is, that my sister is with?'

Klara took Esther's phone. Her face filled with raw emotion. 'Of course, Esther.' Klara looked at her. 'That's Sophus.'

'Sophus,' Esther repeated.

'Yes?' Klara questioned, as if Esther should know the name. Esther shook her head.

'Sophus.' Klara repeated his name. 'My brother, in the Faroe Islands. Aura's fiancé.'

The fifth skin:
Discovery

What was stolen can never really be taken.

29

Alone, Esther walked the spiral ramp to the top of Rundetaarn. She sat on the viewing platform, looking out over the rooftops of Copenhagen. The sky was a descending gradient of deep blue, violet and, at the horizon line, a bright, pale turquoise green. The sun had just set. Esther took a few deep breaths and tilted her head back to watch the first stars begin to appear.

'So?' Esther inwardly asked her sister. 'Am I going to the Faroe Islands now?'

It was three blurry days since she'd met with Klara in the café and the ground beneath her feet had been rewritten.

'Aura wasn't engaged,' Esther had retorted.

Klara had studied her face. 'Are you serious? You really didn't know this? Aura never mentioned my brother?'

'No.' Esther gripped the edge of the table between them. 'No,' she said again.

'Okay. Let's talk this through,' Klara said. 'Start anywhere. First question that comes to mind.'

'When did they meet? Where? How?'

'I introduced them. Sophus flew to Copenhagen for one of my exhibitions, which Aura also came to.'

'When was that?'

'Not long after Aura and I met at uni, in 2008. I think she'd been in Copenhagen for about a year, then?'

'What were they like together? What's he like?' Esther asked.

'They were inseparable right from the beginning. After my show, when Sophus was due to fly back to Tórshavn, where he lives in the Faroes, he told me he didn't need a lift – Aura was going to see him off at the airport. So, he went home, and a couple of weeks later, I met Aura for a drink, and she told me over wine that she'd booked a flight to go to the Faroes to see Sophus.'

Esther tried to run Klara's words through her mind, film through a projector. She tried to see and feel her sister in Copenhagen, meeting up with Klara, radiant with new love, and adventure. She couldn't see it. Or feel it. Everything was black and numb.

'As for what Sophus is like,' Klara said, her face filling with joy, 'he's my favourite person. I was so happy when they fell in love. He and Aura complemented each other. You know? Like, all their edges fitted together.'

Esther put her head in her hands.

Klara leaned forward. 'Are you okay? Esther?'

She lifted her face. 'I don't know anything about him, apart from your photo of them. Aura and Sophus. At Liden Gunver. That's how I found you. I found that photo of them on your website.'

'But, Esther,' Klara said, searching her eyes, 'why didn't Aura tell you? About my brother?'

Esther was silenced by the truth laid bare on the table between them: Aura hadn't told Esther about Sophus because, at that time, they weren't close. And hadn't been again.

Esther and Klara sat together in silence, the café bustling around them.

'I remember that day,' Klara said after a while, eyes glazing. 'When I took that photo of them. That was special, the weekend they flew back here to tell me they were engaged. We went for a walk at Rosenborg Castle Gardens and I took their photo with Liden Gunver, at Aura's request.'

Esther reeled, trying to manage her emotions and absorb

what Klara was telling her. A thought struck her. 'What do you mean, they flew back?' she asked Klara.

'From Tórshavn,' Klara said. 'Where Aura was staying with Sophus.'

Esther rubbed a knuckle against the edge of the table. Abelone hadn't mentioned anything about Aura moving out. Esther knew nothing about the Faroe Islands; when she tried to imagine a life Aura had made there, she had nothing but white static.

She reached into her bag for Aura's journal. Showed Klara the image of the seal woman sculpture.

'Kópakonan,' Klara said. 'One of the best-known stories in the Faroes.'

'Did my sister go here?' Esther tapped the photo of the sculpture.

Klara nodded slowly. 'Esther,' she said, touching Esther's hand, 'you don't know any of this?'

Esther looked down at the journal open in her lap. At the sculpture of the seal woman, strong, tall, powerful. On the opposite page, Aura's words in her own handwriting. *What was stolen can never really be taken.*

She ignored Klara's question and showed her Aura's writing instead. 'Do you know what this means?'

Klara read it. Shook her head. 'Not really. I mean, I don't know what it meant to Aura. It fits the story though, from the Faroes, that the sculpture portrays. About a seal woman who has her seal skin stolen on land by a fisherman. But not even stealing the thing that makes her a seal can change that essential truth about who she is.' Klara tilted her head to better see Aura's journal. 'What is this?'

'It's Aura's. My mother found it … after.' Esther took a breath. Filled Klara in on Aura's journal, her teenage entries and the Seven Skins. She showed Klara the images. 'Is there anything else in here you recognise?' she asked her.

Klara swallowed. 'Not really.'

'Klara?'

'Esther, I think, given what you didn't know, you should really talk to my brother. Talk to Sophus. I'm going to send you his details, okay? He knows I'm meeting you today. But I'll leave it to you to contact him when you're ready. He's really the best person to speak to about Aura, about their relationship.'

Desperation clawed at the back of Esther's throat. Constantly being locked out of her sister's life every time she was close to understanding something was taking its toll. She tried to breathe lightly. 'Sure. Please. Send me his details.' They'd parted ways at the café with a promise to speak soon.

That night, back in the loft at Abelone's, Esther stayed up late, reading on the couch, until it was a decent morning hour in Salt Bay to call Nin. She answered on the second ring.

'Starry?'

'Nin.' Esther closed her eyes, taking in the morning screeches of cockatoos in the background. 'It's so good to hear your voice,' she surprised herself by saying.

'Likewise,' Nin said. 'I'm glad you finally remembered how to use a phone.'

'Fair call,' Esther said.

'I know.' There was a smile in Nin's voice.

They talked easily. Esther filled Nin in on finding Klara's photo of Aura and Sophus online and contacting Klara.

'Text it to me,' Nin said. 'The photo.'

Esther hesitated on the line.

'It's in the vault,' Nin said. 'Goes no further than me.'

She sent the photo to Nin in a text. Listened to the whoosh of it leave and, on the other end of the phone line, the ping of it arriving on Nin's phone.

'It's here, I'm just opening it,' Nin said. 'Oh,' she breathed.

'I know,' Esther said, softly. 'Did you know about him?'

'No,' Nin said. 'She cut herself off from me as much as any of you while she was over there.' Nin was quiet for a moment. 'Who is he?'

Esther told Nin she'd met with Klara that day. 'Sophus is her brother. Who lives in the Faroe Islands.' Esther took a sharp breath. 'Nin, he was Aura's fiancé. They were engaged.'

'What?' Nin's voice was full of cold-water shock.

'Aura was engaged. To Sophus. Here.'

'But ... hang on, no ...' Nin sounded rigid with disbelief. 'She wouldn't have kept that kind of thing, so much of her life, from us. Surely?'

'She did,' Esther said, flatly.

'But ... engaged? Aura didn't do relationships. Her longest one, ever, lasted for, like, six weeks.'

'I know. But she was engaged. Here. To Sophus.' Esther got up from the couch and went to the window in the loft. Searched for the stars.

'So ... Okay ... She was engaged. To a bloke from the Faroe Islands. Where's that?' Nin asked.

'Two-hour flight northwest from here.'

'Was Aura there with him? With Sophus?'

'I asked Abelone about it after I met with Klara, but she said Aura never moved out of the loft here. Always kept it as a base. But travelled a lot through her studies. Apparently, Aura told her that her trips away were for writing retreats with uni friends. To get space for her ideas and research. For her stories.'

They sat in silence on the line together.

'What now?' Nin asked.

'Klara's sent me contact details for Sophus. Said it's best I learn about their relationship from him.'

'Have you contacted him?'

'Not yet.'

'But you will?'

'How can I not?'

'Please, will you let me know what happens? Stay in touch? Please, Starry. Promise me.'

'I promise.'

~

In the dusk light at the top of Rundetaarn, Esther pressed Aura's journal to her chest.

'So,' she asked inwardly again, as she looked up at the stars. 'Am I going to the Faroe Islands now?'

'Excuse me, miss,' a staff member interrupted. 'We're closing in five minutes.'

Esther nodded. After a moment, she gathered her things and stood.

On the street, Esther checked her map. The bar at Nyhavn was a fifteen-minute walk.

Her body twitched with old instincts. She looked at her map again. Searching for something, any alternative.

In the opposite direction to the bar, a familiar name caught her eye, a five-minute walk away. Night had fallen. It was dark enough; Abelone had said it had been Aura's favourite time to visit.

Esther memorised the way to the canal and slid her phone back into her pocket.

To anyone in Copenhagen walking over Højbro Bridge unaware, the Frederiksholm Kanal below was unremarkable, in the sense that it appeared to be just like any other canal in the city. But for those in the know, it was as far from unremarkable as a canal could be. It was the watery home of love, abandoned.

As Esther walked down Højbro Place, closer and closer to the canal, her heart began to race. She tried to imagine what it must have been like for Aura, who had loved the story of Agnete and the merman so much when they were young, to years later discover that her beloved Helena Nyblom had written a version of the story about Agneta and her underwater lover. How fated it would have felt to Aura, making that discovery. How assured Aura would have felt about her life in Copenhagen.

Coming to the cobbled roundabout, Esther crossed the wide street to the canal side of Ved Stranden. Passed couples walking arm in arm, friends chatting loudly on their bicycles whooshing by. A gaggle of women came out of a restaurant, spilling onto the street, the collective energy of their laughter charging the air. Esther wrapped her arms around herself.

The canal was dark, its surface glittering and opaque. As Esther walked to the edge of Ved Stranden, looking down, beams of alluring blue-green light illuminated dark, ghostly figures under the water. She blinked, staring. The merman held the youngest of their seven children. The other six gathered around, contorted in their grief. Frozen in their waiting. At their feet, in the quiet, eerie light, small, silver fish darted between moss and algae. Beyond the merman and his children, the black depths.

Esther sat, arms hanging over the lower guard rail, legs dangling over the edge of the canal. She closed her eyes. Tried to even her breathing. Opened her eyes and looked down at the grief-stricken figures, caught in watery eternity. Agnete was not featured in the sculpture, but, in her absence, she was the sculpture. It was a story of correspondence: above, Agnete's life on land caused love and grief in her watery world below. Below, her life underwater caused love and grief in her world on land above.

Abelone had told Esther that Aura had loved to visit the sculpture at night. Seeing it for herself, the thought of Aura's love for the sculpture filled Esther with a hot fizz of rage; the toll of grief that Agnete's disappearance took on the ones she left behind was palpable.

The themes of the seven water stories in Aura's journal, and of her seven tattoos swirled through Esther's mind. She shivered. Her mind ran through the same questions, again and again. Why was Aura so besotted with these watery tales of seduction, entrapment and transformation? Why did she tattoo herself with reimagined versions of each?

Esther took her phone out of her pocket and opened a new text message. *Hi Sophus. This is Esther, Aura's sister. Who you loved. I'm sorry for your loss.*

Esther rolled her eyes. Deleted.

Dearest Sophus, hi, this is Esther, I'm Aura's little sister. I'm sorry she's gone. My sincere condolences. Klara gave me your number.

Esther cringed, stabbed at the delete icon to get rid of her words. 'Your "sincere condolences"?' she asked herself. 'Were you born last century?' She took a deep breath.

Hi Sophus, this is Esther Wilding. I met with Klara, as she's probably told you, and she gave me your details, suggested I get in touch. I'm in Copenhagen and am hoping to come to the Faroes. I'm looking for a flight in the next couple of days. Do you have any free time in the next few weeks when it might be possible for us to meet up? I'd like to check out Tórshavn and the islands, to have a look around, so no pressure. Klara said my sister loved – Esther considered typing 'you' – *it there so much. I understand if it might be a lot to meet with me, so take your time. I'll text again when I get there.*

She glanced from her phone to the silhouettes of the sculptures underwater, backlit by the eerie blue-green light. Imagined getting his reply. *Don't come.*

'Fuck,' Esther shouted at the canal. Passers-by took a wide berth around her.

She deleted the text. Started a new one. *Hi Dad. Sorry I haven't texted. I'm going to the Faroe Islands. Trying to get a flight in the next couple of days. I'll call you when I get there. Love, Esther.*

She stayed a while. Watched the water. Opened her bag and took out her travel wallet.

When the night chill started to make her shiver, she stood and began walking back to Abelone's.

Left behind on the inky surface of the canal, a black swan feather floated over the merman and his seven children.

30

Esther took her seat on the plane next to the window in an empty row. The view of the tarmac was rainy and overcast. Damp felt like it had crept into Esther's bones. The cabin staff closed the door and ran through the safety briefing. First in Faroese and then English.

'Thank you for your attention, a very warm welcome to everyone on this Atlantic Airways flight from Copenhagen to Vágar. The flight time today is two hours and fifteen minutes.'

Esther gripped the arm rests as the plane began to hurtle down the runway. Rivulets of rain streamed across her window. She squeezed her eyes shut as they took off.

'I'm proud of you for doing this, Esther.' Abelone had hugged her tightly before they parted at the airport.

'I haven't done anything yet,' Esther said.

'Facing the unknown is never nothing. It's what all great art is about. What would Hilma af Klint say about this?' She smiled.

Esther scrunched her face up in resistance. 'I dunno,' she groaned. 'What would Hilma say?'

Abelone put a hand on Esther's shoulder. 'I think Hilma would say apathy is the easy choice. And no one else can make the hard choice for you. Want it, want more – the abstract, the strange, the large, the small, the beautiful, the mysterious, the pain, the loss, the grief, the discovery, the freedom, the joy. Want it, choose it – or accept confinement of your own making. Accept your cage.'

'Alright,' Esther said, holding up both hands, laughing. 'Accept your cage? Geez. Pep talk done.'

Abelone chuckled. 'Okay, okay. Let me try again. Hilma would say this: "I lived in the unknown as much as the known. Remember the beauty that I brought back from the darkness."'

They hugged again, and Esther thanked Abelone for her care and generosity.

'A gift, for your adventures,' Abelone said, as she took a wrapped object from her bag and put it in Esther's hands.

'You've already given me everything, Abelone,' Esther protested.

'Open it. Rip and tear,' Abelone said, picking at a corner of the sticky tape with a glint in her eye. Esther tore away the wrapping to reveal a guidebook to the Faroe Islands.

'I hadn't thought about getting a guidebook.' Esther engulfed Abelone in one last hug. 'Thank you.'

'You come back to me before you go back home, ja?' Abelone held her tightly. 'No pulling a ghost town and going straight from the Faroes.'

'Ghostie?' Esther called, chuckling as she walked away, guidebook pressed to her chest. Abelone gave the thumbs up. She waved until Esther was through customs and out of view.

Esther peered out through her window on the plane into mist and cloud, and down to the immensity of the opaque sea. As she watched the ocean roll by below her, she remembered something Queenie had told her once. *All water is ancient, Starry. It holds the memory of the Earth.* Trying to grasp the age of the sea reminded Esther of how she felt watching stars with Jack. How impossible it was to fathom that when she was looking up, she was looking back into time, at the same stars that people had gazed at thousands of years ago. How impossible it was to fathom that looking below into the ocean, she was also looking back into time, like Queenie said, into every ancient story of water. Almost without thinking, Esther pressed her thumb and index finger together in her lap.

'Coffee?' One of the cabin staff interrupted her thoughts.

'Please.' Esther accepted a paper cup of black coffee and two sugar sachets. 'Thank you.' As the refreshment trolley was wheeled away, Esther heard a voice behind her.

'Excuse me?'

She turned and peeked over her seat.

'Is this your scarf?' A man seated in the row behind her with greying hair and tortoiseshell half-rim glasses offered her a friendly smile. He held Esther's scarf.

'Oh. Thanks,' Esther said, reaching over the seat to take it. 'Must have caught on the trolley.'

'No problem,' he said. His English sounded like Abelone's. Maybe Danish or Faroese, Esther guessed.

She returned to her coffee, stirring in her sugars. Looking again at the sea below. She started humming a tune that came to mind, trying to place the song. She closed her eyes to concentrate and sang a few of the lyrics to herself. Saw a CD cover on Aura's bureau in her bedroom: illustrated waves of sea water surrounded a woman's face, like flowing mermaid hair. Esther stayed on the cover art in her mind until she remembered: Sarah Blasko's album *What the Sea Wants, the Sea Will Have*. The LED display on Aura's boom box – Track 8, 'Woman by the Well'. After Aura returned from Denmark, she stayed in her bedroom and played it on repeat. Esther, home from uni, had called Nin, desperate for help. She'd arrived at the Shell House not long after, announcing she was taking them for a spontaneous afternoon at Queenie's with family. Insisted they go. When the three of them got to Queenie's, they fell into the soothing familiarity of telling stories around Queenie's kitchen table while women sorted and strung shells. Until Aura had interrupted.

Queenie saying, 'We all came from the stars,' as she sorts iridescent shells on her sorting tray. 'Men fell to the land, and women and children to the sea. Sea country is women's country.

And we all go home to the stars, from the sea. It's no wonder all the physicists say we're full of stardust. Our people have known that since the beginning.' She threads marina shells onto string. They shimmer in her hands, luminous in the afternoon light filling the kitchen.

Esther glances at Aura. She's transfixed, hanging on Queenie's every word. It almost feels like it's old times.

'We've always—'

'Where do you want to go when you die, Queenie?' Aura interrupts.

Queenie stops what she's doing and looks across the room at Aura. Glances at the others gathered around the table. 'There's no want about it, bub. Like I said, I'll go back to the stars. Back to my Old People.'

Someone changes the subject. They talk about other things. Make tea. Pass around biscuits.

Aura is polite and more animated than she's been since she came back. To anyone who isn't looking closely, Aura almost seems happy to be in everyone's company.

But Esther sees how Aura's hands shake. Esther hears the slight wobble in her sister's voice.

She finished her coffee and crumpled the paper cup in her fist. Looked through the window again at the sea, keeper of Aura's life. And her death.

Esther turned to her new guidebook from Abelone, eager for distraction. Thumbed through the pages. Her heart-rate began to slow as she read about the geology of the Faroe Islands.

An announcement from the captain: their flight was beginning its descent. Esther folded down the corner of the page she was reading and glanced through the plane window to see that they'd flown under a cloud bank.

She leaned closer to the window, watching as the islands came into focus. The horizon was indistinguishable from the sea, both silver, white and swirling. Islets of volcanic bedrock jutted from the ocean, forming towering sea stacks with dramatic, jagged silhouettes. Esther pressed her forehead and nose to the window as she watched an islet come into view, its towering peaks reminding her of the spine of a giant, curled-up sleeping dragon. Its body was made of black basalt, covered in greenish, golden grass. At its sides, waves crashed against its black rocks in a swirl of startling white. Jack's voice came to mind. *To reach the treasure she seeks, our hero must first get past the dragon.*

The feeling Esther had carried in her body every day since she'd left home tightened a notch in her chest: Aura had done this. Taken this flight, had maybe seen this view. Had looked upon Esther's sleeping dragon with the eyes of someone about to be reunited with the person they loved. From sea to stars, everything was Aura's.

Esther watched as they descended into a sweeping valley, at the base of which was the lone runway of Vágar Airport. With a few bumps and the rushing lurch of the brakes, the plane touched down and came to a halt. Esther took her time disembarking.

As she walked out of the plane, Esther breathed in a shock of bracing, cold air. Vágar Airport was small and quiet.

'Welcome to the Faroe Islands,' the customs officer said with a smile after a cursory glance at her documents. Esther said nothing, smiled in thanks and went on her way.

While she waited for her baggage at the conveyor belt, Esther looked up Sophus' profile on social media, as she'd been doing since the day Klara had given her his details. He only had one account, which was set to private, but showed public posts from other profiles connected to his. Like Tórshavn Football Club's post about their win, including a team photo on the pitch, full of jubilant faces. Sophus' was one of them. The photo looked superimposed: behind them towered the dark bulky shapes of the snowy fjords, and beyond, the white caps of the sea. There were a couple more photos from a bar called

Flóvin, one showing Sophus pulling beers and another of him with a guitar on a small stage, singing to a packed room. Esther had looked up the bar on the internet: Sophus co-owned it with someone named Flósi. She kept·scrolling through the photos, her heart flip-flopping when she recognised one from Klara's photography account: a portrait of Sophus on a trawler boat in hi-vis overalls, hard hat and gumboots, grinning in the sun, low cloud eclipsing the fjords in the background. He held a line of giant kelp high; it made Esther's head spin with a sense of worlds colliding, and a deep yearning for home. For a warm afternoon at the beach, with Nin and Queenie, and tea, Iced VoVos, Aunty Ro, and jars upon jars of unpolished shell treasure. All that iridescence waiting quietly to shine. Had Aura felt the same way? The final photo of Sophus on his feed was maybe Esther's favourite. He was sitting in a green meadow, looking directly at the camera, smiling. Beside and around him were half a dozen sheep. She zoomed in on his face. The face her sister had loved. Had said yes to seeing every day for the rest of her life. Had kept a secret from everyone who loved her.

Esther looked up, realising her bags were the last circling on the baggage claim belt. With them in tow, she walked out of the airport and into air so fresh and clean she instantly felt like she was at home, walking out of Launceston airport. As she followed signs to the bus stop, she looked up. The silhouettes of birds wheeled high overhead. Esther saw Lille Heks' tattoo in her mind's eye again.

She reached the bus stop, where a group of people were already waiting. Opposite was a car park and then nothing but rolling green under a silver sky. Esther stood to the side, arranged her bags around her and took her guidebook out of her bag, turning to the page she'd dog-eared. She wanted to read more about the myth and folklore of the islands; Aura's image of the seal woman rose from the sea grasping her seal skin in hand.

'First time here?' a friendly voice next to her asked.

Esther flicked an eye over the edges of her book, barely glancing sideways. 'Yep,' she said. Went back to her page.

'Well, a very good welcome to our islands.'

Esther sighed, closed her book. Turned and realised the man talking to her was the same one who'd picked up her scarf on the flight. 'Oh, hi. Again,' she said, with more warmth.

'Hi.' He smiled, adjusted his glasses. 'On your way to Tórshavn?'

Esther nodded.

'It's a great town. You'll like it. Our small capital with a big name: literally means Thor's Harbour.'

Esther cast a quick glance at the small carry-on bag at his feet. 'Tórshavn is home for you?'

He nodded. 'I've been in Copenhagen for a marathon I do with my colleagues every year. We run along the water around the city and then jump into the sea baths, and then spend a night eating and drinking and undoing every bit of the running and swimming.'

'Sounds great. Except for the running and swimming parts.'

'If I guess, I think you are Australian?'

'Impressive. No South African or New Zealand first guesses.'

'I chat with colleagues on Skype in Australia.' He smiled. 'So, you are Australian, but you don't swim? Most of you live around the coast, yes?'

'Yep,' Esther said, offering no more. A blue bus came into view.

'Well, if you like nature and the outdoors, we are spoiled for choice here. So many amazing hikes.'

'What's your favourite?' Esther asked, using all the energy she could muster to be polite.

'It's not far from here. Sørvágsvatn. The lake above the sea.'

Esther raised her eyebrows, unable to mask her curiosity.

'Yes,' he said, 'that look on your face is why everyone goes to this place. It has everything: depressing Viking history, a waterfall, views of a witch's finger, and an optical illusion that makes the lake look like it is floating over the ocean.'

Esther couldn't help but smile at his affable nature. 'Thanks for the tip. I'll make sure I go.'

'Great,' he said, standing. 'You're here at a beautiful time of year, when everything is coming to life again after winter.' He gestured around them. 'The mountains are getting greener, and the nights are growing shorter. It's a hopeful time.'

His gentle energy reminded Esther of Jack.

'Hey.' He took a pen and scrap of paper from his bag and scribbled on it. Offered it to Esther. 'If you need anything while you're in Tórshavn, these are my details.'

Esther took the scrap of paper from him. '"Pastor Jaspur Olsen",' she read aloud.

'That's the address of my church,' he said, pointing to his note. 'Visitors always welcome.' Pastor Jaspur smiled.

'Thanks.' She kept her face impassive as she tucked the paper into her pocket.

The pastor motioned to the bus. 'After you.'

Esther boarded, bought a one-way ticket to Tórshavn and stored her bags in the luggage hold. She walked to the back of the bus, took a seat by the window and filled the empty seat beside her with her handbag. Pastor Jaspur took a seat at the front and the bus closed its doors and drove away. Esther relaxed into her solitude.

Along the journey, she was enraptured by the harsh but dramatically beautiful landscapes. Mountains that rose so high Esther couldn't see the tops through her window. The bus route travelled through villages of colourful houses and passed bays where boats were moored. Surrounding green fields were dotted with shaggy sheep. Grass-roofed houses huddled together, some with lit candles in their windows. The bus entered a tunnel and travelled for a while in darkness. When they emerged, Esther caught glimpses of the ocean through some fjords. She drank in the sights. Black basalt rock and sand, accentuated by turquoise waves in the shallows and, in the deep, the dark blues of memory and forgetting. Her fingers twitched as she took in the colours, the textures. Immense sea stacks tumbled into the sea, which rolled and broke against rock, an unending conversation. Deep valleys ran between pristine fjords, the tops of some still dusted with winter snow. At one point the sun disappeared behind high-level clouds and reappeared, transforming the dull lower crags of a peak into a jewel-like green.

As they approached Tórshavn, a raven cawed past the bus and flew alongside it for a few wing beats. Esther sat up, leaned close to the window, one hand splayed on the glass, looking backwards, watching the raven fall behind as they sped ahead. Did Sophus pick Aura up from the airport? Did they stop at any favourite places on the way home? Her stories were embedded in this place; Esther would never know them firsthand. All she had were crumbs to follow. The grief of it pressed on her chest, with the weight of volcanic basalt stacks in the sea.

When the bus arrived at the terminal in Tórshavn, Esther gathered her things and was the last to leave. She checked the map in her guidebook, then, with some sense of orientation, headed for the hostel she'd found in the old part of town.

As she walked, the presence of the sea permeated her senses. It was in front of her, surrounding her, but also in the wind, the salty weight of it. It saturated her senses, catching the light like pieces of mirror, glittering its light on her skin, its taste on her tongue, its heaviness in her lungs and hair. Her mouth watered with longing; there had been a time when barely a day would go by in Salt Bay that she wasn't in the sea. In every season. Before or after school. She'd never been drawn to diving like Freya and Aura. Esther loved to swim in the shallows, up to her waist, to be of the shoreline, with the kelp, sand, pink-tipped shells and driftwood. *My little swan*, Freya used to say playfully, when Esther was younger. *My little*

swan who loves land, sea and sky. As she'd grown up, and Aura
had spent more time learning to dive with Freya, out in the
mystery and depths, Esther's love of swimming along the shore
became something she kept to herself. While every time Freya
and Aura came home and hung up their wetsuits, they seemed
to share a growing secret.

She clattered along the street with her suitcases and arrived
at her hostel, where a disinterested receptionist checked her
in. Esther took her key to her shared bunk room and found it
empty; her roommate's half of the room was neat and bright.
A pot of flowering nasturtiums sat on the windowsill. Aura
running through Freya's garden, the bowl of her skirt full of
velvety red, gold, orange petals. *We'll put them in our salad,
Starry, eat them all up and our lungs and ribs will fill with flowers.*

After she'd unpacked a few things by her bottom bunk
bed, Esther lay down and stretched out with Aura's journal.
She flicked through the pages to her fifth tattoo. The seal
woman. And Aura's verse. *What was stolen can never really be
taken.* Esther ran her fingers over the tape holding two corners
of the seal woman's image to the paper. By the look and feel,
Aura had retraced the letters in the words over the image –
The fifth skin: Discovery – over and again with her biro. Esther
ran her fingertips over the indents her pen had made on the
paper.

Reluctantly, she turned the page to the sixth image. The
one she could least stomach.

She ran her thumb over Aura's handwriting.

The sixth skin: Resistance.

Below, another black and white photocopy of an illustration
taped to the page, drawn by a different artist from the previous
images of Agneta and the Swan Princess.

In the illustration, a young woman in a long dress walked
into the sea. Her hair streamed behind her; the expression of her

face was one of trance-like yearning. Her arms were outreached towards the waves, as if begging.

On the opposite page, Aura's verse. Her sixth tattoo.

Know me now. I am the wild wave.

Esther glanced back and forth between the illustration and Aura's corresponding written verse. Goosebumps rushed over her skin as a reimagined version of the illustration drew itself in Esther's mind. Instead of being submissive, the young woman was in control. There was a tilt to her wrists as if her hands were commanding the waves; her arms were bent as though she was conducting the swell. Instead of yearning in her face, there was the glint of determination in her eye. The sea obeyed.

She shut the journal. Sat up, took deep breaths. The silence of her bunk room pressed in on her.

Esther checked the time on her phone. Salt Bay was asleep. But any respectable local bar would be open.

She jiggled a knee. Checked her phone again. Considered reading more of her guidebook. But she needed air, she told herself. She'd just go out to get her bearings. Flóvin, the bar Esther had seen photos of Sophus in, was less than a five-minute walk from the hostel. A coincidence, she also told herself.

Esther left the hostel and walked purposefully out of her way to bide her time. She strolled into view of the harbour, which felt like the centre of Tórshavn. The rest of the town was built around it, inland, and north and south, following the curve of the waterfront. A long row of what Esther imagined might once have been trade warehouses were dotted with a couple of cafés. Their colourful façades reminded her of Nyhavn with their bright reds and mustards and blues. The water in the harbour was silver-green and crammed with boats. The Faroese flag flew high on a building, rippling in the wind. Red and grey planter boxes dotted street corners.

Esther had to shake the feeling that she wasn't really there. As if she might suddenly jolt herself and be back in her loft at Abelone's. Or burying a dead swan in Salt Bay. Or watching the moon from her window in her share house at Calliope. Everything had unfolded so fast. Nevertheless. There she was, on an archipelago in the middle of the North Atlantic. The feeling of it – newness, wonder and awareness of how temporary her time there was – was exhilarating. She found herself smiling at a car that passed her by. A child in the back seat stuck out their tongue.

She checked the map on her phone and followed the narrow streets from the harbour onto lanes that led her to a cluster of wooden, grass-roofed houses. One had a golden door with a diamond shaped window in it. Above, a painted hanging sign showing the sun rising over the sea, its rays of light in the sky spelling Flóvin. She'd read online that it was a beloved bar selling local beers in a five-hundred-year-old building; the sounds of laughter and chatter from inside could be heard on the street. Her palms were immediately sweaty.

Esther tried to walk inconspicuously past the ground level windows to get a glimpse inside, but it was too dim to see. She hurried away, then walked slowly around the block, trying to shake off her nerves, trying to distract herself with the charm of the tiny, black-tarred houses with white window frames and grass roofs she found along the way.

'Just to recap,' she said to herself as she walked. 'You haven't texted him. You haven't let him know you're here. It would be absolute fucking madness to just show up unannounced at the bar he works in. He's likely to be a total bastard. He's likely to have broken her perfect fucking heart.' Esther swallowed. Kept walking. 'You will not do this. You will go to the supermarket, get some food and just go back to the hostel to cook. You will text him first, before you show up at his bar.'

Esther flashed forward to see herself using the hostel's communal kitchen to heat tinned spaghetti for one. She completed a full lap around the block, back to the golden door of the bar. Stood out of view of the diamond window.

'You will not stalk your sister's ex-fiancé.' She squeezed her hands into fists and let go over and again. The tinned spaghetti bubbled in a pot in her mind.

Esther shook out her limbs, rolled her neck to release tension. Watched herself as she walked to the golden door, opened it and went inside.

31

Flóvin was more charming than its photos online. The room Esther walked into reminded her of fairytale illustrations of cottages long ago; the walls were made of stones in varying sizes, pointed with mortar. The ceiling was low with exposed beams of dark timber. Light bulbs hung in lamp shades made from repurposed crystal decanters. In the hearth, a fire crackled, warming the stone walls. No bar, just people flopped, languishing on vintage couches. Others were gathered around mismatched tables set with candles burning in coloured glass jars. The atmosphere was warm, humming with laughter and chatter in a symphony of languages. Groups of locals talked and laughed alongside huddles of tourists with puffer jackets unzipped, cameras and phones on their tables among pint glasses, and backpacks at their feet.

From the overhead speakers, the opening chords of 'This is the Sea' started to play. Esther stood in the middle of the room, her eyes filling as she sucked in a quick breath of yearning for her father. For his old silver boom box that he played his Waterboys tapes on in the stargazing shack. For his sandalwood soap smell and his flannel shirts. For the look on his face when she swore. She needed him there. She needed to call him. And tell him what?

'Fuck,' she whispered to herself, hearing his voice in her mind. *Swearing, Starry.* She looked around. There were stairs at one end of the room. The bar, she realised, was of course upstairs. Sophus was likely upstairs. 'Fuckitty fuck,' she said as she walked towards them.

The bar was wood-panelled, with an open A-frame ceiling and more crystal decanter lamps hanging at varying lengths from timber beams, casting fragmented golden light around the walls, warming the colours in the wood. Tables were occupied by more groups of locals and tourists alike. On the window ledges sat pot plants and stacks of board games. Behind the bar, a row of a dozen or more beer taps lined the wall. Flóvin was evidently a labour of love, and, it was clear, a much-loved place in return.

Esther stood idle in the corner of the room. Her heart hammered in her chest as she scanned the room for him. Was she about to lay her eyes on the man responsible for Aura's pain? For sending her home sunken-cheeked and hollow-eyed? Sophus wasn't behind the bar, which was staffed by a young woman with long dreadlocks. He wasn't at any of the tables, wasn't one of the faces in the huddles. Esther clung to the safety of the shadows, behind a table of tourists. She pretended she was waiting for someone, making a show of peering out the window into the street and repeatedly checking her phone. She imagined how many times Aura must have walked down the cobblestones, nose rosy from the chill, and pushed through the golden door downstairs, clumping up the staircase to stand where Esther was; both scanning the room for the same man.

Her eyes darted from face to face in the small space, back and forth again.

Sophus was not there.

The sting of failure started to spread through Esther's body. As she made her move to leave, the swing door behind the bar to the kitchen opened outwards.

She turned just as a man walked through.

The profile. The dimple. The smile.

There he was. The man her sister had loved.

He whistled along with 'This is the Sea'. Carried a tray of small dishes from the kitchen in the direction of the table of tourists.

Esther froze. He was headed straight for her.

She tried to turn, too late. Ducked her head to take the opposite way to him, around the table. To get to the stairs. To flee. But her erratic movements only drew attention. To her horror, she was right in front of him.

Esther stared, frozen by panic. He handed out the tapas dishes, asking in English if everyone was okay and who needed more drinks.

The next moment was one Esther would replay for years to come: Sophus looked up and locked eyes with her, standing there, staring pale-faced at him. It was fleeting, their eye contact, no more than a second or two. He looked away, back down at the group, to take their orders. But a frown formed on his brow. He looked up at her again. A shadow crossed his face as he clocked her twice. He looked back down at his order pad. But he wasn't writing. His hand shook, pen poised over paper.

Esther rushed around the group, past him, nearly sprinting to the stairs.

'Hey,' his voice called. His footsteps came down the stairs after her.

Outside, in the street, Esther darted left and right on the spot, not sure which way to go. When she heard the door open behind her, the last crescendo from The Waterboys spilling into the street, she made a snap decision and bolted down the nearest lane.

'Hello?' Sophus called after her.

Turning to look over her shoulder at him was the last thing Esther remembered clearly; what came next was a blur: she tripped and landed hard in something wet and slippery. Shooting pains rose so sharply from her tail bone it caused her stomach to cramp. She retched a few times, vomiting down her scarf. Her hair was in her face, stuck to her cheeks, her palms stung.

'Are you okay?' Sophus approached, crouching in front of her.

She glared at him. Struggled to get to her feet. He gave her space but took her elbows gently to help her up. Esther squeezed her eyes shut, her face hot with horror and humiliation.

'Are you okay?' he asked again.

Esther looked down at the white and sickly green splotches she'd landed in. Slow realisation sank through her. Her eyes watered as she fought the gag reflex again and twisted to try and check the back of her coat. Cursed at the smear across her bum.

She turned back to face Sophus, barely able to meet his eyes. 'I'm fine,' she said. 'Apart from being covered in what I can only guess is ...'

Sophus fought back a smile. 'Bird shit.'

Esther muttered under her breath. Lifted a hand to push her hair out of her mouth, but Sophus caught her by the wrist before she could rub the slur on her palm across her face.

'As far as shit goes, bird is one of the better ones to fall in around here. Horse, or dog, and you're done for.' Sophus looked her over. 'It's just on your hands. And your coat. Oh, and your scarf.'

'No, no, that's vomit on my scarf, not shit,' Esther said. She might have wanted to laugh, but couldn't be sure that, if she started, she wouldn't cry. Sophus was staring at her so intently that it was impossible for Esther to sustain eye contact with him. Did he know who she was? Why wasn't he saying anything? Esther wanted to scream, *Did you hurt her?* Up close, she noticed the dark circles under his eyes, the flatness of pain in their colour.

'Come inside,' he said. 'Get cleaned up. I don't think I'll serve a pint today to anyone who deserves it as much as you.'

An opening, a crack of warmth in Esther's chest. She tried to shut it away, refasten the latch. The wings of things she wanted to say to him beat at the back of her throat.

'Okay,' was all she could muster. She hobbled alongside him, back to the bar.

Sophus led Esther through Flóvin's kitchen to a living space
behind the bar, with a home office set up in one corner, a
couch in the other and a bathroom off to the side. He opened a
cupboard, took out a clean towel and gave it to Esther, gesturing
for her to use the bathroom.

'Let the water run in the basin; it'll warm up quickly, but be
careful, it gets very hot.'

'Got it.'

'Your coat. Scarf,' he said. She handed them over. 'Do you
have a t-shirt under your sweater?' he asked.

Esther nodded.

'Give me it as well. There's something on your front, too.'

Looking down, Esther swore at herself, seeing the mark.

'I've got a spare sweater behind the bar you can borrow.
Once you're vomit- and shit-free,' Sophus said, deadpan.

Esther took her jumper off and gave it to Sophus.

He held her clothes away from his body. The adrenaline
from the fright of her fall started to recede; Esther shivered in
her thin t-shirt. He met her eye. They studied each other's faces.

'Klara told me you might get in touch. I didn't think that
would mean you'd show up in my bar without warning, then
run away from me.'

'I was looking for the supermarket,' Esther said, her face
flaming as she heard her own words. Jennifer Grey appeared
in her mind and delivered her iconic line about carrying
watermelons.

Aura sitting in front of the TV gripping the VCR remote, poised
to pause recording for the ad break; *Dirty Dancing* is the Sunday
night movie on WIN, and they've been allowed to stay up and
tape it. Afterwards they watch and rewatch it until they know
every line of dialogue and the set-up of Johnny and Baby's lift.

It's their last summer holidays together before Aura goes to high school and leaves Esther behind in primary. They spend every day at the beach. *Ready?* Aura asks, limbs glistening in the saltwater. She opens her hands. *I've got you*, she calls. Esther runs and leaps through the air into her sister's arms. Aura stumbles under her weight, and they both collapse into the sea, convulsing in laughter.

'Come into the bar when you're ready,' Sophus said. His expression was conflicted but kind as he walked away.

Esther gripped the sink with her shit-free hand and waited for his footfalls to fade. Turned the tap on and leaned over the basin to wash her hands. She soaped her arms, her face, splashing scalding water over her skin, smarting at the sting. Breathed in the steam.

'What the fuck are you doing?' she spoke to the opaque mirror, fogged and unyielding. 'Confront him,

She wiped her face and arms, hung up the towel and left the bathroom before the mirror could clear.

On the counter at the end of the bar, Sophus had a pint poured and a trio of small dishes waiting. Esther walked to the stool waiting for her and took a seat. Folded next to her meal was a woollen jumper. She unfolded it and slipped it over her head. It hung to her knees; her hands came to the mid-lengths of the sleeves. Behind the bar, Sophus watched her as he dried a tray of pint glasses with a tea towel.

'It belongs to my best friend,' he said. 'He co-owns this place with me and regularly leaves his belongings everywhere.'

'Outgrew the land at the top of the beanstalk, did he?' Esther swirled the loose ends of the sleeves around in circles.

Sophus' laugh lit up his face. 'You're funny,' he said, coming to stand behind the bar opposite Esther. There was an awkward pause. Esther couldn't look at him.

'So,' Sophus said. 'Tapas. Spanish omelette, garlic mushrooms, marinated olives. A pint of our finest local beer.

Oh, and … one second.' Sophus went into the kitchen and came back with a plate of soft, sliced bread. 'Still warm.'

Esther held a hand to her stomach. The last thing she'd eaten was a sandwich in the airport that morning.

'Thank you,' she said. 'I wasn't expecting Spanish food here?'

'That's one thing you can count on in the Faroe Islands,' Sophus said. 'They will always surprise you.'

Esther eyed the bread and square of glistening butter. The omelette. Mushrooms. Olives.

'Do you need any painkillers?' Sophus asked.

Esther shook her head. 'No, I'm okay, thanks.' The beer was dulling the tenderness from her fall.

'Hallo,' a customer at the other end of the bar called for Sophus' attention.

'Hi,' he replied, walking towards them. 'Hang around,' he called back over his shoulder to her. 'We can have a drink together when I finish, Esther?'

Something bright shot through her body, hearing him say her name for the first time. She nodded.

'Good.' He focused on the customer's order, glancing over at Esther as he pulled beers.

She watched him watching her, and turned to her food. Suddenly she was ravenous.

32

Esther sat at the end of the bar, full-bellied and replete as she sipped her pint. Through the windows, the colour of the sky was bright, violet blue. She checked her watch; it was nearly eight o'clock in the evening, but the sunlight was strong enough to feel like early afternoon. Esther took a photo of the view through the window, out to the sea. Texted it to Nin, who she'd figured would still be asleep, as it was early morning in Salt Bay.

I'm sorry, you're where now? Nin immediately replied.

Why are you awake so early? Esther texted back.

Nin answered with a map emoji.

I'm in the Faroes. Tórshavn. Right now, sitting at the bar watching Sophus work.

OMFG! You can see him? Right now?

He's right in front of me. It's his bar.

What's he like? Mind-blown emoji.

He doesn't seem … like an arsehole.

How was it when you met?

Esther looked out of the window, choosing what to say. *He helped me out of bird shit.*

WTF?

I tripped and fell in bird shit in the street. Now I'm in his bar, and we're about to meet properly and have a drink and a chat. I'm shitting myself, Nin. No pun intended.

Esther watched three dots appear on her screen as Nin typed. Then two emojis appeared: a bird and a smiling poop.

A pause.

Don't forget what you already have in common, Starry.

Esther's eyes filled. In her peripheral vision, Sophus walked out from behind the bar, as other staff walked in. *Gotta go. More soon.*

She clicked her phone screen to black. Drained the last sip of beer from her glass.

'Hi,' Sophus said, coming around the bar to stand by her.

'Hi,' Esther replied.

'Can I get you another beer? You nursed that one for a while.'

'Are you having one?' ·

He nodded.

'Sure, then, I'll join you.'

'Why don't you grab that table in the corner? It's quieter.'

Esther agreed. Took her bag to the table and sat.

Sophus went back to the bar, pulled two more beers and brought them to join Esther. 'Skál,' he said, raising his beer to hers.

'Skál,' she replied. They clinked glasses and drank.

Joy Division came through the speakers. Sophus ran his fingers along the grain in the wooden tabletop. Esther had the seat at the table with the clear view through the window. Over the rooftops of surrounding houses, down to the harbour and across to a mountainous, windswept island, silhouetted in the distance. A thought crystallised.

'Trees,' Esther said, turning to Sophus. 'I've just realised. I haven't seen any wild trees.'

Sophus took a sip of his beer. He shook his head. 'They don't like the North Atlantic wind. Or being eaten by wild sheep. They don't grow here. We have trees around town and in various places, but any that you see have all been planted.' He shifted in his seat. 'It freaked Aura out too.'

There she was. Spoken. Present. The third place at the table with them.

Esther spun her sweating beer glass on the table surface. Waited, gathered her voice. 'Why didn't I know about you, Sophus?'

He inhaled deeply. 'That's a big question.' He sighed.

Esther took in the slouch of his shoulders, the lines around his eyes, the pallor of his skin, and the way he trembled, the slightest shake, every time he lifted his beer glass. It was familiar to Esther, the toll it took to face the world.

'Maybe we can start with what you're doing here?' Sophus redirected.

Esther caught drops of condensation on her glass with her fingertips. Considered all the ways she could answer. 'Klara gave me your details, told me you owned a bar in Tórshavn. I was going to let you know I was coming, but I ...' She let her sentence go. Shimmering underwater, the merman and his seven children waited in eternity for Agnete to come home. 'I wanted to say,' Esther began. Sophus looked at her. 'I'm here because I wanted to tell you in person. That I'm sorry. For how you'll have found out about Aura. From Klara, I'm guessing, after I first emailed her a month or so ago. I'm sorry. For your loss.'

'Tak.' Sophus took a long drink of his beer. 'We, Aura and me, broke up ... a year and a half ago. After ... I mean, before she went home.' He took another drink of beer. 'Sometimes it still feels like yesterday,' he said quietly.

'Can I ask how long you were together?' Esther struggled with mistrust of Sophus and compassion for him.

'Same amount of time since we broke up. Eighteen months.'

Esther frowned. 'The timing of things happening in Aura's life here is just one of the things I'm in the dark about,' she said.

Sophus took another sip of beer. 'I'm sorry for your loss, too,' he said. No elaboration.

'Tak,' Esther repeated. Her turn for a long drink of beer, as if courage was at the bottom of her glass. 'I also came here,' she said, wiping the beer from her top lip, pushing herself to continue, 'because I want to know who my sister loved. Who she was engaged to, but for some reason kept a secret from our family.'

Sophus cringed, the sight of which caused a pull in Esther's side.

'You have to understand,' Esther said in a softer voice. 'My family and I ... we ... We had no idea she was engaged.'

'These must have been very confusing years for you and your family,' Sophus replied.

'It's broken us,' Esther heard herself say. 'Ever since Aura started distancing herself while she was here. We don't know much about her life before she came home. What happened to her. Before she ...' Esther couldn't say it to him. To his eyes.

He leaned back in his chair, rubbed his face with his open palms. 'I'm sorry, Esther,' he said. 'This is—' He couldn't meet her eye. 'I want to help you out, I really do. This is just a lot.'

'I get it, but—'

'No,' Sophus interjected. 'I don't know that you do.'

His words stung. She waited for the feeling to pass before she spoke. 'So, help me understand then.'

'Esther, the thing you don't—'

'Hi, hi, hi,' a voice called across the bar. Esther was pained to see how Sophus' face flooded with relief. A tall, lanky man in football gear approached their table with a beer in hand. He wore a sweat band around his forehead, fluffy earmuffs, leggings under his football shorts and vintage Nikes. He looked to Esther like he'd walked into the bar straight out of a Wes Anderson film.

'Flósi,' Sophus said, standing. 'Join us.' He pulled out the third chair. 'Okay?' he turned to check with Esther.

'Why not,' Esther replied drily. 'We weren't talking about anything important,' she muttered under her breath.

Flósi held a halting hand up to Sophus before he sat. 'By the sound of that, you were, and I've just interrupted. I'm sorry. I'm happy to leave and let you continue?'

Thrown by the stranger's sincerity, Esther balked. 'It's fine,' she said.

'I'm Flósi,' he said, holding out his hand to her. 'The much more likable one.'

'Esther, this is my best friend,' Sophus said, 'who I co-own this place with. Flósi, this is Esther. She's—'

'Aura's sister,' Esther said, taking Flósi's hand and shaking it. Flósi studied her face as he clasped her hand in both of his. 'Yes, yes, you are Aura's sister.' It dawned on Esther that, being Sophus' best friend, Flósi would have known Aura too. 'When Annika texted me to say Sophus was in an intense conversation with a strange woman in the bar, I didn't guess for a second this would be the case. May I?' he asked, gesturing to the third seat.

'Someone texted you about me?' Esther looked to the bar where the woman with the dreadlocks was pulling beers. She gave a sheepish wave.

'We're a family here.' Flósi sat. Put his beer on the table and gave all his attention to Esther. 'We take care of each other.' He glanced at Sophus. 'Esther,' Flósi said, 'I'm very sorry about Aura. She was our Moon Child.'

Esther looked at Flósi, bewildered.

'Aura and I shared a love of the eighties, and *The Never Ending Story*,' Flósi explained. 'We miss her so much.' He reached forward to raise his beer. 'We honour Aura; we honour you. Skál. To Esther. Coming to our little island. How lucky we are.'

Taken aback by such openness, Esther looked from Flósi to Sophus. He nodded in acknowledgement. 'How lucky we are,' he repeated.

She raised her glass, sipped her beer. Unable to speak.

'And,' Flósi continued, 'to tonight's drinking saga.' He stood, raised his glass again to the bar around them. 'Skál,' he bellowed.

'Skál,' a few locals cheered.

Flósi stayed standing and guzzled his beer.

'Drinking saga?' Esther whispered to Sophus.

Sophus smiled, wary.

'Just be grateful we're not making you drink your beer out of a ram's horn, Esther,' Flósi said, deadpan.

'I can't tell if you're joking?'

'Shots,' Flósi boomed, clapping his hands over his head. 'I need shots. For the table.'

One of the newly arrived bar staff materialised with three full shot glasses. Esther took hers, dazed by the joy and grief flooding her body. She clinked her glass against Sophus' and Flósi's before knocking it back. Coughed as the burn spread through her. Over Sophus' shoulder, through the window, the sun continued to shine, high in the sky.

Hours later, Esther couldn't explain to herself why or how they'd progressed from shots to the whole bar dancing to 'Lady Marmalade' – Flósi had turned up the loudspeakers and pulled her onto the dance floor – but somehow that's how the night had played out.

After Flóvin closed, Flósi, Sophus and Esther stumbled into the street where the party seemed to continue. While they'd been dancing the sun had gone down, but only briefly. The sky was rosy as it began to rise. People stood around talking and laughing, steam tumbling from their mouths.

'Sophus, Sophus,' Flósi slurred, one arm around Sophus' shoulders.

'Yes, Flósi?'

'Is it Saturday night, Sophus?'

'It's now Sunday morning, Flósi.'

'French hot dogs,' Flósi boomed. He pointed a finger forward and led the way.

'What?' Esther giggled drunkenly.

She followed Sophus and Flósi down the street to a
fluorescent-lit takeaway shop. Flósi entered and soon after
emerged, three paper-wrapped parcels in hand. They sat
together on a bench nearby.

'Breakfast in bed,' Flósi said, passing a parcel to Sophus,
then Esther, before hoeing into his hot dog.

'Why aren't you eating?' Sophus asked Esther, out of earshot.

'I'm vegetarian,' Esther whispered.

'Ah.' Sophus wiped his mouth with his serviette. 'Sorry.'

'Do you want mine?' she offered.

Sophus shook his head but still reached for her hot dog.
'I've got friends at home who will enjoy it,' he explained. 'I
could go back in and make you something at the bar?'

'Oh no, I'm fine.' His thoughtfulness made her giddy. The
image of Baby in *Dirty Dancing* returned to her. 'Do not make
watermelons ~~and eat this,~~ she mumbled to herself.

'Sorry?' Sophus asked.

'How are your hot dogs?' Flósi leaned forward and asked
them.

'So good, tak.'

'Yeah, tak.'

Flósi groaned in satisfaction as he finished his last mouthful.
He scrunched the paper packet from his hot dog into a ball in
his fist, nestled his head into Sophus' neck and started to softly
snore.

'Where are you staying?' Sophus yawned.

'At the hostel, just around the corner,' Esther said. The
sun was breaking over the horizon, tips of the sea beginning to
glint. 'Sunrise? Already?'

'We only have a few hours of darkness at night this time of
year.' Sophus smiled. 'Can we walk you home?'

'I think you've already got your hands full,' Esther said. 'Do
you have far to go?'

'No, our place isn't too far away. Nothing we're not used
to in this state. We have football practice soon.'

'Good luck with that.'

'We'll need it.' Sophus nudged Flósi awake, helped him to his feet.

'Goodnight, little moon moth,' Flósi murmured, kissing the air near Esther's cheek. 'See you soon. Yes?'

'Yes,' Esther said.

'Are you sure you're okay to get back?' Sophus asked.

'I'm sure. The hostel's a stone's throw. Thanks.'

'Okay. See you soon,' Sophus said. He didn't look back.

They lurched away, up the hill. Esther stayed where she was, standing in the street, watching until they were out of view. The town was quiet. The sky lightened with the sun, its light reflecting off the mossy green flanks of the mountain rising from the sea. It moved and curled, beckoned and sparkled. Esther pulled Flósi's jumper around her body for warmth, for protection, as if she could insulate herself with all the folds of wool, enough to make her immune to the allure, the pull of the ocean. She checked the time. Nearly five.

Esther walked aimlessly. Her body was unsteady with booze and with fatigue, but her mind was buzzing. From Sophus and Flósi's company. From the recognition in Sophus' eyes. From the lingering of Aura's life underfoot, overhead, in these rugged islands. She meandered down a road that followed the waterfront.

A quiet hum filled Esther's chest as she took in the richly toned green landscapes, the colourful houses, the dots of white sheep on the hillsides. The sea was molten. Esther wriggled her toes in her boots, eyes towards the horizon, and breathed in the salty air. Imagined herself from the view of the seagulls above: a dot standing on this northern island, on the edge of the world.

Esther came to a sandy beach. She stopped and watched gentle waves roll in. Movement caught her eye; a few cars stopped and parked on the road. Alone, or in groups of two and three, women got out of the cars and walked down to the beach. A few more cars pulled up, and more women walked onto the sand where they all met in a group. Set down thermoses, towels and bags. They chatted as they got undressed, their laughter ringing out, bells in the morning. Some already had swimming caps on. They walked to the shallows with their heads bent together, talking, pointing at the sea. Esther moved closer, as if she was being pulled along by an invisible tide.

Some of the women didn't jump or flinch as their skin met the ocean. They went steadily in, step after step, sure of their place and belonging. Others gave a playful scream at the shock of the cold sea water. Esther curled her hands into fists in her pockets, as if she might be able to squash her envy. The memory of water was in her body, the gasp of it in her lungs, the immersion of it in her ears, the taste in her mouth, the ripple of it over her scalp and in her hair. The saltwater sting and bliss. The shock, the buoyancy, the calm. In her mind's eye, the photo in the View-Master reel: Aura standing with her back to the camera, facing the sea.

Esther blinked. One of the women had hung back on shore. Had noticed her. She began to walk towards Esther as she twisted her long grey hair up into her swimming cap. She stopped and waved from the sand. Esther tottered on her feet. Delirium had begun to kick in.

'I'm sorry,' Esther called to the woman. 'I don't speak Faroese, I'm sorry.'

The woman smiled. Shook her head. She pointed to the sea, gesturing for Esther to join them.

'Oh, no, no thank you. Nei, I don't swim. No. Tak. You enjoy. Brrrrr,' Esther overcompensated for her lack of language with cartoonish actions.

The woman eyed her, curious and silent. Gave her a small smile and walked away, down towards the shore. Into the sea.

Esther watched their swimming caps. A bob of dark heads above water. A finger of sunlight reaching out to them across waves.

33

Nin Robertson swam in the turquoise shallows, looking back to shore and revelling in the colours and crystalline light of the autumn afternoon in Salt Bay; the shell-white sand, the blaze of gold and orange algae on the silver boulders, the muted tones of the gums. Above and below her, the sky and sea mirrored each other in an endless conversation between blue and green; yula had begun their migration north, embarking on the long flight around the curve of the Earth, and inland, on the forest floor between dry eucalypts and she-oaks, the autumn bird orchid was flowering. Endings and beginnings. It was Nin's favourite season.

She dove under the sea, letting herself be carried, giving her body to the buoyancy and current of another slow and gentle wave. It had been an hour since she'd left the hospital. She'd driven straight to the bay for a swim to settle her nerves. The sea was the place where she felt most at home, her ancestral country. Nin surfaced and floated on her back. She gazed upwards at the sky, and inwards, contemplating how her body floating in the sea mirrored what was happening within her body.

When her fingers were pruned and the chill of the saltwater had started to make her teeth chatter, Nin caught a wave in. She wrapped herself in her towel on the sand and sat with her back to the sun, feeling its warmth reach her bones. A text message beeped on her phone. She reached into her bag and checked it. Queenie. She read her mum's words through the blur of happy tears.

My colleagues are calling me Nana Queenie!

Nin replied to her mum – baby emoji, crown emoji, love-heart emoji – then scrolled through her inbox to the message that had started her day. She'd been lying awake at dawn in knots of nerves ahead of her hospital appointment when Esther's name had lit up her phone screen, with a photo attached. Nin looked at it again, zooming in on the view through a window, over roofs to a boat-filled harbour and, beyond, a distant mountain in the sea. It all looked otherworldly. It had been Aura's other world. Nin tried to picture Esther there. Looking at that view. Looking at the man Aura had loved and kept to herself. Even from Nin. She started to type a new text to Esther, to ask how her time with Sophus had worked out, but it was the early hours of the morning in the Faroes and, Nin figured, Esther would either be too drunk to reply or asleep. Not for the first time, Nin marvelled at how Esther had surprised her, finding the guts to go overseas, to undertake the painful, beautiful journey of following in Aura's footsteps.

She tapped on the other photo Esther had sent her, of Aura in Copenhagen, looking joyous, standing wrapped in Sophus' arms. It was beautiful. Nin hated it. A reminder of everything Aura had hidden from her: the new life she'd made for herself on the other side of the world, a life Aura severed from everyone she'd left behind.

Nin closed the photo and instead opened another in her phone. From before Aura left. Their last photo taken together, a few months before Aura flew out. Arms around each other at the end of their waitressing shift; Nin wearing a tiara for her twenty-sixth birthday. Both of their faces lit by their smiles.

She zoomed in on Aura's face. After what had happened to her when they were fifteen, the light of Aura's smile never reached her eyes again, not in the same way it had when they were kids. But she'd tried, Nin thought, caught in a wave of emotion. That brave girl; she'd really tried. In the first year out of high school, Aura had moved to Nipaluna, Hobart, for uni but had only lasted six months before the panic attacks started. She moved back home and got a full-time waitressing job alongside Nin at Marco's restaurant. Nin knew Aura was fragile, but thought she'd made her own kind of happiness in Salt Bay. Until, one day – out of the blue, it felt like to Nin – she said she wanted to go and study in Denmark. She promised she'd email or call every day. Nearly three long years later, with very little contact over that time, Aura came home.

Nin tried everything to reconnect with her. Suggested all their favourite things to do together: road trips, walks in the bush, afternoons at Queenie's. Nothing brought back the closeness between them; Aura remained withdrawn and unreachable. It was like when she was fifteen, but worse. *Sometimes a hurt can go too deep in a person, bub, they can't come back from it*, Queenie told Nin. She refused to believe it. The friendship she and Aura had shared for most of their lives couldn't be over. Then one morning, Aura left the Shell House and never came home.

'Ra-Ra, you're going to be an aunty,' she whispered to Aura's smiling face in their photo. Her chin wobbled as she spoke the words, wishing Aura could hear her. Nausea cramped in her stomach. Nin put her phone away and reached into her bag for the ginger pastilles the doctor had recommended, and her water bottle. Popped one in her mouth and took a slow drink. Burped and rubbed her chest.

'Did you feel this too?' Nin murmured, looking out to sea. 'Those first few months when we didn't know?' Nin sucked on the ginger, trying to calm herself by focusing on the rhythms of the tide coming but all she saw was the bright, terrible colour of Aura's blood. She squeezed her eyes shut against the memory. The fear in Aura's eyes; how tiny her voice had been in the dark when she'd called out to Nin that night.

She started shaking. It wasn't the morning sickness, or the chill from the sea. It was the weight Nin had known too well for too long, of carrying the burden of untold memories in her body. She packed up her things and hurried up the foreshore to her car.

Nin adjusted the light in her workshop to better see the edges of clay she was moulding with her hands. Glanced at the clock. It had been a couple of hours since she'd left the bay, but her mind was still a storm of thoughts. She couldn't shake the memory of Aura's voice or the salty, sharp smell of her blood. Couldn't stop herself imagining Esther sitting in a bar on an island in the North Atlantic, with the man Aura had loved walking towards her. Nor could she soothe the sting of how it hurt, to not have known about him. To have been shut out by Aura too. *You and your baby are both in good health. All is exactly as it should be*, the doctor had told her earlier at the hospital. *No, it's not*, Nin had wanted to say. *No, it's not at all. She should be here with me* Nin thought again of the photo of Aura with Sophus. The pure, unfettered joy on her face. She'd seen that kind of radiance in Aura once before. When they'd been teenagers.

It had happened after school one day in year ten. Nin remembered it clearly: it was Free Dress Day, when high school students were permitted to ditch their uniforms and wear clothes of their choice for one day to raise money for charity; everyone in free dress made a gold-coin donation. Nin and Aura had planned their outfits for weeks, scouring local op shops.

'We're after a kind of Janis Joplin, Shirley Manson, Alanis, Christine Anu look,' Aura earnestly told the elderly Vinnies volunteer. They found pastel night gowns they wore as dresses, with combat boots, matching candy necklaces, black kohl eyeliner and love-heart shaped sunglasses.

It was a fun day at school. They did no work and ran around on their recess and lunch breaks, giddy at seeing everyone in their own skins. After school, they went to the corner shop where the unspoken rule was that only year tens to twelves could hang out. Aura and Nin sat under a gum tree around the back of the shop, with cans of Pasito and a packet of Winfield menthols. They were hidden from street view, next to the car park, sharing cigarettes and headphones, listening to *Jagged Little Pill*. They tried to blow smoke rings as they debriefed about everyone's outfits, dissolving into intermittent fits of giggles over the boys in their class who'd shown up to Free Dress Day in their pyjamas. That's when it had happened.

The low growl of the shimmering blue Holden Commodore comes down the street, surfboards strapped to the roof and windows tinted dark. Silverchair playing so loud on the car stereo Nin feels the bass from 'Tomorrow' in her belly. The Commodore pulls into the car park at the back of the shop. The engine and music cut. All four car doors open, and five boys from year twelve get out. Barefoot, long sun-bleached hair dripping, skin glistening and eyes bloodshot from saltwater. He's the last to emerge, the driver. Tucks his wet golden hair behind his ears and strolls right by them. Michael Tully. Everyone at school knows his name.

'Nice sunnies, Lovebug,' he says to Aura. As if Nin doesn't exist.

Aura sits unmoving, mouth in a half-smile, eyes hidden behind pink plastic love-hearts. When she doesn't reply, Michael Tully smiles to himself and walks off to join his mates in the corner shop. Nin rolls her eyes and resumes chatting, but when she glances at Aura, she realises her best friend hasn't moved. Nin snaps her fingers in front of Aura's face. No response. She leans forward and slides Aura's sunnies down off her nose. Aura looks at her, eyes sparkling.

'He just spoke to me,' she breathes. 'Right? Michael Tully? Just called me a lovebug?'

Nin nods, trying to mirror Aura's excitement, but a deeper feeling she doesn't recognise makes her wary. It's something about how lit up Aura is, just because Michael Tully's muttered a few words to her. As if his attention is the first time that Aura has ever felt the warmth of the sun on her skin.

~

Nin pinched the clay's edge too hard. Again.

She sighed in frustration. Let her shoulders fall. Tried to focus.

A few days after he'd called her a lovebug at the corner shop, Michael Tully found Aura in the school library and offered her a ride home in his Commodore. He did the same thing the next day. And the next. Soon he was taking her home from school every day. They started spending weekends together. And school nights; Aura told Jack and Freya she was staying at Nin's but met Michael Tully at the beach instead. Aura started calling him River, a code name taken from the Tully River on the west coast. She wrote I ♥ River all over her schoolbooks, and on her thighs in biro pen where it was hidden by her school skirt. If anyone asked her, she proclaimed her love for River Phoenix. A few weeks after Aura and Michael Tully started sneaking around together, he threw an eighties house party.

Aura promised Nin it wouldn't be all about Michael Tully; they'd get dressed up as Cher and Tina Turner and dance the night away together. As soon as they arrived, Aura started drinking vodka shots. They danced to one song: Fleetwood Mac. Aura said she was going to get another drink. Nin waited, then went looking, but couldn't find Aura anywhere. She was alone on the deck of Michael Tully's house among groups of seniors when she spotted Aura under a streetlight, leaving the party with him, headed for the seven boulders on the beach. Nin called a taxi and left the party by herself; hours later, Aura tapped on her bedroom window, her face dreamy and her make-up smeared.

After the weekend of the party ended and they went back to school on Monday, Aura was giddy to see him. But on their lunch break, when they went to the corner shop, Michael Tully ignored her. His eyes didn't even flicker when Aura walked by. They went back to school and Aura locked herself in a toilet stall. It scared Nin, how hard Aura cried over him. A week after the party, Michael Tully was seen kissing a senior named Katie Cannon on the basketball courts. The next day he drove Katie home from school in his Holden. Michael Tully never acknowledged Aura again.

Three months after Michael Tully's eighties party, Aura was at Nin's for a sleepover. She didn't cry so much anymore, and sometimes Nin caught a glimpse of the Aura she knew in her best friend. Mostly, it just seemed like the light had gone out in Aura. They'd ordered Domino's and watched *Empire Records*, then gone to bed; the sound of Aura whimpering Nin's name in the middle of the night woke her. Queenie drove white-knuckled to the hospital while Aura lay haemorrhaging in Nin's arms in the back of the car.

Nin fretted the clay. She'd overhandled it, again.

As she tore the piece she'd been working with from the whole, she was gripped by a wave of nausea. Clutched her stomach and doubled over. Breathed deep, through another queasy spasm. Stood and stepped away from the mould before she could take her frustration out on it. Reached for her water bottle and more ginger pastilles.

She paced in circles. The past was too close.

Nin reached for her phone. Reopened her message thread with Esther. Studied the photo again that Esther had sent of her view from Sophus' bar. Aura had been there. Esther was there. Nin remembered when they were all kids, the eagerness in Esther's face to please her and Aura. To keep up. To be included. Nin's eyes welled.

She went out of the side door to the workshop and sat under the gnarled, giant gum in the garden. Her mind crackled with colliding thoughts. Rain was coming; the rich scent of it was heavy in the air.

~

It had been a rainy afternoon, a few months after Aura had disappeared and Esther had left for the west coast, when Freya had knocked at the door of Nin's workshop.

'Hi love, Queenie said you were here,' Freya called. 'Mind if I come in?' She looked uncharacteristically nervous.

'Freya,' Nin said, putting her sketch book down where she was seated in her dad's old armchair. 'This is a nice surprise.'

'I hope so,' Freya said, fidgeting with the shell necklace she was wearing. One of Queenie's pink-tipped green marina strands. 'Can I get straight to the point?'

'Please,' Nin said.

'I wanted to share an idea with you that I have. An idea about a memorial gathering for Aura, and about Esther.'

Intrigued, Nin made them tea. Opened a packet of Iced VoVos.

'I want to be clear, this isn't about lying to Esther. That's not what I'm asking of you,' Freya said. 'This memorial is for Aura; that's true. But it's also about making the space for Esther to come home, to talk with Jack and me, and to begin to find things out on her own.' Freya cleared her throat. 'I can't lose another daughter, Nin.'

The way Freya's face crumpled then, like she was a child, not one of the stoic matriarchs she was known to be in the community, filled Nin with compassion. When Freya took Aura's journal out of her bag and offered it to Nin, she was shaking.

'Esther's in a bad way, you know that. You saw her. After Aura's … death. She won't speak to us. I … I feel like I'm watching it all over again, and this time I can't just sit by and do nothing about it.'

Nin looked at Freya's grief-stricken face. 'What can I do to help?' she heard herself say.

Freya's eyes filled with relief. 'Help us plan an eighties memorial party?'

~

Drops of rain splattered onto Nin's face. As the rain belted down, she sheltered her head with her arms and hurried across the garden into her workshop. Fatigue hit her suddenly and hard.

She patted her clay sculpture in apology. Gathered her things, readied to leave, and felt a surge of gratitude to think Queenie would be at home, waiting for her.

As Nin went to pull the studio door closed, she paused. Turned to face the large, framed photo hanging on the wall. She and Aura were teenagers on a day at the sea together with Nin's family, when Aura was still wild and free before Michael Tully had happened to her. Wriggled in between them was a young Esther, her grinning face turned up towards Nin and Aura, a sunflower searching for light. Hanging over the frame was the necklace Aunty Ro had made when Aura came home from hospital. Nin savoured the pale, iridescent glow of the marina shells, contrasted by the matte jet of the black crow shells. Her focus shifted to Esther's young face, the uncontained joy in her expression.

Nin welled up as Aunty Ro's voice filled her mind. *We hang our necklaces over photographs of the ones we love to protect them.*

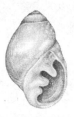

34

A rhythmic tinkling sound, like chimes, woke Esther. She stirred. Her eyes were hot and gummy, her body heavy and sluggish. The pounding in her head was merciless. She tried to drift off; the sound roused her again. She rubbed her eyes, rubbed the pain in her temples. Focused. She was in her bunk bed in her hostel room. In Tórshavn. A slow awareness: there was someone else in the room. She rolled over. Squinted. A woman stood in the doorway with her back to Esther. Her arm moved back and forth. Esther angled her head to better see: the woman wore silver rings on every finger, which chimed against each other as she rhythmically sprinkled tiny white crystal flakes. A pinch from the box in her hand, the crunch and crackle as she rubbed the crystals between her fingers, breaking them down. A slight pause, then her silver rings clacking together and the small crumple as the crystals landed. They glittered, almost invisible, on the floor.

Salt, Esther realised. The woman was sprinkling salt over the threshold of the room.

'Hello?' Esther propped herself up. A desert had formed overnight in her mouth; her tongue was dry and sticky.

The woman turned. Dusted her hands off. She had damp hair tied back in a knot, pinned with a posy of yellow wildflowers behind her ear. Around her neck hung a large carved green stone pendant with paua shell accents.

'Hey,' she said with a smile. 'Are you hungry? I was just about to head out to get some late lunch.'

'Sorry?' Esther shook her head, wincing from the pain of sudden movement.

'I said, are you hungry? Do you want to come with me to get a feed?'

Thrown by the woman's easy, casual tone, as if they'd been mid-conversation and were picking up where they'd left off, Esther ran through her memories of the night before at the bar with Sophus and Flósi, trying to recall if she'd met the woman then. But she came up with nothing.

'Uh,' Esther mumbled, her head pounding, 'yeah.'

'Cool as. Take your time. Meet you downstairs?'

After a quick, scalding shower, a change into clean clothes and a glass of water with paracetamol, Esther went downstairs into the hostel common room. An eclectic mix of people lounged on couches reading, sat together eating and laughing in booths along one of the walls, and gathered around tables littered with half-full glasses and coffee cups. There was a hum in the air, a collective energy; everyone on the cusp of something. Possibility. Adventure. Discovery.

Esther pulled her sleeves down over her hands as she scanned the room. A raised hand caught her attention. The salt woman waved from one of the booths where she sat with three other women and their bulging backpacks. She got up, hugged the women in the booth and crossed the room to meet Esther. Her eyes were wet.

'Ready?' she asked Esther.

'Are your friends coming too?' Esther asked, looking at the women in the booth, their arms around each other in comfort.

'No.' The woman shook her head. 'We've just said goodbye. They're flying to Iceland tonight.' She wiped her eyes, waved over in the direction of the booth as she walked out of the room. 'Let's go; I need bread.'

Esther followed her, glancing back at the women and their bags, together and waiting to take their next journey.

Outside the hostel, the afternoon was fresh and clear with a light, cool breeze. Esther took in lungfuls of it. Her mind strayed to Sophus. Wondering how he and Flósi had pulled up, how their soccer game had gone that morning. Whether he was at the bar that afternoon. Should she go and see him? *See you soon*, he'd said. Esther frowned through the persistent pain in her body. She needed food. Hair of the dog. The brisk air helped, and the warmth, however weak, of the sun. She held her face up to it as they walked. Let thoughts of Sophus go.

Strolling under the dappled shade of trees in town, Esther considered what Sophus had told her about no wild trees growing on the islands. She looked up at interlaced boughs and recognised rowan, sycamore and willow. Once they'd been seeds, Esther imagined, carried in packets and pockets until they were planted there, in Tórshavn, far from their ancestral lands. Johanna and her voyage to Australia came to mind. And Gull, left behind in Copenhagen, with her secret tattoos in her fairytale house.

As Esther surfaced from the depths of her thoughts, walking alongside the salt woman who'd offered her kindness, she realised they hadn't spoken much to each other yet. She side-eyed the woman. Noticed how content her face was in their companionable silence. A compulsion immediately bubbled in Esther's chest to fill the space between them with conversation, questions, politeness. She exhaled slowly, falling in time with the salt woman's step. Willing herself to play it cool, willing herself to take in the sights and sounds of the place and people around them.

'Here,' the salt woman said, gesturing towards the double-door entrance to a grass-roofed red wooden building. Esther read the sign above. Lumiere Café.

'I just love this place,' the woman said to Esther. 'Paris meets Tórshavn. Plus, bread and books, what more could we want?' As if they were lifelong friends.

'Books?' Esther craned her neck to look around the café.

'There's an adjoining bookshop,' the woman said, leading them to a table by the window. 'The coffee, the beer, the bread. All heaven on a plate. So is the carrot cake.'

They sat together at a table by the window and mused over their menus. The café had the styling of a French patisserie and the hygge Esther had come to recognise; white, grey and black décor with wooden furniture and warm lighting. The view through the window extended across a narrow courtyard by the footpath and up to an arch of trees. Maybe Aura had sat there, writing in her journal. Writing lines to tattoo into her skin.

'I'll order for us.' The salt woman stood.

Esther blinked back tears. As she looked over the menu prices, she roughly calculated the cost of a meal and began to itch with awkwardness. The currency conversion was more than she'd realised; being with Abelone had sheltered her from the realities of daily accommodation costs and having to count out a food budget. She had newfound respect for Aura working and saving to support herself and her studies in Copenhagen.

'What'll you have?' the salt woman asked.

Esther scanned for the cheapest side options on the menu. 'Croissant, please. Plain. And tap water. Thanks.' She took some krona from her pocket and put them on the table. As the salt woman took Esther's money, her expression softened. She went to order and returned from the bar carrying a tray of two beers and a dish of salted peanuts.

'There was a queue, so I bought two for myself, but it's yours if you want it,' she said, sliding a beer across to Esther.

Esther glanced at the bar. No queue. 'Thank you,' Esther said, flushing. 'That's really kind of you.'

'It's nothing,' the woman smiled. Offered her hand across the table. 'We should introduce ourselves, eh? I'm Liezel Te Whiu.'

'Esther Wilding.' She shook Liezel's hand. 'Thanks again for this.' Esther raised her beer and clinked it against Liezel's before taking a long, cold glug.

'You're welcome.' Liezel joined her.

'So,' Esther started. 'I'm guessing we're roommates?'

Liezel smiled. 'Only until tomorrow. Tonight's my last night here.'

'You're heading home?' Esther asked, surprised by her disappointment.

Liezel shook her head. 'I'm going back to the UK, where I'm living and working. I left home, Auckland, with an open-ended ticket.'

'Me too,' Esther said. 'The open-ended ticket, I mean.'

'Cool,' Liezel said. 'How long have you been travelling?'

Esther counted in her mind. 'About four weeks,' she said, straightening her posture with a quiet sense of pride. 'How about you?'

Liezel thought about it. 'Going on five years,' she replied.

Esther took a long drink of cold beer, though it did little to cool her embarrassment. 'So, you just left home one day, knowing you wanted to travel for years?'

'I don't know if it was that cut and dry.' Liezel smiled. 'I was bored out of my mind with my life and realised no one else was going to change it for me.' She took a sip of beer. 'You know how when we're growing up everyone asks us what we want to do?'

Esther nodded.

'Travelling was always my answer. Took me until I was thirty-five to listen.'

'Wow,' Esther said.

'Why wow?' Liezel smiled. She exuded a deep sense of ease with herself.

'In all the times I've been asked that question, I don't think "to travel" has even occurred to me as a possibility,' Esther marvelled.

'And yet' – Liezel raised her beer – 'here we are.'

'Here we are,' Esther agreed. They clinked glasses. 'So, nothing happened that made you want to just pack up and leave?' Esther asked.

'What, like a heartbreak?' Liezel teased.

'I guess, maybe, yeah,' Esther laughed.

'Nah, no romcom plot for me.' Liezel traced the edges of the table with her fingertips.

'I can't imagine having that kind of faith in myself, to just pack up and go,' Esther heard herself say, taken aback by her own candour. 'What did you do before you left New Zealand, if you don't mind me asking?'

'I was an IT technician in the public service. Like "Hotel California", you know, the song? You can clock out but never leave? It was the golden shackles, mate: an addictive pay cheque in exchange for your soul. After ten years doing the same thing in the same place, I just decided I was done. If I could do tech in New Zealand, I could do it in Edinburgh or Paris or Berlin. I've got a sweet gig in London just now, but I've worked contracts in Amsterdam, Lisbon and Oslo.'

'That's amazing,' Esther breathed. 'Can I ask, what gave you the guts to go? You know, without anything driving you, like a heartbreak, or a crisis?' She felt like her story was written on her face in capital, neon letters. ESTHER WILDING WAS TOO CHICKEN SHIT TO EVER SEE ANY BIG DREAM THROUGH ON HER OWN MERIT, LIKE STUDY SCIENCE OR TRAVEL THE WORLD.

'I'm the youngest of five,' Liezel explained. 'I've got four brothers. Yes, all sympathies deserved and welcome.'

Esther chuckled.

'I grew up watching the world tell my brothers that they could go and do whatever they wanted when they left home. But no one really said that to me. And I never really questioned why it was one story for my brothers and another story for me. I went to school, went to work, went to house auctions, went speed dating. Got my education, job, house and – now ex – husband. But something still niggled away at me. That niggle is where my guts, as you said, came from. I don't ever want to feel that way again, that I'm going against myself instead of towards myself.'

Esther made a mind-blown gesture at her temple with her fingers. 'This feels like I'm hearing a song I've known all my life that I've been singing along to but never fully realised what the lyrics were about,' she said.

'That's a great way of putting it.' Liezel laughed. 'What about you?'

'Me?' Esther blanked.

'Where's home for you?' Liezel asked.

'Tasmania.'

'Lutruwita,' Liezel replied.

'Yes!' Esther exclaimed.

'Loved it. I travelled Oz when I first left home, to cut my teeth. Backpacked all over Tassie.'

'No way,' Esther said, invigorated by the connection.

'Yes way.' Liezel smiled. 'I hiked up and down the west coast. Stayed for a while at this tiny place on the river in the Tarkine.'

Esther stilled. 'Calliope?' she ventured.

'That's it.' Liezel snapped her fingers. 'Calliope.'

'That's where I was. Just before I left to come here. Calliope,' Esther said, hand on her chest. 'I was working there, at the river lodge. For the last year.'

'No way,' Liezel repeated, laughing. 'Oh man, travelling will never fail to amaze me. This happens more than you'd believe.'

'What, being in an archipelago in the North Atlantic and meeting someone who knows the exact same remote place as you on an island in the south Pacific?'

'Pretty much.' Liezel grinned. 'Oh, that sky, that river,' she reminisced.

'Right,' Esther said, remembering the black green of the water. The reflective glassiness of it. The lure.

They were interrupted by café staff bringing plates of food to their table. Esther stared as they set down baguette sandwiches and two thick slices of carrot cake.

'One's cheese and tomato, the other's smoked salmon. My eyes might have been bigger than my belly when I ordered, so help me out?' Liezel asked.

Esther sat, unmoving and quiet. Floored by Liezel's generosity.

'Listen, Esther,' Liezel said. 'You might know this already, but travelling is a different way of living. It can be brutal and lonely and sometimes everything goes wrong. The generosity and kindness of strangers are often how you get by. It's cheesy' – she paused, nudging the baguette filled with thick slices of cheese for emphasis – 'but it's true. Paying it forward is a thing. Someone did this for me once when I was in Greece, on my first day there. I was a red-hot mess then too. I know what a good meal and good company can do.' Liezel offered the sandwiches to Esther.

'It's that obvious,' she said, 'that I'm a mess?' Esther took the cheese and tomato baguette.

'No judgement: it took you three attempts to open our bedroom door when you got in this morning. And it wasn't locked.' Liezel bit into her salmon baguette. 'Then, when you eventually got into our room, I asked you if you were okay, but you'd passed out half in and half out of your bed.'

Esther groaned, covering her face with her sandwich. 'I'm sorry.'

'Don't be,' Liezel said with a genuine smile. 'I hope your night was worth it, though?'

Esther replayed Sophus running around the corner to find her covered in bird shit. The look on his face. Horror. Confusion. Amusement. Recognition. Tenderness.

'What was with the salt?' Esther changed the subject. 'When I woke up, earlier. It was salt you were sprinkling on the floor, right?'

Liezel nodded, chewing. 'It's just a thing I do. For safe passage. For protection. For housewarming and farewelling. When I arrive and when I leave a place. Or when I see someone who needs good juju.'

'That would be me.'

'Clearly.' Liezel grinned again. 'I carry salt with me everywhere I go.' She rifled through her handbag and took out a small, cork-topped glass vial, filled with salt crystals. 'I've got dozens of these. It's my granny's fault. She instilled it in me: the ritual of salt. It always reminds me of her. Of the ocean at home. Where I come from. My ancestors. Keeps everything close. When I leave wherever I'm staying, my checklist is like, tickets, passport, salt.' She laughed, deeply, open mouthed, from her belly. 'So, I always have plenty to spare and am happy to share.'

'Well, thank you,' Esther said. Whether it was the buzz of the beer, the relief of her hangover easing or the surge of gratitude, for a moment sitting there in the café with Liezel, on her own and so far from home, felt purely wonderful.

'So, what about you?' Liezel turned the conversation again to Esther. 'What's your story? What are you doing here? How long are you staying?'

Esther considered how to respond. Liezel's generosity of spirit was contagious.

'Budget be damned, I'm buying us another round for that answer.'

A while later, having moved from their rounds of beers to pots of tea, Esther was still sitting with Liezel at their table by the window. It was nearing evening time and still bright outside. The long hours of daylight made Esther giddy. She took another sip of tea. Liezel had listened to her story, eyes focused and sharp while Esther had talked. And talked. She'd shared everything: growing up in Aura's light, falling apart when she left. Dropping out of uni after she disappeared. The menacing hum of the quiet in the Shell House after they called off the search. After the coroner's open finding came in. The ticking clock in the kitchen, the merman burdened with eternal waiting. The slow collapse of her mind; the day of darkly golden light rippling down the walls when neither of her parents showed for her session with the psychologist. Moving west. Coming home. The memorial party. Aura's journal. Her teenage love-heart punctuation. Her seven images, *Seven Skins*. Her tattoos. Esther's arrival in Copenhagen. Discovering Sophus in Aura's life.

'Esther, I don't know what to say. I'm sorry. I'm so sorry this has happened to you,' Liezel said.

'And now, I'm here.' Esther smiled tearily. She'd shared almost everything. Not Aura's note. Esther didn't go near that place inside, pushed away, deep down, beneath tangles and thickets and thorns. 'I'm here,' she repeated, more for her own benefit than Liezel's. 'Sorry, I've just never said so much of that to anyone before. No one. And I'm pretty much purging my heart with you, a stranger.'

Liezel gave her a sad smile. 'Welcome to hostel life, Esther. The odd magic of living in transience, moment to moment, making choices based purely on how you feel right now, not in the past, or for any reason in the future. Just because we're here, now, together, in Tórshavn, sharing a cuppa. It feels good.'

'It does.' Esther smiled. Rubbed a hand over her chest. 'It's also weird though? Sharing your deep belly truth with someone you've just met?'

'You get used to it. It becomes your norm,' Liezel said. Sipped her tea. 'I like that, "deep belly truth".' She tipped her cup back and swallowed her last mouthful. 'So, can I ask you a deep belly question?'

'Sure.'

'What now?'

'What do you mean?'

'I mean, this guy, your sister's ex-fiancé you didn't know about until a couple of weeks ago, Sophus, he's, what, a couple of blocks away, with everything you want to know about your sister in cards he's keeping close to his chest?'

Esther nodded.

'When are you going to meet up again?'

'I turned up without giving him any notice; I feel like I need to let him make the next contact. He knows where I'm staying.' Esther sighed. 'I'm trying to keep in mind how this must be for him, too. Even though he and Aura broke up over a year ago, finding out about her death is fresh. Even though he broke it off with her, that must still be such a shock for him.'

'But you don't know if that's how it went down, though. Right? That he broke it off with her?'

Esther paused. 'You're totally right, Aura could absolutely have initiated their split. But it just makes the most sense, that he broke up with her – that he's responsible for what a mess she was when she came home to us.'

A waiter came and asked if they wanted more tea. Esther said yes.

'I'm really curious about her journal,' Liezel said, after the waiter had left. 'Do you have it with you?'

A flare of panic before remembering it was in her bag, at the hostel. A strange sensation: she hadn't thought to bring it with her.

'I left it back in our room,' Esther said.

'It sounds like it's, what, like, a map or something, of your sister's tattoos?'

'Maybe it is? I don't know. I don't know how to follow it to find answers because I don't even know the questions to ask.'

Their new pots of tea arrived. Liezel and Esther each poured themselves fresh cups.

'Her journal,' Esther said, leaning forward, 'it's like holding my sister's heart and all her stories in my hands, right in front of my eyes, in plain sight, but I can't read them. They're right there, but I can't see them clearly. I don't understand. I don't know why I'm here.'

A flicker of jewelled wings. Heartlines.

Liezel reached forward and put her hands over Esther's. 'But you said yes, Esther. To life. When it was presented to you. You're here. For yourself. For your sister. What more could you ask of yourself? You've shown up when it matters most.'

'I'm still living the niggle, though, that you talked about,' Esther said with an ache in her throat. 'I'm going against myself instead of towards myself, Liezel.'

Liezel regarded Esther with a steady gaze. 'It's not that cut and dried though, right? Sometimes crisis is the only way we meet our edge.'

'Do we need to switch back to beers for this conversation?' Esther half-joked.

'The thing about crisis is that sometimes it's the only way we can reach the point where we have to choose,' Liezel said, taking a sip from her tea.

'Choose what?' Esther asked.

'To stay in pain. Or to live beyond it.'

'But how?' Esther asked tearily. 'How do you stay in it and not be destroyed by it? How do you live beyond it?'

'That's where rock bottom can surprise you,' Liezel said. 'Sometimes it's the only place where we can find the courage in ourselves to choose change. To choose to transform ourselves.'

She took in Liezel's words. Remembered running into a bar in Nyhavn, blinded by panic. Drunk, following a tattooed barman. Coming home to Abelone's house, reeking of booze and sex, hours late. Smashing a vase, throwing up in the shower. Waking up, hungover. Desperate. Strung out. Considering the edges. Then came another memory. Herself at thirteen, brave, loving, forgiving, adventurous, joyous. Followed by more: laying a feather at Liden Gunver's feet, meeting Tala, buying Abelone peonies, drinking Russian Caravan tea, considering the horizon line between the light and dark parts of herself. Finding her way through the library, piecing together parts of Aura's journal. Meeting Lille Heks and Klara, calling Nin. Booking a ticket and flying into Vágar by herself, watching mountains rise from the sea like dragons. Walking into Flóvin, meeting Sophus, and Flósi. And now, she was sitting with one of the coolest women she'd ever met.

Everything in the café became sharper and brighter: the smell of coffee, the dream-like evening sunlight, the skip and hum of chatter rising and falling from the people around them. A horizon line in her mind's eye: Hilma af Klint's swans shimmied their wings.

'You might have started your travels in crisis, but even knowing you for' – Liezel glanced at the clock on the café wall – 'going on seven hours now, I'd bet my salt you're already different than you were when you left home.'

Esther grinned at Liezel in gratitude.

'Through crisis she transforms,' Liezel announced, clinking her teacup with Esther's. 'Skál,' she said, winking.

'Skál,' Esther repeated.

Later when they got back to their room at the hostel, a folded piece of paper with Esther's name scrawled on one side waited for her under their door.

Liezel picked it up. Handed it to Esther, an eyebrow raised.

Hey Esther,
*   I hope you were okay today. I could barely run at practice. Flósi threw up mid-game on the pitch.*
*   Tomorrow, I'm out on the boat, maybe. You've been lucky since you arrived, the weather's been good. Either way, I'll be at the harbour in the afternoon. Would you like to meet there for coffee? 3 pm at Havnhúsið?*
*   Sophus*

35

A vacuum cleaner in the hall outside their door woke Esther from dreams that had left her clammy with cold sweat. She peeled her sheets off her skin, heart racing. Blinked hard. Aura. Right there, almost within reach. And not there at all.

Esther sat up and gripped the edge of her bed. Looked frantically around the room, recounting Queenie's advice in the early days after Aura had disappeared: name something you can see, something you can hear, something you can taste, touch, smell. As her heart-rate began to slow and the cruel clarity of her dreams faded, Esther became aware she was alone in the hostel room. Liezel's top bunk bed was made, her backpack gone. A hollow formed in Esther's chest. How could she be so affected by someone she'd known for less than twenty-four hours?

When she stood to gather her things for a shower, she saw Liezel's note. Folded on the floor beside her bed, propped beside a cork-topped glass vial of salt and a posy of small, dried yellow wildflowers, the same kind Liezel had pinned in her hair the day before. Esther opened the note. It was a photocopy of a page from an old wildflower reference book. In the margin Liezel had drawn three check boxes and ticked them all.

Tickets ☑
Passport ☑
Salt ☑

Esther picked up the glass vial and shook it. Salt crystals. *For safe passage. For protection. For housewarming and farewelling. When I arrive and when I leave a place. Or when I see someone who needs good juju.*

Below Liezel's list, in the photocopied text from the wildflower reference book, she'd underlined the name of a particular flower and a few sentences.

Caltha palustris. Marsh-marigold.

Thrives in habitat near water. Dies back in autumn but survives harsh winters due to buds remaining near to the surface of marshland soil. These buds become cheerful yellow flowers that bloom in spring.

Beneath the photocopied text, in Liezel's handwriting:

Also known as sólja, the national plant of the Faroes.

She survives harsh winters, to bloom near water again. In other words, through crisis, she transforms.

In the bottom corner of the page, Liezel had written her email address: liezelgonequesting@gmail.com. Esther ran her fingers over Liezel's writing in awe. That someone so mesmerising and magnetic wanted to stay connected with someone like her was hard for Esther to fathom. She gathered the dried wildflowers, went to her bag, took out her travel wallet and pressed the flowers and Liezel's note into a pocket, next to her six remaining black swan feathers. Checked the time on her phone; nerves pinwheeled through her stomach at the thought of meeting Sophus that afternoon at the harbour.

Esther took her things to shower. Halfway down the hall, she turned, went back to her room, grabbed the salt vial and, after a moment's hesitation, sprinkled some on her tongue.

She sat at the corner table she'd nabbed at the harbour café where Sophus had asked her to meet. Sipped her coffee. Aura's journal and her guidebook lay open in front of her. Outside, the mild, clear weather had been swallowed by the mouths of thick, dark clouds, heavy with rain, driven from the west over the sea by the force of the North Atlantic wind. Watching the dramatic sky through the window made Esther burrow into the cowl neck of her jumper. She was used to the grey and the cold from winters growing up on the east coast in Salt Bay, but not the sudden rage of the wind. The only time she could remember experiencing anything like it was in winter when she was a teenager, and a depression settled over Salt Bay, bringing storms that had beaten down on the Shell House for days. By the fire, Aura had begged Jack for stories about the Bass Strait and all the ships that had disappeared trying to cross its renowned treachery. Esther spun her coffee cup, remembering the whites of her sister's eyes, the thrill and terror in her face as Jack used great theatrics to relay stories of squalls and those who suffered their peril. Aura's insatiable hunger for the romantic and melancholic.

A loud crack sent gasps through the café as a freestanding sign outside was blown over by the wind. Esther pressed a hand to her chest to steady her heart-rate. Checked her phone for the time. Scanned the harbour outside for any sign of Sophus. They hadn't exchanged phone numbers, so there was no way for him to let her know if he wasn't going to make it. Surely he hadn't been out on the boat in such winds, whatever being out on the boat meant. Maybe something to do with the photo of him Esther had seen on social media, with the kelp.

Desperate to avoid watching the moments tick by on her phone, Esther picked up her guidebook and scanned for things to do in town. She flicked through locations and photos. Catching a glimpse of one that she recognised, she stopped. Kópakonan. Her heart dropped.

For the first time since Freya and Jack had given her Aura's journal, Esther realised how the tone changed in *Seven Skins*: as the fifth of Aura's seven images, Kópakonan shifted the storytelling energy from her predecessors. The Binalong Bay Girl, Agneta, Liden Gunver and the Swan Princess had all experienced having something essential stolen from them; Aura had reimagined and restored them in her retelling of their stories with her tattooed verses. But Kópakonan was different. Instead of sorrow and yearning, there was a distinct reverence in Aura's responding verse to Kópakonan. An admiration. A sense of strength and self reclaimed.

What was stolen can never really be taken.

Esther flicked forward one page, to the sixth image, the illustration of the woman walking into the sea. The power in Aura's verse filled Esther's chest with renewed emotion.

Know me now. I am the wild wave.

'Esther?'

She yelped in fright and knocked her glass of water from the table, sending it flying and soaking Sophus' jeans in the process.

'Shit,' Esther said, her face growing hot. She leaped up and brought him napkins from the counter. 'I'm so sorry,' she said. Her heart pounded in her chest and she could hardly hear for the rush of blood in her ears.

Sophus wiped down his jeans, an amused, confused look on his face. 'Sorry, I wasn't trying to sneak up on you. I didn't realise you were so deep in thought.'

Esther waved his apology away. 'Hi,' she said, starting over as casually as she could.

'Hi.' Sophus took her cue.

'I'd just like to assure you that I can meet up with people without great theatrics, such as falling in shit or throwing water at them.' Esther sat and plucked invisible things from her jumper.

'I look forward to experiencing that,' Sophus said, corners of his mouth twitching. 'Can I get you another coffee?'

Esther asked for a cup of tea. Sophus went to the counter and ordered. When Esther was sure he wasn't looking, she shoved Aura's journal and her guidebook deep into her bag. He returned with their drinks.

'Thanks,' Esther said, taking her cup and small jug of milk. 'You weren't out in this wind today, were you?' She stirred milk into her tea.

'Nei, I ended up working in the hatchery today.'

'The hatchery?'

Sophus shook his head. 'Sorry, you don't know what that means. I forget you don't know about me. Like I know about you.'

Aura filled the space at the table; all the conversations she'd had with Sophus that Esther was oblivious to.

'You know about me,' she repeated.

'Aura talked about you all the time. Of course. Sisters of seal and swan skins.'

Esther stilled. A riptide of emotions tore through her: betrayal, anger, love, yearning, guilt. She cleared her throat. 'Hatchery?' she asked again.

'For seaweed seedlings.'

She pretended to look surprised; she'd studied the photo of him on the boat closely enough to recall the navy stitching in his work overalls. 'Is that some sort of side hustle? For when you're not at the bar?'

'I work part time with an organisation here called Ocean Rainforest. They cultivate seaweed and research its potential impact on the climate crisis.'

'I have a friend back home who works for the University of Tasmania in the same kind of field. And other friends, whose families depended on kelp for survival in Lutruwita for thousands of years.' Esther thought of Tom's giant kelp project, and of Queenie and Aunty Ro's kelp water bowls and carriers.

'Of course, ja, something our islands have in common,' Sophus said. 'There's a lot of important stuff coming out of Tasmania too with kelp and sustainability. Lutruwita.'

'So, you work at a seaweed farm here?'

'Not in Tórshavn, in Kaldbak, about a twenty-minute drive from here. It balances me. If I only had the bar, I'd lose myself in it.' Sophus shook his head. 'Like Flósi.'

'He's a bad influence on you?' Esther teased.

Sophus chuckled. 'We've been friends since we were kids, so I'm immune to him by now.' His smile was the sunlit corner in a cold room. 'He drives me nuts, but he's like family. I love the guy.'

'I can see why,' Esther said, thinking of Flósi's sincerity.

'He's never had an easy time,' Sophus said. Esther waited for him to say more, but when he didn't, she let it be.

'My ignorant tourist assumption was that you're a sheep farmer,' she ventured.

'As a traditional Faroese man, nothing would make my father happier,' Sophus said. 'But it's not for me. Never was. Klara is the same. Our mother is Danish. We were born there, grew up here. And both returned to Copenhagen as soon as we were old enough.'

'But you came back?' Esther asked.

Sophus cleared his throat. 'When my mother got sick.'

Esther handled her teacup. 'I'm sorry,' she said quietly.

'Tak.'

'Is she …'

'Still alive? Ja. Survived a heart attack. And changed everything. Divorced my father. Left the farm. Lives in town here now. Near her friends. It's been hard for them both, but she said she didn't have time to lose. She's joined all sorts of groups. Knitting, arts, sea dipping.'

Esther's ears pricked up. Sea dipping. 'And your dad?'

'Still on the farm.'

'With sheep.'

Sophus nodded. 'My father is a good man. Just the wrong man for my mother.'

Esther thought of her parents. How far Jack and Freya often seemed to be from each other in their orbits, but, then, how unquestionable the gravity was between them. She felt a twinge of pride.

Sophus continued to talk about his family. His aunt, a music teacher and avid knitter. How proud he was of Klara and her photography. As he chatted, Esther sneaked glances at him. The way his hair curled behind his ear; how many times had Aura tucked it there? His dimple when he smiled; had it made her sister's stomach flutter? His week-old stubble, no doubt stroked countless times by Aura's fingertips. The grey-green shade of his eyes; had it reminded Aura also of granite and shallows? His lips. His teeth. His mouth. His mouth had been on Aura's. Had known her body. Had breathed in her breath.

Esther picked at a fingernail. Mentally changed the subject.

Sophus finished speaking and took a sip of coffee. They sat together in silence.

'So.' Esther searched for something to say. 'What is it about sheep farming that isn't for you?'

'Esther, I didn't want to meet today to talk about sheep.' He smiled at her.

Her stomach dropped. 'Right,' she said, swallowing. 'What did you want to meet to talk about?'

'I wanted to see you to say ...' Sophus paused. Studied her face. 'I'm sorry I was so weird the other day when you came to Flóvin.'

'It was a lot, to just show up like I did,' she said quietly. 'I should have called. Given you warning. Preparation. Something.'

'It was,' Sophus said, choosing his words, 'it was just …
a shock,' he conceded. 'When I turned around and saw you,
it was like my mind was split in two. One part knew it was
not possible. The other part though, seeing you standing there
in my bar, that part of me thought that she'd come back. Just
for a second. I thought Aura had come back.' His voice broke.

Esther looked across the café, at people chatting, sipping
coffees, scrolling through photos on their phones. She couldn't
look at him while she breathed through the skin-crawl of
shame.

'It's good you're here.' Sophus leaned forward, seeking out
her eyes with his own. 'I'm glad you just showed up and fell in
bird shit,' he said, smiling. 'I'm glad you're here.'

Esther held his eye contact. She tried to find the gumption
to ask Sophus what had happened between him and Aura.
She wanted and feared his answer. Opened her mouth to ask
something, anything.

'Would you like to come for dinner tomorrow night?'
Sophus blurted out. Esther closed her mouth. 'Flósi and I both
have the night off,' he said. 'We'd like to invite you. For dinner.
Would you like to come? I'm cooking, so there'll be vegetarian
food for you.'

For you. Esther searched his face.

'Sure,' she said, taken aback. Despite his state when they'd
last seen each other, he'd remembered she didn't eat the hot
dog Flósi had bought her. 'I'd love to come for dinner. Can I
bring anything?' Esther asked.

Sophus shook his head. 'I'll come and get you from the
hostel tomorrow night. Is six too early? Flósi wants to give you
the proper tour before dinner.'

Under starry skies, the sea rolled to shore, bioluminescent.
Without effort, or restraint, Esther smiled at Sophus.

'Six is good.'

The next day, Esther unpacked her shopping bags and spread their contents out across the countertop of the hostel kitchen, which she had to herself. Butter, eggs, sugar, lemon, vanilla extract, flour, cardamom, baking powder. Milk, pistachios, powdered sugar. Almond meal and candied ginger. Thanks to local advice, she'd found rose water in a pharmacy, but rose petals were the one ingredient she thought would defeat her, until she had an idea: at Lumiere Café she'd charmed the waiter with her desperation, offering a whole day's worth of her food budget in exchange for her three tablespoons of the edible petals from their café kitchen. Esther took the rose petals from her bag, wrapped in doubled napkins inside a brown paper bag, smiling in reflective gratitude for the waiter who'd given them to her free of charge. The last ingredient: three-quarters of a teaspoon of salt. Esther took the glass vial from her bag and shook it, relishing the quiet crumpling sound of Liezel's salt crystals inside.

On her phone, Esther opened the photo she'd taken of Erin's painted cake recipe. Scanned the method again, repeating the items aloud to herself. Started opening and closing all the cupboards in the hostel kitchen, searching and gathering. Mixing bowl. Spatula. Measuring cups. Whisk. Her face stung in a pleasurable way from the wind she'd been out in all morning, walking around Tórshavn on her own, shopping for all she needed to take with her into the night ahead. She reached to the back of a cupboard, emerging triumphant with a sifter in hand, mimicking the noise of a cheering crowd. As she arranged everything she needed, she spotted a boom box on the kitchen windowsill, next to a pile of cookbooks. A tape sat in the cassette player. Esther turned her head to the side to better read the writing on the tape label, upside down. Men Without Hats. She plugged the player in and pressed play. Turned the volume up. Started bopping along with the opening chords of catchy synth pop. Ducked her head around the doorway to peek into the common room; it was mid-afternoon and mostly empty. A couple were reading together on the couch. A woman by the window was studying a map and writing in a notebook. In one of the booths a group of young men huddled around a phone, talking over the top of each other, their voices a river of language. She didn't seem to be disturbing anyone.

Esther danced back to the cassette player and nudged the volume dial a notch further. Glanced up at the clock on the wall. Four hours until Sophus was due to meet her downstairs. Her palms went clammy. She exhaled. Shook it out; wiggled her hips, rolled her shoulders. The keyboard beats played straight from the tinny speakers and into her heart.

There was one last thing needed. She shimmied from cupboard to cupboard, but each was unyielding. Checked the oven, the most obvious place. Empty. More cupboards. Nothing. Her spirits started to fall. She scanned the kitchen. The idea she'd woken up with, that she'd been so convinced was a good one, started to feel contrived and ridiculous. To go out into the wind and search shops again would take time she didn't have.

Esther had started to pack up the ingredients, resolving to give them to the hostel's communal food box, when she glanced over her shoulder and noticed a concealed cupboard, under the oven.

She crossed the kitchen. Kneeled, pressed her hands together in faux prayer. Snapped open the cupboard and peered in. Synthesiser beats crescendoed in distortion from the cassette player.

'Yes.' Esther punched the air at the sight of a cake tin.

Until she took it out of the cupboard. Turned it over in her hands.

She dived back into the cupboard, rummaging in desperate hope for other cake tins. There weren't any.

At five minutes to six, Esther waited in the crowded hostel lobby for Sophus, a cake container at her side holding her afternoon's baking efforts. She'd cut it into pieces to disguise it. Reminded herself of Erin's words. *The whole point is never the cake; it's the power of the ritual.* It would be fine. It would be fine.

Around her, people checked in and people checked out. A flow of journeys in varying directions. She stood from the table she'd been sitting on and studied her reflection in the wall mirror, again. Tugged at her black t-shirt. Adjusted her scarf. She pulled up her black jeans by the waist, regretted not wearing her belt. She'd washed her hair; why had she thought it would be a good idea to put some of the leftover rose water through it?

'You smell like a scented doily,' she said to her reflection. Stared at her face, resisting the urge to run back to her room and scrub the new eyeliner and mascara from her eyes. Turned her back to the mirror and sat on the table again.

Aura standing in the doorway to Esther's room, watching her get ready for her year nine blue-light disco. 'Can I show you a trick?' she asks. Esther meets her sister's eyes in the mirror and nods permission. Aura comes to stand beside her. Takes the eyeliner from Esther's hand and gestures for Esther to look up. With a gentle touch, she runs the nib of the eyeliner pencil along Esther's upper and lower lash lines.

'If you put it here, instead of on the lid, it makes your eyes look bigger. Where's your mascara?' Aura asks. Esther hands it to her. She brushes Esther's lashes with the applicator. 'There. See?' Aura turns Esther towards the mirror.

She stares at herself, dumbfounded. Her eyes are lined with glossy black kohl, lashes thick and feathery. She looks so different. She looks like Aura.

'In Ancient Egypt,' Aura murmurs, 'Cleopatra believed that by lining her eyes with kohl, just like yours are, the gods would grant her protection against harm.'

Esther smiles at Aura in the mirror. Aura returns her smile, but her eyes are dull as stone.

The hostel door opened. Esther looked up.

Sophus walked in, wind at his back. He pushed his hair out of his face. Searched the lobby for her.

She didn't call out or wave. Just stayed as she was, sitting on the table, legs swinging, watching him, waiting.

At the sight of her, his face lit up.

The sixth skin:
Resistance

Know me now.
I am the wild wave.

36

They walked together out of the hostel to where Sophus' truck was parked on the street. It was battered and rusted in places, with hooded headlights, a wooden tray bed and faded cherry-red paint. As he opened the passenger door for her, Esther caught Sophus eyeing the container she was carrying.

'Oh, I baked something. For dessert,' Esther explained. 'A family recipe. From home.' She cringed. 'It's not exactly how I imagined it would turn out.'

'I'm sure it will be very good,' Sophus said. His smile when he'd first seen her had faded, replaced by tension in his face, a tightness in his movements. As if the ease of their conversation at the café the day before had never been.

'No rain today,' Esther said, settling in her seat with the cake on her lap.

'Nei,' Sophus said.

'Just wind.' Esther rolled her eyes at her attempt to keep conversation going. Sophus gave her a distracted half-nod. Just wind? She looked out of her window. 'I see your watermelons and raise you wind, Baby,' she muttered under her breath.

'Okay?' Sophus asked.

'Fine.' Esther tried to smile.

He drove. Silence filled the cab of the truck. In Esther's lap, the cake seemed to grow heavier and heavier. They passed more colourful houses – red, blue, mustard – and turned onto a narrow road where the landscape opened and houses were fewer. Ewes and lambs grazed in some fenced fields, and horses in others.

After a short distance, Sophus slowed down and pulled into a driveway. 'We're here,' he said. He parked in front of a tall, slate-blue house with a stone-walled garden, which was occupied by three shaggy, grazing sheep. 'Do you need help?' he asked as he swung out of the truck.

Esther shook her head. She watched as he opened a small gate set in the stone wall; at the sight of him the three sheep bleated and trotted over, nuzzling at his legs. He murmured to them as he patted their heads and ruffled their ears. They closed their eyes and seemed to sigh in contentment.

She got out of the truck and stood with her cake in hand at the gate in the stone wall. She thought of the photo she loved, of Sophus in a grassy meadow with sheep, all sitting in the sun, all seemingly smiling.

'Want to meet them?' Sophus looked up at her.

'Of course.' She gave him a warm smile in the hope of dissolving the awkwardness and strain in his face. Had he changed his mind? Did he not want her there?

His shoulders relaxed a little. A hint of a smile. 'This,' Sophus said, walking towards one of the sheep, 'is Meryl.'

Esther shot a look at him, trying to figure out if he was joking.

'And this,' he said, arms open to another sheep, 'is Lady.' Lady walked into his embrace and bleated. He rubbed her head and ears. Then stood and pointed. 'And over there is Frida.'

'Seriously?' Esther asked.

Sophus looked at her, deadpan. 'Meryl Sheep. Lady Maaamaaa. Frida Maaahlo. I introduce to you, Esther Wilding.'

Esther choked back a honk of laughter. Pulled herself together. 'Not Lady Baaabaaa? Or Frida Baaahlo?'

Sophus shook his head. 'Faroese sheep maaa more than baaa.'

Esther snorted. 'Well. Ladies. It's maaarvellous to meet you,' she addressed the sheep, and, before she could stop herself, curtseyed. Sophus watched her closely. She smiled again at him. 'Are their names your doing?'

'It's a running household joke,' he said.

'You keep them as pets?'

'They won't ever be slaughtered, if that's what you mean.' Sophus stood. 'Which makes a lot of people here think we're weird; in the Faroes sheep aren't pets, they're food. But on my father's farm they were rejected by their mothers when they were lambs. I took in one, then another. And another. And now ...' Sophus patted Lady Maaamaaa, then led Esther along the path towards the house.

She studied the back of his head. 'Looks like ewe give them a maaa-gical life.'

'I,' Sophus said over his shoulder. Stopped. Turned. Finally, his smile was genuine. 'Good one.' He scuffed his feet over the door mat and opened the front door.

Behind a narrow window to the side of the door, a plate of pillar candles burned. Esther standing at the entrance to Freya's studio, candles burning in the windows, lilies blooming. Tattoo gun inside buzzing.

'Come in.' Sophus stood in the open doorway.

Esther frowned at her boots as she scuffed her feet over the door mat. How many times had Aura done the same?

She looked up. Met Sophus' eye.

'Come in,' he said again.

A quiet intake of breath. Esther crossed the threshold and stepped inside.

After unlacing her boots, shedding her coat and accepting a pair of house slippers, Esther followed Sophus from the entryway into his home, carrying her cake container. The walls of the living room were wood-panelled and warm, with built-in bookshelves crammed with paperbacks and photography books.

Paintings of various sizes hung on the walls, some framed, some on stretched canvas, many of the sea. Candles flickered on window ledges and a vase of wildflowers was set on the coffee table. Around the base was a gathering of small, whittled animals. A sheep. A raven. A seal.

'Can I take that for you?' Sophus asked, motioning for Esther to give him her cake as they walked through the living room and into an open-plan kitchen dining area. The dining table was long, filled with candles and a vase of fragrant, silver roses and set, Esther noticed, for five. At one end sat Flósi and a woman, deep in conversation with an open bottle of wine between them and half-filled glasses in hand.

'Look who I found,' Sophus said. He carried Esther's cake into the kitchen.

'Moon Moth,' Flósi boomed. 'Come, meet my sister, Lena. Sophus, get another glass, will you, for our guest's wine.'

Sophus saluted as he set the cake on the counter and took wine glasses to them.

'It's good to see you again, Flósi,' Esther said, extending her hand towards him. He looked at it like she'd just offered him the bottom of her shoe.

'Come here,' he said, pulling her into a hug. She let herself lean into the comfort of feeling like she'd been engulfed by a giant. 'Esther,' Flósi said, releasing her from his embrace, 'this is my old sister, Lena.'

Lena whacked him playfully on the arm. 'Old-er. Older sister. It's not my fault you were a change-of-life baby.' She swatted him out of the way. 'Hi Esther,' Lena said. 'It's good to meet you. Welcome to our home.' She offered Esther wine.

'Thanks for having me,' Esther said, accepting a glass. 'So, you live here too, Lena?'

'With my daughter, Heidi,' Lena answered. 'She's fifteen.'

'It's living hell,' Flósi said cheerily.

Lena ignored him. 'Heidi's out the back; you'll meet her soon.'

'Yes,' Flósi jumped in eagerly. 'Come, I'll give you the grand tour.'

Esther sneaked a glance at Sophus, who gave her an I-told-you-so smile.

'I'd love the grand tour.' Esther smiled.

'I'm going to check on dinner.' Sophus headed back into the kitchen.

'Great, I'll be back in a minute.' Flósi hurried away.

Esther and Lena stood together, wine in hand.

'The boys haven't stopped raving about you since you all met at the bar,' Lena said. 'Flósi mostly, of course. His general levels of excitement in life are either zero or kid-on-Christmas-morning.'

'He's made me feel very welcome,' Esther said. She tried not to obsess over how much Sophus might have participated in the raving Lena referred to

'We've just met, Esther,' Lena said, 'but I hope it's okay to say that I'm very sorry about Aura. We were shocked when Sophus told us. It's so hard to believe. I'm so sorry about the pain you and your family are in.'

Esther swallowed a mouthful of wine, finally realising that, living with Sophus, Lena would of course have known Aura too. 'I appreciate it,' she said quietly. 'Thank you.'

'Okay, little Moon Moth, I—' Flósi stopped mid-sentence as he returned and saw Esther's face. 'I left the room for three minutes and you're both crying? What did you do?' he accused Lena.

Esther laughed. She looked at Lena. 'Thank you,' she said again.

'No more new friends for you,' Flósi said to Lena, who poked her tongue out at him as she wiped her eyes. 'Here,' Flósi said to Esther. 'These are Lena's and should fit you. Will save you putting your boots back on.' He offered her a pair of yellow garden clogs to slip on. Esther looked to Lena.

'Of course, please,' Lena said, gesturing to her clogs.

Esther looked down at Flósi's feet. His clogs were covered in holographic unicorn stickers.

'What have I told you about taking my stuff, Flósi? I use those stickers for the kids at work,' Lena complained.

'Quiet, Nurse Ratched, real men need unicorns too.' Flósi clinked his wine glass against his sister's and bustled Esther towards the door that led into the back garden. 'She's a nurse in the children's ward. I steal all her fun things,' he whispered. 'But always replace them.'

Caught up in the buoyancy of Flósi's energy, Esther felt lightheaded. As she stepped outside, she looked back at Sophus in the kitchen. They held eye contact until she was out of view.

Outside, the day's blustering wind had scrubbed the sky clear. Esther breathed in the light, the sky, the clouds, the vastness of the sea in the distance. The novelty of nearly eighteen hours of daylight wasn't wearing off. Flósi walked ahead of her, through a small, protected vegetable garden, fenced off from a grassy paddock. Near to the back of the house sat a shed and, behind it, Esther spied the gable of what looked like a glasshouse.

'Basil, strawberries and lettuce,' Flósi explained. 'We can't grow anything anywhere the girls roam. They eat everything in their path,' he said, gesturing to the fenced-off garden. 'So, this is all the space we get.'

Esther smiled, heart-warmed by the priority the sheep clearly had in the family.

'Heidi,' Flósi called as they went through the gate in the fence to the paddock. 'Where are you, devil child?'

'Here,' a gleeful voice replied, out of view.

Flósi and Esther walked around the side of the shed to find Heidi kicking a soccer ball with four sheep following her, nuzzling the ball. One, with platinum fleece, seemed more committed to playing than the other three.

'Come and meet our new friend, Esther.'

Heidi ran over to them, cheeks flushed, long purple hair swinging over her shoulder. 'Hi,' she said.

'Hi,' Esther replied, offering her hand.

'Welcome to our humble abode, it's all a lark to meet you.' Heidi took Esther's hand and gave it a vigorous shake. 'So pleased you could join us for dinner. Should be quite the evening of nanty narking.'

'Sorry?' Esther shook her head, confused.

Flósi groaned. 'Heidi, just say we're going to have fun. Nanty narking? You promised. One night off, while our new friend is here. One night without any Victorian-*Downton-Abbey*-English.'

Heidi shrugged, grinning. 'I kruger-spoofed.'

'She's obsessed.' Flósi rolled his eyes at Esther. 'It's a sickness,' he said to Heidi, wagging his finger. He walked towards the sheep who were nosing the soccer ball around on the grass. 'I'm going to hang with my friends here who aren't kruger-whatevers. Liars. Esther, come meet the girls,' Flósi said over his shoulder.

Esther hung back with Heidi. 'Lady Violet Crawley, right?' she asked. After she'd dropped out of uni, she'd filled her days with more episodes of *Downton Abbey* than she'd ever admit.

Heidi looked at Esther, impressed. 'You presume correctly!'

'Esther,' Flósi called, laughing as he kicked the soccer ball around with the sheep.

Esther squeezed Heidi's arm with a smile and walked to Flósi. 'I met Meryl, Lady and Frida out the front.'

'Very good. Let me introduce you to the rest of the posse.' Flósi put his hands on one very woolly ewe. 'This is Shagourney Weaver.' He walked around to the next sheep with a blonde coat. 'Dolly Maaarton. She's quite famous around here for her smash hit, "Maaalene".'

Esther started to laugh.

'This is Michelle Omaaama,' Flósi said, patting another sheep.

'And this,' Heidi said, joining them, 'is Megan Maaapinoe. She's my football teammate. And secret favourite.' She wrapped her arms around the platinum-fleeced ewe.

Esther laughed, enamoured with Heidi.

'Tour continues this way,' Flósi bellowed, waving to Esther from across the paddock where he'd wandered.

'Tell me more about Megan Maaapinoe, over dinner?' Esther asked Heidi.

Heidi nodded with a smile and turned back to the soccer ball. As Esther strode to catch up to Flósi, she watched Heidi return to playing with the ewes.

'She's great,' Esther said as she reached him.

'She is,' Flósi said. 'I thought you might like this view,' he motioned towards the horizon.

Esther turned. 'Wow,' she breathed. From the highest point in the paddock, they looked down over the valley and outskirts of Tórshavn to the sea, and a mountain in the distance. 'Where is that?' Esther asked, pointing.

'Nólsoy,' Flósi answered. 'There's only one village there, also called Nólsoy. Creative, right? A ferry connects it to Tórshavn, only twenty minutes. Everywhere in the Faroes is connected, by road, or boat, or helicopter.'

Esther observed the island in the distance. Rising from the sea, its shape reminded her of an illustration in one of Aura's favourite childhood books, of a brown hat, which really was an elephant inside a boa constrictor. *The Little Prince.*

'I go sometimes, over to Nólsoy, just to see the birds. It's a special area, that island, because it's a breeding ground for puffins and other birds.'

'Puffins,' Esther murmured in wonder.

'Have you ever seen one?'

'A puffin? No.'

'They are my favourites,' Flósi said with unrestrained joy.

'Why?' Esther asked, uplifted by his energy.

'You want fun facts?'

'Sure.'

'What do you call a baby puffin?' Flósi asked.

Esther shrugged.

'A puffling,' he said, grinning.

Esther repeated the word, laughing. 'Outrageously cute.'

'Puffins have one puffling per year, and usually only one partner for life. The parents fly far distances to catch fish, sometimes making one hundred trips a day to feed their puffling. I don't know if I've ever been that committed to anything.'

Esther glanced at Flósi. 'I'm not sure I believe that.' She nodded over her shoulder towards Heidi.

Flósi feigned nonchalance. 'She's alright.'

Esther rolled her eyes playfully. 'Any more fun facts?'

Flósi considered his answer. 'Two more.' He held up a single finger. 'One: puffins are widely loved. I'm half Icelandic and have family in Iceland, where more than half the world's puffin population breeds. My relatives live in a village on Heimaey where people have made a puffling patrol, to help rescue pufflings that get lost or separated from their family.'

'Are you making that up?'

Flósi shook his head and held up a second finger. 'Two: the Atlantic puffin's Latin name, *Fratercula arctica*, means, in English, little brother of the north. Some birdwatchers have said it might come from how their feathers resemble a friar's robe.' Flósi shook his head. 'I like to take it more literally. I always feel better in April when the puffins come back. Like family, returning after winter.'

Esther shook her head in wonder. 'Pufflings? Puffin patrol? Where am I?' she murmured.

'On the edge of the world with us, Moon Moth.' Flósi smiled down at her.

'Why do you call me that?' she asked him, curious. 'When we met at Flóvin, you called my sister Moon Child. Right? After *The NeverEnding Story*?'

'Yeah. As I said, we bonded over our mutual love of eighties films.'

'But later you called me Moon Moth in the street when we were saying goodbye.'

Flósi looked out to sea, suddenly sombre. 'Being around you that night felt so much like being around her again. But so different. It just happened, calling you Moon Moth. I don't know.'

Esther tensed as she let his words go through her. 'So, my sister reminded you of the Childlike Empress of Fantasia and I remind you of a ... moth?'

Flósi frowned until he caught Esther's eye and saw the playfulness in her face. He smiled. 'What can I say, I'm not a poet.'

'Okay. But if you were ...?' Esther pushed, compelled by a need to know how it had felt different, sitting with Aura compared to sitting with her, drinking beer in a bar on the edge of the Arctic Circle.

Flósi shrugged. 'I'd probably try to say something about the moon and moths, and the darkness that brings out the light in them, all their unseen magic. When we met, you reminded me of these things. Moon moths.'

Esther side-eyed him. 'You're not a poet, huh?'

Flósi shrugged again. 'Like I said, it's just a feeling I had the night we met. Being around you. The way Sophus was with you.'

Esther stilled. 'The way Sophus was with me?'

'No,' Flósi hurried to say, 'no, I just, I mean, I could just tell, there's a lot going on for you. Being here. Meeting us. Him. Is it a weird nickname for you? I will stop.'

'No,' Esther said. 'It's beautiful. Thank you. I was just curious.'

The sun shone down. Esther breathed in the blue tones of the sky. She looked across the paddock to the gable she'd spotted earlier. 'Is that a glasshouse?' she asked.

'Now you've done it,' Heidi called, appearing suddenly nearby.

'Shut your sauce-box,' Flósi called back.

'Sauce-box?' Esther raised a brow.

'Mouth,' Flósi said. 'You spend enough time around a kid speaking Victorian English, it rubs off on you. You want to see?' Flósi started walking in the direction of the glasshouse.

'I'd love to.'

As they crossed the paddock, a deep, rasping sound echoed through the air.

'The dressing bell,' Heidi exclaimed, kissing each of the sheep on their heads and running inside.

'Thanks, Carson,' Flósi called after her. He glanced at Esther. 'I'll show you the glasshouse next time?'

'Sure.' A quiet thrill went through Esther at the thought of visiting again. 'What was that sound, Flósi?' she asked as they walked back to the house.

'You don't blow a Viking horn to announce dinner where you're from?' Flósi asked her.

Esther couldn't remember the last time her face had ached from smiling.

37

Lena, Sophus and Heidi were seated by the time Esther and Flósi came in and kicked off their clogs. Candles were lit and the dining table was laden with steaming, glistening dishes.

Sophus cleared his throat. 'Esther, it's not a traditional Faroese meal, but it is all vegetarian.'

'It's what?' Flósi retorted.

Sophus ignored him. 'It's the best I could do with what was in at the supermarket. Most fresh produce here is imported and the next boat delivery comes tomorrow, so I hope it's okay...'

A platter of grilled eggplant halves sat beside a deep pot of miso soup, next to a tray of satay tofu skewers and a large bowl of sesame broccoli and noodles. Before she had the chance to speak, Esther's stomach growled at a volume that made everyone look at her.

'I'd take that as a compliment,' Flósi said to Sophus and sat.

Esther pressed a hand to her abdomen. 'Sorry.' Her face was hot. 'This looks amazing, Sophus, thank you.'

He smiled and busied himself with the table settings.

'Here, Esther, allow me,' Heidi said, drawing Esther a chair at the table.

'More wine?' Lena offered.

'Just a bit, thanks,' Esther said.

Flósi raised a glass. 'So, Moon Moth, even though catering for you means we're all going to starve ...'

Lena laughed, shaking her head at her brother.

'Right?' he said out of the corner of his mouth, turning to his sister. 'We might as well go out and join the girls to eat grass for dinner. No meat? We're basically living that story ... that book of yours, Heidi, what's it called?'

'*The Hunger Games*,' Heidi chimed in.

'Are you doing a toast, Flósi, or should I?' Sophus sighed.

Flósi resumed, eyes twinkling. 'Welcome, Esther.' He tipped his glass in her direction.

'Welcome, Esther,' Lena and Heidi repeated. Sophus raised his glass; Esther could feel his eyes on her.

'Skál,' they chorused.

'Here's to our felicitous evening, dear chaps,' Heidi said, ducking the napkin Flósi threw at her.

After everyone had eaten seconds and then thirds, they sat around the dining table moaning about overeating.

'I take it back, I take it back. Who knew plants could be so filling?' Flósi groaned and undid the top button on his trousers. 'Thanks, Sophus. That was a vegetable feast fit for Vikings.'

Sophus smiled, smug. 'Who wants coffee?' he asked. 'If anyone has space left, Esther baked us a cake for dessert.'

Murmurs of appreciation went around the room. Esther inwardly prayed they were all too full, until their chorus of wanting left her with no hope. Maybe there was something she could still do if she served the cake ...

'Flósi, come and help me serve, good sir.' Heidi jumped up and dragged Flósi by the sleeve before Esther could volunteer herself.

'Fine, you wretch,' Flósi answered.

Esther looked back and forth between Lena and Sophus at the table, who were doing her the kindness of speaking in English to include her in their conversation. But she was distracted, listening to Flósi and Heidi chattering in the kitchen. She watched from the corner of her eye as they gathered

serving plates, cutlery and, eventually, opened the lid on the
cake container.

There was silence, then tell-tale sniggering. Esther sneaked
a look at them: Flósi grinned over Heidi's shoulder while she
arranged the pieces of Esther's cake on a serving plate. Their
sniggers lasted for another couple of seconds until Flósi burst
into belly laughter.

'What's so funny, you two?' Lena asked.

'Esther brought us a dick-and-balls cake,' Heidi answered,
matter of fact.

'Heidi,' Lena scolded, getting up to go into the kitchen.
Esther scrambled after her. Confused, Sophus followed.

'I'm so sorry,' Esther said to them all, wringing her hands. 'I
was really hoping you wouldn't notice. It was the only cake tin
they had in the hostel. I didn't have time to buy another one.'

'I bet it was that Scottish hens' party that came to the bar
and nearly drank us dry,' Flósi roared with glee at Sophus.

'I've never seen a penis made of cake before. It's great,
Esther. Also, anatomically correct,' Heidi said. Lena's jaw
dropped. Heidi grinned and looked at Flósi, serving trowel
in hand. 'Esther's already cut it into pieces, so here are your
options: head, shaft, or balls?'

'Heidi,' Lena exclaimed, pressing her fingers to her temples.

'Ball, please,' Flósi said cheerfully, holding out a serving
plate.

'Flósi,' Lena hissed, 'don't encourage her.'

'Mamma, it's a penis. I'm fifteen.'

'What is that supposed to mean?' Lena retorted. 'Can we
please not act like we live in a zoo in front of our guest?'

'I'm sure Esther knows what a penis is too. Don't you,
Esther?' Heidi looked at Esther.

'I'm so sorry,' Lena said to Esther.

'No, I'm sorry,' Esther replied.

'I thought you said it was a family recipe?' Sophus asked
quietly.

'It is.' Esther's voice was strained.

'Penis cake is your family recipe?' Heidi asked, impressed.

'I'm just looking on the internet here,' Flósi said, scrolling on his phone, 'and you didn't have to cut it up, Moon Moth. There's a whole article here. You could have turned it into a crocodile or an elephant. Or' – Flósi paused, scrolling further down – 'a wizard.' He turned his phone screen to face her, his eyes glittering with amusement.

Looking at the little iced wizard in a hat on Flósi's phone, made of a cake shaped like testicles and a penis, Esther felt the tickle of laughter press into her ribs. She turned to Flósi, held his eye. 'The problem is, we've only just started getting to know each other, Flósi. I only make penis wizards for my closest friends.'

Heidi guffawed, an expression of awe on her face.

Flósi shook one finger above his head, as if Esther had scored a goal.

Lena threw her hands in the air. 'I give up. Does anyone in this god-forsaken household want coffee?'

'Again, I'm so sorry,' Esther tried to say to Lena with a straight face but dissolved.

'I'm not at all sorry about these rose petals. Divine. Also, these candy pieces, what are they, ginger? And the nuts. The nuts are great.' Flósi picked a pistachio off his piece of cake and popped it into his mouth. 'No pun intended.'

Lena groaned and went to the kettle. 'This house is a sheep trough. Esther, I'm sorry to say you fit right in.' A smile played at the corners of her mouth.

'Oh sis,' Flósi soothed, standing to put an arm around Lena. 'Why be such a killjoy?' He glanced at the others, a wicked look on his face. 'Can't you just let us enjoy our hap-penis?'

Sophus, who had remained composed to that point, doubled over.

'I've had enough penis for one night!' Lena yelled.

A momentary silent pause was shattered by Heidi's outburst of squawking laughter, which sent everyone into wheezing giggles. Lena included.

When their coffee cups and cake plates had been cleared away, and Heidi had fallen asleep on the couch, Esther made a move to gather her things. She'd tried to insist on walking back to the hostel, for night air and the stars, but Sophus had refused, saying he'd deliberately not drunk too much wine so that he could drive her. To hide the heat in her face, Esther had pretended to look for something in her bag.

As she put on her coat and boots by the front door, Esther noticed Flósi and Lena nudging Sophus. She straightened up. 'What is it?' she asked them.

Sophus sighed, hands in his pockets. Flósi and Lena leaned against the wall, waiting.

'Esther,' Sophus started. Sighed again. 'We have something we'd like to ask you.'

'Okay,' she said, her stomach dropping.

'The thing is, you are here,' Sophus said.

'Nailing it, Shakespeare,' Flósi whispered.

Sophus glared at him and spoke in a torrent of Faroese. Flósi held up his hands in surrender. Made a motion as if to zip and lock his lips.

'You're here, Esther,' Sophus tried again. 'And you're family. You are.'

Esther's eyes filled. Embarrassed, she blinked the tears away.

'We have a spare room here that isn't being used. If you need your own space and want to stay at the hostel, we get it. But we want you to come and stay with us while you are here. For as long as you need. You can come and go whenever, save your money, and feel like you have a home in the Faroes. Because you do.'

'I also have a drawer full of ordinary cake tins,' Lena offered. Sophus shot her a look.

To Esther's horror, her chin started to wobble.

'Is this a good or bad sign?' Flósi asked Lena. She shrugged. Esther looked at their faces. 'Thank you, that's so kind. Can I think about it?' she heard herself ask. She shouldn't stay with Sophus. She still didn't know what had happened between him and Aura. He hadn't offered the information and she hadn't found the right moment to ask him outright.

'Ja, think about it, of course,' Sophus said, his expression unreadable. He reached for his keys.

'Ja, of course,' Flósi and Lena agreed.

'Great,' Esther said. She thanked Flósi and Lena again for the evening. Apologised again for the cake. Turned to Sophus. Her heart hammered against her chest, screaming at her to be heard. The thought of leaving Sophus, Flósi and Lena, Heidi, Dolly Maaarton and the other sheep made Esther feel cold inside.

'Ready?' Sophus asked her. He opened the front door. The night poured in, bringing the scent of the sea. In Esther's mind, a flock of black wings fluttered between silver-skinned stars. A murmuration.

'Uh,' Esther said, coming to a halt in the open doorway.

Ahead of her, outside on the garden path, Sophus turned back. She held his gaze, then turned to look at Flósi and Lena.

'Esther?' Sophus asked.

'I, uh, I've thought about it,' she said to him.

38

At her kitchen counter by the open window, with the sea breeze on her skin, Erin chopped onions, cloves of garlic, carrots and a few stalks of celery into bite-sized pieces. She hummed along with the song on her stereo, the honey-fire voice of Shellie Morris, as she slid the contents of her chopping board into a saucepan. Nodded with satisfaction at the rising sizzle. She strained the cannellini beans she'd had soaking and readied her seasonings and sugar kelp flakes. Queenie had a rare afternoon off and was coming for veggie chowder.

For as long as Freya and Queenie had known each other, Erin and Queenie had been friends. Since Aura disappeared, they'd grown closer. Their shared meals had started during Aura's search party and had continued after Aura's case was closed. Over time, eating together had become ritual: as regularly as their schedules would allow, they met up to cook, eat and share how their families were doing over a glass of wine. They'd come to depend on their time together as a source of resilience and support.

Once her chowder was simmering, Erin took a bottle of sauvignon blanc from the fridge and popped it into the freezer for extra chill. Set the table. Checked the time again. Queenie was due any minute.

Erin's eyes drifted to the books and folders on her coffee table. Maybe she could delve into them for just five minutes and continue the research she'd been immersed in all morning.

Her mind was still whirling with Helena Nyblom's stories of women and water. She went to the coffee table and opened a few folders, sliding John Bauer's artworks from the paper pile, marvelling again at their evocative beauty.

As she began to feel pulled into the otherworld of her research, a loud, sharp knock at the front door interrupted Erin's thoughts. She smiled to herself; Queenie was always right on time.

'I brought us a tub of that seaweed salad we love, a fresh wholemeal loaf from Banjo's and two macadamia chocolate brownies for balance,' Queenie announced when Erin opened the door.

'Wine's on ice,' Erin added.

'Who needs therapy?' Queenie kissed Erin on the cheek as she came in.

Erin snorted. 'Everyone.'

'Touché.' Queenie strode towards the freezer.

'So,' Erin said as she mopped up the last of her chowder with a buttered wedge of bread, 'how's Nin doing?' They'd eaten, drunk some wine, chatted and laughed about work, internet dating, insomnia and Queenie's complaints about medical inaccuracies in the latest season of *Grey's Anatomy*. It was time to talk family.

'Ninny's good,' Queenie said, taking a sip of her wine. 'Her three-month scan brought up a lot of stuff. She's been reflecting a lot on her and Aura growing up together.' Queenie took a longer sip of wine. 'Nin's missing sharing this with Aura, especially since she's going to raise this baby on her own. Told me that since her scan, her shock that Aura is gone feels fresh.'

'That makes sense,' Erin murmured. The day after Aura, white-faced and shaky, had been discharged from hospital, Nin had shown up in distress at Erin's door, asking for a ritual. A spell.

Anything to help her best friend get over her pain, rejection and shame. 'How are you doing in all of this, Queenie?' Erin asked.

Queenie's face flooded with joy. 'I am out of my skin excited about this baby coming,' she replied, laughing, and dabbed at the corners of her eyes.

'It's just such beautiful news.' Erin passed Queenie a napkin. 'How's Aunty Ro?'

'Bossing Nin about the baby already.'

'I can well imagine.' Erin chuckled. 'Is Nin still working on her next exhibition?'

'She's in her workshop every day,' Queenie said. 'Plans to keep working right up to her due date, I think. Who knows who'll have the last say there? Oh wait, I do. It'll be Baby.'

'What's she working on at the moment?' Erin asked.

'A sculpture for the kanalaritja exhibition.'

'I can't wait to see it.'

'It's exceptional,' Queenie said. 'We're having another fundraising market day soon. Lots of us have been busy stringing. You'll come?'

'Of course,' Erin said. 'I can never have enough of your treasures around me, Queenie, you know that. Or the art Nin is making, I wear her silver shells every day.' Erin lifted a long silver chain from beneath her blouse, on which hung a raw amber pendant and three marina shells Nin had cast from sterling silver.

Queenie shone with pride. 'Nin's spirit just doesn't run out, in any direction. Not in her art' – she gestured at Erin's necklace – 'or for her family, or her passion for the exhibition. Her energy keeps us all going, I'm sure of it. I've just got to keep an eye on her that she doesn't burn out. Especially now. She doesn't have an off button, that girl.'

'Huh,' Erin said, deadpan. 'Can't imagine where she gets that from.'

Queenie waved Erin's words away with a wry smile.

'Has Nin told Esther yet? About the baby?' Erin asked.

'Not that I'm aware of. Nin wants to wait until she's home to tell her. They've been texting. She says Starry's got enough on her plate.'

'She's not wrong,' Erin said.

Queenie dipped her spoon into the chowder pot in the centre of the table for another mouthful. 'Nin says Esther's met Sophus, the fella Aura was in love with over there?'

'Apparently.' Erin leaned forward, braced her face with her hands and groaned.

'I know it's a lot, Erin. What's happening with Esther. Hang in there,' Queenie said.

'I just can't help but worry. About how this is all going to play out. Esther. Over there. Freya, here. The gulf between them. Freya can be so ...'

Queenie nodded. 'I know.'

'I don't know what to do other than bury myself in work, to try to find Esther some more answers about Aura's journal.'

Queenie looked carefully at Erin. 'Nin says Esther sounds like she's holding up okay.'

Erin rubbed her face. 'I guess so. I've chatted to her a bit, texts here and there. It's keeping me awake at night though, wondering if she's really coping? Or is she in a bar? Is she alone? Who's she with? Is she putting any pieces about Aura together? How could she when there's so much that she doesn't know about Aura's life? I mean, at least we know something about where Aura's grief came from. Right? We know the pain Aura carried in a way Esther doesn't. I guess I'm just ...' Erin ran out of words. Covered her face with her hands. 'It feels like all of this would be so much easier if Esther knew about ... everything.'

'That was the decision that Freya and Aura made,' Queenie said. 'Who's to say if it was right or wrong.' She leaned forward. 'Give Starry some credit. She can hold her own. Look at her, making the decision to go to Copenhagen alone. And now to the Faroes. That takes nerve.'

Erin sighed. 'You're right.'

Queenie sipped from her wine. As a thought came to her, she frowned. 'Could Esther know already? And hasn't said?'

Erin shook her head. 'Both Freya and I have talked with Abelone since Aura disappeared – she's never mentioned anything about what happened to Aura when she was fifteen. I just don't think Aura would have told her. My guess is that if Aura confided in anyone she met overseas, it would have been Sophus. She was clearly besotted with him. You saw how happy they looked in that photo of the two of them in Copenhagen.' Erin fidgeted with her napkin. 'If Esther finds out, I reckon it'll be Sophus who tells her.'

Queenie's face filled with empathy. 'Must feel like you're waiting for the other shoe to drop every day. Not knowing when it will.'

Erin nodded. 'It'll be so much for Esther to process. I'm scared she'll feel betrayed by us not telling her. Plus, trying to understand why Aura wanted to protect her from knowing. It's been hard enough for us, and we've known from the night Aura was in hospital. I've always wanted to tell Esther. But ...' Erin's chin wobbled.

'It was Freya's and Jack's call to make,' Queenie said quietly.

Erin thought about the haunted look Freya's eyes had recently taken on. The way Jack seemed to be running for penance. 'How's Freya's anxiety? She doesn't talk about it much with me. Is she still on medication?' Erin asked.

Queenie shot her a look.

Erin waved her question away. 'Okay, okay. Doctor–patient confidentiality blah-blah,' she said, pulling a face, trying to bring some levity.

'Erin, you of all people know the strain that's always been there between Freya and Esther. It was there right from the start,' Queenie said.

Erin nodded, remembering the bleak days after Freya's own miscarriage. Jack with eighteen-month-old Aura on his hip, his face full of despair, opening the front door to her and leading her down the hallway of the Shell House. In the darkness of their bedroom, Freya lay motionless on their bed, her body curled around unused baby clothes. It took almost a year before Freya conceived again, and Erin remembered how rigid with worry she'd been during her pregnancy with Esther. And then, nearly a decade on, after a day at the beach with the girls, Freya had called Erin, inconsolable. *I found a seal pup on the beach, Erin. I buried her with paper daisies,* she'd sobbed on the phone. *The grief never leaves. It never ends.*

'It's okay,' Queenie said, her voice gentle.

Erin realised tears were rolling down her cheeks. She patted them away. 'I just wish Esther was going through this with proper support. I was chatting to Jack the other day. He told me he's been sending Esther emails suggesting therapists. But she hasn't replied.'

'She might not have the head space for support, until she's more settled. Right now, everything around her is new and demanding all of her senses to process. Reflection will come later. It might just be timing.'

'I hope so,' Erin said, her voice hoarse.

'She's going to be okay,' Queenie said, reaching for Erin's hand across the table. Erin met Queenie's eye. Magpie song and the sound of the waves breaking in the distance filled the dining room.

An hour after Queenie had left, Erin sat at her dining table, long cleared of lunch, and pored over the books and papers she'd brought home that morning from campus.

She sifted through the illustrations that Aura had collected in *Seven Skins*. John Bauer was a nineteenth-century Swedish artist who had drawn two of them, one for Helena Nyblom's fairytale 'Agneta and the Sea King', and the other for her fairytale 'The Swan Suit'. The third illustration in *Seven Skins* was the work of Charles Folkard, a twentieth-century English artist who had started his career as a magician. He had drawn Helena Nyblom's character Violanta walking into the sea, in her devastating fairytale 'All the Wild Waves of the Sea'. The third story Esther said she hadn't been able to find in English, when Erin last spoke to her.

Erin sat back in her chair. Rubbed her brow. She couldn't concentrate.

A sweet and pungent gust came through the window. Erin looked out to her back garden where the last of her fragrant roses were in bloom, and the pile of dried seaweed that she'd gathered from the shore waited for her.

Outside, Erin put on her gardening gloves and began mixing the dried seaweed through her compost pile. The wind nudged at her back. At her sides. She sat on her heels and pushed her hair out of her face. Looked up at the gums and mulberry tree in her garden.

'Have you seen her?' she asked. The wind rustled and hushed the leaves.

Erin began turning the soil with her spade, covering her autumn garden beds with the seaweed compost to protect and nourish her plants and flowers through winter. It was a trick Abelone's mother had taught her and Freya when they were teens in Copenhagen. After a wild storm during their stay, Abelone's mother had driven the three girls to the west coast on a trip to gather seaweed from the shore for her garden. She'd explained that the seaweed fed the soil nutrients and minerals they needed to survive the long, cold months. After walking the shoreline and filling bags with dried seaweed, Erin had been crouched down fossicking through kelp for driftwood and shells when she'd spotted something gold and glistening in the sand. It was raw amber, Abelone had explained to her. The gold of the North, they called it. Tears of the Gods. Ancient tree resin buried in the seabed that wild storms dislodged and washed ashore. That was when Erin had first believed in magic, holding a piece of raw, ancient amber in her hands from the bottom of the sea, from the life of ancient trees; beauty washed ashore by violent chaos.

Erin stuck her spade in the earth. Her hands shook as she felt for the raw amber pendant hanging around her neck from her silver chain, along with Nin's silver shells. Every autumn in Salt Bay, Erin gathered seaweed and kelp from the shoreline and laid it on her garden beds to prepare for winter. The first frost was coming, the night skies were raw with the smell of ice. Is that what the skies in the Faroe Islands smelled like? Did the air feel as wild on your skin as the staggering green mountains jutting from the dark sea looked?

As the afternoon light began to fade over the lichen-covered silver rocks in the bay, Erin leaned forward on her knees, hands in the dirt. She couldn't stop the image of a wild storm barrelling over the sea, headed for Esther on shore in the Faroes. She could see Esther's eyes, her smile, her bare feet on the sand. The storm was headed straight for her. Erin drew in and exhaled long, slow breaths. She closed her eyes and willed herself to imagine the storm breaking up, dispersing and cracking the sky open, lavishing Esther in light. Garlands of kelp and a trove of raw amber laid by the sea at Esther's feet.

Erin's breathing returned to normal. Queenie's words rang in her mind. *She's going to be okay.*

Erin picked up her spade and dug furiously in the soil as if, by sheer will, she could make it so.

39

Esther carried a tote bag from the guest bedroom through to the kitchen. She put her bag on the dining table and went to the cupboard, searching for the coffee percolator. Pale silver mid-morning light poured through the glass doors by the dining table. The house ticked and hummed. There was the occasional bleat of a sheep outside. Maybe Frida Maaahlo. Lena was at work, Heidi at school. Flósi was at Flóvin, and Sophus was putting in extra hours with Ocean Rainforest. A few days earlier, Flósi had remarked over breakfast that Sophus was working more hours than usual; Esther had fallen quiet, her suspicions confirmed. Extra shifts had become a convenient way for Sophus to continue to avoid her, as he'd done for the ten days since Esther had checked out of the hostel and moved into their guest room.

Steaming coffee in hand, Esther sat at the dining table and unpacked the contents of her tote: her phone, Aura's journal. The View-Master and reels Erin had made for Aura's memorial. Esther's six black swan feathers. She took the last object from her bag. *Evidence*, a book of Mary Oliver's poetry that she'd bought from the bookshop connected to Lumiere Café, when she was doing her best to fill her days earlier that week. While she'd been waiting for Sophus to make time for her. Waiting for the conversation they needed to have to happen.

Esther drew Aura's journal close on the table and, as had become ritual, laid her hand over the cover of She-Ra.

'Sisters of Seal and Swan Skins,' she whispered. 'Séala and Eala. Raise your swords and your voices.'

Esther skipped over the pages as she always did, avoiding Aura's teenage words. Nevertheless, she glimpsed the red ink of her list. *Put Starry through star school and support her dreams of becoming a scientist so that the whole world knows her name, like Carl Sagan.*

Esther lay the journal open at Kópakonan. The seal woman. She'd been looking into renting a car to drive to Mikladalur to see the sculpture, but Lena had offered Esther her car in a few days when her nursing roster switched to day shift. The thought of seeing the sculpture firsthand made Esther shiver inside.

She turned the page, to Aura's sixth skin. *Resistance.* The illustration of the woman walking into the sea. *Know me now. I am the wild wave.* Esther brushed a hand over the black and white photocopy of the illustration, tracing the woman's hair caught in the wind, the yearning on her face, the outreach of her arms as she went into the sea foam and waves.

'What's your story?' Esther asked. She sipped her coffee and reached for her phone. Opened the unread email from Erin that had arrived overnight; she'd sent Esther some thoughts on Helena Nyblom's three fairytales. Esther skimmed the parts she'd already read to get to what Erin had written about 'All the Wild Waves of the Sea'.

Starry, I've attached an English translation I've found of 'All the Wild Waves' for you. I think it's more a cautionary story than fairytale. As you'll read for yourself, Violanta, a young woman, grows up with her mother and brother among cherry trees in the mountains. She wants more than domestic bliss: she's full of desire for a life of adventure. Violanta yearns for vastness and mystery, so she finds the courage to leave the safety of her home and set off on a journey to get to the sea. Along the way, she is interrupted by opportunities – a marriage proposal, a good job – but Violanta refuses to settle.

*At every intersection where there's a choice to be made in her
journey, she chooses herself. When you remember this story
was published in 1912, doesn't it blow your mind? All
she wants in her heart of hearts is to get to the sea. It's her
dream. She doesn't let anything stop her. Violanta chooses
herself above all else.*

*This is where the story and Aura's reverence for it will be
as hard for you as it was for me, Starry.*

*When Violanta reaches the sea, when she finally gets
there, the sea is a malevolent, punishing thing. She is filled
with terror and consumed by the black-green waves that crush
and swallow her, that scream at her in the story's last lines,
'Do you know us now? All the wild waves of the sea!'*

*The thing that Violanta wanted most and pursued with
all her courage, determination and heart, is the thing that kills
her.*

Esther set her phone on the table, her hand shaking. She
looked again at Aura's journal, at the trance-like yearning on
Violanta's face as she walked to the sea. At the churning waves,
their foreboding malice. Her eyes darted to Aura's handwriting.
Know me now. I am the wild wave. With her tattoo verse, Aura
had disempowered the waves in the story and instead inked
their power onto her own skin. A shiver went down Esther's
spine. Her sister was refusing to be punished for her desires and
was instead declaring her own power. Was *that* what it was
about?

'Most kind madam, good day to you,' Heidi bellowed as
she came like a gale into the kitchen.

Esther covered Aura's journal with the Mary Oliver poetry
book. 'A good day to you, m'lady,' she said with forced
brightness. 'School finished early?' She glanced at the time on
her phone.

Heidi opened the fridge and stood in front of it, staring at its
contents. Shook her head as she disappeared behind the doors

and emerged with arms full of bread, cheese and mayonnaise. 'I'm quite partial to returning to my hearth for nooning.'

'You came home for lunch?' Esther translated.

Heidi nodded. Made her sandwich and joined Esther at the table.

'How's school?' Esther asked.

'Agony, were it not for my chuckaboos.'

Heidi's confidence and ability to be who she was, to express herself with such assuredness left Esther giddy with an old and familiar sense of awe; she reminded Esther of Aura at the same age.

'Chuckaboos are friends, right?' Esther asked.

'Yetf,' Heidi said around a mouthful of sandwich.

'Friends are the most important thing about school,' Esther said, remembering what it was like to be fifteen. How vital belonging was, wherever you could find it. Tom. Tom. Out of nowhere his name rang like a bell in her heart.

'What's all this?' Heidi asked, gesturing over the dining table. Before Esther could stop her, Heidi had picked up the View-Master and looked into the eyepieces. 'Oh.' Heidi put down her sandwich to hold the View-Master with both hands. 'Aura,' she said in a small voice as she clicked through the reel.

A tremor of emotion went through Esther's body. She sat, unmoving, unsure of what to say.

Heidi put the View-Master down. Returned to her sandwich. They sat together in silence.

'Did you spend a lot of time with my sister?' Esther ventured to ask.

Heidi nodded. 'We talked about Victorian fairytales a lot. She was really interested in Scandinavian stories from that time.' Something in front of Esther caught Heidi's eye. Esther looked down to see the illustration of Violanta poking out from underneath the poetry book.

'You know this illustration?' Esther asked, moving the book away and showing Heidi Aura's journal.

Heidi glanced at it. 'I remember her making that.'

Esther's body went cold.

'She was sitting right here when she stuck that illustration of Violanta into her journal and wrote that verse onto that page.' Heidi's face fell. 'She was happy then.'

'She was?' Esther asked, her voice breaking. 'Aura was happy when she made this?' She flicked through the journal.

'She was happy when she made that page, with Violanta,' Heidi clarified.

'What about the next page?' Esther turned the page to the seventh image. 'Do you know this sculpture?'

Heidi nodded and looked away. 'It's at, um, Listaskálin. The art museum. In town.'

'It's here?' Esther asked, struggling to keep her voice steady. 'In Tórshavn?'

Heidi nodded again, but still wouldn't look at the seventh image in Aura's journal.

'Heidi? Did Aura put her seven stories together in this journal here? Did you see her making all of it? Do you know about *Seven Skins*?'

Heidi wrapped the remains of her sandwich in a napkin. 'I'm sorry, Esther, I'm not allowed to talk to you about this.'

'Why? Who told you not to talk to me about this?'

'I have to get back to school.' Heidi stuffed her lunch in her bag and hurried from the kitchen.

Esther watched Heidi go, her mind unravelling.

'Toodle pip,' Heidi called. The front door slammed behind her.

Esther glanced back down at Aura's journal, open to the pages of her final image and tattoo verse in *Seven Skins*.

The seventh skin: Homecoming

A photocopied photograph of a sculpture: a naked pregnant woman stood on the edge of a cliff, the shape of a ship's bow.

Below her in the implied depths, where the cliff fell inwards and away, her mirror image stood, upside down.

On the facing page, Aura's lines. The seventh tattoo on her spine.

As she was above, so she is below. So she is below, as she was above.

Through the roar of noise in her head, Esther focused on one thought: get to the art gallery. She threw everything on the dining table back into her tote and hurried out of the kitchen towards her room to get her things together. Her chest was tight. There was a prickling in her hands.

'Keep it together,' she instructed herself. As she laced up her boots and wrapped her scarf around her throat, a sharp knock came at the door. She jumped with fright.

Esther opened it, struggling to even her breathing.

A woman with long grey hair stood on the step.

'Hey,' she said. Regarded Esther with a cautious smile. 'I'm Greta.'

'Hi,' Esther replied. 'I'm Esther.'

'I know. I'm Sophus and Klara's mother. Can I come in?'

Esther followed Greta into the dining area, unwinding her scarf as she went, and sat at the table. Greta went into the kitchen and started making a pot of tea.

'Sophus isn't, um, he's not here,' Esther said.

'I'm not here to see Sophus.' Greta took two cups and the brewing tea to the table and went to the fridge for milk. 'I'm here to meet the woman who's made such an impression on my children.' She sat with Esther at the table.

'Oh?' Esther's stomach dropped. She took the cup of tea Greta poured for her.

'Klara and Sophus have both told me about you. I wanted to come and meet you.' Greta took a sip of her tea.

Esther blew the steam rising from her cup. Took a small sip. What had Sophus told his mother about her?

They sat together drinking their tea. Greta's presence seemed to fill the room. Esther thought back to what Sophus had told her, about how his mother had divorced his father, survived a heart attack and started to live life on her own terms. *She said she didn't have time to lose. She's joined all sorts of groups. Knitting, arts, sea dipping.*

'Oh,' Esther said as her bleary memory of her first morning in town by the sea surfaced. 'We've met before. Kind of.'

Greta scrutinised Esther's face. 'By the sea,' she murmured. 'Ja? That was you?'

'That was me,' Esther said.

'You looked so much like you wanted to swim. You had so much longing in your face.'

Taken aback, Esther could only nod.

'But you didn't want to swim that morning.'

'Too cold for me,' Esther lied.

'Ah,' Greta said, drinking her tea.

'You swim every day?'

Greta nodded. 'Even if it's snowing.'

Esther shuddered. Shook her head.

'Ja, it's cold,' Greta said. 'But the saltwater and our souls go together here. Life on these islands exists around the sea. We swim and use the sand like this,' Greta said, rubbing a hand up and down along her arm, 'to keep our skin soft. And we never shower afterwards. The saltwater must be kept on our skin. The salt and the minerals from the kelp stay on our bodies. Keeps us well preserved,' Greta said with an outburst of throaty laughter. 'I didn't know the women I swim with until I started sea dipping. It's as much about friendship as it is about the sea.'

Esther watching Freya and Aura heading off together, going diving, while she paddles in the shadows. 'Sounds wonderful,' she said.

'So,' Greta continued, 'you should come with us while you are here. It will make you feel alive. I don't know how to best say it in English, but it's like, when I'm not in the sea, I'm not in my skin. Ja?'

Esther tried to give a polite smile. The sea was gone from her. She fidgeted with her teacup as thoughts jostled in her mind: 'All the Wild Waves of the Sea', her conversation with Heidi, and the image of Aura sitting at the same dining table Esther and Greta were sitting at, making her journal. Cords of anxiety pulled tight through Esther's body.

'I wanted to say,' Greta said, interrupting Esther's thoughts, 'I would like to give you my deepest condolences. Aura was a big part of my son's life, which meant she was a big part of my life.'

Esther could see Sophus in the warmth of Greta's eyes. And Klara in her smile. These people who had known and loved her sister. These people Aura had also left behind.

'Could I ask you what happened?' Greta asked. 'We know so little.'

Esther's mind skittered back to Heidi's reaction to seeing the illustration of Violanta in Aura's journal. *Know me now. I am the wild wave.*

'There's nothing to know,' Esther said curtly. Sighed. She didn't want to be rude. 'The last time Aura was seen she was walking by the sea. At home, in Lutruwita. Tasmania. Her clothes were left on shore. She disappeared. No trace. The police found no signs of suspicious circumstances. They couldn't confirm whether it was an accident or ...' Esther ran out. Of breath, of words, of courage, and capacity. The words she didn't say twisted through her gut. *She left me a note. Which I ignored.*

Greta reached her hand across the table to rest it over Esther's. 'I'm so sorry for your pain and loss, Esther.'

Esther took her hand away. She was impatient with condolences and tired of feeling her head was filled with the cotton wool of confusion. Frustration made her skin itch. In her mind's eye, the naked pregnant woman stood on the edge of the cliff, her mirrored reflection below, waiting for Esther.

'Sophus is avoiding me,' Esther blurted out. She sucked her lips together behind her teeth, as if taken aback hearing herself speak the words. 'Sorry.'

Greta's face softened with compassion. 'Ja. That's his way.' She shook her head. 'When he's overwhelmed, he snaps shut like a fish in a shell. He was the same with your sister.'

Esther sat rigid. Drank her tea.

'There's no such thing as a perfect relationship, of course, but Sophus and Aura had something special. He worked hard at opening himself up with her. She changed him for the better in that way. After Aura left him, he wasn't himself for a long time. He—'

'Wait.' Esther interjected. 'What do you mean, Aura left him?'

Greta looked at Esther. 'Yes. She left him. He was devastated. It totally broke his heart.'

Esther sat slack in her chair. Aura had left Sophus. Not the other way around.

It took her a moment to realise. The feeling in her body was relief.

'When Klara told us that you emailed her, and what happened to Aura,' Greta went on, 'it brought everything back to the surface for him. He's afraid. Fear keeps him closed up.'

'Fear of what? Of me?' Esther's brow furrowed.

'No. Of feeling big emotions when he talks to you. About Aura. You might not realise how much you are like her, Esther. It's a shock, even for me. To sit here with you. It is the feeling like someone is playing a trick on my mind.'

Greta's words popped something in Esther like a pin. What was she doing? Living in Sophus' house, hanging around, just waiting for him to talk to her? The feeling she'd started to allow herself to believe, that she had a place there, that she belonged in the Faroes, was just an illusion. How could she have been so wilfully forgetful? This was Aura's life. Flósi, Heidi, the sheep,

Lena, Sophus – they were Aura's. Esther looked away from Greta, out of the glass doors to the sheep grazing and the sky beyond the garden. Her eyes filled. One of the sheep – Esther guessed Dolly Maaarton – was nosing Heidi's soccer ball on the grass with Megan Maaapinoe.

When she felt Greta stand at the table, Esther looked back at her.

'I'm sorry, Esther, I didn't mean to upset you. Maybe I shouldn't have come.'

'No, it's not you, Greta. It's nice that you made the time to come and meet me. Thank you.' Esther wiped her nose. 'It's just everything. It's very hard. Being here.'

'It must be,' Greta said quietly. 'I hope so much you find what you came here for.' The tone of a text message beeped in Greta's bag. She took her phone out and read it. Smiled to herself. 'I should go,' she said to Esther. 'My knitting class starts soon. That reminds me,' Greta said, reaching into her handbag for two skeins of pale silver wool. 'Can you make sure Sophus gets these?'

Esther took the wool. 'Sophus …?'

'Ja. He's the best knitter out of all of us. Not that he admits it; he got teased so much growing up and still does, I am sure. He made this sweater for me when he was a teenager.' Greta smiled proudly, stroking her sleeve.

The sharp edges inside Esther's chest were softened by the thought of an adolescent Sophus, growing up in the wild and unrelenting Faroese weather, landscapes and traditions, sitting at home knitting the delicate green jumper Greta was wearing.

'I'll let him know,' Esther said. 'If I ever catch him in the same room as me.'

Greta pressed her lips together, as if she was trying to stop herself speaking, but then changed her mind. 'He is very happy you are here.'

The desire to ask for more from Greta about her son burned at the back of Esther's throat. But, as Greta readied to leave,

Esther couldn't bring herself to risk saying anything that would give her feelings away.

She followed Greta to the front door. They faced each other.

'Thank you for coming, Greta. For the tea.'

'No problem,' Greta said as she swung her hair over her shoulder. Something on her arm caught Esther's eye, a bird tattooed on the underside of Greta's wrist. She noticed Esther staring.

'Sorry, I was just admiring your tattoo,' Esther said.

Greta pulled her sleeve up. 'I got it in New Zealand, a couple of years ago. After my divorce.'

'On your own?' Esther asked, not able to withhold the awe in her voice.

Greta smiled at her. 'I went to an artist's retreat on the South Island, in Hokitika, pretending I was all about "the art"' – she made quotation marks in the air with her fingers – 'but really, I just wanted to meet new people. The friends I made there, and the stories they shared with me, felt like' – Greta paused, pressing her hands on her chest – 'one of those machines that brings your heart back to life. You know?'

Esther nodded.

'So. One of the women I was on retreat with, Jude, had a chin tattoo. A moko kauae. She shared with me what tattoos mean to her people, in Māori culture, that it is believed every Māori woman has a moko on the inside, near to their heart, and when they are ready, getting their chin tattooed brings their moko from their heart to their skin.'

Esther rubbed goosebumps from her own skin.

'I loved Jude's story, her electricity, ja? In her skin? When she told me her day job was as a tattooist, I asked her to give me my first after our retreat was over. I chose a tūī bird. I befriended one while I was there, on the South Island. They sing at night, often at full moon, and have two voice boxes, which makes their calls and songs unique and strange.' Greta ran a hand over her tattoo. 'She makes me feel more comfortable about being me. About the choices I've made. And reminds me to sing, even if I sound strange.' Greta laughed.

Esther studied the finely lined bird and its vivid colours on Greta's skin. 'She's beautiful,' Esther said, preoccupied with thoughts of Freya. Memories of her mother's studio; the looks on the faces of women in front of the mirror for the first time with their new skin.

Greta opened the front door then turned back to Esther. 'It's funny you spotted my tattoo this first time we meet. Your sister did that too. She loved it. Asked me to talk about it all the time. When did I get it, how did it feel, what did it mean to me? She was like a child asking for their favourite story over and again. But I guess it made sense, since she was in the process of getting her seven tattoos,'

A rush of blood went to Esther's head. 'You know about my sister's tattoos?'

Greta's eyes glossed over with memory. 'I thought it was fascinating. Her way of telling the story she'd been carrying for too long. Ja? But never found the words to tell.'

40

After Greta had left, Esther leaned against the front door and let herself slide to the floor. She put her head in her hands, trying to make sense of her conversations with Heidi, and then Sophus' mother. When her thoughts did nothing but endlessly loop, she got to her feet. Considered going out, to see the last sculpture in Aura's journal that Heidi had told her was at the art museum. Apathy overwhelmed her. No museum visit. She briefly contemplated going to a different bar in town, but couldn't summon the energy required to lie to herself about how the burn of liquor and the hands of a stranger would make her feel better.

Instead, Esther shuffled through the house. Stood in front of the open fridge listening to the oven clock tick. Eventually filled her pockets from the crisper.

Outside, the day had turned dark and blustery. The wind was rough and cut through Esther's clothes. She walked, through the garden, to the open paddock behind the house. Her shoulders were hunched, her eyes were heavy. The wind pushed her around. When they saw her, Shagourney and Dolly trotted to Esther, sniffing, and nudging their snouts against her pockets.

'Hi, ladies,' Esther said. She reached for the grapes and lettuce leaves she'd brought them. 'Sorry, no oats and pears today.' Michelle Omaaama and Megan Maaapinoe gathered around her, and, beside them, Frida and Meryl.

Lady came bleating across the paddock and looked almost as if she was grinning when Esther held an open palm of grapes out to her.

'You're always so happy to see me,' Esther said to them, rubbing their heads and patting down their flanks. Her eyes filled with wanting. Wanting to belong. To be at home in her own life, which she was sick of feeling locked out of.

She kicked the soccer ball around with the sheep until they started to tire, then walked the rise of the paddock, holding her face up to the chill in the wind, trying to cool the heat of frustration in her skin. Breathed lungfuls of salty air, wanting to soothe and loosen the tangle of questions knotted in her stomach, in her mind, in her heart. Why wasn't Heidi allowed to talk to Esther about Aura? Who'd told her not to? What had changed for Sophus since the night he'd asked her to move in with them? Was it all for nothing? Why had she come? How would it ever stop? The endlessness of living without her sister. The knots and tangles, binding her tighter and tighter to a life without Aura, without answers, without closure. It wouldn't. Esther pressed her hands to her temples, pressure rising in her chest. It wouldn't ever stop.

'Fuuuuuuuck iiiiiiiiittt,' she bellowed into the wind. A mouthful of her own hair blew down her throat, making her cough. 'Fuck off,' she croaked as she spat out her hair. 'And fuck all of this.' She swept her arm wide. 'Fuck it all.'

Esther faced the view of Nólsoy, crowned by cloud in the distance, skirted by the foaming sea. Aura running an open hand over the page in *The Little Prince*, looking from the illustration up at Esther with shining eyes. *Promise you'll never become a Grown Up and see a brown hat, Starry. Promise me you'll always believe in magic.* Esther shoved her cold hands deep in her pockets. 'Fuck your hat elephant,' Esther muttered. 'Fuck magic.' She paced. Turned to the sea. How long had she felt so out of place in her own life? 'Fuck you,' she shouted, angry tears rolling down her cheeks. The wind howled back at her.

Esther hung her head, hands on her hips. Her fingers were numb from cold. Her face stung. She took a few deep breaths to calm herself. Took a few more.

Stopped. Sniffed the air.

Turned. Sniffed again.

Esther started to walk, following the tell-tale scent up the paddock and around the corner to Flósi's glasshouse. After she'd moved in, he'd mentioned wanting to show her inside a couple of times but always when he was rushing out the door to work. As Esther walked closer to the glasshouse, she realised the walls and roof were lined with bubble wrap, giving the interior an unclear, dream-like appearance. But Flósi's profile inside was unmistakable. The distorted sound of music playing through cheap speakers travelled on the wind. The tune was haunting.

She knocked on the door frame.

'Ja?'

Esther opened the glasshouse door and took a step back as a billow of smoke engulfed her.

'Moon Moth,' Flósi announced through the haze with a grin. 'You've come for your tour of my glasshouse.'

'Green house might be more fitting,' Esther quipped, waving the smoke from her face.

'I see what you did there.' Flósi stood in the doorway and held the door open for her. 'This is frowned upon here, so our secret?'

'When you say frowned upon …?' Esther asked.

'It's very illegal,' Flósi conceded.

Esther snorted. 'Okay. Our secret …' she trailed off as she walked into the glasshouse, quietened by wonder.

Each bubble-wrapped wall was lined with shelves of potted plants. Plastic containers of black water were placed sporadically between knobbly cacti, vines, glossy broad leaves and pale closed flowers. From the steel beams of the roof hung more potted plants at varying levels, some thick with flower buds. Two faded floral-print camping chairs sat aside a knocked-about coffee table bearing a thermos, a bowl, scissors, tobacco papers and a lighter. Next to one of the chairs was a small, open cabinet, its narrow shelves lined with similar wooden figurines to those in the house: seals, birds, boats, flowers. On top of the cabinet was a whittling knife, a carved puffin's head emerging from a small piece of wood, and a scattering of wood shavings and chips.

'Flósi,' Esther said, awed.

He giggled as he closed the door and took a seat, gesturing for her to do the same. She ran her hands over the velveteen leaves of a plant hanging next to her and joined him.

'Did you build this glasshouse? And you look after all these plants?'

'I did, and I do,' Flósi said, rolling a new joint. 'But it's not glass.'

'It's not?'

'Glass would never survive the North Atlantic wind or weather. It's made of polymer. So, technically, it's a plastic house. But Heidi said that doesn't quite have the same charm.'

Esther chuckled, looking around and above where she was seated, at the thriving plants that Flósi had taken such care to protect from the extremities. 'What's with the bubble wrap?' she asked. 'And containers of black water?'

'Insulation and thermal mass,' Flósi said matter-of-factly as he licked the edge of his tobacco paper.

'Obviously,' Esther said, looking at him blankly.

Flósi giggled again. 'Most of it came from deliveries at the bar.' He pointed at the sheets of bubble wrap lining the walls. 'I read on a gardening blog that it's good for insulating glasshouses. The water is dyed black, it absorbs more warmth from the day that way, and releases it when the temperature drops. A degree or two can make all the difference to my night-blooming friends.'

'Night blooming?'

'Ja. This is a night garden.' Flósi lit up his joint and took a deep drag. 'My night garden.'

The tension in Esther's jaw loosened. 'All of these plants bloom at night?'

Flósi nodded, exhaling smoke upwards. 'Not all at the same time, but yes, mostly only at night.' He pointed out the different plants to Esther. Queen of the Night cacti, moonflower vine, night jasmine, midnight candy, tobacco flower, angel's trumpet. 'There are others I'd love to have, like night-flowering orchids, but they need pollinators.' Flósi gazed through the glasshouse roof at the low-hanging bruise-coloured clouds. 'I wish moths could live in here too. Like the luna or the atlas. Ethereal little workers making their magic in the shadows.' Flósi took another drag, then offered the joint to Esther. 'Moon moth,' he wheezed as he exhaled.

'Ha. Well, yes. You got a moth in here after all.' Esther took the joint from him. Inhaled, listening to the crackle, watching the tip flare. The beautiful, distorted music continued to play through Flósi's cheap speakers, the single beat of a drum. In her mind's eye she sat with her dad at the stargazing shack, the heartlines on the wings of southern old lady moths fluttering in the shadows. Esther grimaced through a rush of lightheadedness. She swallowed an immediate rising giggle. 'What made you want to build a glasshouse?'

'My secret therapist asked me where my place was.'

Esther looked at Flósi, questioning.

'Faroese men generally don't go to therapy.'

'I see.' Esther thought of Jack. 'So ... your place?'

'Yeah. My therapist asked me if I had a place in my life that I was responsible for tending.'

Esther studied his face, her mind humming with curiosity. 'Where was it? Your place?'

'I didn't have one. I had other kinds of places. Flóvin. Home. Football. Plenty of wild areas on the islands. But none that I was solely responsible for taking care of. So I built this a few summers ago.' Flósi's giggle turned into a wheeze. 'I had no idea how much hard work it would be. Plants need a light–dark cycle to develop properly so I have to create enough darkness for them in spring and summer, and enough light and warmth for them in autumn. In winter my plants come inside the house. It's a whole thing. Blackout tarps. Grow lamps. But I can't stop.'

Esther listened, admiring Flósi's commitment. Took another drag. 'Why did your therapist ask you where your place was?'

Flósi reached for the joint. She handed it back. 'Because I'd told him it felt like there was nowhere in the world where I belonged.' He took another drag, his eyes half closed. 'We talked about hobbies, and I mentioned the gardening blogs I'd been reading. He asked me what my favourites were about, and it was this.' Flósi swept his arm overhead. 'Night gardens.'

Esther sat quietly. Her body softened. 'I know that feeling. In my own way. Like there's nowhere on Earth you can go where you might be at peace. Nowhere that feels like you belong.' She rubbed her forehead, her skin tingling as the high hit her. 'That's how being at home has felt to me for years. Ever since Aura left and came overseas. It didn't feel like home anymore.' Esther held a hand to her mouth, clacking her dry tongue.

'Now you're overseas too,' Flósi said, pouring her a cup from his thermos.

'Thanks,' Esther said, accepting the cup and taking a sip. 'Mint tea?' she said in surprise.

'What? I drink mint tea. What were you expecting? Ouzo?' Flósi asked with an impish grin.

Esther sipped her tea, grinning. Her face felt like it was collapsing in on itself.

'I love it here. But I don't belong here, Flósi.' She ran a finger around the rim of the thermos cup. 'This is Aura's place. Her life. I'm just a ghost here, lingering in her place, where I don't belong. Boooo.' Esther imitated a ghost noise while she batted in irritation at the tears rolling down her cheeks.

Flósi leaned forward with his elbows on his knees. Sat with her for a moment in companionable silence. 'When I started building this glasshouse, everyone at the bar and the harbour who heard about it called me crazy. Said nothing like this could outlast the weather here. Once it was built and didn't collapse in the first ten storms that came along, everyone then said I was crazy for spending all my money and time on plants that needed so much care and effort and only came out at night. But that's the thing about this being my place. It only has to make sense to me. And it does. This glasshouse. These plants. It might not last its hundredth storm, but neither might I. That's one thing for sure the Faroes teach you: no one escapes the weather.'

Esther looked across at him. 'I guess not.'

'Everyone has something that hurts, right? And everyone has to find a way to live with it. This is mine. Maybe yours is coming overseas, to find your way through the pain of losing your sister. Sure, she had her place here. But so do you, Moon Moth.'

'Do you always turn into an oracle when you're high?'

'*The* Oracle,' Flósi corrected her. They slouched in their camping chairs, gripped by giggles. When their gasps had subsided, Flósi reached for the thermos cup from Esther and poured himself tea.

'Stoned or not, here is a truth,' Flósi said.

'Okay, okay,' Esther said, pulling herself together.

'This place keeps my mind strong.' He swept another arm around the glasshouse. 'That's why it matters. Why having this place matters. Whenever I'm in here, I'm reminded: there's a certain kind of beauty that can only exist because of darkness.'

Esther stared at him for a second then rolled her eyes. 'Yeah, and you're not a poet.'

He smiled. 'Can I ask you some things, Moon Moth?'

She nodded.

'Are you in therapy after everything you've been through losing Aura?'

'Don't hold back, eh?' She fidgeted with her sleeves. Laughed, though this time Flósi didn't. Esther shook her head. 'My dad's a therapist. I hate it. It's always put me off.'

Flósi shook his head. 'Nice try.'

Esther laughed, waving away his protest.

'Next question,' Flósi said. 'Do you have your place? That you're responsible for tending?'

Esther groaned. 'I just told you Dad's a therapist and I hate it, then you try and psychoanalyse me?'

'You're avoiding the question.'

Esther sighed. Jack tended the stargazing shack. Freya tended her tattoo studio and every woman who walked inside. Aura had tended places ... everywhere. The seven boulders at the secret lagoon in Salt Bay. Abelone's loft in Copenhagen. Everywhere Esther had been in the Faroes. There was no space Esther had created, or place she'd tended, that Aura wasn't a part of. A place where Esther belonged. A place all her own. Did Calliope count? An image of Kane made Esther shudder. He was suddenly replaced by the black swan's grave near the stargazing shack. Esther shook the thought loose from her mind. Glanced up at the overcast sky. Closed her eyes and ascended, above the paddock, observing the glasshouse shrink to a speck on an island of jagged edges hemmed by the vast, unknown velvet of the sea. Higher still, through the clouds, above the blue curve of the Earth, into the silence, the darkness. The light of stars.

'You're welcome in here anytime.' Flósi's voice brought her back to herself.

'Thanks,' she murmured. Opened her eyes. 'Can I ask you some things, then?'

'Sure.'

'Who told Heidi she wasn't allowed to talk with me about Aura?'

Flósi met her eye. 'I did.'

Esther sat back in her chair. 'Why?'

'Because it's Sophus' story to tell,' Flósi said simply. 'No one else.'

'But he's avoiding me,' Esther said, heat rising to her face. 'And has been since I moved in.'

'He's avoiding the conversation he knows you need to have. He's not avoiding you.'

'You think?' Esther inwardly cringed at how whiney she sounded.

'He's getting his head right, Moon Moth,' Flósi said quietly. 'He doesn't want what's between you two to get in the way of the very important reason you're here.'

Esther's stomach dropped. She searched Flósi's face, taking a moment to gather her voice. 'What's between us?' she asked, her heart racing. 'I'm not imagining it?'

He relit the joint. Took a drag. 'You have to remember,' Flósi said gently, 'that you showed up here without any warning. Asking about your sister. Asking Sophus to have a conversation with you about his life with her that he didn't ever expect to have. It will bring up a lot. For you both. The time has to be right. On top of that, every time you two are near each other the energy between you is too' – Flósi gesticulated with his hands – 'loaded? No. Heavy. It's too heavy. It can't carry itself.' Flósi looked at her. 'Maybe ease up.'

Esther folded her arms. Thick grey clouds pressed on the glasshouse. Her skin was clammy. 'This feels like a warning,' she said.

'Only of what you both already know, Moon Moth. I've said this to him too. Ease up. Whatever you're feeling towards each other doesn't come first right now. There's time for that later. Right now, you have other responsibilities that are more important for both of you.'

Esther eyed Flósi evenly, jutting her chin in an effort to subvert the discomfort of the heat creeping up her neck. 'You're pretty switched on for someone who plays the clown all the time.'

Flósi's eyes glittered. 'Is that a promise?'

'To you?'

'Not to me. To yourself. To do right by yourself. Sophus. And Aura.'

Tears sprang to Esther's eyes. 'You don't think I'm awful?'

Flósi frowned at her. 'How do you mean?'

'For having feelings for him?' Esther fidgeted.

He held her gaze for just a second before looking away. 'We don't choose who we love.'

'Why do you care so much about this?' she asked.

'He's my family,' Flósi said simply. 'And now, you know, so are you.'

Esther stared at him. 'Fuck, Flósi.' Her chin wobbled. 'How could I not promise everything after that?'

She reached for the joint. Flósi handed it to her.

They leaned back in their chairs and sat together in the company of flowers waiting for darkness to bloom.

41

Esther tossed and turned in bed. Checked the clock. Four am. She drew the curtains back. The morning sky was pearlescent, lined with pink clouds, punctuated by the occasional streaks of a raven's wings. Flósi's words from their conversation the night before in the glasshouse echoed through Esther's mind. *Right now, you have other responsibilities that are more important for both of you.* She'd acknowledged the truth of his words with a promise made. To herself. To Sophus, and Aura. Esther had tossed and turned through the night feeling it, the promise, lodged in her windpipe, then, later, a solid thing between her rib bones. She forced it down, into a place where a stubborn sense of resolve began to do its work. Oyster flesh around grit.

She pressed her fingertips to the cold glass of the windowpane. Allowed herself a secret smile that warmed her face, her skin, her belly. *Every time you two are near each other the energy between you is too ... heavy.* She'd heeded Flósi's words but in solitude all she could focus on was the iridescent truth beneath them: Sophus felt for her too. The knowing shimmered through her body, beauty in darkness. Until questions rose, unbidden, from the shadowy depths of her thoughts. Why were she and Sophus drawn to each other? Was it a feeling beyond, or because, of Aura? And then, as ever, the same question that had beaten inside Esther's body every day since Aura hadn't come home from the sea: had her sister meant to leave her behind?

She struggled for breath around the tightening in her chest, the prickling at her temples. Esther refused the questions. Denied herself answers. Shut her eyes, refocused her thoughts. Rolled over in her warm bed and tucked her fingers between her legs. There was only the wanting. She pushed everything else away. Except the wanting. Knowing Sophus felt it too kept her from the shadows.

Later, flushed, she flung her doona back, dressed, and swanned into the kitchen for coffee. Opened the fridge, filled her pockets. The house was empty, everyone at work or school. There was levity in Esther's step as she walked outside into the paddock.

'Girls,' she called. 'Dolly, Michelle, Shagourney.' They trotted to her. Snuffled and nuzzled the pears, oats and lettuce from her hands, their soft breath tickling her palms. Esther let herself laugh. The shock of her throaty cackle caught her off guard, the feel and volume of it rising free from her belly, carried on the wind. Out to sea. She watched the vast blue in the distance. All the wild waves. Something prickled under her skin, rising from her feet to a shiver at the back of Esther's neck. She looked over her shoulder, around the paddock.

It was empty except for the flock. But Esther knew she was there.

On the periphery of her vision, Aura lingered. Waiting.

Esther shut her eyes. Willed herself to stay with how she was feeling. Light. Unburdened. Wanted. *Whatever you're feeling towards each other doesn't come first right now. There's time for that later.* Esther opened her eyes, rubbed Lady Maaamaaa's ears. Watched the sea, taking steadying breaths. Considered the perceived but unspoken understanding she'd reached with Sophus: he would tell her about his life with Aura when he could. Creating space for that to happen came first. But that didn't mean Esther couldn't allow herself the pleasure of knowing she was not alone in her wanting. She just needed to find a way to move her craving for him through her body.

The memory resurfaced an hour later, under an oyster-shell sky, while she was kicking the soccer ball around with Megan Maaapinoe. When she was out of breath, Esther doubled over, hands on knees, gazing across the crashing slate of the sea to the golden hues of Nólsoy. Rugged hills rose around her, the edges of their silhouettes cutting into the sky, separating everything she could see from the mystery beyond. It was then that Aura was beside her, again, her eyes clear in the light. *Sometimes the simplest way to face something you don't know how to face is to start by going for a walk.* Esther took a few sharp breaths through an ache in her ribs. Around her, the land, rock, sea and sky beckoned. *Remind yourself how the look of something changes once you're moving, step by step by step.* She bit on the inside of her cheek, studying the lines between land and sky. Struggled to hold the memory of her sister's voice.

Esther took another sharp breath. Looked to the edge of her view over Nólsoy.

Decision made. She would walk.

The next morning, she packed her dog-eared guidebook, cheese sandwiches, some of Flósi's dried strawberries, a few locally handmade chocolates she'd bought from a café in Tórshavn, and a thermos of strong, sweet coffee into her backpack.

'Running away from home?' Sophus asked with a smile as he came into the kitchen, his face filled with curiosity.

'I just feel like walking,' Esther said with a light shrug. 'Thought I'd check out the nearby coastline.' She waved her guidebook in the vague direction of the sea.

'Esther. I'm sorry. I've been so busy with work; I should have offered you a tour. Or pointed out places to go, to visit while you're here.' He leaned against the counter, coffee in hand. 'Be careful when you go walking, okay? It can be dangerous here. Don't wander off, and make sure you only follow paths marked with cairns.'

'Got it.' Esther kept her tone light. 'Maybe if I'd let you know I was coming in the first place, you'd have had some time and headspace to think about being my tour guide.' She offered a genuine smile. Drank in the sight of him, his face still creased from sleep, the sleeves of his woollen jumper pushed up. A thought occurred to her.

'Before I head off,' she said, leaving the kitchen and returning a moment later, 'I met your mum a couple of days ago when she came round. Asked me to make sure you got these. For your knitting.' Esther handed Sophus the skeins of silver wool, joy bubbling in her chest to see his face flush.

'Thanks,' he mumbled, taking the wool from her, not meeting her eye.

'Apparently, you're quite the knitting star,' Esther said.

Sophus spluttered into his coffee.

'I'll see you later,' she called as she forced herself to walk out of the kitchen, away from him to the front door. Her heart strained against her chest. *Ease up.* She pulled on her boots and headed out into the cool morning. Kissed Meryl and Frida on their heads as she went through the front garden and gate.

Esther walked along the road until she was out of view of the house, then stopped and tugged her guidebook from her backpack. Went over the map and details again. There was a nearby trail she could connect to that would take her to a path marked by cairns that led to two small lakes; in summer they were favoured by kittiwakes in such numbers that the lakes themselves were said to turn white. Further on, her guidebook promised, she'd find a chair built of stones, which marked the site of open-air public meetings that had taken place with national speeches and songs since the late 1800s to the present day. But what Esther was most drawn by was promised views of two islands she hadn't yet seen, Hestur and Koltur, and the legend of a love story that remained in the ebb and flood tides between them.

She tucked her guidebook into the pocket of her windcheater. *Step by step by step.*

Aura followed in the edges of her vision, in the space between her heartbeats. Esther fought the twin urges to draw her sister close and leave her behind.

She walked the road, uphill, looking for the trailhead. All the while breathing through the guilt and contradiction burning in her body.

For the next few days, Esther followed the same routine. Woke, packed a cut lunch and thermos, and headed out to walk. In wind, in sun, in rain. She followed the same trail to the same view. Step by step by step. And came home every day at dusk; she needed a full day of the light, the sea, the pinwheeling oystercatchers, the shimmering black wings of ravens, the whisper and chatter of the sea breaking over and over again on basalt rock. Every day it drew her out of the house. The longing for it. The pull and pulse of it. The sea. Towards and away from Aura.

On Esther's fifth day of walking, Heidi intercepted her in the kitchen before she set off.

'Where are you walking every day?' Heidi asked, plucking an apple from the fruit bowl and twisting the stem off.

'To the edge of the island. To see Hestur and Koltur.'

'You're walking the same trail, every day? You don't get bored?'

Esther smiled. 'It's the same trail but I notice something different every time I walk it. The birds, the lakes, the colour of the clouds, little pink flowers growing between rocks. The smell of the sea. The look of it. The current, the colour. The sea is always changing.'

Heidi considered Esther's response. 'I love the lakes. With all the white birds. I go there sometimes when I need to think.' Her face filled with a dreamy expression. 'There's a story about those islands and the sea between them. Hestur and Koltur.'

'I read about it in my guidebook,' Esther said. 'Is it really a true story?'

'People say it's true, but who knows.'

'What's true?' Sophus asked as he came into the kitchen.

'The story of Magnus and his island girl, on Hestur and Koltur,' Heidi said.

'Ah,' Sophus said. 'Hey.' He rested a light hand on Esther's arm as he brushed by her at the counter to get to the coffee machine.

'Morning,' Esther replied, unable to look up until the heat in her face had begun to cool. She steadied her hand as she sliced cheese for her sandwich. 'What was the girl's name?' Esther asked. 'My guidebook talks about Magnus, but only refers to the girl he loved as "girl".'

'Extra, extra, read all about it: local legend remembers boy's name and not girl's.' Heidi rolled her eyes as she tore a piece of buttered toast into strips and ate them. Esther gazed at her in adoration.

'Did your guidebook tell you the part of the story about Grísarnir in Koltursund?' Sophus asked.

Esther frowned. 'No, just that it's a true story, about Magnus, the local boy who lived on Koltur and fell in love with a girl on Hestur. Right? Her father didn't know about their love affair, so they met in secret. Magnus would swim on the ebb tide from his island to hers, they'd spend several hours together until the tide turned again, then Magnus would swim home, carried by the flood tide.' Esther buttered her bread for sandwiches, glanced at Heidi. 'Can I just say, gold star for effort goes to Magnus? I struggle to get a bloke to summon the effort to call me for a second date.' Heidi snorted. Esther smiled, whipping her butter knife in the air like a conductor's stick. 'True story.'

'What sort of "blokes" have you been hanging out with?' Sophus muttered.

'Sorry?' Esther asked him. Sophus looked away, drank his coffee.

'Anyway,' Esther said, turning back to Heidi, 'you know the rest of the story. Magnus and his love met their doom when the girl's father discovered their meetings. One day as Magnus came to shore, the father threatened him with an axe, and Magnus had nowhere to go other than back into the sea – but can I just pause at this point to call bullshit? I feel like this is the Faroese version of Rose not squeezing over so Jack could fit on the door with her in *Titanic*.'

Heidi applauded. Sophus chuckled, appraising Esther, a depth to the look in his eye.

'Heartbreaking. I'll never get over it. Just move the fuck over, Rose,' Esther griped. 'In answer to your question, Sophus, that's where my guidebook story ends: Magnus was never heard of again, and legend says a current took him and carried him out to sea. I want to know though what happened to the girl.'

'Extra, extra,' Heidi repeated.

'Ja, so,' Sophus said, 'around here, the story goes on that after Magnus was taken by the sea, an eddy formed in Koltursund. Magnus's act of revenge. Locals say Grísarnir still exists to this day.'

'What's an eddy?' Heidi asked Sophus. He answered her in Faroese.

'A whirlpool, right?' Esther clarified. Sophus nodded. 'Can you see it? From shore?'

'Nei, I don't think so.'

Esther fell quiet as she wrapped her sandwiches. The seven boulders in Salt Bay huddled around the secret lagoon came to mind. The turquoise tranquillity of it. The last place her sister was seen alive. As Sophus and Heidi chatted around her, Esther was overwhelmed by yearning, for guidebooks to know her sister's name, for a whirlpool, wild and mysterious, to exist in the sea that took Aura's life. Her thoughts fluttered, a velvety shawl of purple, gold, blue wings beating. Heartlines in the shadows.

Esther shook the images away. Focused on her day ahead. Focused on getting out of the house and into the clean, fresh air of the islands. It felt like the air at home on the northeast coast. A familiar, comforting tether. As was walking. She'd spent less than a week exploring by foot, and yet, in that time she'd spent outside in the wind and sun, wandering the fields towards the sea, she'd noticed a shift inside the house: she'd begun to settle into the rhythms of the household, like her conversation with Heidi and Sophus that morning, without as much agonising or second-guessing her belonging. Breathing in lungfuls of sky and sea spray seemed to soothe the sharpness of her desperation; the more Esther relaxed, the more she felt everyone else relax too. The collective breath it seemed that Lena or Flósi or Heidi held every time Esther and Sophus interacted with each other let go. The tension in Sophus' face had softened. Flósi had been right to tell her to ease up. Buried deep within her, the grit of Esther's resolve had begun to take on an iridescent skin of its own. She just needed to keep walking.

'Can I see your phone for a sec?' Heidi's voice brought Esther's thoughts back into the kitchen. She took her phone out of her pocket and gave it to Heidi, who tapped the screen a few times, then handed Esther's phone back to her.

'What's this?' Esther asked, looking at her phone.

'Omma said you're most partial to the sea but deny yourself the pleasure of swimming. So, we made you a playlist to help.'

'Sorry?' Esther packed her sandwiches and dried strawberries into her backpack. 'Who is Omma?'

'My mother,' Sophus said, chewing on a mouthful of toast as he carried a cup of unasked-for milky tea to Esther. He smiled as he handed it to her. She wrapped her hands around it, trying not to react to the feeling of being known by him.

'I don't have any grandmothers, so I call Greta my omma,' Heidi explained.

'I see,' Esther said. 'And when you say, "We made you a playlist", who is "we"?'

Heidi and Sophus glanced at each other. Both raised a hand. Sophus' eyes danced with mischief.

Esther picked up her phone and opened her music streaming app. Read the name of the playlist Heidi had added. '"In Aid of Esther's"' – she paused, studying the next word – 'something.'

'Accismus. You say it like, ak-siz-muhs,' Heidi corrected her.

'That's not a real word.'

Heidi gasped in faux horror. 'You're not suggesting I'm a flapdoodle? Remain stout of heart, chuckaboo, I tell no lies. Accismus is perfectly good English.'

'What does it mean?'

Heidi narrowed her eyes and wriggled her eyebrows mysteriously at Esther.

Esther couldn't help but laugh. 'Why the intrigue?' She scrolled through the songs. 'You made me a playlist ... about water?'

'Yes, water. And about the sea. Being in it. Loving it. Like you do. Or, used to do. We tried to find as many Australian bands as we could too. It was Sophus' idea,' Heidi said. 'He thought if you listened to songs about water and the sea while you're walking, the two might help with your sadness, and you might walk yourself into swimming again.'

'This is your doing?' Esther looked to him.

'It's just a bit of fun,' Sophus said, 'to keep you company while you're standing to live.'

'Sorry? Have you muddled your English?' Esther laughed at Sophus. Shot a side-wink to Heidi.

'"How vain it is to sit down to write when you have not stood up to live! ... the moment my legs begin to move, my thoughts begin to flow ..."' Sophus took another bite of toast. 'Henry Thoreau wrote that about what you're doing and what we know by instinct in the Faroes: walking, being in nature, is something that makes us better. Something we all need.'

'You're quoting Thoreau at me?' Esther quipped, thinking of Jack's dog-eared copy of *Walden* on the bookshelf in his office.

'Yes, Sophus can read,' he chuckled.

'No, oh, I didn't mean it like that,' Esther groaned. Covered her face with her hands. Heidi looked back and forth between them, smiling to herself as she sauntered to the fridge.

Sophus shook his head, good-naturedly. Dusted crumbs from his hands. 'Your playlist is just a bit of fun. To keep you company while you're walking every day. She loved making it for you.'

'We,' Heidi corrected him as she stood in front of the open fridge.

'Yes. That's right. We,' Sophus said, glancing at Esther. 'We loved making it for you.'

'Well, thanks,' Esther said, face aflame, unsure of what to do with her hands.

Esther spent that day walking the trail through the fields to the southern tip of the island, listening to the playlist Sophus and Heidi had made her. She stopped at the view looking back over Tórshavn and out to Nólsoy while Agnes Obel, Bruce Springsteen and Joni Mitchell sang to her about rivers. The sky was clear; the day was mild. The sea and islands were luminous. As Esther passed the kittiwake lakes, Tim Buckley sang a song to a siren. Velvety brown, blue and purple moth wings fluttered in the shadows of Esther's mind. Tom Waits growled for a sea of love. Following the path by the chair made of stones, through a patch of wild daisies, to the view of the islands, Hestur and Koltur, R.E.M. reminded Esther of the hot summer twilights that she, Aura and Nin had spent night-swimming in the secret lagoon; the moon set behind the silver rocks, Aura and Nin splashing in the moonbeams on the surface of the sea. As she walked, Esther's fingers twitched with the memory of saltwater. The Waterboys sang of Jack's hours in the stargazing shack, and the day Esther and Sophus met at Flóvin. 'This is the Sea'.

She took a break to sit on a soft patch of grass just off the path with a view of the two islands and sound between them. Magnus's watery otherworld. Esther strained her eyes to find his whirlpool. She was wondering what had happened to the girl left behind on land when a new song started on her playlist, just the beat of a hand drum and a woman's voice. A shiver swept over her body as she recognised it, the same haunting song Flósi had been playing in his night garden the afternoon she'd joined him. Esther couldn't understand the lyrics, they weren't English, but the power of the vocals, of the drums, caused a lump in her throat. She checked her phone. The song was called 'Trøllabundin', sung by Eivør. Esther tapped her name into a search engine. Eivør was a Faroese singer, who drew from ancient musical roots in her culture to write her music. 'Trøllabundin' was one of her most beloved songs. In English, it translated as 'Spellbound'. Esther read the lyrics as she listened twice to the song about being enchanted, heart and soul. Rubbed the goosebumps from her arms for the duration.

While she sat and unpacked her lunch, watching the clouds and sea, Esther smiled in surprise as songs from home played: John Butler plucked an ode to the ocean on his guitar, Blue King Brown sang for water, and Merril Bainbridge pined for what was underneath. Esther ate her chocolates first, relishing every rich mouthful as she imagined scenarios of Heidi and Sophus making an Australian catalogue of water-themed songs. For her. Because she loved the ocean but didn't allow herself to swim anymore. Her hands shook as she poured a cup of coffee from her thermos. She was just about to take a sip when the opening chords of the next song started. Sarah Blasko's smoky voice. 'Woman by the Well'. That song, playing on repeat from behind Aura's closed bedroom door. Esther standing in the hallway of the Shell House, fists clenched in rage at her sister's wilful silence, diminished spirit and hollow eyes.

'Hello?' A couple of figures appeared in the corner of Esther's vision.

'Jesus fucking Christ.' Esther startled. Took her headphones off and glared at the person and sheep dog in front of her.

'Hello,' the person said again. 'It's you, from our flight. My Australian friend from the coast who doesn't swim.'

Esther glared at the pastor, her vision clouded by anger and adrenaline. 'Am I wearing a sign that says I don't swim after my sister drowned, please bring it up with me as much as possible?'

'I'm sorry?' The pastor's face furrowed with concern. The dog sat, smiling at Esther, tongue lolling.

As quickly as it had sparked and surged through her, the heat of Esther's rage and exasperation fizzled. She sighed. Put her headphones aside on the grass. Stood, shook her head. 'I'm sorry. Sorry, Pastor. About saying Jesus' name.'

'I'm sorry about your sister,' Pastor Jaspur said carefully. 'That must be very difficult.'

'Never mind,' Esther said, a few rogue tears slipping down her cheeks. 'It's nothing,' she asserted, flicking them angrily away. 'Fuck,' she muttered, immediately sighing. 'Sorry, sorry. Sorry about that fuck. Jesus. Oh, for fuck's sake.' Esther wiped her face with her hands.

'Happens more than you'd believe.' The pastor's dog strained on its leash for Esther.

'Who's this?' Esther sniffed, crouching to the sheepdog.

'This is Carl.' Pastor Jaspur relaxed the dog's lead; Carl accosted Esther with a barrage of licks, sniffs and tail wags, bowling her over. Esther meant to laugh, but a sudden sob made her crumple.

'Are you okay?' The pastor rushed forward. 'Carl, we've talked about how to make friends. I'm so sorry. Are you okay?'

Esther nodded. Dusted herself off. Patted Carl's fluffy, slobbery head. She stood and opened her mouth to lie but heard the truth come out instead. 'It can catch me off guard. How to live without her.'

'Even after many years, grief can sneak up on us as if it's fresh.'

She glanced sidelong at him. 'I don't know how to bear it sometimes.'

'How long ago did your sister die?' Pastor Jaspur asked.

'More than a year now.'

A flicker crossed his face. 'It's still very fresh.'

Esther shrugged. 'It feels like yesterday. And ten lifetimes ago. Her death took time away from me. I don't know what I'm doing,' she muttered. 'Most of the time I don't really know how to get through the day.'

'In my experience, we don't know how to bear grief while we're in it. It can feel like a mountain. Immovable, unchangeable. But one day, we find it's not as insurmountable as we thought. We get a toehold. Change is always happening. Life is always moving. Grief is no exception.' The pastor's voice was calm and gentle.

Esther squinted at him. 'You're annoyingly easy to talk to.'

He smiled. 'Apologies. Occupational hazard.'

Esther gave him a small smile. Folded her arms across her chest as if she might be able to contain the pain in her centre. She looked the pastor over. He was wearing running shoes. The neckline of his t-shirt was damp from sweat. Carl sat at his feet, tongue still lolling, still smiling. 'You two are running this trail?' She stated the obvious.

He nodded. 'I never got your name.'

'Esther,' she said, offering a hand.

The pastor shook it. 'It's very nice to meet you, Esther. Are you going to be okay on the rest of your walk?'

'Yes. Thanks.'

The pastor turned to the view. 'Have you been enjoying your time in the Faroes?' he asked.

'I have. I mean, as much as I can. I'm here for my sister, really. But that's another story.'

'One I'd love to hear. You can come by the church anytime.'

'I don't go to church.' Esther set her jaw. .

The pastor took in her response. After a moment he gestured around them. 'Yet here you are enjoying nature,' he said with a genuine smile. As he turned to the trail he looked back at Esther. 'Have you made it to the lake over the sea yet?'

'Not yet.' She had it on her list of places to explore once she could borrow Lena's car.

'Don't miss your chance to go if you can. The lake runs into a waterfall that flows over a cliff into the wild sea. When you see it, it's hard to believe your eyes.'

She is filled with terror, and consumed by the black-green waves that crush and swallow her, that scream, do you know us now? All the wild waves of the sea!

Esther rubbed her arms. 'Thanks again for the tip,' she said.

The pastor waved and, with Carl, began to jog away. 'Take care of yourself, Esther.'

She packed up her coffee and uneaten sandwiches. Put her headphones back on but checked the remaining track names first. No more surprises. There was one that caught her eye. 'Heidi and Sophus' Disclaimer'. She tapped it. Heidi's giggle tumbled through her headphones. Sophus cleared his throat.

'Hi Esther,' they said in unison. 'We're adding this voice note to say that we also wanted to include songs in your playlist to remind you how much water, in all its forms, can bring you joy,' Sophus said, a smile in his voice.

'And so, without further ado,' Heidi announced.

While she walked, Esther was unable to stop herself chuckling at some of the water-themed choices Heidi and Sophus had made for the rest of her playlist. Billy Joel's 'River of Dreams'. Vanilla Ice, 'Ice Ice Baby'. Milli Vanilli's 'Blame it on the Rain'. And the song that made her stop and laugh out loud: Enya's 'Orinoco Flow'. Imagining Heidi and Sophus putting the playlist together for her filled Esther's chest with an intensity of emotion she couldn't bear to name.

Later, as she walked home with the sun at her back, Esther stopped by a field of pink flowers. She'd noticed them coming into bloom, their delicate colour striking against the vivid green of the lush grass in the fields. *They're a wetland flower. We call them reyðaakkuleya,* Flósi had told her when she'd mentioned seeing them one night after her walks. It had been a rare night when everyone was gathered around the dining table for dinner together. *In English, they're called ragged robins. Because of their untidy looks.* Wine in hand, Esther had laughed. *I know how they feel,* she'd said. *I doubt that,* Sophus had said quietly.

As the light began to soften, casting the pink flowers in gold, Esther recalled the look on Sophus' face that morning when he and Heidi had given her the playlist. She took her phone from her pocket to check the spelling. *In Aid of Esther's Accismus.* Esther opened a new browser window on her phone and tapped the word into the search bar.

Accismus. Noun. *Ak-siz-muhs.* Sixteenth-century English. *The act of feigning refusal of something truly wanted.*

42

Through the next week, Esther continued to walk. In silver rain and pale sun, under dense woollen clouds, and clear blue skies. Yearning for the sea under one foot. Guilt and missing her sister under the other. Her resolve held. Aura's journal remained closed on Esther's bedside table. Her black swan feathers and View Master stayed tucked away in her bag. Her laptop remained closed on the floor of her bedroom, her emails long neglected. She'd broken her promise to stay in touch. Salt Bay and everyone she loved there felt far away, belonging to another life. Another Esther. Jack had started leaving voice messages on her phone asking for updates, asking if she'd considered any of his suggested colleagues as potential therapists she could work with. The strain in his voice, the pleading in his messages stacked up, unanswered. In the evenings, Esther shared wine with Lena, helped Heidi with her homework and sometimes joined Flósi in his glasshouse.

One night when everyone was home, Sophus cooked again. Grilled garlic tofu with creamy potatoes, and pickled red onions on a bed of kelp noodles.

'Local recipes with a vegetarian twist,' Sophus said to Esther as he served her plate.

'No meat again?' Flósi asked, making a show of lifting his plate and checking underneath. 'At all?'

Esther grinned, clinking her chilled beer against Sophus', knowing she held his gaze for a few seconds too long.

After dinner, heavy rain started to fall. Esther curled up on the couch with Heidi and introduced her to the complete eighties series of *She-Ra*. On a pause between episodes, Heidi turned to Esther.

'I love her Sword of Protection. The power of it. Her power.'

'Me too,' Esther said.

'She reminds me a bit of Eivør.' Heidi grinned.

'I get that,' Esther agreed. 'Listening to Trøllabundin while I'm walking makes me feel the same way,' she mused.

Heidi nodded enthusiastically.

'It's a song that sounds like how I imagine She-Ra felt every time she raised her sword.' Esther lifted her arm, her hand closed in a fist around an imagined sword.

Heidi leaped off the couch, threw her head back and crowed.

'I don't get why you added "Trøllabundin" to my playlist, though – it's not about water?' Esther asked.

'Not technically,' Heidi said as she sat back on the couch. 'But it's very connected to the story of Kópakonan, the seal woman, here on the islands. Eivør sang it live when the sculpture was installed at Mikladalur. It was a big event; lots of us went and watched her perform.'

Something about a change in Heidi's tone caused Esther to listen closely. 'Lots of you?' she reiterated.

'Ja,' Heidi said excitedly. 'Sophus planned it that way, so we were all there when he and Aura—' She looked in horror at Esther. 'Sorry, Esther.'

'Heidi, it's okay. You can talk about Aura with me.'

Heidi pressed her lips together and avoided Esther's eye. She pressed the remote and a new episode of *She-Ra* started to play.

Esther waited until after Heidi had gone to bed before she went searching online. Found a clip of Eivør singing 'Trøllabundin', beating a frame drum at the base of the seal woman sculpture.

She hunched over her laptop and went through the video frame by frame, scouring the audience for any glimpse of Sophus and Aura. They were unseeable, pixellated faces.

The following morning, after a restless sleep, Esther awoke to a calm and clear sky, something she'd learned to treasure in the Faroes, a place of four-seasons-in-one-day weather. She got out of bed, driven by her need to walk, to clear her head.

Esther barrelled into the kitchen, expecting it to be empty, but found Sophus making a thermos of coffee.

'Hi,' she said.

'Morning.'

'You're up early.' She tried to keep her distance from him as she moved around the kitchen making a cup of tea.

'I hoped to catch you before you headed out. Maybe I could tempt you to not go walking today?'

Esther turned. Tried to mask her surprise. 'It'd have to be a better offer.'

'Come with me instead.' He put the lid on the thermos and offered her his smile.

She kept her tone casual. 'Where?'

He took his jacket off the back of a dining chair. 'Help me run some errands?'

'Errands,' Esther rolled her eyes with a playful smile, anything to hide her nerves. 'How could a woman resist?'

As they drove in Sophus' truck along a narrow road away from Tórshavn, Esther noticed a light on his dashboard.

'Your headlights are on,' she said.

Sophus nodded. 'It's illegal to drive day or night here without them.'

As they drove Esther sneaked furtive glances at Sophus' profile. *No one escapes the weather*, Flósi had said to her on her first visit to his glasshouse. What did Sophus know of Aura's weather? Why would he have included a song in Esther's playlist that was so bound up in his story with Aura?

'Where are we going?' she asked. An easy one. A simple start.

'Vágar,' Sophus answered.

'Where the airport is?' Esther asked, confused.

'And my aunt's village.'

'We're going to your aunt's house?'

'She's got a leak and needs to borrow my pipe wrench. After the rain.' Sophus motioned to the toolbox at Esther's feet, beside which were nestled two tall brown glass bottles of beer.

'Okkara risi. Okkara kelling,' Esther read aloud from each beer label. 'We were drinking Okkara the other night with the dinner you cooked, right?'

'Right. But not these. Risi and Kelling are Rakul's, my aunt's, favourites. They're named after the story of two famous sea stacks nórth of here, Risin and Kellingin. The giant and the witch.'

Recognising the story, Esther nodded. 'I've read about them in my guidebook. I'm starting to think these islands are made of stories as much as basalt rock.'

'Aren't all islands?' Sophus smiled at her. 'We say here that a place is its stories.'

A clear image of Queenie and Aunty Ro gathering shells from kelp in shallow water played in Esther's mind. *Sea country is women's country. Muka luna.* Aunty Ro's warm, wise voice. The paper-crinkle of her eyes when she smiled, fingers running over the garland of iridescent shells always around her neck. A pit opened in Esther's stomach and filled swiftly with the salt of homesickness.

'I can't remember the story,' she said, shaking her hair out of her face, trying to shake the feeling away. 'Tell me about the giant and the witch?'

As they drove, Sophus told Esther about Risin and Kellingin, the giant and witch from Iceland, who, in ancient times, tried to steal the Faroe Islands. One night, after travelling through stormy seas from Iceland, they reached Eiðiskollur, the mountain farthest to the northwest of the Faroes. The witch climbed the mountain and tied a rope around it for the giant who was in the sea, waiting to start dragging the islands to Iceland. But it was not easy. The witch pushed the mountain and the giant pulled, but the mountain would not move. All their efforts created too much pressure and the mountain itself cracked. The giant and the witch worked through the night, without success. They worked so hard that they were oblivious to the approaching dawn.

'Dawn was a problem?' Esther interjected.

'Of course,' Sophus said. 'Everyone knows giants, witches and trolls turn to stone if even one ray of sun falls upon them.'

'Of course,' Esther repeated.

'I guess it's a story about Faroese resilience and pride, you know, how we're a small but mighty – immovable – nation,' Sophus said. He glanced at his watch.

'You think otherwise?' Esther asked. Were they late for something? 'How does the story end?'

Sophus shrugged. 'As the witch realised daybreak was coming, she jumped from the mountain into the sea to be with the giant just as the first rays of sunrise travelled across the ocean and touched them. They turned immediately to stone, and stand there still. Some say we should remember what could have happened if the sun hadn't risen that morning. But sometimes when I see them, the sea stacks, I think it's nice. At least Risin and Kellingin are together. Not like Magnus and his girl.' He pulled up in front of a small white house with a red roof, which was nearly the same bright shade as his cheeks. 'We're here.'

'Great.' Esther's heart pounded in her ears. *At least they're together.*

Sophus took his toolbox and handed Esther the two bottles of beer to carry to the house. He hurried her to the front door, a slight look of concern on his face.

'Sophus, why are you—' Esther was cut off by singing coming from inside the house. It caused her step to falter. An unmistakable, haunting voice.

'Sophus,' Esther said, gripping his arm. He gave her a knowing, satisfied smile. As Esther continued to listen, her heart raced. She widened her eyes at him. 'That's not ... Sophus. Is it ... it sounds like it's live?' she hissed.

He opened the front door to the house, taking Esther inside to a cosy living room filled with bright light, crammed bookshelves and musical instruments. He gestured for Esther to sit. He sat beside her. Their knees were touching. The singing reverberated through the wooden frame of the house, through their bones. Esther's skin stung from the intensity of her goosebumps as she listened to the song that she'd come to know so well on her walks, being sung in the next room. That, thanks to her conversation with Heidi the night before, now reminded her of her sister with Sophus.

Esther tried to keep the moment for herself. Looked at Sophus, wishing she could make it so.

'Eivør is here?' she whispered, miming the explosion of her mind with one hand by her temple.

'It's not such a big deal for us; the islands are small in many ways. Rakul is a well-known musician and music teacher. She taught me to play the guitar when I was young,' Sophus whispered back. 'Rakul's known Eivør since she was a girl dreaming of becoming a singer. Sometimes she rehearses here.'

The power of Eivør's voice reverberated through the walls, through Esther's body.

'What's she rehearsing for?'

Sophus smiled at Esther. 'Flósi and Eivør are friends; he's convinced her to make a special appearance at our eighties night. She always draws a crowd.'

'Flósi's friends with Eivør?'

'Like I said, the islands are small.'

Esther imagined Aura in his arms, the two of them together watching Eivør perform. Did everyone know Aura? She closed her eyes before Sophus could see them shine with tears. Pretended to focus on the breathless power of Eivør's voice.

'This song is very famous here,' Sophus said.

Esther forced herself to reply. 'You don't just hear it, you feel it.'

'Once, our music was just the voice and stomping feet. Eivør's known for using the old ways in her music. That's why you can feel it, like you say. It's something your body recognises. Primal.'

Esther looked at him. She became keenly aware of their proximity to each other on the couch. Ever so slightly let the weight of her knee lean against his. 'I looked up its meaning in English. Trøllabundin. It means spellbound,' she said in a near-whisper.

He shifted closer, seemed about to answer, when the song ended in the next room. Followed by a chorus of joyful applause and a torrent of conversation in Faroese.

A cold wash of air came over Esther. Sophus stood. The spell was broken.

Esther forced a bright smile. 'So. We just happened to arrive this morning at the same time as the country's national musical treasure happened to be rehearsing at your aunt's?'

'That's about it,' Sophus said, beaming. 'Heidi told me you'd mentioned how much you love "Trøllabundin".'

She held her words behind her teeth. Bit back her regret over bringing it up with Heidi.

Esther questioned him with her eyes, wanting to ask him what the song meant to him and Aura. But then a woman bustled past the doorway to the living room. Flowing pale hair and strong stride.

'Hey, Sophus,' she called backwards, waving over her shoulder as she went by. Sophus stepped into the hallway and waved as Eivør slipped out the front door. Esther watched on, starstruck.

'Rakul,' Sophus called out. 'We're here.'

A woman called back in Faroese.

'They're in the music room,' Sophus said, gesturing for Esther to follow him.

'They?' Esther asked, head spinning.

'My mother is here too,' Sophus said with a sheepish smile.

'Any more surprises up your sleeve you care to share?'

Sophus made a pantomime of checking his shirt sleeve.

'You dag.' Esther couldn't help but laugh.

A puzzled look crossed Sophus' face as he led them out of the living room to Rakul's music room. 'What does "dag" mean?'

'Sheep shit,' Esther said.

'You're calling me sheep shit?'

'No, but we don't have time for a lesson in Australian slang.' She cordoned off sections of her heart and, despite her instincts, pushed thoughts of Sophus with Aura away. Esther wanted this day that Sophus wanted to give her.

They walked into another room. Grand piano in a corner, a few music stands, and a plush couch on which Greta sat beside a woman with the same smile and pale green eyes as her but darker hair and glasses with a thick mint-green frame. Rakul.

'Sophus,' Greta said, standing to embrace her son. Sophus hugged her.

'Rakul, this is Esther. Esther this is my aunt, Rakul.'

'Hello, Esther,' she said, offering a hand. 'Welcome to our islands.'

'Thank you.' Esther remembered to offer the Okkara beers.

'Ah, you are especially welcome when you bring my favourite beer.' Rakul boomed with laughter. She hugged Sophus. Spoke to him in Faroese. He replied, gesturing to his toolbox.

'It's good to see you again, Esther,' Greta said, coming to Esther's side. 'You look well. A glow in your face.'

Esther touched a hand to her cheek. 'Thanks, Greta. It's good to see you too.'

'You're doing well?' Greta asked. 'Sophus said you have been walking?'

'I have. The landscapes here are so beautiful. I started walking and I haven't been able to stop. I'm enjoying it so much,' Esther said.

'It gets under your skin,' Greta agreed.

A flash of the seal woman sculpture. Seal skin in hand. Of Liden Gunver in Copenhagen. Aura in Sophus' arms.

'Have you been for a swim yet?' Greta asked, enthusiastically.

Out of the corner of her eye, Esther saw Sophus looking over a piece of knitting laid over the back of an armchair. 'No.' She briefly met Greta's eye and shook her head.

'Rakul is one of the women you saw swimming with me that morning. So, now you know you have two friends in the sea waiting for you.' Greta smiled warmly.

Esther tried to return the smile.

'You dropped a stitch,' Sophus said to Greta, pointing at the knitting.

'No,' she retorted, 'I did not.' She tsked at him.

'You did.' He unpacked the pipe wrench from his toolbox. 'Rakul, do you need me to help you with the leak?'

Rakul shook her head. 'I can fix it.' Sophus nodded, closed his toolbox.

'Do you two want to stay for lunch? We've made enough for four just in case,' Greta offered.

Esther opened her mouth to accept but Sophus answered first. 'We have to keep going; I've got to check on the boat after the rain.'

There was a twinkle in Rakul's eye. 'Will we see you at knitting circle tomorrow night?'

Sophus shook his head as he headed for the door. 'Too much to do for eighties night. You're coming, right?'

Rakul murmured something to Greta in Faroese, then turned back to Sophus. 'Of course.'

'Good.' Sophus turned to Esther. 'Ready?'

'Sure,' Esther replied. 'Really nice to see you both,' she said to Sophus' mother and aunt.

'And you, Esther,' Rakul said, linking arms with Greta.

Esther followed Sophus out to his truck. 'You didn't want to stay for lunch?' she asked as she put on her seatbelt. 'Also, you have your own boat?'

'I packed us a picnic and thought we could eat it by the lake,' Sophus said as he put the truck in reverse. 'And yes, we inherited the boat from a regular at Flóvin. I can show you later.'

They pulled up at the lake Esther had passed in the bus on her first day in the Faroes.

'Is this the lake with two names?' she asked Sophus.

'Ja. Leitisvatn and Sørvágsvatn,' he answered.

Esther observed the peaks in the distance and the far end of the lake, the point where Pastor Jaspur had told her it looked like it was floating. *The lake runs into a waterfall that flows over a cliff into the wild sea.*

'I've been told to come here,' Esther said as Sophus parked.

'It's a tourist hot spot,' Sophus said. 'Everyone hikes to go and see the optical illusion on the other side, where the lake looks like it hangs over the ocean. That's probably what you've heard, right? It's impressive. But sometimes I think simplicity can be impressive too.' Sophus reached for a bag stowed behind their seats.

They walked from his truck to a bench with a view of the lake spread out before them, a calm mirror of the world. Reflections of the sky, mountains and the occasional raven flying overhead obscured everything beneath. Sophus unpacked his bag in the space between them.

'I think I got this right,' he said. 'Cheese sandwiches and dried strawberries. That's what you take walking, right? Oh, and those fancy chocolates you like. From the chocolatier in town.' He turned back to the bag and retrieved a thermos. 'And coffee. Of course.'

Esther's stomach flip-flopped. 'You know what I take walking for lunch?'

'It's not hard to pay attention,' Sophus said simply. 'Plus, there's not many Australians wandering around Tórshavn right now visiting the local chocolate shop saying they're staying with the "blokes" who run Flóvin. I'm friends with the owners, and they told me you always buy the same double-dipped chocolates.' He smiled effortlessly.

'What would you have done if I'd said no and not come?' Esther countered.

'Luckily,' Sophus said, 'I love cheese sandwiches. And chocolate.'

His loveliness grated against a sharpness in her chest. Esther toyed with her sandwich, appetite gone. 'Why did you ask me to come with you today?'

Sophus glanced at her and then out to the lake. 'I wanted to spend some time with you. I've been distant since you came to stay with us and not a good host. I wanted to make up for that.'

'I … um …' Esther stumbled. She hadn't been expecting a direct answer.

'Ja?'

'Nothing.' Esther shook her head. 'That's nice of you, Sophus. This is nice. Thank you.' She clenched her jaw. Swallowed the words down. *Fuck your sandwiches and chocolates and fuck your beautiful mum and aunt, and fuck everyone knowing everyone on these fucking beautiful islands and fuck you for loving my sister first.*

'You're welcome,' Sophus said.

They finished their lunch. Drank their thermos of coffee. When Esther stood to stretch and take in the full view of the lake, she turned.

'Holy shit,' she said. 'What's that?' Around a bend in the shore, rising from the lake behind them, was a sculpture of a large horse, made of stones within wire caging, rearing out of the water on its hind quarters. Esther pressed a hand to her heart.

'The Nix,' Sophus said loudly.

Esther glanced around to see who he was booming at.

'If you say his name, he can't take us under,' Sophus explained. 'The Nix is a water creature that can transform into many shapes, mostly to trick you and steal you from shore to drag you deep into the lake. The only way to save yourself is to say his name. Once his name is said aloud, you take all his power away.'

'If only,' Esther said under her breath. 'You like your cheery stories here, don't you?'

Sophus chuckled. 'The Nix tricked two children into thinking he was a horse and tried to take them under. One of their names was Niklas; by accident the other child called out, "Nix", and that's how we came to learn the way to break the spell if The Nix ever gets hold of you.'

Esther looked at the horse sculpture rising from the lake. A warning of what can lie beneath calm water.

A jewelled moth wing flashed in Esther's mind.

On their drive to the harbour, Esther kept her eyes fixed on the views through her window. Jade-green fjords. Moored boats. Sheep. Craggy mountains, tumbling, ever crumbling, into the sea. Otherworldly hues she knew no names for, somewhere between silver and blue.

Sophus broke their silence. 'You're quiet. Are you okay?'

Esther nodded.

'Do you still want to come with me to check *The Terminator?*'

'Sorry?' Esther raised a brow. '*The Terminator?*'

'Our boat. I lost a bet: Flósi got to name her, and Heidi got to choose what colour we repainted her.'

'Well, obviously, I'm coming with you to see this boat.'

The witch pushed and the giant pulled but the mountain would not move. All their pushing and pulling created too much pressure and the mountain itself cracked. Esther imagined it, the cracking, going through her insides.

At the harbour, Esther followed Sophus past rows of boats. Until, ahead, she glimpsed a bobbing red and pink hull. The thought of Flósi naming it *The Terminator*, the thought of Heidi choosing a pink and red colour palette, the thought of Sophus honouring his lost bet with them was almost unbearably endearing. She was entitled to none of it. To none of them.

Sophus crossed the gangway to the floating jetty and greeted a group passing by, who laughed playfully at him and kept walking. Sophus looked to Esther, standing at the edge of the harbour. '*The Terminator* is slow, has sails and is pink; people either shake their heads or laugh when they see us coming,' he explained. 'But we have a lived-by rule here: if you have a boat, you must use it. So that's what we do.'

'You don't fish?' Esther asked.

'No. *The Terminator* is for joy rides only. We take her out when the weather is good to get off the land for a while and remember our sea legs.'

Esther stayed where she was on solid ground and walked back and forth to get a better view of the retro font painted in strawberry red along the sherbet-pink body of the boat. *The Terminator*. Painted across the bow were red hot lips and a pair of lashy, coquettish eyes.

'Take a tour inside if you want while I check her over?' Sophus called as he stepped on board.

Esther closed her sweaty palms into fists. 'I'm fine here.'

While Sophus checked the motor and sails, Esther took in the sights and sounds around the harbour. Families walking the waterfront, enjoying the calm, still afternoon. Occasional laughter. Boats coming in full of tourists in matching life jackets. She crouched by the harbour edge and stared into the water, releasing a small gasp when she spotted an orange starfish clinging to one of the jetty pontoons, like a splayed hand. She and Tom had been kids when Jack had taken them to the south coast for a weekend Space Club trip. They'd watched the stars at night and combed the rockpools in the low morning tides. Jack had bellowed with childlike wonder when he'd spotted a tiny sea star and lifted it on his fingernail to show Esther and Tom. *It feeds on the algae that's on the surface of the rockpools, kids, and do you know how? By pushing its stomach out through its mouth and eating.* Tom had nudged Esther, his face full of awe. *Your dad is so cool.*

'Dad,' she whispered, her mouth souring with self-loathing. 'I miss you.'

'Esther,' Sophus called.

She stood and turned to him.

'Let's go out,' he said. 'Let me take you out for a short ride.'

'No.' She shook her head. 'I don't go into the sea, Sophus.' Her fingertips twitched with longing.

'We're not going into the sea. Just out on it. You might enjoy seeing where you've been all this time in Tórshavn from a different perspective?' Sophus offered. 'We don't often get such calm conditions.' He swept an arm towards the sky.

She rocked from foot to foot.

Sophus held her gaze. 'You'll be safe,' he said.

Before she could fully acknowledge to herself what she was doing, Esther started walking towards the gangway. Stepped onto the floating jetty. Walked to where *The Terminator* was anchored. Didn't look down.

Sophus reached out a hand to her. 'You're safe,' he said.

She glanced back at the starfish beneath the water. *In the North Atlantic, starfish can regenerate their own arms, which they can lose when they're trying to hide from or escape threat.* But, Jack had told Esther and Tom, his eyes twinkling, *maybe even more incredible is that if the severed arm is not harmed, it can not only heal but also completely regenerate and create a genetically identical starfish.*

Esther took Sophus' hand and stepped on shaky legs from land to sea.

The seventh skin: Homecoming

As she was above, so she is below.
So she is below, as she was above.

43

Under a bright sky, they motored out of the harbour and followed the waterfront. Sophus sat by the engine, steering the rudder. Esther sat to one side, looking back at the mustard, red, white, navy harbour buildings receding in the distance. She leaned back. Small waves broke at the bow, peeling away from the boat, whitewash like curls of torn paper on the dark glass of the sea.

'*The Terminator* is great,' Esther said to Sophus.

'I think so too. She only has a four-stroke motor so she's slow compared to others in the harbour, and she has sails that we never use. But she goes well. We have fun with her in the summer. Take her out when the wind lets us. Flósi and Heidi love her.'

'I can see why,' Esther said.

For a while they puttered along, quiet. Esther watched gulls flying over sea, their wings catching the light. Sophus pointed out Sandagerð, where Esther had seen Greta, Rakul and their friends swimming on her first morning in Tórshavn. Patches of colour clung to black rock in the distance where spring wildflowers were in bloom. White ribbons of thin, unnamed waterfalls cascaded from mossy green and black cliffs to turquoise and indigo sea.

After a while, the sensory loss of solid ground beneath her made Esther's head spin. She squeezed her eyes shut, but it was too late. Questions she couldn't push out to sea engulfed her, a set of relentless waves. Where was Aura's body? What had happened to her sister's smile? Her eyes? Her elegant hands. The spatter of freckles along one collarbone. How could she have left Esther behind? *Wait for me, sister, wait for me.* Esther swallowed down the swell inside her and didn't soften her grip of the sideboard until they turned and began a slow idle back towards the harbour. Even then, her knuckles stayed white.

As the engine quietened, Esther looked at Sophus. He smiled at her. She didn't smile in return. Her sister's name filled her mouth. Pressed against her teeth.

'Did you bring Aura out in this boat?' Esther asked quietly.

Sophus looked away. Across to Nólsoy. Up at the soft clouds. Eventually he nodded.

'Tell me about my sister.' Esther sat across from him, gripping the edge of the boat as they rocked on the water, the sky throwing gold over their heads. The look on Sophus' face suggested he knew it wasn't a request; it was time.

He exhaled. 'Where do you want me to start?'

'I don't know what I don't know, so start wherever you want.'

Sophus rubbed a hand over his jaw. 'I've been thinking about how to have this conversation with you. It feels important to say first, before anything else, that Aura intended to tell you this herself. Her story.'

Esther sucked in a breath as if she'd been winded.

'If this is too hard—'

'No.' Esther shook her head. 'That's why I'm here.' The weight of the truth sank through her. 'To find out what my sister kept from me. To try to understand what took her from me.' Her voice cracked. 'Start anywhere, Sophus. Just tell me. Please.'

He nodded, and continued to nod, as if winding up courage to speak. 'When Aura was fifteen,' he began.

'Fifteen?' Esther echoed, confused.

Sophus went on. 'When Aura was fifteen, she went to a party. Her first big high school party.'

Nin and Aura scurrying down the hallway, giddy, arms entwined as Tina Turner and Cher. 'I remember,' Esther said.

'She had a big crush on the guy whose house the party was at. He was a couple of years older than Aura. They'd met and had been hanging out for a while.'

Esther drew a blank at first. Until Aura's heart-dotted handwriting in her journal came to mind. *I kiss River!!! Which I'm going to do at his 80s party tonight.*

'She left the party with him at some point in the night and went to a special beach where you grew up. Seven boulders. A secret sea?'

'A hidden lagoon,' Esther murmured, gazing over the side of the boat into the water, seeing the curve of the bay at home. Aura with her backpack when they were kid~~n. *I'm going to the water to cast a spell for my selkie sisters.*~~

'Aura went to the hidden lagoon with this guy. They had sex. Her first time.'

Esther looked sharply at Sophus.

'She was very clear: it was consensual.'

Esther picked at the skin on the underside of her wrist.

'After they'd been hanging out, and then slept together at his party, Aura thought this guy had the same kind of feelings for her. But back at school, he ignored her, and soon he was with someone else. Aura said the pain of his rejection changed her. She tried to be her usual self. After a couple of months, she was starting to do okay. Then one night she went and stayed at her best friend's house. Nin?' The colour had begun to drain from Sophus' face.

'Nin,' Esther confirmed.

'She was at Nin's and in the middle of the night, she woke up in pain and started to bleed. Nin's mother, the doctor, she got Aura to hospital.' Sophus took a moment. 'That's where she found out she was pregnant and miscarrying her baby.'

Esther went still.

'There were complications. The hospital had to call your parents for permission to do surgery to save her life; Aura was underage.' Sophus hung his head. Rubbed his hands together. 'After surgery, the doctors told Aura that the complications with her miscarriage had been serious. They weren't sure it would be possible for her to have children.' He glanced up at Esther. 'They discharged her, she went home with your parents, and tried to go back to her normal life.'

He paused, giving Esther space to speak.

She stared at him, every one of his words blowing apart the carefully constructed compartments in her heart. Allowed herself time to find her voice. 'I don't know anything about this.'

'Aura made your parents promise they'd never tell you.'

'No,' Esther said quietly. She shook her head.

'I can only imagine how much this hurts to hear. Try to remember she was only fifteen, Esther. Heidi's age.'

Heidi's age. Esther's vision watered with quick, rolling tears. She flicked them away.

'Aura's teens were suddenly over. In one night, she went through a physical trauma that she was told would affect the rest of her life. All because she'd had a crush, gone to her first high school party and hooked up for her first time with the boy she liked. She carried the pain of being used and the aftermath of the miscarriage alone. Never told the boy. He finished school, left town. But Aura lived with what had happened between them every day. Carried it in her body. In what she'd been told her body might not be able to do again in her future.'

A searing pain went through Esther's chest. She squeezed her hands into fists. Light travelled over the sea, revealing the world as it went. Esther took a breath. Imagined the lungful of salty air going down her throat, into her lungs, turning muscle and tissue to stone.

'Aura talked about you every day. I felt like I knew you, before I knew you. She talked about hiding this part of her life from you. Had the fear we all have of disappointing the people we love the most. She didn't want you to think less of her, Esther. She didn't want to let you down. She wanted to stay as she'd always been for you. The older one. Brave. Strong.'

Esther didn't move. Didn't speak.

'Do you remember what she was like before that party?' Sophus asked.

Her seal sister at fifteen: playful, curious, magical. Fire under her skin and an unsatisfied hunger for life. Wild, smart, powerful. Heart-shaped sunglasses, kohl eyeliner, chipped nail polish, army boots. Necklaces made of plastic charms and sherbet candy.

'She was heavenly,' Esther whispered.

Sorrow weighed on Sophus' face. 'Do you remember a change in her around that age? Sometime after she went to that party?' His voice was raw. Tender.

Esther's senses flooded with the scent of blue gums. Sitting in the stargazing shack, watching the sky. Jack pointing out the southern old lady moths, hidden in the shadows. *Maybe you just weren't seeing what was right in front of you, Starry.*

'Esther?' Sophus asked.

She frowned as a memory surfaced, one she couldn't clearly recall.

'Their wing markings look like heartbeats,' she murmured.

'Their wings?' Sophus asked, his voice sounding far away.

A vague hospital memory. The garish light, the beeping machine, its green jagged line. Aura lying in bed, sleeping.

Esther sucked in a deep breath. Breathed out. 'Sophus.' She focused on his face. He searched her eyes, held her hands.

'You're safe,' he said.

Cold Chisel singing about flame trees at Aura's memorial. Esther clicking through a reel on a View-Master labelled *The Teens*. *Click*. Aura, a freckled teenager, her open, joyous face. *Click*. Aura, her arms wrapped round her knees, face turned away. *Click.* Aura looking straight at the camera, eyes piercing. The difference in one reel.

Memories kept coming. Thick and fast. Hushed conversations between Freya and Jack, after Aura dropped out of uni, which stop the minute Esther walks into a room. Aura and Freya with their heads bent together, walking to the sea. Aura on her twenty-first birthday, dressed as the Princess of Fantasia, calling with manic, drunken joy to her friends, *Say my name.* The day they all drive her to the airport, colour in her face, a sparkle finally returned to her eyes. *I'll find Agnete for you, Starry.* Three years later, she comes home from Denmark, all the colour and sparkle gone.

'Sophus, what happened to her here? Why did she come home so broken? Why did she leave me?' Esther asked him.

He looked at her, tormented. Held her hands.

'Tell me,' she urged.

'Esther,' Sophus stalled.

She squeezed his hands. 'Tell me.'

'It happened not long after we met. Only a few months. After she came to the Faroes.'

'What did, what happened?'

Sophus sighed. 'Aura fell pregnant. With our baby.'

Esther's hands went slack in his.

'I was overwhelmed. We'd been careful.'

She took her hands back into her lap.

'Aura told me straight away she wanted to keep it. The doctors here told us there were risks, there always are, but that Aura was healthy. That's when Aura told me what happened to her when she was a teenager. What it meant to her that we'd conceived. Our baby was a miracle. Aura's joy was up here,' Sophus said, gesturing above his head. 'Her happiness was infectious. Those weeks were the best I had with her. It was like she sprinkled fairy dust on everyone she crossed paths with.'

Esther chewed on the inside of her cheek until she tasted blood.

'I loved her. I knew that. I just didn't know if I was ready for a baby. But Aura was so sure of us becoming parents that I got swept up in her certainty. That's when I proposed to her. Whenever I asked her about her family at home, she didn't say much. As I've said, she talked about you every day. I had no clue she'd cut ties. I can only guess it's because it might have been too much for her, trying to hold her past and future at once, there and here.'

Esther looked up at the fairy floss sky. 'The baby?' Her breathing shallowed. A cold sweat formed on her top lip.

Sophus pressed his hands together at his mouth. 'We had a daughter.' His voice was hoarse. Esther held a dreadful breath. 'She was stillborn,' Sophus said.

Light travelled over the sea. Revealed the world. Turned skin to stone.

'After the funeral, Aura stayed for as long as she could. But we were no good. Nothing was any good anymore.' Sophus wiped his eyes. 'We didn't know each other well enough to go through something so hard and so personal. We both suffered loss, but each of us differently. I was heartbroken, I grieved. I grieve still. But it didn't bring up past trauma for me. The loss and grief were visceral for Aura. It had happened in her body, to her body, again. Pain consumed her. We stopped being able to have simple conversations without them turning into arguments. I couldn't talk to her. I couldn't get her to talk to me. I wasn't an angel either, I'm sure. I didn't know what to do to help her. Us. She couldn't tell me what she needed. She didn't know. I didn't know what to say. It was like I was watching her slowly disappear right in front of me. It went on that way until I came home from work one day, and she was gone. She just left. Went home. To you. Our last conversation was about something stupid, an argument over what we were having for dinner. We never spoke again. I tried. She wouldn't answer any of my calls, emails. I didn't have your address in Tasmania. I had to let her go. I didn't know anything about Aura until Klara rang me from

London a couple of months ago and told me you'd reached out to her. That's when I found out ... Aura was gone.'

Esther put her face in her clammy hands. Breathed through the knots and spasms in her stomach.

'When you showed up at Flóvin that day ... when I saw you ...'

Though she clenched her jaw against them, the waves of nausea Esther had been fighting tore through her body, hot and urgent. She scrambled for the side of the boat and vomited. Cried out against the burn in her throat.

Sophus was by her side. Held back her hair. 'You're okay,' he said.

'I'm fine.' Esther spat into the sea. 'I want to go back. I want to go back.'

'Okay.' He wrapped an arm around her. 'Here,' he said, as he took his seat by the motor, gesturing to a space by his side for her.

'I'm fine,' Esther repeated. Wiped her mouth. Stayed where she was.

As they motored back to the harbour, Esther yearned for darkness and stars instead of the bright northern night sky.

When they got home, Esther followed Sophus through the sheep happily gathering to greet them in the front garden.

'Not now, girls,' he said softly, patting them gently out of the way.

Inside, Esther took her coat off. Slowly. Every movement felt burdened.

'Are you okay?' Sophus asked her as he hung their coats.

'I'm fine.'

'Can I get you anything?'

'I want to show you something.'

'Okay,' he said. 'We'll have privacy in my room. Go ahead.

I'll make some coffee to warm up. Unless you want tea? With
some honey for your throat?'
   Esther nodded.
   While Sophus was in the kitchen, Esther went to her room
for Aura's journal. Walked down the hall to Sophus' bedroom
door. Something she'd imagined herself doing night after night,
as she lay awake, but in very different circumstances. At the
sound of laughter ringing through the house, Esther paused
in the hallway, listening as Heidi regaled Sophus with stories
Esther couldn't understand; the jubilation in her Faroese was
unmistakable.
   Try to remember she was only fifteen, Esther. Heidi's age.
   Esther pressed a hand to the wall to steady herself. Clutched
Aura's journal to her chest. She opened Sophus' bedroom door,
closed it behind her. Felt the wall for the switch and squinted as
her eyes adjusted to the lamplight.
   His bedroom was neat. Minimal. Cosy. A double bed. A
single armchair. Small coffee table aside. A full bookshelf. An
open wardrobe of folded jeans and woollen jumpers. One hung
over the back of the armchair. Esther ran her fingers over it.
Lifted it to her face and inhaled the smell of his shampoo, the
sea and bar smoke. She made herself put it down. Turned to the
window where some of Flósi's whittled sheep almost made her
smile until she saw that they sat on the sill gathered beside a line
of pastel-pink queen scallop shells.

Esther listening to the clacking sound as Aura collects scallop
shells from the shore in Salt Bay. Aura's just turned thirteen, a
threshold Esther can't see but at almost ten years old can feel.
They've gone to the beach together. Aura's suggestion, an
increasingly rare occurrence. On the cooling sand, light molten,
skin warm, they've fallen into the rhythms of childhood with
each other. Combing the shore, squawking with delight at
discoveries. Neptune pearls. Swan feathers. Blue gum seed pods.
When Aura unearths a pastel-pink scallop shell from the white

sand with her toe, Esther, who's been keenly watching, can't stop herself from begging.

'Tell me the story, Aura,' she repeats over and again. 'Please.'

With a deadpan expression but a great flourish of her hand, Aura clears her throat. 'Once upon a time,' she declares, cloaking herself in washed-up fronds of bronze kelp yet to be fully sundried.

Esther claps. They aren't so different. Her big sister isn't outgrowing her.

'The sea was full of white scallop shells,' Aura continues. 'One day a white scallop got stuck on shore at low tide, before dawn. She panicked, but no matter what she did, the scallop couldn't reach the water.' Aura pauses, lifts the scallop shell in her hand. 'As the sun rose, the scallop was so frightened she snapped her shell shut, fearing danger. Fearing the worst. But after a while, when nothing had happened, the scallop opened her shell. Found she'd been carried back to sea on a new tide where all the other scallops were cheering for her return and exclaiming over her shell.'

Esther knows her part. 'Why were they cheering? Why were they cheering?' she chants.

Aura weaves gum twigs together into a garland. 'Because,' she says, 'the little scallop had been brave and returned from the great unknown. But not only for that reason. Oh no.' The delicious pause. The garland complete. Aura wedges a pink scallop shell between two entwined twigs. 'It was because the sunrise had painted the little scallop's shell all the colours of the first light of day. A reminder forever of her courage.' Aura walks to Esther, cheeks dimpling as she grins. 'From then on, that brave little scallop was known as Queen.' Aura lowers the garland on Esther's hair and holds her face close. They rub noses, giggling.

Esther stands and roars. 'Ra-Ra and Starry.'

Aura throws her arms in the air and crows. 'Sisters of Seal and Swan Skins.'

And together: 'Raise your swords and your voices!'

Two sisters run, ever wild. Along the sea in cloak and crown.

~

Another peal of Heidi's laughter wafted through the house. Esther blinked. Stared at the sill and counted the seven pink scallop shells fanned against the glass. An instinct, a knowing washed over her: Aura had collected the shells. For Sophus. She was everywhere.

She didn't want you to think less of her, Esther. She didn't want to let you down. She wanted to stay as she'd always been for you. The older one. Brave. Strong.

'Ra-Ra,' Esther said aloud, her mouth puckering.

She looked back to the bookshelf. The wardrobe. The bed. Where Aura had lived, breathed, loved. Grieved.

'You are everywhere,' Esther whispered. 'And nowhere.'

'Sorry I took so long,' Sophus said as he opened the door with two steaming cups in hand. 'Heidi had an eventful day at school and was like a wind-up toy.'

Esther kept her back to him as she pushed the tears from her cheeks. Turned when she was ready. 'No worries,' she mumbled. Took her tea from him, nodded in thanks.

Sophus sat on the end of his bed and cradled his coffee in his hands. Esther sat, keeping her distance. She put Aura's journal on the bed beside her.

'What do you need right now, Esther?' Sophus faced her with an intent expression. 'Is there anything I can do?'

She set her tea on the sill, away from the scallop shells. Picked up Aura's journal and turned to Sophus with it in hand, an offering. His face smarted at the sight.

'You can tell me about the seven stories my sister collected in this book, and her seven tattoos.'

44

Although it was early in the morning, the sky had shed its brief night skin by the time Sophus drove them north in his truck. Esther sneaked a sidelong glance at him, silhouetted against emerging views of silver ocean and green fjords through his window. The sun was high and filled the cab of his truck with warm light. Around them, the mountainous islands to the northeast of Tórshavn towered from the metallic sea, lined with gold by the sun. Esther's first views of the dramatic, isolated and unforgiving peaks through her plane window came back to her. The spines of ancient sleeping giants. Jack's voice in her ear: *To reach the treasure she seeks, our hero must first get past the dragon.* Esther's was shaky with fatigue. How was he feeling? She glanced again at Sophus. He took a sip of coffee from his thermos.

'Will we make the ferry?' she asked.

He nodded. Looked as haggard as Esther felt. They'd stayed up most of the night talking, going through Aura's journal.

'Her teenage diary,' Sophus had said, sitting beside Esther on his bed. A small smile at She-Ra on the cover, sword raised. A heavy sigh, bewildered, as he turned through the pages. 'I can't believe this is back in my hands, again. This piece of her. From when she was here.'

Esther watched him closely, envy burning holes through her for memories he had of Aura that she didn't.

'She showed it to me after we'd conceived. After she'd told me about her first pregnancy.' The tenderness in his fingertips as he traced Aura's handwriting turned a screw in Esther's chest.

'Aura stopped writing in it after the party when she was fifteen. I remember asking her why she'd kept it all this time. She said she didn't want to forget who she was before her life changed. Said she wanted to keep the teenager that she was once close to her.' Sophus cradled the journal in his hands. 'I think that desire is also where her seven fairytales and tattoos came from,' he said.

'She got her tattoos because of what happened when she was a teenager?' Esther's heart began to pound.

Sophus shook his head, unsure. 'Maybe. The stories come from her dissertation at university, seven fairytales about women, water and transformation. They came to mean so much more to her than research. These stories,' Sophus said, thumbing through the latter half of Aura's journal, 'spoke to her and for her. That's why she was inspired to write her own line for each one. And why she wanted her words tattooed on her body.' He stopped on the page with the seal woman sculpture. 'She talked often about growing up watching your mum change women's lives through decorating their skin. Once she got the idea of connecting the fairytales with her story and tattoos, it became unstoppable. She became unstoppable.'

Esther nodded, pained by sweeping recognition. 'That's exactly what she was like once she set her heart to something.'

He turned to the fifth image and stopped on Kópakonan. The seal woman. '"What was stolen can never really be taken",' he read. Shook his head sadly. 'She was obsessed with this story.'

'She always loved seals. Selkies. They were part of her sense of self.' Esther told Sophus about following Aura out of her room when they were kids, the night she'd run away to the sea to cast a spell to call to her selkie sisters. And the Selkie Tree in Aura's teenage years. 'It's no wonder though. Aura was born into seal stories.'

'She told me about this, when she explained where your Seal and Swan Sisters game came from. Aura was born in summer, at the same time as the seal pups, right?' Sophus asked.

Esther nodded.

'And you were born in winter. With the swans.'

'Aura Sæl. Esther Svane. Our ancestry on Mum's side is Danish. And Celtic. Big pagan energy.'

The intensity in Sophus' eyes fuelled Esther's chatty delirium.

'When we were kids we used to call each other Séala and Eala. Always thinking we were calling each other "seal" and "swan" in Irish. I only recently found out that instead of the mammal, séala means "fixture". As in "to seal a window". Turns out we spent our lives running around calling each other the window sealant and the swan.' Esther tried to laugh but her voice fell flat. She glanced at Sophus. The intensity in his eyes was gone. His face had paled. 'Sorry,' she mumbled, not knowing what she was apologising for.

Sophus didn't seem to hear her. He looked down at Aura's open journal. 'Esther, do you know this story? Ours, of Kópakonan?'

'Your standard selkie fairytale. Right? About a seal woman who comes to shore, sheds her seal skin to take human form and has it stolen by a fisherman.'

'It's a little bit different.' Sophus didn't meet her eye. 'In our culture, selkies are humans who end their lives by drowning in the sea.'

Esther stilled.

'After death, they take on the form of seals and can only become human again when they come back to shore and shed their seal skins. That can happen on just one night a year, on the eve of Three Kings, when rules and social orders don't apply. There's playing, singing and dancing, but just until the sun rises.'

Sophus went on, telling Esther about a young farmer from the village of Mikladalur on the island of Kalsoy, who once heard about a nearby cave where it was said that the selkies came to shore and shed their skins.

'On the next eve of Three Kings, the farmer went to the cave where he hid and waited. After a while, he watched in amazement as a large bob of seals swam close to land, peeking their dark, black eyes above the waves to make sure it was safe to emerge from the sea. One by one the selkies came to shore, shed their seal skins and walked in human form on the sand. There were more than the young farmer could count, male and female, young and old, a huge family, all taking part in singing, dancing and revelry. That's when a seal approached the rock he was hiding behind, and, not seeing him there, took off her seal skin, transforming into a beautiful young woman. As the young farmer watched her run off to play with the others, he decided. "This woman will be mine." From his hiding place, he stole her seal skin and continued to wait. At dawn, when all the selkies slipped their seal skins back on and hurried into the sea, the young woman couldn't find her skin. She searched for it, panicking as the sun rose, while the other seals called for her from the water. In that horrible moment, the young farmer came out from his hiding place, carrying her seal skin. She was trapped. There was no other choice but to go with him. Back to his village, his house, where the young farmer locked the woman's seal skin in a heavy wooden chest and attached the key to his belt which he wore every day.

'The farmer and young woman married and had children. She did her best to adjust to her life on land as a housewife and mother. But every day she went to the sea. Where, every day, a large male seal was seen swimming close to shore as if to greet her. Her life went on this way until one day, the farmer went fishing and forgot to take the key to the wooden chest with him. When he got home from sea in a panic, his children were sitting alone in the house, not answering when he asked where their mother was. He noticed the fire had been put out and the sharp knives had been put out of reach so the children would not come to harm. He found the chest, open and empty, and immediately knew his selkie wife would never come home.

'Time passed. One night, before the farmer was due to go seal hunting with other men from Mikladalur, his selkie wife came to him in a dream. She begged him to spare the lives of the large male seal guarding a grotto, and the two pups inside. Her mate and sons. When the farmer woke, he didn't heed the selkie's plea in his dream. The first seal he slaughtered was the large male guarding the grotto. The hunting party killed every seal they found in the cave. Including two pups the farmer clubbed to death in his rage. Back on land that night the village came together to feast on seal meat. Just as they were about to start eating, the selkie raged upon their banquet in the form of a wailing spirit. When she saw the head of her mate and the flippers of her pups on platters, she let out a terrible shriek of grief and damned the farmer, the whole village and every future descendant.

'As revenge for their unforgivable cruelty to her kin, the selkie cursed people from the village to drown at sea until the dead would be able to hold hands and reach around the island of Kalsoy.' Sophus ran his hand over the image of Kópakonan in Aura's journal. 'After this sculpture was installed, it caused some upset.'

'Why?' Esther asked, shaken by the story.

'Kópakonan was stolen from the sea, enslaved by her captor, or "husband", and had two land children, but all she wanted was to return to the sea. To herself and her kind. Some people feel that Kópakonan should be facing the ocean, not the village.'

Esther looked at the image of the selkie sculpture in Aura's journal, remembering the moment she'd had in the harbour café, feeling struck by her perception of the sculpture as empowered. The grip of Kópakonan's hand holding her seal skin. The set of her jaw. Her naked body stepping over rock, the sea and mountains at her back, her gaze on the village of Mikladalur. The thought that she'd been disempowered, again, facing land rather than the home she longed to return to, brought tears to Esther's eyes.

She looked at Aura's handwriting, imagined the loopy lettering inked into Aura's skin. The first tattoo Freya had given her. Esther ached with a yearning to understand.

'Did you tell Aura this story too?' Esther asked.

Sophus shook his head. 'Nei. She knew about it before we met in Copenhagen. It was one of the first things we ever talked about when we met at Klara's exhibition, the story of Kópakonan. Aura asked me if I had webbed toes. I couldn't tell if she was joking.' The hint of a smile flickered over Sophus' face.

'Why would she ask you that?'

'Sorry. That's the last part of the story. The children the selkie had with the farmer grew up and had children of their own. To this day people say we can see who has descended from the seal woman when someone is born with webbed toes. Evidence, they say, that we carry the blood of seals in our veins.'

Esther resisted the question. 'Is that why you took Aura to the seal woman sculpture to see Eivør play?' she asked instead.

Sophus looked at her, caught off guard.

'Heidi told me,' she explained. 'You took Aura to Mikladalur when the sculpture was installed. Eivør sang "Trøllabundin". It was a big ceremony. A commemoration. For the village. Also, for you and Aura. But I don't know why, or of what.'

Sophus ran his hands roughly over his face. He didn't look at Esther. 'I took her there to propose. After Aura told me we were pregnant. Later, we went to Copenhagen to buy a ring. That's where Klara took our photo, that one you found on her website. Aura wrote her line inspired by Kópakonan after we got back from Copenhagen. And her remaining verses.'

Esther took Aura's journal from him and snapped through the pages as images of Aura and Sophus together clouded her mind. The journal had become a blur. She'd studied every page, each line, so closely that she couldn't see clearly what was right in front of her. A paragraph in her guidebook about winter in the Faroes came to mind. *Be mindful of 'snow blindness', pain and discomfort in the eyes caused by exposure to too much ultraviolet light.*

Sophus put his hand over hers, stopping her again on the Kópakonan page. 'Aura was rewriting her story, Esther.' He pointed to the line. '"What was stolen can't really be taken."'

'You can say it as many times as you like. I don't understand it,' Esther said. 'I don't know what any of it means.'

'Our baby was what Aura had been told was impossible; everything she thought had been taken from her had returned.' Sophus turned the page and pointed to Violanta. '"Know me now, I am the wild wave." All Violanta wanted was to get to the sea and, when she did, it destroyed her,' Sophus said. 'All Aura wanted was to live free of the shame and guilt of her teenage pregnancy. And she got there. In Copenhagen. Here, with me. She turned the tide. She was the wild wave.' Sophus looked at Esther. 'All of this, the fairytales, the tattoos, it was Aura's way of remaking what she'd lost. Of being her own key, chest and seal skin. That's why she loved Kópakonan so much, and why our seal woman story inspired her to gather these seven fairytales in her teenage journal, to honour the teenage skin she lost, and to write her own tattoos. It gave Aura strength and resilience.'

Later, after Sophus fell asleep on his bed, Esther stayed awake, sitting in his armchair with her sister's journal, going through Aura's teenage handwriting, her love hearts, her seven stories and seven tattoos. *Her own key, chest and seal skin.*

At some point in the early hours of the morning, Esther fell into shallow sleep, neck at a crooked angle. Until a terrible shriek in her dreams startled her awake.

'Esther?' Across the room Sophus' voice was thick with sleep. 'You okay?'

She sat up, shaky with fatigue. 'I need to see her. Kópakonan.'

Sophus stretched. Rubbed his eyes. 'Okay,' he said, reaching for his jumper and keys. 'I'll take you.'

Esther turned from the sea to Sophus again as they drove. It was every little thing: his focus on the road to take her where she needed to go. The way he tucked that curl of hair behind his ear when he was deep in thought. The look in his eyes whenever he saw her, a mix of surprise and joy. The lives he'd lost: his baby's, Aura's, his own – meant to have been lived out with Aura. Esther saw her sister wrapped in his arms, together in Klara's photo, standing in front of Liden Gunver. The love and happiness in Aura's face. She'd known then she was pregnant. And had accepted Sophus' proposal. Unlike Liden Gunver, she'd found her way to the surface.

'Nearly there,' Sophus said. Esther pressed her lips together in a tight smile. Her heart pounded in her throat, in her stomach, in her thighs. It was shared grief. That's all it was. He wasn't hers to love.

By the time they reached the ferry in Klaksvík, the sun was hidden behind a thick, oyster-shell sky. Sophus drove on to the ferry and parked. They got out of the truck and headed for the deck. 'It takes about twenty minutes to get to Kalsoy. I'm going to ring Flósi, let him know where we are and ask if he's all set for tonight. He should be awake by now.'

Esther remembered. 'Eighties night.'

'It's fine. Flósi can take care of things until we get back.' Sophus took his phone from his pocket and began to walk away.

Esther wandered towards the railing. 'Say hi for me,' she called over her shoulder.

Esther leaned against the railing of the ferry. Checked her pocket for the black swan feather she'd thought to bring with her. Watched the rows of red, white, mustard and blue houses and buildings of Klaksvík village shrink from view as the ferry sailed away, into the folds of emerald-green fjords under dense sky. She ran her eyes over the ridges of the mountains, layer upon layer of rock,, scars from the volcanic violence of their creation. Watched herself walk up the steps of the stargazing shack, with Aura, each holding one of Jack's hands. They brushed the blue gum leaves from the top step and sat. Their skin covered in fine salt swirls from a morning playing by the sea in the wet-eyed watch of curious seals and cautious swans, whose ancestors had been slaughtered under the roof of what the stargazing shack had once been. Aura hated the thought of the seals and swans being brutally hunted so much that she refused any mention of it in her company. But Esther, three years younger, often quietly asked Jack to tell her the story of how he'd made such a place of violence into a sanctuary she loved, where she could sit and watch the stars. Holding the possibility of such transformation close was the only way Esther could counterbalance the shivery knowledge of how cruel people – life – could be. Aura's journal was no different from a mountain formed by violent eruption in the sea, or a slaughter shack repurposed as a haven for gazing into the fires of the universe, under sentinel gum trees who had seen it all. Beauty from malevolent force. Aura's creation from destruction. *Promise me you'll always believe in magic.*

It was when Esther turned to watch the lull of the wake trailing behind the ferry that she realised, with the effect of an afterthought, that she'd left land for water again.

Sophus came to lean on the railing beside her. They stood together, silent.

'Flósi okay?' Esther eventually asked.

He nodded.

She ran her hands near to his on the railing. 'Are you?'

'Ja. It's just ... memories.' He looked up at the mountains, the sky. 'There was this old Faroese proverb I told Aura when she first mentioned her series of seven tattoos.' He stared down into the sea. 'Kann ikki ráða sær heldur enn kópur, tá ið hann sær húðina.' Sophus drummed his fingers on the railing. Looked at Esther. 'It means to have as little self-control as a seal that sees its skin.'

She breathed around the paper cuts each new detail of the intimacy he'd shared with her sister issued to her insides. 'Aura would have loved that,' Esther said.

'I teased her about it all the time, being a seal without self-control. "How's your seal skin coming along?" I'd ask. It always made her laugh. But it was true. She was awake late at night with her seven stories, this journal, her laptop. And first thing in the morning. Our dining table looked like a map of fairytales, from Tasmania, to Denmark, to the Faroes.' Sophus' eyes were cloudy with memory.

'A map,' Esther mused. The seven stories, the seven tattoos, fell into place on the topography of Aura's body 'My aunt called them that The stories Aura chose In her journal. The lines she wrote about them.' She traced the words on the railing with a fingertip. *The Seven Skins.* 'A map,' she repeated. 'Directions. Ways for Aura to face what she couldn't bear, that loss of innocence, that grief in her teens. To claim the hard-fought joy she found here. With you.' Esther was lightheaded. 'By getting tattooed, she was telling her story. Making her own map. To transform herself. Her life.'

'That's right,' Sophus said. 'She was so excited about her tattoos. She got her first before we knew each other. '"If you want change, raise your sword, raise your voice." She had her second done just after we met. "He will give you flowers to forget. You plant seeds, to remember." And her third after we'd been together for about six months. All at the same place in Copenhagen. Tattoo Stjerne.'

'I met Lille Heks, the owner,' Esther said.

'Aura loved her.' Sophus paused. 'She planned to get her remaining four verses after our baby was born. But Aura wouldn't get tattooed while she was pregnant, she was too nervous to do anything that might affect the baby.' His voice faded. 'So. It never ended up happening. She only got three of her seven tattoos done.'

Esther looked at him. 'What? Sophus. No. She didn't only have three tattoos.'

He frowned. 'What do you mean?'

'Our mum tattooed the last four verses on Aura after she got home from the Faroes. She had all the verses tattooed. All seven. On her back.'

His eyes searched hers. 'She got the series finished. Before she died?' His voice broke.

Esther nodded.

Sophus leaned on the railing. Hung his head.

She wrapped an arm around him. Looked away, into the wind and up at the towering fjords, but made sure she held on, tightly, while his shoulders shook.

Their fifteen-minute drive from the ferry dock was a silent, brief pilgrimage through three narrow tunnels. Mikladalur was nestled in a u-shaped valley, on cliffs overlooking the sea and across to Kunoy, the island opposite. Esther kept her eyes trained on every glimpse of coastline, waiting, waiting. She recalled a note in her guidebook. The sculptor, Hans Pauli Olsen, descended from Kalsoy ancestors and had made Kópakonan using his bare hands and clay. Piece by piece, she came into being, before being later cast in bronze and stainless steel. Built and installed to withstand thirteen-foot waves. There was a video Esther had found online of a hundred-year North Atlantic storm battering the coast of Kalsoy, and Mikladalur. She'd repeatedly rewound and replayed footage of the eleven-and-a-half-foot wave that had hit Kópakonan. The seal woman had remained standing, unscathed.

As Sophus slowed on approach to the village, Esther sat up straighter in her seat. Ahead of them, she recognised the view of Kunoy across the sea, from the island terrain behind Kópakonan in the photograph from Aura's journal. Sophus parked and cut the engine.

'We're here,' he said. He'd barely spoken a word on the whole drive from the ferry.

Esther got out of the truck. They were high on a cliff. She looked down to the sea. The wind had picked up, the sea was ruffled. She followed Sophus along a narrow stone path, between black houses with white shutters and grass roofs perched on the edge of the cliffs. Grateful they had the path to themselves.

They descended one short flight of stone steps which turned to face the sea. Searching. Searching.

Then walked down another short flight. A sharp intake of breath.

Kópakonan rose from a knoll of basalt rock, over two metres tall. Her once-bronze skin had been covered by the striking blue-green hues of verdigris. She stood with her back facing the sky, mountains and the sea, her longed-for home. The set of her gaze faced the cursed village of the young farmer who'd once stolen what was not his to take. One of her legs stood on rock. The other remained in her seal skin, which she clutched in one hand.

'Aura,' Esther called for her sister. She ran, down the last long flight of stone steps to the rocky knoll jutting out into the sea. Where Kópakonan stood, staggering in her size and exuding power.

Esther clambered over rock to her, reaching for the seal woman's hand. Cold. Unyielding. At full height, Esther stood level with Kópakonan's forearms. She squinted in the wind up at the emotion sculpted into her face – loss, rage, power – the embodiment of the stories Aura had loved most in her life. Esther pressed her hands on Kópakonan's seal skin. Ran her fingers over the seal's eyes. This was where her sister had accepted Sophus' proposal. Had stood in his arms and listened to Eivør sing 'Trøllabundin'. Had written a new future for her life. All in the presence of the seal woman's story.

Esther wished for the strength to turn the sculpture. To enable Kópakonan to face the sea. She took the black swan feather from her pocket. Tucked it into a crevice between Kópakonan's seal skin and thigh.

She turned to Sophus, who was behind her. 'Thank you.' She steadied her breathing. 'Thank you for bringing me here.'

His mouth pinched with emotion. 'Esther, I have to tell you,' he started. 'This isn't just where I asked Aura to marry me.'

Esther held on to the seal woman as a fresh gust of wind hit. She wiped a few drops of rain from her forehead.

'This is where we scattered our daughter's ashes.' Sophus swallowed.

His words cut straight through her body, like the wind. She didn't speak. Couldn't look at him. She leaned her weight against the sculpture, looking into the waves breaking against the black rock. The weight of an unasked question rose and broke over her, hard. Esther turned back to face him. His eyes.

'What did you name her?' she asked. 'Your daughter? My niece?' In the second before he answered, Esther heard Aura's voice.

'Eala,' he answered. 'We named her Eala. Our swan.'

Esther stared at him.

'I wanted to tell you sooner,' he explained. 'It's never felt like the right time. Then we talked last night, about Aura and you being Séala and Eala. But the words still wouldn't come.'

When she was able to speak, Esther's voice didn't sound like her own. 'The last time Aura was seen on the day she died, people said she was down by the seven boulders, walking the shoreline. Crying the name Eala.' She pinched the skin on the underside of her wrist between her fingernails until she felt the wet sting of blood. 'She was calling for her baby.'

'Aura named our daughter after you, Esther. She was calling for you both.'

Esther sucked in her breath. 'But I wasn't there,' she exploded in dry-eyed rage. 'I wasn't there. She asked me to be there, to meet her, and I didn't go.'

Sophus' face filled with sorrow. 'Oh, Esther.'

'She left me a note that morning, asking me to meet her at our spot, the hidden lagoon, but I was too angry with her for leaving me, for shutting me out, for keeping her life a secret from me. I wanted to punish her for leaving me behind. So, I abandoned her.' Esther heaved for breath. 'I'm no better than the farmer in this fucking story.' She waved an arm towards the village houses on the cliff above them. 'I didn't do as she asked when she needed me most. So now I'm cursed. To live the rest of my life without her. I'll never see her again. My fucking beautiful sister.' She faced the seal woman. Swallowed a gutful of wind. 'I'll never see you again,' she screamed up at Kópakonan.

Sophus waited for her to catch her breath. 'You're not cursed, Esther.' He moved towards her 'It's not your fault. None of this is your fault.'

Esther struggled with his words, with the wind whipping around her ears, with the pressure of unshed tears pounding behind her eyes. 'I should have saved her. I should have been able to save her.' Her throat ached. 'How could she leave me?' Esther yelled.

Sophus looked at her. Helpless. Despairing. Maddened, Esther pressed her forehead against Kópakonan's arm until it became painful. And then pressed harder. Begging. Pleading.

'Esther,' Sophus said, his eyes filling. 'What do you need?' He offered her his hand.

She searched his face, as Aura must have done so many times while feeling the same pull in her being towards him as Esther did now.

'What do you need?' Sophus asked again, his voice soft. His hand reaching.

Hands reaching. Holding. Digging. A fluttering of memories.

~

'Is she dead, Mum?' Aura asking in a shaky voice as Freya approaches.

The look on Freya's face makes Esther cold all over. Their mother drops to her knees, cradling the seal pup in her arms.

Later, behind the shack, Freya digs a grave and gathers the paper daisies she'd asked the girls to pick. Grips them in her fist until her knuckles pale, then throws them into the pup's grave. Takes up her shovel and begins filling in the dirt.

'My love will not leave you,' Freya whispers again and again. Sometimes her voice breaks into a sob. Esther stands very still, watching the dirt fall and cover the soft pink bundle in the ground; Freya has wrapped the seal in one of their baby blankets from the back of the linen closet. It gives Esther a strange feeling to think of it being under all that cold dirt.

Esther tries to snuggle into Freya's body, but her mother looks at her with eyes like empty rooms.

A fluttering.
Their wing markings look like heartbeats.

The garish light, the beeping monitor and its green, jagged heartline. Aura lies in bed, sleeping. Freya curls around her; a second skin, a protective shell.

Esther leaned her body against the sculpture; Kópakonan protected her from the wind. The feeling came, swift, all-consuming. Knowing.

'Mum,' she heard herself say to Sophus. 'I need to talk to my mum.'

45

Freya Wilding lifted the tattoo needle from Queenie's skin and wiped the ink away with a piece of damp paper towel. Inspected her line work up close, then sat back. Wiped Queenie's skin over again. Met her eye.

'We're done,' she said. 'Your grandchild's story is ready.'
Queenie held Freya's gaze.

Freya nodded, an unspoken exchange, her eyes welling.

Queenie squeezed Freya's arm. 'We're done,' she called out to the others, her voice giddy.

Around Freya's partition screen, painted with the gilded cranes that Esther had always loved, flew Erin, Aunty Ro, Coral and Nin with her growing belly. Cool afternoon light poured through the windows of the studio. Ruby Hunter sang through the stereo speakers. The faint, clean smoke scent of peppermint gum leaves lingered in the air.

'Let's see, let's see,' Aunty Ro instructed, fussing over the strands of marina shells glimmering around her neck.

Freya stepped back and peeled off her gloves. 'You know where the mirror is.' She motioned to Queenie. Her skin warmed with pride as the women flocked around her dearest friend.

'Ready, Nana?' Nin asked Queenie, who shook the tension from her limbs after hours on the tattoo bed.

'Ready.' Queenie took a deep breath.

'This is for you, Baby,' Nin spoke to her stomach.

Standing by Queenie's side, Erin looked back over her shoulder, seeking Freya's eye contact across the room. Freya pointed at her welling tears while she rolled her eyes in self-deprecation at Erin; her stoicism was gone. Ever since Esther had left, her emotions had, been uncharacteristically skin-deep, constantly spilling over. Erin gave her an empathetic smile, rolled her eyes back in solidarity.

'Oh,' Queenie breathed as she stepped in front of the mirror and took in the sight of her arm, her skin, transformed. 'Oh,' she said again, turning this way and that. 'Freya …' She pressed a hand over her heart.

'It's perfect, Frey, thank you.' Nin walked to Freya, kissed her on the cheek, then returned to her mother. Hand always resting on her stomach.

Queenie leaned her head against Nin's. Coral and Aunty Ro crowded around. Queenie leaned down to speak to Nin's stomach. 'Your nan has so many stories to tell you, little one. This will be our first.' She turned back to the mirror.

'It's good,' Aunty Ro announced. 'Very good.' She clapped her hands once as if drawing business to a close. Rocked back and forward on her heels for a few seconds before leaning towards Nin. 'Now that the tattoo's done, do we get to eat at this party? Where are the biccies?'

Freya wrapped Queenie's arm in cling wrap and ushered the women into the lounge area of the studio where Erin ferried wrapped plates of cut sandwiches and slices of her home-baked honey cake from the fridge to the coffee table. As Nin's baby-shower festivities began, Freya hung back with the excuse of needing to tidy her station before she could join in. Although she'd insisted on hosting the gathering when Queenie had first mentioned the idea of her tattoo, when it came to actuality, Queenie being tattooed for her unborn grandchild was too confronting for Freya. All afternoon her breathing had been shallow, like something was tightening around her lungs, restricting her breath.

As she put away her bottles of ink, her mobile phone vibrated against the counter. When Freya looked at the screen her heart skipped beats. She tapped the green answer button, pressed her phone to her ear.

'Esther?' Her voice shook.

'Mum?' Her daughter's voice. Small. Far away.

'Min guldklump.' Freya closed her eyes as relief washed through her body. 'Where are you?'

'On a ferry. On our way home from the seal woman sculpture.'

'Our?'

'I'm with Sophus.'

Freya searched the darkness behind her eyelids, trying to see the unseeable: her youngest daughter on a ferry at sea with the stranger Aura had loved. There was something in the way Esther said his name.

'Mum,' Esther said, 'I know.'

Jolted, Freya opened her eyes. Nausea seized her gut.

'About Aura's pregnancy when she was a teenager, and her haemorrhaging. Her miscarriage. That you told me was her appendix.'

'Hang on, Esther, okay? Hang on.' Black spots of panic obscured Freya's vision as she slipped unnoticed out of the studio, across the garden, into the cool shadows of the Shell House. 'I'm here. Hang on just a minute more. I'm here.' She pressed her phone hard against her ear to hear over the rush of blood to her head.

'Mum.' Esther sounded uncertain.

Freya hurried down the hallway, pausing at Jack's closed office door. He was in a session with a client. Should she knock? Interrupt? She kept going, rushing into their bedroom. She closed the door behind her. There was a long pause on the line. 'Esther? Are you still there?'

'I know what happened here before Aura came home. I'm calling to tell you. It's going to be hard to hear.'

Freya's knees jellied. She dropped to the edge of her bed. 'You can tell me. I'm here, Esther. I'm here.' Her hand ached from the tension of her grip on the phone.

'Aura had a baby. Here in the Faroes. With Sophus. A daughter. She was stillborn. They couldn't survive their grief. Aura left Sophus and came home to us afterwards.' Esther's voice was monotone. 'They named her Eala. That last day Aura was seen alive, down on the beach, at our spot. Calling out for Eala. It wasn't just for me. Aura was also calling for her daughter.'

Freya pressed her knuckles to her teeth, holding back the howl in her chest.

'After she was cremated, Aura and Sophus brought Eala's ashes to the island of Kalsoy and scattered them into the sea where Kópakonan, the seal woman sculpture stands. That's where I've just been. That's what Sophus has just told me. He's told me everything in the last couple of days.'

Freya breathed through nausea, lightheadedness, black spots. Breathe. Breathe.

'Mum?' Esther sounded like she was speaking in a windy tunnel. 'Mum?'

Freya opened her mouth. Closed it again. 'I'm here.' She coughed up the words. 'I'm here, Esther.' Her skin was numb. Her mouth was dry. She closed her eyes again and this time saw Esther, at the bow of a ship, sailing over the sea that held the ashes of Freya's granddaughter. She took a shaky breath and spoke slowly, around the sob in her throat. Tried to get the words out before the hurt swallowed her ability to speak altogether. 'I hope you can understand why we never told you. It tormented us. We were never able to reconcile inside ourselves that to keep a promise to Aura meant that we kept a truth from you.'

'But you understood it, though.' Esther's voice cracked. 'Aura's need for what had happened to her be kept from me. Her shame. Her grief. You understood it, Mum.'

'Of course,' Freya said, heart racing. 'That's my job as your mum. To understand.'

'No more.' There was a tremor in Esther's voice. 'No more shame. No more secrets. I can't handle one more fucking secret, Mum.'

Freya dug her fingernails into her thigh. 'What do you mean, Guldklump?' She cringed at herself.

'Stop keeping secrets from me.' Her voice was sharp. 'The seal pup. That day on the beach when we were kids. That you buried in our baby blanket. And cried for over its grave. "My love will not leave you."'

Freya hung her head. Her daughter's name, unspoken, filled her mouth with longing and sorrow.

The wind roared down the line from the Faroes to Salt Bay. Esther waited.

'I miscarried a pregnancy between you and Aura.' Hot tears ran down Freya's cheeks. 'She was due in October, along with the irises I waited for every year to come into early summer bloom. When I found out her due date, I decided to name her after the flowers in my garden.' Freya wiped her nose on the back of her hand. 'Are you still there?'

'I'm here,' was all Esther said.

'I lost Iris in autumn, at sixteen weeks. It was a bright, sunny, cold day.' A small, misplaced laugh escaped her. 'After I miscarried, I was no good. I couldn't get out of bed. I couldn't do much of anything. Jack and Erin helped me look after Aura.'

'Aura knew about Iris?' Esther asked.

'Not until she was fifteen. After she lost her own baby.'

'Why didn't you ever tell me?'

'You were only twelve then.'

'I was old enough.'

'I didn't think you were.'

'Why didn't you tell me later?'

Freya sighed. 'Everything became entangled, I suppose. With respecting Aura's privacy and putting her miscarriage behind us.'

'But you could have told me. I could have known about Iris, too. I could have known about Aura.' Esther's voice buckled under the strain of her composure. 'You say you put it behind you, and you might like to believe that Mum, but it's not true. You and Aura had your own secret club that I wasn't a part of. Never welcomed into. That's what it was like, after she was in hospital, seeing you two always with your heads bent together, going into the sea together, leaving me behind. Like you had your own secret language. Which you did. Your shared experience. That you excluded me from.'

The burden of consequence weighed on Freya's shoulders. In her mind's eye she sat in Queenie's GP office, a year after losing Iris. *Your blood tests came back, Freya. The headaches and chills that you've been experiencing aren't a virus. You're pregnant. You're getting your rainbow baby.*

'Esther,' Freya said. Pinched the bridge of her nose between thumb and forefinger. 'Have you ever heard the phrase *rainbow baby?*'

A pause. 'No,' Esther replied.

'Neither had I. Until I found out I was pregnant again. With you.' Freya lay back on the bed, stared at the ceiling. 'That's what Queenie called you when she told me the results of my blood test. And explained it's a name commonly given to a healthy baby born after a miscarriage. Like a rainbow that appears in the sky after a storm.' '

Esther was quiet. 'I was your rainbow? After Iris?'

'You were,' Freya's voice cracked. 'My rainbow baby.'

There had been countless days during her pregnancy with Esther that Freya had spent at Queenie's kitchen table, drinking herbal tea while Queenie and her family strung their stories from piles of iridescent shells. Freya had become besotted with the luminous colours, hidden beneath the unassuming outer layer of each shell, waiting to be revealed in the light. She'd mentioned it to Jack one night, her growing obsession with iridescence, the shimmer and flash, hidden, then revealed; how it felt timely to her, waiting for their rainbow baby to be born. Jack's eyes had filled with meaning. *Frey, you know the word* iridescent *comes from the Latin word* iris. *Which means rainbow.* Freya had stared at her husband while she cradled her stomach with her hands. It was a connection, she discerned, between Iris and their next child. A connection she clung to while she waited for her due date to arrive.

'You were as magic as any rainbow to me, Esther.' Freya took a jagged breath. 'But I struggled towards the end of your pregnancy. You became a kind of magic I couldn't believe. I didn't dare. What if I lost you too?' Freya willed herself to continue. 'Just before you were born, Queenie talked to me about the possibility of mixed emotions around your birth. Joy, healing, hope. Guilt, fear, anxiety. She warned me that for many parents the birth of their rainbow baby caused conflicting emotions as they grappled with grieving their loss while celebrating the birth of their new child. Not me, I thought. Just give me a healthy baby, I bargained with myself, and we'll be fine. But I wasn't prepared for the intensity of the experience when you were born. You, your life, was everything Iris and her life never got to become. The polarity of my emotions haunted me. I suppose that's another reason I justified not ever telling you about Iris. To talk about her death was to talk about how hard I found your birth.' Freya lifted a hand in front of her face. She was shaking.

'Mum.' Esther's voice was thick with tears. 'I just always thought you never liked me much.'

Freya covered her face with her shaking hand. 'Min guldklump,' she whispered. 'How could you ever think that?'

'We've never been close. Not like you were with Aura. After she was gone, it just got worse. The distance between us. '

Freya dropped her hand from her face and stared at the ceiling. Ran her eyes over a crack in the plaster that widened along the skirting board.

Over the years she'd told herself many stories: sometimes daughters just liked their fathers more than their mothers, the way Esther had favoured Jack ever since she was small. Or, Freya just didn't have that much in common personality-wise with Esther. That happened sometimes, not all mothers and daughters were as close as she was with Aura, she'd reasoned with herself. The truth was a submerged thing, deep, dark and buried: Freya hadn't ever allowed herself to step fully into the skin of mothering Esther. She'd kept her at arm's length from the day she was born. In case something happened to Esther. In case Freya lost her too. It had happened in the moment when Freya first saw Esther's newborn face: the raw, bloody love that had torn through her body was a merciless, dangerous, all-consuming life force of its own. Gripped by fear, a part of Freya had shut down. Esther couldn't have all of her. The consequence had been self-fulfilling. As she grew, Esther instinctively learned not to need her mother. In turn, Freya resented Esther's independence from her. Over the years the crack between them widened into a chasm.

'Esther,' Freya said, tears closing her throat. She didn't answer. 'Esther,' Freya said again, panicking that the line had gone dead. Thoughts of her daughter filled her mind and body, vivid and sensorial. The flecks of fire in Esther's hazel eyes, her dark honey-coloured hair. The dash of freckles over her nose, the light-giving force of her smile. How her laughter sometimes set the kookaburras off in the trees when she was a little girl. How her skin flushed whenever she was heated with emotion. Every detail; a flash of magic.

'I'm here, Mum.' Esther sounded close. Clear.

'I'm ... Esther, I'm so sorry.' She listened to her daughter breathe. For a while, neither of them spoke. Freya cleared her throat. 'You're carrying so much, skat. You're so far away. Everything that's come at you in the last couple of days, learning about Aura, her life, her pregnancies, Sophus. And now me, our family.' She sat up. 'This is too much. You shouldn't have to carry this alone.'

'I'm not alone,' Esther said.

Freya heard it again, the tone in her daughter's voice she'd noticed earlier when she'd said Sophus' name. 'I know. But you should be with us. Your family. Don't you think? Come home, to your dad, and aunt Erin, and Queenie and Nin. They need you. We need to grieve for Aura and Eala now, together.'

'Why can't you say it?'

'Say what?' Freya asked, her throat pinching.

'Dad and Erin and Queenie and Nin? *They* need me?'

Freya took a deep breath. Her own advice, something she told every single one of the women who went under her needle. Breathe. Transformation hurts. Don't forget to keep breathing.

She took another breath. And another. The words were at the back of her throat.

'Mum.'

'Come home to me, Esther,' Freya blurted. '*I* need you.'

Half an hour after Freya and Esther hung up, Freya followed Jack into the bathroom. He ran a basin of warm water. Took a clean face cloth from the cupboard and soaked it, wrung it and gently wiped Freya's red, teary face. She'd told him everything Esther had told her. About Aura. Sophus. Eala. And what she'd told Esther. About Iris.

'I'm scared for her, Jack. This is too much for her mind to hold alone.'

'She'll be okay,' Jack said, his voice uncertain, his face ashen. They sat together in silence.

Freya held his hand. 'I should go back into the studio and tell Erin and the others.'

He nodded. She traced invisible patterns over the back of his hand with her fingertips.

'Our granddaughter.' Jack looked at Freya, his eyes drained. 'Eala.'

She whimpered. 'Did Aura think Eala's death was her fault? Did our baby die thinking she was to blame?'

Jack pulled her into his tight embrace. Freya let herself be held.

'You'll be doing my next tattoo,' Queenie was saying to a beaming Coral when Freya walked back into her studio.

She watched Queenie nurse her newly tattooed arm as if she was already cradling Nin's unborn baby. The placement of her tattoo was deliberate and meaningful: at the top of her arm, Freya had tattooed a dense bouquet of wedding bush flowers, with their brilliant white five-petal flowers and thin green leaves. Rich with story for Queenie, the flowers would be directly in the baby's view when Queenie held the infant for the first time. From the day they were born, the baby would begin to learn their story, as well as their grandmother's face.

The flowers were radiant beneath the cling wrap on Queenie's skin. Hues of pink and grey to shade and illuminate the white petals. Citrus yellows and tawny browns to line the waxy green leaves. Wedding bush flowers burst into bloom, forming bushes of glowing stars in the dunes of the northeast coast, and for generations of Queenie's family heralded the southern migration of the humpback whales. For Queenie, they would now and always also commemorate the birth of her first grandchild.

Freya hovered in the doorway, wringing her hands.

Erin spotted her first. 'Where'd you run off to?' She got up from the couch. 'Freya?'

Aunty Ro put down her cup of tea. Coral and Nin turned.

'Freya.' Queenie's tone was no-nonsense as she came to stand at Erin's side. 'What is it?'

Freya stepped tentatively into the room. 'Esther rang,' was all she managed to say, before she stumbled into their open arms.

46

A few hours after they returned from Mikladalur, Esther sat on the floor of her bedroom and laced up her boots. The murmur and hum of Sophus and Flósi's conversation travelled through the walls of the house. She tucked her wallet, an extra jumper and a bottle of water into her backpack. *We were never able to reconcile inside ourselves that to keep a promise to Aura meant that we kept a truth from you.*

She stood and looked around, checking she had everything. Fatigue had made her lightheaded, absentminded. She'd been restless since their return from seeing Kópakonan. And mostly silent after her phone call with Freya. She'd tried to nap after they'd got home, with no luck. Too much noise. Screeching tyres, smashing glass, the sound of the swan's body hitting her truck. *Eala*, Aura called. The remorse in her mother's voice. *Have you ever heard the phrase* rainbow baby? Esther's temples pounded.

As she readied herself to leave, Heidi swished into the open doorway of Esther's bedroom, all blue velvet, cheap polyester and the brimming hopefulness of teenagerhood. Her lilac hair was piled in tight coils on top of her head, pinned under a blue hat with white flowers. 'Mayhap you'll join the felicitations this eve?' she asked, her eyes sparkling.

At the sight of her, Esther softened. 'Don't you look incredible,' she said.

Heidi beamed, curtseyed. 'So? Are you coming tonight?'

'Sorry, chuckaboo,' Esther said. 'No eighties party for me.'
She didn't explain any further. 'I'm going for a walk, then early
to bed.' She lifted her pack onto her back. 'But promise you'll
tell me all about the party tomorrow? I'll make you breakfast.
Pancakes. Extra syrup.'

Heidi's face fell.

'We made the right choice with your costume, didn't we?
Would a young Violet Crawley give me a twirl?' Esther tried to
lift Heidi's spirit.

Heidi obliged, her smile partially returning.

'Has your uncle seen you yet?' Esther asked, holding Heidi's
hand in the air as she spun.

She stopped, stumbled. Laughed. 'He says I'm not allowed
to come because my costume doesn't count.'

'You let him get away with that?' Esther asked.

'I simply pointed out that Flósi and Sophus failed to specify
which century of eighties, so I'm perfectly within my jovial
right to attend as I see fit. Lady Crawley from the eighteen-
eighties.' Heidi adjusted a polyester ruffle.

'Well.' Esther breathed around the ache in her chest. 'You
win Costume of the Night in my scorebook.'

'Yeah, but you haven't seen Flósi yet,' Heidi countered.

Esther was almost tempted to go into the kitchen where she
could hear Flósi's booming laughter. 'Take photos for me.' She
reached to her bedside table for her house keys, hanging on her
Space Club keyring, and put them in her pocket. 'I'm going to
try to slip out the front door – tell everyone I said goodbye? I'm
guessing you'll all be gone by the time I get back from my walk.
Sophus knows I'm not coming.'

Heidi bit on a fingernail. 'Are you okay, Esther?'

They lingered together in the doorway. Heidi's question
went unanswered.

On impulse, Esther leaned forward and kissed Heidi on
the forehead. 'You are magnificent, Lady Violet. Have fun
tonight.'

The evening air was cold. Esther inhaled deep lungfuls of it as she walked briskly through the garden, promising Frida Maaahlo and Dolly Maaarton she'd bring them treats soon. She didn't know where she was going, only that she had the compulsion to walk. To keep walking. Her eyes burned in the glare of the night sun.

Freya's voice rang in her mind. *Come home to me, Esther. I need you.*

She walked harder. Faster.

What was it like? To disappear?

Esther followed a path by the river Sandá, which Sophus had told her led to the waterfront. Her heart strained at the thought of him. The grief in his face, the warm grip of his hand when she took hold and hung on as she clambered down from where she'd been clinging to Kópakonan; the few seconds his hand had lingered in hers as they'd walked together before he'd let go.

Her thoughts swirled. What would it have been like to grow up with two sisters? To be one of three Wilding girls.

Esther tried to imagine Iris. Maybe she would have been more like Jack and Esther, with darker hair and greener eyes. She tried to envision what being the youngest of three might have been like. Three of them at the beach. Three of them in the stargazing shack. Sisters of Seal, Swan and … Flower Skins?

The futility of her thoughts made her head pound. Esther tried to clear her mind; the questions still came. What would it have been like to live knowing Iris had come before her? Honouring her. Talking about her. How many conversations had Esther missed out having with Aura about their middle sister? What depths of connection had their family missed out on by not commemorating together that, for a time, Iris had existed? If Esther and Aura had grown up talking about Iris, would Aura have been more likely to talk about her miscarriage when she was fifteen? And her life in the Faroes with Sophus?

With Eala? What else had misplaced shame and secret-keeping stolen from them?

Esther groaned, pressed her hands to her temples. She stopped and turned to face the wind. The sky. All the hues of blue. Aura. Iris. Eala. Her unlived life with two sisters, with a niece, was a ghost ship that had sailed without her; a voyage she would never know.

She kept walking. Glimpsed the sea ahead. Clouds gathering, conspiring. Closer, a flock of sea birds spinning, diving, disappearing under the surface of the waves. Memories joined them, spinning, diving, disappearing.

Deep in thought, Esther rounded a curve in the path and looked up. Realising where she was, she almost laughed; the path by the river had led her to Sandagerð.

She scanned the almost-empty beach. Down at the shore, where the shallow water and sand were the same shade of silver, a cluster of figures were gathered. Tucking their hair into their swimming caps. Rubbing grains of wet sand over each other's arms and backs.

Esther sat on the grassy headland and watched them enter the sea. Steadily, one foot after the other, the women walked into the gentle waves. A few screamed with joy as the cold water engulfed their bodies. They bobbed and swam, wiping the saltwater over their faces, some daring to splash, and dived under the surface for seconds at a time.

Compelled, Esther got up and walked closer. When the grass reached the sand, she unlaced her boots, peeled off her socks. Her heart started to hammer as she hurried down the beach. One of the women in the sea spotted her. She raised her hand in a wave. Esther waved back. Greta.

'This is nice, to see you here,' Greta called as she waded into the shallows. As she came closer, her step faltered. 'Esther. Are you okay?' She frowned, shaking off sea water. 'I see why Sophus is worried.'

'I'm fine.' Esther kicked her feet in the sand.

'He told me you've had a lot going on these last couple of days?' Greta looked Esther over.

'I'm fine.' Esther turned to the women swimming in the sea. She recognised Rakul, who waved. Some of the other women gave friendly waves too. She gave a small wave back.

'Maybe you'd like to join us?' Greta asked. 'It's cold, we won't be in for long.' She extended an arm, gesturing for Esther's jacket, her tūī bird alive in ink on the underside of her wrist. 'The worst part is the first step. After that, it's easier.'

Esther didn't allow herself time to change her mind. She set down her boots and socks. Let Greta take her jacket. She took off her jumper. Unhooked her bra and pulled it through the armhole of her t-shirt, which she kept on. Unzipped her jeans. Left her clothes, still holding warmth from her body, folded on the sand. Aura's dishevelled dress, found where she'd last been seen pacing on shore, had been given back to them in a sealed plastic evidence bag, grains of sand still clinging to the fabric.

'Are you ready?' Greta asked, by her side.

Esther started walking towards the sea. The sand changed from dry to wet.

A gasp as the cold water lapped over her feet. She walked further into the shallows. Another sharp intake of breath. The shock of cold.

'One step at a time,' Greta murmured. She gave Esther space, walking apart from her but staying nearby.

Esther looked down, at her feet under the water. *Know me now.*

She took another step. Further into the sea.

Up to her knees. Her thighs. Her groin. Her hips. Belly button. The raw burn of the cold.

There was a sharp cracking sound that made her flinch, though when she looked around, she seemed to be the only one who heard it. Needling pains in her feet shot upwards through her body.

She stepped forward again. The sea water touched her sternum, tugged gently on the ends of her hair.

Alongside her, Greta hovered. Beyond Greta, the other women bobbed, rubbing their arms for warmth.

One more step and the water covered Esther's heart. Reached her collarbone. Another sharp cracking. Another painful upwards rush. Esther winced, pressed a hand to her chest. The pain inside made it hard to breathe. It was just the cold water, she reasoned with herself. It was just the cold.

To talk about her death was to talk about how hard I found your birth.

Esther let her knees collapse and sank under the sea until she hit bottom. Exhaled the air from her lungs and opened her eyes to watch the bubbles rise and vanish.

What was it like? To disappear?

She looked around her, underwater. Searching. Yearning.

The world below was dark and unknowable. Endless. The cold made her head ache.

She looked up, through the rippling surface of the sea to the white sky, crossed by the flight of small black birds. Esther closed her eyes, imagining the sky filled with iridescent black wings, enough to block the sun. That flash of aqua, violet, green in the light. The colours of marina shells, waiting to be strung on Queenie's kitchen table.

Suddenly, Esther's lungs burned with an urgency for air. Shooting pains went through her chest. She stayed where she was. Stayed. Stayed. Until instinct made her stand and push through the surface, gasping for breath.

Esther wiped the water from her face and eyes. Greta was there, at her side. Rakul was close by, and behind her were the other women.

She kept wiping the water from her eyes, until Greta gently touched her arm. Esther realised she was crying. Lungs raw, heaving for air. Shivering. Achingly alive.

Racking sobs went through her body as she tried to catch her breath. Greta took hold of Esther's hands and didn't let go. Rakul waded over to them, then was joined by another woman, and another.

As the night sun blazed, the women circled around Esther in the northern sea. Stinging from saltwater, she let herself be held as she cried a cracked-open dam of grief from her body.

Back on the sand, Esther stayed close to Greta, who wrapped her in a towel, and then a woollen blanket. Rakul and the other women gathered nearby.

It had been so long since Esther's skin had been soaked in saltwater, and she couldn't stop marvelling at both the strangeness and the familiarity of the sensation. She touched her fingertips to her cheeks and the skin around her eyes; her face was puffy from crying.

Greta unscrewed a thermos of coffee and offered Esther a cup. They exchanged a small, understanding smile. Esther murmured her thanks.

The women chatted and laughed as they dried off and dressed. Cups of thermos coffee were passed around. One of the women opened a plastic container and offered it to the group. Esther drank her cup of the hot, strong brew and took a slice of sweet butter cake from the container. The bitter and sweet flavours made her eyes roll with pleasure; her body tingled from satisfaction and saltwater.

Soon everyone started dispersing. As the women walked back to their cars, words swelled in Esther's chest.

'Thank you,' she said softly. Cleared her throat and tried again. 'Thank you,' she said with greater strength. 'Tak.' The sea-dipping women stopped, turned. 'Tak.' Esther pressed her palms together in gratitude, gesturing to them. Some returned the gesture. Others smiled and waved.

'Can we drive you home, Esther?' Rakul asked.

'Of course, we're driving her home,' Greta stated.

'That'd be really nice,' Esther said.

She glanced back, over her shoulder, at the sea. *Know me now.*

Rakul and Greta stayed on either side of Esther all the way back to the car.

'Thank you again,' Esther said as they pulled up at Sophus' house. 'For the towel and blanket. And to you both and your sea-dipping friends, for the whole afternoon.'

'Remember, no showering,' Rakul said. 'The sea stays on the skin.'

Esther nodded.

'We're heading home to get dressed then going straight to the eighties party at Flóvin. Do you want us to come back and pick you up?' Greta asked.

Esther shook her head. 'Thanks. But I'm not going.'

Rakul and Greta exchanged a look. 'Are you sure that it's good to be alone right now?' Greta asked. 'You've had a very hard couple of days.'

'That's why I don't feel like being at a party,' Esther said quietly.

'It might be good for you to be with people who care about you. You don't have to be a party animal,' Rakul offered.

'Klara has come from Copenhagen for the weekend to join us. She would love to see you,' Greta added.

'Has she? I'd like to see her too. But not tonight. Maybe over the weekend. I'm just going to go to bed. But thank you both, so much, again.' Esther got out of their car.

'See you soon, Esther,' Greta called as they drove away.

She waved them off and turned to the house. Someone had left the outside light on for her, even though it wasn't dark. The simplest consideration. Welcome home. To be thought of made her eyes well.

Inside, all was quiet. Wafts of cologne and the scent of hairspray lingered.

As she went through the house, the thought of Heidi in her costume as Violet Crawley made a small smile dance across Esther's face. Another fleeting thought: who was Flósi dressed as?

When she walked into her bedroom, it was the first thing she saw: the costume she'd bought online for the party, that had been hanging in the back of the closet, was laid out on her bed. With crown. Gold boots. Lipstick. Cape. Sword.

A handwritten note was placed beside it.

In case your apanthropy lifts and you find yourself in state of betweenity, herewith one question, my most ardently favoured chuck: what would She-Ra do?
Love, Heidi

47

She stepped out of a taxi. Adjusted her red cape around her shoulders. Flóvin was tucked around the corner, just out of sight down the laneway of black-tarred and turf-roofed buildings. The soft strains of Cyndi Lauper's celebration of girls just wanting to have fun played under the sunny night sky.

Esther scrunched the ends of her hair, full of wild waves and dried saltwater. Pressed her red-lacquered lips together. Before she'd left home, she'd found and glugged from a bottle of wine in the kitchen; the burgundy taste lingered in her mouth. She tried to ignore the places where the cheap vinyl embellishments of her costume dug into her skin. Took a deep breath, walked down the laneway and around the corner.

People spilled out of Flóvin, milling around the entrance. Big Bird and Mr T drank together. Bon Jovi wrapped his arms around a human Rubik's Cube. Music played through the open upstairs windows: she recognised 'The Safety Dance'. Esther smiled – the song would forever remind her of the night she'd baked painted cake in the penis tin at the hostel. As if on cue Flósi's laughter rang in the air. She looked up. He was near the window, mostly out of view – was he wearing a hat? – but Sophus' silhouetted profile beside him was clear. Nerves needled her skin. She hadn't spoken to him since they'd driven home, mostly in silence. Standing in the lane, she stalled, long enough for doubt to begin to creep in. She smoothed down the short white skirt of her polyester dress, adjusted her gold belt and straightened her plastic gold crown. Moved her weight from one foot to the other in her gold block heel boots.

Men Without Hats ended. Esther held her breath, waiting for the next song to begin. 'If You Love Somebody Set Them Free'. She rolled her eyes.

'Thanks for nothing, Sting,' she muttered.

Esther stalled for a few more moments. Took a steadying breath. Strengthened her grip on her plastic sword and strode through the heavy golden door.

Inside, the downstairs section of the bar was hazy from the heat of gathered bodies and the outputs of a coloured smoke machine. The syrupy flavour of the punch at Aura's memorial clouded Esther's senses. She swallowed it down. Pushed through the crowd, pushed the memory away – Jack's eyes behind his Doc Brown goggles, Freya's radiance in her grief and Stevie Nicks chiffon – and searched for faces she recognised. Clusters of costumed people danced and lounged.

Esther made her way past Madonna in her fishnets and tulle sandwiched between Goose and Maverick in their aviator whites. She nudged past Prince Akeem chatting to Princess Leia on the staircase and went upstairs where the bar area was crowded and buzzing. Neither Flósi nor Sophus was working the bar; everyone in Flóvin was being served by Boy George and E.T. Esther was standing on her tiptoes, straining to see over the crowd, when she heard Flósi's squeal behind her.

'Moon Moth,' he exclaimed. She turned to see him grinning. 'You came.' He pulled her into a big hug.

'I'm here.' Esther hugged Flósi tight and stepped back to take in his costume.

Black cowboy hat with a band of sharp, plastic faux-animal teeth, a necklace strung with more of the same plastic teeth, a pleather crocodile-skin waistcoat and matching pleather armband. Large plastic Bowie knife tucked into his belt, and black jeans. But the thing that made Esther laugh until her false eyelashes clumped with tears was the large, inflatable plastic crocodile Flósi was carrying around like a beloved.

'Croc Dundee,' Esther snorted.

'Goodday, mate. Throw another shrimp on the barbie?' Flósi smiled with smug satisfaction after his attempt at an Australian accent.

'Oh god, terrible, on so many levels,' Esther wailed. 'And no one actually calls them shrimp.'

Flósi looked at her, confused.

'Never mind. I'll teach you about prawns another time. You look amazing.'

'Well, you inspired me.' He twirled, with the crocodile, and leaned closer so she could hear him over The Pointer Sisters' excitement. 'I'm glad you came. I heard it's been a rough couple of days. Are you okay?'

A scratchy corner of polyester pinched the tender skin under Esther's arms. She didn't answer his question.

'Speaking of amazing.' Flósi took the hint and changed subject. He stepped back to make space before he kneeled, the crocodile bending with him. 'She-Ra, our Princess of Power,' he said, doffing his hat.

Esther knighted his shoulders with her sword with great theatrics, then pulled him to his feet. They both laughed.

'Moon Moth, I have to keep going, it's so busy, and if I don't help Sophus, he'll kick my arse.' Flósi hugged her again. 'I'll come back soon with more drinks.' He looked down at Esther's hands. 'Wait, why are you empty-handed?' Before she could answer he turned and bellowed towards the bar. 'E.T., get She-Ra whatever she wants.' E.T. gave a thumbs-up in the air.

Esther watched Flósi wend his way through the crowd, inflatable crocodile bobbing along beside him, to the stage area. He put a hand on Sophus' shoulder and leaned in to speak to him. Her stomach flip-flopped; Sophus looked up, straight at her. His face brightened with surprise. He lifted a hand. She returned the wave. He said something to Flósi and started moving through the crowd towards her, while Flósi took over prepping the stage. It wasn't until Esther got a full view of his costume that it registered.

'You've got to be fucking kidding me,' she said under her breath. Pete Townshend started singing 'Let My Love Open the Door'.

'Esther,' Sophus said with a dimpled smile. 'You came.'

She looked him up and down. 'I don't remember Marty McFly being tall.'

'Height is no obstacle when it comes to being a *Back to the Future* superfan.' Sophus raised his hand with a sheepish smile as if confessing.

'Define superfan,' Esther challenged him, with a playful raised brow.

His eyes twinkled while he considered his answer. 'Well, for example, only a superfan would know that the power level Doc's flux capacitor needs for time travel—'

'—is one point twenty-one jigowatts,' Esther interjected. She tried to remain deadpan, but Sophus' laughter made it impossible. Inside her chest, waves caught in a net of gold light breaking through clouds.

'She-Ra suits you,' Sophus said.

'Thanks.' Esther held his gaze, searching his eyes for meaning. She only just stopped herself from asking, *More than she suited Aura?*

'What made you change your mind?' Sophus asked.

Esther shrugged. 'The persuasive powers of a certain fifteen-year-old?'

'That'll do it.' Sophus grinned. 'She's around here somewhere with her friends, having a better time than any of us, I think. There's a boy ...'

'There is?' Esther asked. 'I didn't know. Oh, geez ...'

'Flósi's not coping,' Sophus said, chuckling. Their banter was so easy. He tucked his hair behind his ear. 'Listen, Esther,'

he said, 'I'm so glad you're here. I also get why you didn't
want to come. So, if you change your mind, if the party energy
becomes too much, or if you just need a quick exit, or anything,
just come and find me.' His brow furrowed with concern.
'Okay?'

'Sophus,' Flósi bellowed from the stage in a break between
songs.

'I better get back to it.' Sophus looked at her apologetically.
She waved him on. 'You came at the right time,' he said over
his shoulder. 'Eivør's on soon.' The expression in his eyes was
mixed. 'See you again soon, okay?'

Esther nodded, standing empty-handed in the crowd.

'Hey you.'

She turned to see Molly Ringwald, ready for the prom,
smiling at her with open arms.

'Oh my god,' Esther laughed. 'You look fantastic.' Under a
short copper wig, in head-to-toe pink lace, tule and polyester,
was Klara.

'So good to see you again, Esther,' she said as they hugged.
'I love your costume. How are you?'

'Do you want to get a drink?' Esther countered. They
pushed together through crowds to the bar.

'She-Ra,' E.T. greeted her. 'What can I get you?'

Esther asked for two beers and handed one to Klara.

'Skál,' they said in unison.

Klara moved her shoulders to the beat of the next song;
Carly Simon sang 'Let the River Run'.

'Our song,' two voices cheered beside them; Greta and
Rakul kitted out as Melanie Griffith and Joan Cusack from
Working Girl. Teased mullet coifs, blue eyeshadow, leather,
tassels and shoulder pads.

'Esther,' they both exclaimed. 'You came.'

Esther raised her beer.

'You're okay?' Greta asked Esther. 'This is strong and brave
of you. Being here with everyone. It's good.'

'Hi, Mamma,' Klara greeted Greta in her Melanie Griffith wig and coral lipstick with a kiss on the cheek and laughed as she said something in Faroese to Rakul, who swatted her away playfully. 'I was just telling Rakul that I think she needs more eye make-up.' Rakul's blue eyeshadow reached her brows.

'Hi everyone,' Lena said as she joined them, head-to-toe in Joan Jett blacks.

'Hi Lena,' Esther said, hugging her tight. 'You look so great.'

'So do you,' Lena said warmly, fluffing out Esther's cape.

Esther finished her beer and ordered another round. Lionel Richie started dancing on the ceiling. The group danced together until they were interrupted by Flósi.

'Shots for all,' he declared, delivering a tray of full shot glasses to them over the bar. Greta scrunched up her nose. Rakul gave her a nudge and handed her a glass. The memory of what it was like to follow the sun of an older sister burned a hole through Esther's centre. She downed a shot without waiting for anyone else.

'Where's mine?'

Esther felt someone take her hand; Lady Violet Crawley was beside her, heckling Crocodile Dundee for a drink.

'Where's mine?' she asked again. 'You uncouth rogue.'

'Heidi,' Lena warned.

'Nice try.' Flósi made an elaborate show of pouring a shot of lemonade to reassure Lena and slid it across the bar to Heidi. 'You're all pushing your luck just being here.' Flósi nodded towards Heidi's three friends at the other end of the bar sipping their sodas through straws: Ripley, one of the Teenage Mutant Ninja Turtles and Spiderman.

'Just throw this lemonade in a glass with a double vodka on the rocks, young man, and we'll have no trouble.' Heidi winked at her uncle. Flósi snorted.

Watching the two of them, Esther forced a laugh. *You're alright, Esther. You're alright.* Nin's voice rang in her mind, her eyes full of fear under her Tina Turner wig and eyeshadow. Esther's heart raced; she pinched hard at her wrist.

'Hello, Esther.' A voice behind her made her turn.

'Pastor Jaspur.' Esther smiled in surprise. The pastor was dressed in a blue suit and tie. Her smile widened when Esther looked down to see Carl smiling back at her, panting by the pastor's side.

'I didn't realise you'd be here.'

'Everyone loves an eighties night,' the pastor said. 'Even God.'

'And dogs, by the looks of things. But ... your costume?'

'Carl comes with me most places around here. He and I are a two-for-one kind of deal. And the clue is there,' Pastor Jaspur said, pointing at a card tied around Carl's neck with string, on which was written one word: *Hooch*.

Esther chuckled. 'Hooch. Turner and Hooch. Of course.'

'Hi everyone,' Sophus' voice came across the speakers.

The room rose in cheers. Esther turned, straining to see the stage through the crowd.

'Welcome to our annual eighties party, our way of celebrating these longer days and brighter skies.' He seemed to be searching the crowd. 'Thanks for being here.' More cheers. 'This is one of the busiest nights we've had in the last few years, and while I'd like to think it's because I'm going to be singing for you a bit later' – a smattering of kind laughter went through the crowd – 'we all know it's because we have a very special guest here tonight.' The room clapped and howled. 'So, enough from me. Here she is, from our own islands, the widely beloved Eivør.'

The lights went down; the room fell into darkness. Murmurs and whispers of anticipation ran through the crowd. Esther felt Heidi lead her by the hand. They bumped through bodies, until they stopped. Heidi squeezed Esther's hand once. Esther squeezed back. *Friends*, Freya is saying, her voice strong and clear. *Tonight has been a long time coming. It's been a year since our daughter, our firstborn, Aurora Sæl Wilding, was last seen. Walking to the sea.*

'No,' Esther said sharply.

'Esther?' Heidi whispered. 'You okay?'

Esther squeezed Heidi's hand again as the steady beat of a frame drum came over the speakers.

The crowd started to clap in time. Some started stomping: the single rhythmic beat reverberated from the floorboards up through Esther's body as she recognised the song. 'Trøllabundin'. To hear Eivør's drum firsthand made Esther's skin prickle.

The lights came up; Esther gasped. She and Heidi were front and centre in the crowd. Straight ahead of them on stage, Eivør stood in front of a microphone, wrapped in a black glittering cloak, her blonde hair swept back off her face, her eyes lined with black. She beat her frame drum. Took a breath. 'Spellbound, I am, I am.' Eivør's voice swelled and soared, filling the room, floating into the air, accompanied only by her drumbeats. Listening to 'Trøllabundin' on her playlist, Esther thought it was performed by a whole band, but she was wrong. It was just Eivør's voice and her drum. Nothing else. The rich layers in her timbre and the percussion created by her throat singing had a visceral effect.

Esther shivered, struck by the song's magic. Though it was sung in Faroese, Esther knew enough to understand the lyrics were about feeling enchanted; how it felt to fall under someone's spell. Yet she couldn't help but feel that the song itself was a spell all its own. The intention in the music, in Eivør's voice and throat singing, was hypnotic, powerful and primal. Esther's eyes glossed over with tears. How it felt to hear 'Trøllabundin' live was akin to how living in the Faroe Islands felt to her; the landscapes, the sea, the stories, the people had cast a spell that had transformed Esther's life. A spell she never wanted to break. Or leave.

She glanced sidelong at Heidi; the joy in her face illuminated by the glow of the stage lights. Esther's focus lengthened. Beyond Heidi, standing to the side of the stage, was Sophus. Looking straight back at her.

Esther didn't look away. Neither did he.

'Trøllabundin,' Eivør sang, 'Trøllabundin.'

The song ended. The room roared with applause. Eivør pressed a hand to her heart in thanks to the crowd and waved as she walked off stage. Sophus reappeared at the microphone.

'Eivør,' he said, raising his beer. More applause and raised glasses everywhere. 'While you're feeling generous,' Sophus said, putting down his beer and picking up his acoustic guitar. Someone wolf-whistled. Someone else called out something in Faroese that made people laugh.

'Throw your underwear on stage and just see what happens, Marius.' Sophus adjusted the microphone and strummed a few chords, raising a few more whistles. 'Since that's such an easy act to follow for amateurs like us …' He looked at the crowd deadpan. More laughter. 'I thought that now's probably the best time to keep our tradition of performing for you, before I've drunk too much and can't. Flósi's already there.'

'Hey.' Flósi's shout from the side of the stage was followed by his entrance, appearing by Sophus with a tambourine and pair of maracas raised. Laughter and cheering surrounded Esther in the crowd.

'So here we are,' Sophus said, 'Crocodile Dundee and Marty McFly, your humble, favourite pub owners, to sing you our number for the night as is our custom. We're borrowing, or ruining, you guys can decide, from The Waterboys, a personal favourite eighties band, to say thanks for coming, thanks for being here. Thanks for keeping us going and making this bar what it is in Tórshavn. And happy spring.'

'Heidi, where are you?' Flósi shook his maracas and framed his eyes with his hands, searching the crowd.

Heidi waved a hand.

'Get up here, Lady Crawley. This tambourine has your name on it.'

Heidi looked at Esther.

'Go, go,' Esther said, laughing and urging her towards the stage.

People stepped aside to let her pass. Esther moved forward into the gap that had opened. Right in Sophus' eyeline. He looked at her, down at his guitar, back to her face.

'Here we go,' he said softly and started strumming. Flósi and Heidi started the beat in triple time.

When Sophus started to sing, the crowd surrounding Esther roared. Covered in goosebumps, she watched him play, listened to him sing; the melody tied knots in Esther's stomach. 'This is the Sea'.

For the duration she stood mostly unmoving, unable to look away from him. Flósi's and Heidi's antics, occasionally whacking each other with their instruments, made Esther laugh along with everyone else around her. But the emotion knotted in her centre brought her back to Sophus. To the lyrics of the song. He sang them to everyone, but every word hit Esther square in the chest with resonance. Around her, people swayed. Some opened the flashlights on their phones and held them in the air.

It wasn't until the song was nearing its end that Esther realised. Sophus had changed the words in the chorus.

Her heart began to race. She stared at him, waiting for the chorus to come around again.

He played the guitar hard and loud. As the chorus crescendoed, Sophus' drifting gaze came back to her.

He looked her straight in the eye.

'She was the river,' he sang. 'You are the sea.'

A jolt went through Esther's body. An imagined flash: Aura smiling at the camera, her face replete with joy, her hands on her stomach, standing wrapped in Sophus' arms.

'She was the river,' Sophus sang again, not taking his eyes off her, standing in front of him in the crowd. 'You are the sea. You are the sea.'

~

Afterwards, with eighties hits once again blaring from the speakers, the dance floor was crammed. Everyone gathered at the bar: Lena, Greta, Rakul, Klara, Heidi and her friends, Flósi, Sophus and Esther. She couldn't look at him. Flósi got drinks for everyone, feigning ignorance when Heidi and her friends swiped some shots. Esther could feel Sophus watching her. She kept her attention focused solely on her conversation, catching up with Klara. But when The Psychedelic Furs started singing 'Pretty in Pink', Klara squealed and shook her Molly Ringwald wig, knocked another shot back, and corralled everyone onto the dance floor.

They stayed there as a group dancing, song after song. Esther kept her distance from Sophus, dancing with Klara, Heidi and her friends, and Lena. The more she drank, the more her memories blurred. Flósi kept her topped up, ferrying drinks from the bar to the dance floor. Heidi got a hold of Esther's She-Ra sword and danced around knighting everyone with it. Greta and Rakul did an out-of-time drunken tango to 'I Wanna Dance With Somebody'. Esther looked around at them, their faces, these good people she had come to love. Who'd welcomed and cared for her. Was it only because of Aura? Esther danced the question away. A giddy sense of relief flooded her limbs. She laughed, twirled and drank, craving more and more.

Whitney ended. The heavy synthesiser beats of Wang Chung started. Recognising the song, Esther threw her hands in the air and bellowed like Flósi. The memory came, vivid and unstoppable. She was maybe five years old. *Dance all day, Dad*, she said to Jack as he twirled her around their lounge room overlooking Salt Bay. *Dance Hall Days, Starry*, he corrected her, chuckling. *What? That's just silly*, she exclaimed with a giggle. Esther tried to dance away the ache in her chest for Jack.

'Esther.' Marty McFly was suddenly in front of her. He slid his arm around her waist and offered his hand to dance. Her resistance lasted a second or two. She leaned in. Clung to him. They spun through 'Dance Hall Days' and the continuing eighties playlist. She didn't want the songs to end if it meant that he'd take his hand away from the small of her back.

At one point during '(I've Had) The Time of My Life' she leaned back to steal a glimpse of his face. Caught the look in his eyes.

She was the river. You are the sea.

In the early hours of the morning, Greta and Rakul discarded their teased mullet wigs and left with Klara. After three extensions to their curfew, Heidi and her friends had talked Lena into letting Heidi sleep over at one of their houses and left.

'Banshees,' Flósi slurred after them.

'Come on big brother, home time for us.' Lena winked at Esther as she and Sophus led Flósi, stumbling, out to their taxi in the street.

Esther hung back with Boy George and E.T., helping to gather empty bottles and glasses at the bar. Nerves swirled at the thought of being alone with Sophus. Outside, car doors opened and closed. There were some jovial shouts from last stragglers before Sophus' footsteps came up the staircase.

'Oh, leave that, Esther. Really. Thanks, but we can clean up tomorrow.'

Esther dusted her hands. Sophus spoke to E.T. and Boy George in Faroese, and after a few laughs and friendly waves at Esther, they finished up and left.

'What a night,' Esther said, trying not to slur.

'Yeah. We're just lucky Flósi was done in before he tried getting everyone to do some traditional circle dancing. That's a favourite party trick of his.'

Esther chuckled. Fidgeted with the edges of her cape.

'I'm in no shape to drive. Taxi?' Sophus asked.

'Oh, please god, yes.' Esther grinned drunkenly. 'Not even She-Ra could do the walk home in these boots.'

The taxi dropped them off at the garden gate. Esther drank in deep breaths of cold air, trying to will herself into being sober. It was finally, briefly, dark. While Sophus paid the driver, she looked beyond the shadowy outline of the house and up at the night sky. A small flare of light flashed in the corner of her eye, but when she turned to look where she thought she'd seen it, low to the sky behind the house, there was nothing but the dark blanket of the sea in the distance.

They stumbled through the gate, giggling, hushing each other through the garden, to the front door. He unlocked it and they crept inside, taking off their boots, puffer vest and cape. Esther followed him through the house to the hallway where they paused, cast in low light from a lamp left on in the lounge room.

She looked at him. He looked back at her. In their drunkenness there was nowhere to hide.

'You called her the river. And me the sea,' she murmured with a shake of her head.

'Ever since that day you walked into Flóvin.' Sophus reached for one of her long curls, hanging over her shoulder, his fingertips grazing her skin. 'You are everywhere,' he whispered.

Esther teetered on the edge of self-control. She'd brought up Aura. He hadn't. Her heart was beating so hard she could almost taste it.

'I want this,' she whispered. A declaration. 'I want this with you.'

The resistance they'd maintained between each other dissolved in the single step he took towards her. His lips. His fingertips on her face. Her arms wrapped around his neck; the fistfuls of his shirt gathered in her hands.

He threaded his fingers through hers, led her down the hallway to his bedroom. Opened and closed the door behind them.

A raw and long-forgotten sense of joy tore through Esther's body. *I want this.*

48

Sunlight played across Esther's closed eyelids. Shallow water, shallow dreams, shallow sleep. Aura weaving gum twigs together into a garland. *Because*, she says, *the little scallop had been brave and returned from the great unknown.*

Esther startled awake, a film of cold sweat on her skin. She relaxed against her pillow and looked at the pink scallop shells on the windowsill. *Ra-Ra and Starry.* Aura stood and crowed. *Sisters of Seal and Swan Skins.* In unison: *Raise your swords and your voices!*

'Morning,' Sophus said groggily, stretching. 'Ooooogh,' he mumbled, holding his head. He rolled onto his side, reaching for her.

'Morning.' She made herself malleable; he scooped her body into the shape of his, little spoon, big spoon. Threaded her fingers through his, relishing the feel of his skin against hers. *Don't break the spell. Don't break the spell.*

A face appeared at the bedroom window. And another.

Meryl Sheep and Michelle Omaaama stared at Esther and Sophus through the glass for a few moments before they started bleating.

Esther burst into laughter. Sophus lifted his head from his pillow to look at the sheep then propped himself up on one arm.

'Thanks girls,' he said to them, as if they were in conversation. 'The matriarchs are happy for us,' he said to Esther.

She laughed again. Her smile subsided. Esther turned her face to his. 'Are you? Happy for us?'

He studied her face. 'I am.'

'I am too,' she said, touching her fingers to his beard, running her hand over his face.

He looked down at her, looking up at him. 'I've thought about waking up with you so many times,' Sophus said.

Esther kept her back to the windowsill and pink shells. 'I've thought about doing this with you so many times,' she said, running her fingers down his stomach.

'Look away, girls,' Sophus said to Meryl and Michelle at the window, who'd already lost interest and were grazing.

Later, after a shower together, Sophus gave Esther a pair of his trackies and one of his jumpers to wear. She got dressed, rolled up the pant legs and sleeves and did a catwalk saunter and twirl towards the bed where he was lying.

'Even She-Ra turns back into a pumpkin at some point,' she joked.

He smiled at her. 'She-Ra or pumpkin; I don't care. I'll take either.'

Tears pricked the corners of her eyes. 'You're going to have to give me a warning first if you're going to say things like that.'

He pulled her close. 'Ready for coffee? Breakfast?'

She groaned. 'Both. I feel seedy as hell.'

'Seedy? You want to garden?' he asked, confused.

Esther snorted. 'Seedy. As in, hungover.'

'You realise English is ridiculous, right?' He went to the bedroom door, held out his hand to her.

Esther's smile fell. 'Is that a good idea?' she asked. 'For everyone to see us? Together?'

'I'm not ashamed of us, Esther.' He said it so simply and plainly.

She took his hand. 'Neither am I,' she said, almost believing herself.

~

When they walked into the kitchen together, Lena and Flósi were sitting around the dining table chatting and laughing. Crumb-filled breakfast plates and coffee cups piled up between them. An empty pill sheet sat on the table in front of Flósi who was cradling his head in his hands.

'Morning,' Sophus said, holding Esther's hand as they came into the room.

Lena's brows shot up in surprise, though she quickly recovered with a warm, knowing smile. 'Good morning, you two.' She glanced warily at Flósi, whose laughter had turned stony-faced. He stared at them, silent.

'Morning,' Esther said too brightly.

'Any coffee left, Flósi?' Sophus asked.

He didn't answer.

'Okay,' Sophus said under his breath. Still holding Esther's hand, they went into the kitchen to make coffee. Esther tried talking to Sophus with her eyes. He was calm, his eyes clear and sure.

'Here you go,' he murmured, pouring her a cup of coffee. Handed it to her and watched her take a sip. She smiled in thanks; he tucked her hair behind her ear. Her body tingled in response to his touch.

'This is bullshit,' Flósi muttered at the table.

Sophus sighed. 'Flósi, c'mon,' he said gently. Shook his head at Esther as if not to worry.

'Come on, what?' Flósi asked, louder, leaning back in his chair, looking back and forth between Esther and Sophus.

'Are you seriously upset?' Sophus didn't let go of Esther's hand.

'Yes, Sophus,' Flósi snapped. 'I'm seriously upset.'

'Why?' Sophus asked, narrowing his eyes.

Flósi took a beat, as if he was deciding whether to say something or not. 'Because you've put me in this position, again. I'm the one who'll pick up the pieces after' – he paused, gesturing at them – 'this.'

'What is that supposed to mean?' Esther couldn't hide the sting from her voice.

Flósi stood, pushed his chair back and went to stand at the glass double doors leading into the back garden and paddocks.

'Flósi?' Esther asked again, her face hot with hurt and anger.

He turned to face her. 'Esther, if you don't know why what you've done is only going to lead you both to more grief, I'm not going to explain it to you.'

'Watch it, brother,' Sophus said quietly.

'I could say the same thing to you, brother,' Flósi shot back.

'That's enough,' Lena interjected, holding up her hands.

'Come on, Lena. Like you're not thinking it too.' Flósi turned back to the view through the glass doors.

'Thinking what, exactly?' Esther asked, her voice rising.

'Esther,' Sophus started.

'No, Sophus. I want Flósi to say what's on his mind. Thinking what, exactly?' She walked towards Flósi, unable to mask her emotion. He didn't turn. Didn't answer. 'Flósi,' she demanded.

He kept his back to her. 'You're going to leave and break his heart, Esther.' Flósi's voice was brittle with quiet anger. 'Just like your sister did.'

Esther's mouth gaped open as if she'd been winded. 'Why are you being like this?' she breathed, incredulous.

Sophus put a protective arm in front of her and stepped towards Flósi as if he could shield her from the blow already dealt. Flósi turned from the door and he and Sophus switched to a slinging argument in Faroese. Lena, in the middle, tried to mediate.

At first Esther was the only one to hear the knock at the door. On the second knock, louder and more urgent, everyone fell silent.

Sophus left the room to answer the door and came back with two of Heidi's friends who'd been at the party the night before, Ripley and the Ninja Turtle. Both were fidgeting, skittish.

'Hi girls,' Lena said, her voice edged with instant concern. She stepped forward, talking to them in Faroese. Her tone turned urgent. She spun around to address Flósi before she hurried from the room.

'What? What is it?' Esther asked Sophus, her hand on his arm, a sick pit of fear opening in her stomach.

'Heidi didn't stay at Danvør's place last night, as they'd agreed she would. After they left the bar, Heidi told them she was coming back here to get her sleeping bag, but she never showed up. Now Heidi's not answering her phone, so Danvør and Birgit have come to see if she's here '

Lena yelled in Faroese from the hall. Came rushing back into the kitchen.

'Lena thought she might have come home, but she's not in her bedroom,' Sophus said.

'Well, where is she then?' Esther asked, panic shooting through her limbs.

Sophus' face paled. He asked a question in Faroese. Danvør answered. 'I just asked about the Spiderman kid. They said he's not answering his mobile, and no one's answering the phone at his house. His parents are in Copenhagen for the weekend.'

Lena ran for the phone, started punching in numbers and pacing as she made phone call after phone call.

Flósi asked Sophus a question, his tone softened.

Sophus grabbed his keys off the counter. 'Will you stay here in case she comes home?' he asked Esther, his eyes tense with worry.

'Of course,' Esther said, caught between conflicting emotions.

'I'll call you,' Sophus said, kissing her quickly and heading for the door with Flósi, Lena, Danvør and Birgit.

~

Nearly an hour later she paced the length of the dining room. The living room. Waiting. Going over when she'd seen Heidi the night before, and if she'd noticed anything awry. But all Esther could recall was Heidi almost levitating with joy at the bar, being with her family and friends.

Esther rubbed her brow until her skin began to hurt. Sophus had called a couple of times since they'd left: Heidi wasn't with any of her other friends, or in any of their hang-outs around town. Lena had been to the local police; they were preparing a search message for national radio. The last time Sophus had called they were at the harbour, checking *The Terminator*. No luck.

Furious with her sense of helplessness, Esther put on her boots. She couldn't sit still at home doing nothing. After she scribbled a note, Esther grabbed her phone and keys and left. Through the garden gate to the road. Which way? Where might Heidi have gone? Something nagged at her mind. The lakes. The kittiwakes. Heidi had said she'd loved them. Esther set off, half-walking, half-running, down the trail.

'Heidi,' she called repeatedly, the whole way along the trail. After forty-eight hours had lapsed, the SES had combed the beaches of Salt Bay, walking in uniform lines along the coast and the surrounding bushland searching for any sign of Aura. Every day that she was out looking for her, all day long Esther had shaken with the unrelenting fury of being so utterly helpless. Of being such a total failure, unable to find her sister.

At the point in the trail where the pink flowers, ragged robins, were in bloom, Esther doubled over and vomited. She sat on the grass and took out her phone. Called the house. No answer. Called Sophus. No news. They were driving along the waterfront, checking the beach.

'Where are you?' Sophus asked.

'I couldn't sit at home doing nothing. I thought she might be at the lakes, so I came to check but she's not here.' Esther's voice wobbled. 'She's not here,' she repeated.

'Esther,' Sophus said, 'it's going to be okay. She's going to be okay.'

'How do you know?' Esther whispered.

Sophus went quiet on the line.

'I'm going to head back,' Esther said. She got to her feet. Took a sharp intake of breath. 'Call me if you get any news.'

'You too.' They hung up.

As Esther made her way home, flashes of the night before came back to her. Heidi squeezing her hand before Eivør's drum started beating. The look on Heidi's face, of love and joy, as Sophus played, singing straight to Esther. The lightness in Heidi's step as she and her friends had left the bar. The drape of Spiderman's arm around her waist as he stepped aside for her to go downstairs first.

The trailhead led back to the road. Esther walked, watching the house come into view. The sheep grazing in the rear paddock. The finial on the glasshouse.

Esther's pace slowed. The flash of light. Low in the sky when she and Sophus got home.

Her heart began to race. There'd been a flash of light behind the house.

Tears gathered in her throat. 'Heidi,' she yelled, as she started running.

Esther crossed the paddock behind the house, weaving between Frida, Dolly and Megan. At the door to the glasshouse, she halted.

'Please, god,' she panted, hand on the door latch before she flung it open.

Inside, among the discarded gown of Lady Crawley and Spiderman's suit, was Heidi. Curled up in the arms of a young boy. Asleep in a single sleeping bag. Both bare-skinned.

Esther's first reaction was to smile, before her face crumpled from relief, love, anger, exhaustion. Heidi stirred, opened an eye. She blinked up at Esther until realisation set in. Glanced, stricken, at the boy beside her.

'Please don't tell Mamma,' she begged.

'Sorry, chuckaboo.' Esther shook her head. 'They're all out looking for you after you didn't show up at your friend's place.' She took her phone out of her pocket. 'Get up, both of you.' The boy stirred. 'Get dressed. Come into the house.' Esther closed the door to give them privacy. She walked out of earshot and called Sophus, shaking as she lifted the phone to her ear.

'Esther?' Sophus answered.

'I found her, Sophus. She's here; she's safe,' Esther sobbed. 'I found her.'

She chose a spot in the sun on a grassy knoll by the harbour, overlooking the sea. A pair of ravens circled and landed on the railing of the red and white lighthouse behind Esther. Signage told her the lighthouse was part of Skansin, a historic fortress once used to protect Tórshavn from pirate raids. She watched the sea, almost smiling to herself at the thought of how much Heidi might wish she had a fortress to protect her from Lena's ongoing inquisition back at the house.

Esther had left not long after Sophus, Flósi and Lena had returned, when the torrent of Faroese between Heidi and Lena had intensified and she'd sensed that her non-understanding presence was an intrusion. No matter how Sophus had tried to translate for her or protested otherwise, she didn't belong in the family circle around the dining table. As she'd quietly excused herself from the room, Flósi hadn't taken his eyes off her.

She stretched in the mellow sun before folding her legs back up to her chest. The thought of Flósi pained her; the disappointment and hurt in his eyes. After she'd found Heidi and everyone had come home, he hadn't said anything to Esther. He didn't have to, his cutting words kept repeating in her head.

You're going to leave and break his heart, Esther. Just like your sister did.

'Esther, hi.'

She looked up.

'Pastor Jaspur,' she said, quickly wiping away a few rogue tears. She was surprised by her relief on seeing his friendly face. 'And Carl! Hi, Carl; have you recovered from your partying?' She opened her arms to the sheepdog who ran into her embrace and launched a licking tirade on Esther's chin. 'I lost you guys in the crowd last night. No running today?' she asked.

'Nei.' Pastor Jaspur chuckled. 'Just a couple of gentlemen taking a brisk walk together, after a little too much indulgence last night.'

'Ah,' Esther said, scratching Carl behind the ears.

'May we join you?' the pastor asked, gesturing to the grass beside Esther and Carl, who clearly had already made himself at home.

'Of course.'

The pastor sat beside her. Together they watched the sea.

'How are you today?' he asked.

She saw herself through the pastor's eyes: tangled hair pulled back in a top knot, oversized tracksuit, face in need of a hundred-year sleep, scratches and scars on her wrist. She pulled her sleeves down over her hands. 'Nothing new. Ongoing existential crisis, fucking up everything I touch.' Esther clenched her jaw.

'There's something to be said for consistency,' Pastor Jaspur mused.

Esther almost laughed. 'Why do I always feel with you that even with the simplest question, like "How are you?", you can read my mind or see into my soul or something?'

'I get asked that a lot,' the pastor answered. 'I call it "the gaze of God".'

'Catchy.' Esther looked out to sea. Carl did three circles and lay nestled in the space between Esther's arms and legs. 'Someone needs a break from their brisk walk.'

'He's not the only one,' Pastor Jaspur said. Held his face up to the sun.

'Can I ask you a question?' Esther looked at the pastor.

'Yes.'

'How do you know so much about grief?'

The pastor looked down at the grass, and out to sea. 'My wife died,' he answered. 'Five years ago. We took Carl out for a run here together one morning, and she never came home. She was alive, and then she wasn't. Afterwards we learned she had hypertrophic cardiomyopathy. A heart condition that often goes undetected but can cause sudden cardiac death. We'd been married for a year.'

Esther stared at the pastor. 'That's so cruel. I'm sorry,' she managed to hold her voice steady enough to say.

'Thank you.'

'How have you survived it? The grief?'

'I relearn my answers to that question every day,' Pastor Jaspur said. 'Faith. Nature. Helping others in our community. This guy.' He ruffled Carl's ears. 'Talking to stray visitors on aeroplanes and at bus stops and around the islands.' He smiled at Esther. 'And running. Malla is why I still run. It keeps me close to her. Helps me move grief through my body. Helps me to honour her. And to process the weight of the grief others suffer and share with me through church. Running is where I find my answers.'

Esther caught a glimpse of Jack lacing up his shoes to run along the sea; of Freya walking out the back door of the Shell House into her studio; of the women she'd tattooed stepping in front of the mirror, the look on their faces on seeing their skin transformed. Nin and Queenie collecting shells in the shallows. Erin tracing lines of ink and saltwater over her wrists. Abelone swimming in icy saltwater, Kristina's favourite words inked onto her body. Sophus driving Esther at dawn to Kópakonan.

'Oh, and therapy,' the pastor continued. 'Years of therapy. This is how I live with the grief.'

Esther didn't catch her reaction quickly enough; she scoffed at his mention of therapy. And felt instantly rotten for it.

The pastor didn't say anything for a while. He looked out at the water and surrounding islands. 'Have you ever heard about the mystery of the monarch butterfly migration over Lake Superior?'

'Is that in North America?'

The pastor nodded. 'Malla always dreamed of taking a trip to follow their migration from central Mexico to Canada.'

Esther swallowed. 'No, I haven't heard of it.'

'It puzzled scientists for years: why did monarchs take a sudden eastward turn at a specific point over the lake year after year? Doing so makes the already tough journey even harder. They could just fly directly south, saving themselves huge difficulty, yet every year at this specific point in their migration they turn east, fly for a while, and then veer south.' Pastor Jaspur glanced at her. 'No one could figure it out until geologists and biologists finally connected their research: thousands of years ago, a mountain once rose from the lake at that exact point where the butterflies turned east. This geological migration memory has been inherited by generations of offspring who have never seen the mountain but remember it anyway and fly out of their way to avoid it. Even though they've never seen it or known it. No one knows how they pass on this knowledge. Just that they do, and it shapes the course of their lifespan.'

Esther couldn't speak for the lump in her throat.

'Malla's death was my invisible mountain. Grief could have kept me trapped in pain patterns for the rest of my life. Therapy is how I learned to change course.'

Esther wiped the tears from her cheeks. It seemed like ever since she'd swum in the sea with Greta and Rakul, she hadn't been able to stop her eyes from leaking.

'When we bumped into each other on your hike, you mentioned you're not in therapy,' the pastor said.

Esther nodded.

'You know what I love about being human?' Pastor Jaspur asked.

She side-eyed him. 'What's that?'

'We have the most wonderful ability to change our minds. About anything. Any time we like. All we must do is make the choice.'

She shook her head, unable to hide her smile. 'You'd get along well with my dad.'

'I'd like him very much, I'm sure.' Pastor Jaspur checked his watch and stood. 'Come on, old boy.' He whistled. Carl leaped to attention. 'We have an evening sermon so we should get going. But it's been nice talking. I always enjoy seeing you, Esther.' The pastor clipped Carl's lead to his collar.

Esther's heart pounded at the thought of what she was about to say. 'Pastor Jaspur,' she said. Silent, slow tears ran down her cheeks. 'I think I'm leaving this week.'

'Oh,' he said, nodding, taking in her words. 'That's sad for us here in the Faroes. But I bet there are people waiting to see you who will be very happy about this news.'

Esther wiped her nose on the back of her hand. *Come home to me, Esther. I need you.*

'I wish you good things, Esther. And I hope we see each other again one day.' The pastor waved.

'Thank you for being my friend,' she called as he started to walk away.

'Thank you for being ours,' Pastor Jaspur said with a smile, before he and Carl walked down the knoll and out of view.

49

When Esther got home, the house was quiet. She went into the dining room: empty, as was the kitchen.

As she started to head towards her bedroom, she looked through the glass doors and glimpsed Sophus outside, in the paddocks, kicking the soccer ball around with the sheep. There was a furrow in his brow, tension in his shoulders. Esther's heart sank. How was she going to tell him? A deeper fear: how would she go through with it?

A familiar sonorous melody started to play in another room. Esther smiled to herself: the *Downton Abbey* opening score. She walked towards Heidi's room, looking back at Sophus as she went.

At Heidi's door, Esther knocked softly. 'Heidi? It's me. Can I come in?' She tried the doorknob, but it was locked. Behind the door, the music volume increased. 'Chuckaboo?' Esther said loudly. 'I'm sorry. Okay? You know I had to let your mum know where you were.' She knocked again. Waited. 'Please, can I come in?'

The music cut. Rustling. Footsteps. An unlocking.

Esther steadied herself and opened the door. Heidi was in bed with her laptop, covers pulled up to her chin. 'Hi,' Esther said.

'Hi,' Heidi said flatly. She tapped a button on her laptop and the music resumed at loud volume.

'Downton's greatest hits?' Esther asked, nearly yelling to be heard.

Heidi huffed. Turned the volume down. 'The complete soundtrack.'

Esther sat on the edge of Heidi's bed. 'How are you feeling, chuck?'

Heidi's eyes turned red with tears. 'Like my life is over.' The absence of Heidi's jovial Victorian English quips was unsettling.

'Why?' Esther asked. 'I mean, which part makes you feel that way?'

'All of it. Everything. What happened with Mamma. After she got home.'

'It sounded intense.'

Heidi snorted. 'You left before the worst of it.'

'If it makes you feel any better, I couldn't understand a word of it anyway.'

The slightest smile drifted over Heidi's face before it disappeared into anguish. 'She said it all in front of Jónas.'

'Jónas is Spiderman?' Esther asked.

Heidi nodded.

'You like him, hey?'

'We met when we were kids, at a youth group for ocean conservation. We've always hung out since then, but this year we started spending more time together.' Heidi shrugged. 'I just haven't said much at home about it. But I do like him. A lot.'

Tom sitting beside Esther in the stargazing shack, wearing his Space Club t-shirt with ironed creases in the sleeves, while they both listen to Jack talk about the space-time continuum. Esther smiled sadly at the memory. She put a hand on the blankets, patted Heidi's leg underneath.

'I know it doesn't make much sense, since anger doesn't seem the same as love, but your mum was only that upset because she was scared that something might have happened to you. She was worried she couldn't protect you.'

Heidi wiped her face. 'I know. But did she have to humiliate me to get her point across?'

'I don't think you need to feel humiliated just because your mum got upset in front of a boy you care about.'

Heidi looked at Esther like she had two heads. 'That's not it. I don't care that she was upset in front of Jónas. What humiliated me is that she asked him whether we used protection. She focused all her rage on him, not me. Esther, she made him cry.'

'What?' Esther tried not to laugh. 'Oh, god.'

'See?' Heidi groaned, put her hands over her face. 'I told you, my life's over.'

'What did Jónas say to her?' Esther asked.

'There was nothing he could say. I had to step in and tell the truth: the condom was mine. There was no way Jónas and I were doing it for the first time without protection.'

Esther tried not to look so impressed. 'How did that go?'

'Mamma seemed disappointed and angry, but also, weirdly, proud. Then she kicked Jónas out and told me I'm grounded until I'm forty. She got in her car and left and that was about' – Heidi checked the time on her laptop – 'an hour ago.'

'Lena will be her normal self again soon. She just needs a bit of time.'

'For what?'

'As weird as it sounds, it's as much an adjustment for your mum that you're old enough to make your own decisions as it is for you.'

'I guess.' Heidi sighed. 'I just … what if he doesn't want to hang out with me anymore after this morning?'

'Oh, love.' Esther searched for words that might soften the anxiety in Heidi's face. 'If this kind of thing is a dealbreaker for Jónas, is he really someone you want to have around?' Was she listening to her own advice?

Heidi scrunched up her nose. 'No. But I know him. He's not like that. I know in my heart he'll be fine.'

'There you go.' Esther smiled.

After a moment, Heidi gave Esther a strange look.

'What?' Esther asked.

'Nothing.'

'What is it?'

'Well ... who was your first time with?' Heidi asked.

'Ah,' Esther said, Tom's face returning to mind. 'The first time I had sex was with my childhood best friend. It should never have happened. Although, I mean, that's not entirely true. I'm glad my first time was with him. Even if it was awful.'

'It was awful?' Heidi asked.

'We were in our early twenties, at a friend's wedding. I was so sick of waiting and wanting to have sex with someone but didn't want to waste my first time on a random hook-up. I got confused and thought that just because Tom and I had always been such good friends, we should be more than that. So, we got drunk and had sex.'

Aura sitting on the edge of Esther's bed with paracetamol and water. *Remind yourself how the look of something changes once you're moving, step by step by step.*

'Why was ...' Heidi paused.

'You can ask me anything,' Esther said, remembering how the light had caught in Aura's eyes that morning.

'Why was it awful, exactly?'

Esther chuckled. 'Well, it wasn't lovely and cosy in a glasshouse with night-blooming flowers.' She shook her head. 'It was outdoors, on a golf course. I got impaled by a thorny plant and he threw up on me.'

'What?' Heidi screeched, throwing the blankets over her face. She pulled them back down. 'Are you still friends?'

'Not really, which is a shame,' Esther said. 'I miss him. He's my oldest friend.' The truth of her words took her by surprise.

As they kept talking, an awareness grew in Esther that Heidi might remember having this conversation with her for the rest of her life, every time she remembered the first time that she had sex. The honour of playing any part in Heidi's life made Esther's chin wobble.

Their conversation lapsed into an easy, shared silence. The *Downton Abbey* soundtrack continued playing on Heidi's laptop.

'Heidi, I have to tell you something,' Esther started. She took a few beats. 'The thing is, it's time I went home. To my family.'

Heidi stared at her.

'They need me. They need to know what I've learned about Aura's life. And I need them.' Saying it out loud made it ring true in Esther's being.

Heidi frowned. 'You can't decide, just like that, to suddenly go home.'

'It's not sudden. It's been on my mind for a while; I mean, I never arrived thinking I would stay. I can't stay. It's not even possible. But I had a pretty big conversation with my own mum yesterday and, when everyone was out looking for you this morning, I realised it's true: my parents and I need each other right now. Seeing how worried everyone was for you, how much love everyone has for you, seeing how everyone came together this morning. My family went through that after we lost Aura. But we never found her.' Esther waited until she could speak again. 'I can take what I know of her life here with you all home to my family and ease some of their worry and fear and pain. Going home now will help my family grieve. Will help me grieve.'

Heidi listened deeply to Esther's words. 'What about us?'

'You will always be my chuckaboo,' Esther said.

'What about Sophus?' Heidi asked more pointedly. 'He loves you.'

'Heidi,' Esther objected, shaking her head.

'What? He does.'

Esther shifted uncomfortably.

'I don't want you to go.' Heidi's voice wavered.

'Part of me doesn't want to go either. But I have to.'

'Will I ever see you again?' Heidi asked.

'Tomorrow morning at breakfast.' Esther's attempt at a joke fell flat. 'I'll be here for a few more days. I need to find flights and pack.'

'You won't leave without saying goodbye?' Heidi asked. *Like Aura* hung unspoken in the air.

'I won't leave without saying goodbye,' Esther said. 'I promise.'

Esther pulled Heidi's door closed and stood in the hall, quelling the sob in her chest. She pressed a hand to the door for a moment. Then turned and walked down the hallway.

Sophus wasn't in his bedroom, or the living room, dining room or kitchen. Esther went out the glass double doors into the garden, and then the paddock. Found him sitting on the grass with Shagourney Weaver, arm around her, scratching her behind the ears. The rest of the girls grazed nearby.

'Hi,' she said, sitting beside him.

'Hi yourself,' he said with a surprised smile. He leaned over and kissed her. Jolts went through her body.

It was late in the afternoon, but the sun remained high in the sky. Esther basked for a moment in the abundance of light.

'What a day,' she said. 'I was just catching up with Heidi.'

'It was eventful around here for a while,' he said with a low whistle.

'How's Flósi?' Esther asked with caution.

'He drew the short straw and is at Flóvin. He'll be fine. I'm sorry about this morning. He is too. But I'll let him talk to you more about that.' Sophus shook his head. 'Flósi just has a big heart and no-filter feelings to match.'

Esther fidgeted. Tried to find her words.

'How was your walk?' Sophus asked.

'I ended up down at Skansin. Bumped into Pastor Jaspur. Had a chat.'

'Nice.'

Shagourney ambled over to Esther for a pat. She looked
into the sheep's woolly face, her deep brown eyes. Esther
blinked back tears.

'You okay?' Sophus asked. 'Hey,' he said. 'Come here.'

Esther couldn't let herself lean into his chest. 'Sophus,' she
cried.

'What is it? Esther?'

She waited until her voice was strong. 'I have to go home,'
she said.

Sophus searched her face. 'Is this because of Flósi this
morning? Because it is—'

'No.' Esther shook her head. 'It's not Flósi.' She fought the
yearning in her body for him, her desire to keep things easy.
'Last night, this morning ... Sophus ... it's ... I ...' She took a
breath. Started again. 'It's been a dream living here. With you.
Being with you. But ...'

'But what?' he asked gently.

'This was Aura's life,' Esther said quietly. She couldn't look
at him. 'I came here to find out what happened to my sister,'
Esther forced herself to continue, 'and now I've got to go home
to be with my family. To talk it all through with them.'

Sophus shook his head, turned from her to look out to sea.

'What does that mean? Shaking your head.'

'This wasn't just Aura's life,' he said quietly. 'It's mine, too,
Esther. And yours.'

The wind picked up; Esther pushed her hair out of her
face. 'You only know me here, Sophus, but I need to face my
life, everything I left behind at home. I need to take care of
my family. And I need to take care of myself.' Her composure
began to crumble. 'I'm such a mess, Sophus, and you don't
deserve a mess. I need to get my shit together. The last thing I
want to do is hurt you.'

He looked at her for a long time. 'You're not a mess to me.'

Unable to take in his words, Esther turned her face to the
wind. After a while, she turned back to him. 'Even if I didn't

leave this week, Sophus, I'd have to go home soon. We both know that. There's no magical visa that doesn't expire. Or a bank account that doesn't empty. I'm on the bones of my arse; I've only been able to stay here this long because you gave me a beautiful home to live in.' She took his hand, threaded her fingers through his. 'This isn't real,' she said, keeping her voice strong. 'You know it's not.' Waited for him to respond. He didn't speak. 'Say something,' she whispered.

'I know you have to go home to your family,' he said. 'I want that for you, that reunion.' He squeezed her hand. 'And you're right. We knew you'd have to leave at some point. I just ... after last night ... I didn't think it would be so soon.'

Somehow, hearing him confirm her feelings made them hit her afresh. How could she leave? Her chest ached with conflicting emotions.

Sophus looked at her. She looked back at him. 'What about us, Esther?' He kissed her again. Held her face in his hands. 'Is this real?'

Esther took in his face, his eyes. The feeling of his hands on her skin. The sky behind him, the memory of his body, the smell of the sea. She took it all in, willing herself to remember every little detail.

50

A few days later, on a violet-hued morning that made the green shades of the islands especially vivid, Esther sat in the passenger seat of Sophus' truck, staring out the window while Sophus drove. They didn't speak. Every now and then, Esther glanced from her view of the islands to Sophus' grip on the steering wheel: white-knuckled. A muscle twitched near his eye. He'd been unusually quiet since she'd told him she was leaving.

The night before Sophus had barely said a word, even though he'd cooked dinner for everyone – Greta, Rakul, Klara, Lena, Flósi, Heidi – who'd come to share a meal and say goodbye to Esther. He'd made another vegetarian feast: garlic, Manchego and potato croquettes, with a butter chive dipping sauce, and platters of smoked aubergine and tofu with grilled carrots, asparagus and a mustard sour cream sauce. Each mouthful made Esther's eyes water and reminded her of something Erin had told her once about baking painted cake: *When someone bakes or cooks with their heart, you can always taste it in their food.*

All evening, Flósi and Heidi were in fine form, asking if there was penis cake for dessert again, which confused Greta, Rakul and Klara, and led to a raucous, detailed retelling of Esther's first visit for dinner. Esther cried with laughter and emotion; she tried multiple times throughout their meal to catch Sophus' eye over the candle flames on the dining table.

After Greta, Rakul and Klara took turns to hug Esther at
the front door, they left together, calling Esther's name up to .
the sky as they drove away.

When Esther closed the front door and turned, Flósi was
waiting for her. 'Can we talk?' They'd both avoided each other
since his outburst. Whenever they'd been in the same room their
mutual politeness was almost unbearable to Esther, but she'd
been too stubborn to make the first move. The sting of Flósi's
words the morning after the eighties party hadn't fully faded.

Esther followed him into the living room. Sat and waited
for him to speak.

'I made you this,' he said. Handed her a small parcel
wrapped in cloth and tied with string.

Esther gently pulled the string and opened the folds of cloth
to reveal a palm-sized moon moth, whittled from two types of
wood: a piece of richer, darker caramel grain for the wings and
body, and a buttery-toned wood for the eye spots on the wings.

'She's made from offcuts of cherry. The pale spots on her
wings are silver birch.'

'Silver birch,' Esther murmured, running her fingertips over
the pale eye spots and turning the pendant over in her hands.
Tom. She'd seen him there at the window, bearing witness as
she'd sat at the base of the silver birch, tearing at its bark. Aura's
reverent voice. *My Selkie Tree.*

'Do you like it?' Flósi asked, fidgeting.

Esther looked at the earnest expression on his face. 'So,' she
said, half-smiling, 'is this an apology moth?'

Flósi returned the half-smile. 'I was so awful the other day.
I was upset and had a loose tongue and I'm ashamed. I'm sorry,
Esther.'

'I know you are.' She ran her fingers over the pendant. 'I
know this has all been very weird, me coming here. I'm sorry I
didn't do better, Flósi. I didn't mean to upset you.'

'No,' Flósi shook his head. 'No, no. Please don't be sorry.'
He sighed. 'When you arrived, that night we met at Flóvin,

you couldn't know this, but you met Sophus at the best version of himself he's been in the last couple of years. Since Aura left. When Klara got that first email from you and rang Sophus to tell him what had happened to Aura, he was absolutely devastated, but it also brought him a sense of resolution.'

Flósi ran his hands over his jaw, his chin. 'Really, Esther. I mean, she was here one day, her life woven through his everywhere in this house, and the next day she was gone. Just gone. She left, without warning. Watching him process that and the craziness he felt not being able to get in touch with her again was agony for all of us who love him. Finding out what had happened to Aura, as tragic and heartbreaking as it was, ended nearly two years of limbo for Sophus; his grief had somewhere to go. Two months later, he seemed like he was returning to himself for the first time in much a long time. And then you walked into Flóvin.'

He hung his head. 'I was just starting to feel like I was getting my best friend back. I didn't want to lose him again. And I could tell from that first night where things between you two were headed from the way you looked at each other.' Flósi opened his hands and shrugged. 'I don't know. Everything about this has been hard. And I wasn't my best self for either of you when you probably just needed my support the most. So' – he leaned forward and put his hands around Esther's – 'I'm really sorry.'

'Oh Flósi,' Esther said, scooting forward and wrapping her arms around him in a hug, 'you make us all better with your big heart.'

Flósi wrapped his arms fully around her. 'By the way,' he said into Esther's hair, 'it's not an apology moth.'

'No?'

'It's a you-always-have-a-home-here-with-us moth.'

Esther adjusted her seatbelt and patted the pocket of her jacket, feeling the shape of the carved moth inside. After they'd talked, while everyone was busy cleaning up dinner dishes, Esther had crept outside to Flósi's glasshouse. She wondered when he'd find the black swan feather left by his whittling tools and partially finished puffling.

She glanced at Sophus again. He was staring straight ahead, focused on the road. Jaw clenched. Was he angry? That she'd gone to his room after the dinner dishes were done and everyone had gone to bed? From her seat in the truck, she wanted to reach across the small space between them. A gulf, a galaxy. Instead, she checked the time on her phone. Heidi would be on recess at school. She'd said goodbye to her, and Lena, before they'd left for school and work.

'Will you write to me?' Heidi had asked.

'Of course,' Esther said. Heidi opened her school bag, wrote something on a piece of paper and handed it to Esther. 'This is my email address. Email me and I'll send you back all my handles. We can follow each other on social media. Not that my feeds are very interesting right now because I'm grounded until I die.'

'I will,' Esther said to Heidi, smiling at Lena as she folded the paper and slid it into her pocket.

'Also, I have this for you.' Heidi pulled up the sleeve of her jumper to reveal countless knotted bracelets and rubber bangles on her wrist. She untied one and handed it to Esther: braided waxed turquoise cotton with lilac plastic beads that spelled out a word Esther didn't know. 'I have one too,' Heidi said, pulling her sleeve further up to reveal her matching bracelet.

'"Quaintrelle"?' Esther asked.

'A woman who prioritises a life full of passion, inspiration and pleasure,' Heidi said, grinning through tears.

Sophus turned the radio on as they went through a tunnel. Esther spun Heidi's bracelet around her wrist. In the darkness she imagined Heidi getting home from school that afternoon. Flopping on her bed only to discover Esther's plastic She-Ra sword under her pillow, LADY CRAWLEY inscribed on the hilt.

After Esther had hugged Heidi and Lena goodbye, she'd gathered her luggage by the front door and gone out the back to say goodbye to the sheep. She'd talked to and hugged each one.

'Esther,' Sophus had called from the double doors. 'If you want to go to the art museum before the airport, we should leave now.'

He took her to see the last sculpture in Aura's journal, *Mirror Image*, also by Hans Pauli Olsen. They stood together, taking in the artwork.

'What do you think it meant to her?' Esther asked him quietly.

'I don't know.' Sophus shook his head, his eyes red. 'I like to think it means that there's more than one way to see anything in life.'

Sophus went back to his truck and gave her a moment alone with the sculpture. Esther took her fifth black feather from her travel wallet in her bag and laid it on the ledge that joined the woman above with her reflection below.

They drove out of the tunnel. Esther blinked in the daylight. She spotted the sculpture of The Nix rising from the lake's edge. *Say his name and break the curse.* If only it were that simple. She watched the surface of the lake, glassy, calm, mirror-like. At the other end, somewhere there ran an overflow, where water rushed over rock and plummeted, crashing into the wild sea. Esther pressed her fingertips to the window. She hadn't done the hike. She hadn't remembered to make the trip. To see the lake floating over the ocean.

As they approached the airport, Sophus cleared his throat. 'Should I come in with you?' he asked, looking at her. She held his gaze for a moment.

'It'll only make it harder,' Esther said quietly.

'Okay,' he said, tight-lipped.

They pulled up at the kerb. Got out of the truck. Sophus unloaded Esther's luggage from the tray and placed her bags at her side.

'Abelone is good to pick you up?' Sophus checked.

Esther nodded. She'd called Abelone to ask if she could stay for a night on her way home, and relished her husky cackle in response.

They faced each other, both unable to meet each other's eyes. The silence stretched out between them.

'I'm sorry,' Esther finally said, struggling to maintain composure.

'For what?' he asked, his voice softening. He stepped closer. Tucked her hair behind her ear.

'For coming to your room last night,' she said.

Sophus shook his head, drew her into his arms. 'It's all I could think about, while I was cooking. While we were sitting through dinner. I just wanted to be alone with you. To be with you.'

She held on to him tightly, her body warmed by the memory of their skin pressed together, the look in his eyes. 'I'm sorry for coming to Flóvin without giving you warning,' she rambled. 'I'm sorry if this has all made your life difficult again.'

'Esther … Jesus …' He sighed, drawing apart from her, looking her in the eye. 'You have nothing to apologise for. I've loved every minute, since I looked up in the bar and saw you standing there. Every single minute.' He kissed her. 'I'm sorry I've been so quiet. I haven't known how to be around you. I just … I don't want you to go.'

Esther's skin prickled with the discomfort of how little else there was to say. Until she remembered. 'I got you something,' she said, flashing him a smile. A delay. From her carry-on bag she took a brown paper parcel. Handed it to him. He looked at her with a curious smile. Peeled open the taped corners.

'The bookshop next to Lumiere Café ordered it in for me.' Esther smiled.

He turned the copy of *The Manly Art of Knitting* over in his hands, shaking his head and smiling. The cover was a black and white photograph of a cowboy, complete with hat and sideburns, sitting in his saddle on his horse while knitting.

'I wrote in it for you, but don't read it now,' she said.

Though he chuckled, Sophus' eyes were dull with sadness. He studied Esther's face for a moment as if he was trying to figure something out.

'What?' she asked.

He opened the driver-side door to the truck and took a wrapped parcel from behind the seat. 'For you,' he said.

'Oh,' she murmured, running her hand over the parcel She unwrapped the soft paper; a scarf of soft, pearlescent wool, threaded with metallic black and silver, shimmered in her hands.

'It's my grandmother's pattern, full of stories from the islands, passed down in our family, of women and the sea. Greta taught it to me.' Sophus put his hands in his pockets.

'You knitted this,' Esther said, running her hands over the scarf.

'It just felt right,' he said, 'that you should have our stories with you.'

She let the scarf fall to its full length. He helped her to drape it around her neck.

'It feels right ...' He trailed off.

She ran a hand over the wool. His stitches.

'I have to go,' she said, her voice strained. She slung her carry-on over her shoulder and extended the handle on her suitcase. Willed herself to move. To walk away from him.

'Wait,' Sophus said. 'Just wait.' He held her tightly. She wrapped her arms around his body, closed her eyes, breathed him in.

'Thank you,' she whispered.

And then, they were apart; everything happened too fast. He got back into the truck. Started the engine. She turned and walked away, towards the airport terminal.

"'Remind yourself how the look of something changes once you're moving,'" Esther recited her sister's words aloud. "'Step by step by step.'"

At the entrance, her step faltered. She stopped. Turned around. Against the backdrop of towering, craggy green volcanic mountains, his red truck was still parked where she'd left him; Sophus stood in the tray, watching her go. When he saw her turn, he raised both arms in the air. She laughed, tearily. Raised both arms back and waved. Stood there waving until there was nothing left to do but wave one last time, turn and walk away.

Two hours later, Esther fastened her seatbelt and leaned to the window as her flight took off. She watched the islands shrink in the distance, her insides shrinking with them. One last time she took in the jagged landscapes that were the green tint of dreams, black basalt rock, turquoise shallows and the white ribbons of waterfalls. Giant peaks rose from the sea; the dragons slept on. She'd found the treasure she'd gone looking for, but it wasn't hers to keep. Esther pressed her forehead to the window, imagining him on land from her bird's-eye view.

When the cabin crew brought the refreshments trolley, Esther ordered a double vodka and soda; the last view of the islands disappeared behind a veil of cloud.

In the same moment, Sophus drove home; *The Manly Art of Knitting* lay open on the passenger seat in his truck where Esther's presence lingered. He glanced down at it, to the opening page titled 'Basics'. A black feather was taped at the quill to the paper. Esther's handwriting below. He looked back to the road; her words kept their own beat inside his chest.

For my Marty McFly,
   Thank you for reminding me that the flux capacitor is fuelled by conviction as much as it is by jigowatts.
   I had the time of my life.
   Love, your She-Ra

51

Esther sat on the green couch in Abelone's living room, taking in the clear and warm afternoon light. On the mid-century coffee table, Abelone's tobacco pouch lay open, tobacco grains scattered beside an old newspaper, a partially finished crossword. The tall potted fig trees and glossy monstera plants seemed to gather around, as if keeping counsel, speculating over Esther's luggage sitting to the side of the pink folk-art rug. Nothing had changed. Everything had changed.

She stared at the framed print of Hilma af Klint's swans, one black, one white, and the blurred horizon line between them, where their beaks met, ever so slightly overlapping.

Esther asking her dad, 'Could I ever become a good enough swimmer to make it all the way to the horizon?' They're at the stargazing shack.

'You could try.' Jack smiles. 'But the horizon doesn't exist, Starry.'

Esther looks at him in disbelief.

'True,' Jack says. 'You can see it, but it's not really there. Just like the end of a rainbow, the horizon is an illusion.'

Esther gazed at the swan painting. Rested an arm on a velvet cushion, running a hand with the grain of fabric then against it. A month had passed since she was last in Abelone's house. That measurement of time felt like the horizon. An illusion, elastic, collapsible. That month-ago version of herself sat too close on the couch, reeking of sex, self-loathing, rage and failure. Esther spun the friendship bracelet on her wrist, tethering herself to the present. *Quaintrelle.*

'Here we are,' Abelone announced as she came through the swing door to the kitchen with a tray of cake and tea. 'Let's try this again, shall we?' She set down the tray on the coffee table and served Esther a slice of Sosterkage. Seven Sisters Cake. Poured a cup of Russian Caravan tea.

Esther inhaled the sweet and smoky aromas; for the rest of her life, she would drink Russian Caravan tea to anchor herself to moments spent sitting in the house of her ancestors by a lake of swans in Copenhagen, with Abelone.

'So, skat,' Abelone said, sitting opposite Esther and sipping her tea. 'Your time in the Faroes. Tell me everything.'

An hour later, only tea leaves left at the bottom of their cups and sweet crumbs on their cake plates, Esther and Abelone sat together on the same couch. While Esther had been sharing what she'd learned of Aura's life in Tórshavn, Abelone had crossed the room to sit with her.

'Esther,' she said, her face filled with sorrow. 'I'm so sorry.'

Esther nodded. 'Me too.'

'She scattered Eala's ashes at Kópakonan?'

Esther nodded again.

Abelone tutted. 'I wish she'd come home to me here.' She sighed. 'On her way back home. I wish I could have done something to help her.'

Esther fidgeted with a thread in the couch covering. 'There's so much I wish I'd done differently, Abelone.'

'Of course. That's what hindsight is. Wishing we could make the past perfect when it can never be changed. You did the best you were able to do at the time.'

Esther sighed. 'That's hard to accept.'

'It is.' Abelone looked at Esther carefully. 'I get the feeling there was more to all of this, to your time in the Faroes with Sophus and his family.'

Esther shifted in her seat.

'You mentioned him a lot. You spent a lot of time with him? That sounds like it was intense. Yes?'

Esther's face grew hot. She couldn't meet Abelone's eyes.

'Esther?'

Eventually, Esther looked up.

'Oh,' Abelone murmured, a knowing expression on her face.

Esther's eyes filled. She wiped them before any tears could fall. 'I don't know what it was.' She looked to the print of the swans. The horizon line between them. 'Maybe it was just grief. Our shared grief.' The look on his face before she walked away from him at the airport. The way her whole body ached with yearning to stay. 'But maybe it was love,' she whispered. Shrugged. 'I don't know.' Wiped her eyes again.

Abelone looked at Hilma af Klint's painting. 'The thing is, skat, when it comes to grief and love, I've found they're one and the same.'

A shiver went down Esther's spine. 'But even if it is love,' she said, a pinch in her throat, 'I'm afraid that we went too far. That I've done the wrong thing. Again.' She picked at the skin around her fingernails. 'Even though it's never felt so right, being with someone. As I felt with him.'

Abelone folded her hands over Esther's. 'Going too far is in our blood.'

Esther searched Abelone's eyes.

'We come from sea-faring people. Vikings, fishermen, women who depended on the sea for their survival. Who relied on going too far, on venturing into the unknown, to learn where the line was, between safety and danger.'

Esther turned her palms under Abelone's so they were holding hands. Where had the line been with Sophus?

'Our ancestors didn't know their limits,' Abelone continued, 'until they went too far.'

Esther threw Abelone a grateful look.

'Only a few generations ago, even our Johanna and Gull lived their lives by going too far. Your family exists in Australia because Johanna decided to marry and sail to the other side of the world. We are sitting in Gull's house; she bought this home because she chose to stay in Denmark and pretended to be a man, sailing trade routes, working as a sailor. Did they go too far? Whose business is it to say? But they made bold choices. They didn't die wondering. Going too far can have its place. You made choices that felt good. Who's to tell you they were wrong? Were you hurting anyone? Did you cause anyone harm? No.' Abelone patted Esther's hand. 'Don't let fear or self-doubt make you regret them.' Abelone's words kindled a flicker of hope in Esther's chest.

'Thank you. Esther looked down at their fingers folded together. A small black bird was tattooed on the top of Abelone's hand. 'Enough about me,' Esther said. 'I don't remember that tattoo.' Looking at Abelone's hand, Esther turned her head sideways to get a better view. 'What is that? A black bird?' She looked closer at the flecks of white and silver in the wings. 'A starling?'

'Oh. This? Oh, well ...' Abelone trailed off, half-heartedly waving the attention away.

'Ummmm,' Esther said, jaw dropping. She kept her eyes fixed on Abelone, leaving her nowhere to hide. 'What's going on?'

'Well,' Abelone said, aloof. 'I've been navigating some uncharted water myself, lately.'

'Romantic water?' Esther's brows shot up.

Abelone didn't respond.

'Who with?' Esther exclaimed. She looked at the starling on Abelone's hand again. Something about it was familiar. Starling. Tattoo. Things slotted together in her mind. 'Oh my god,' she said, looking from Abelone's hand to her face. 'Lille Heks?'

Abelone held her hands up, grinning in radiant surrender. 'I have you to thank, actually. After we all met up that day at the Rundetaarn, Lille Heks and I kept in touch. Texts and calls. We've gone out a bit. It's early days,' Abelone said, rubbing a thumb softly over the starling in her skin, 'but it's going well.'

Esther smiled. 'From the look on your face, and that tattoo, and knowing what starlings mean to Lille Heks,' she mused, 'I'd say it's going very well.'

Abelone giggled behind her hands.

'This should have been the first thing you told me when we saw each other at the airport,' Esther teased.

'Well,' Abelone said, dusting crumbs from her trousers. 'I'm a dark Norse, no?'

Esther was about to correct her when she picked up the twinkle in Abelone's eye. She chuckled. 'You are indeed a dark Norse.'

Later that afternoon, Abelone and Esther made plans to share a late dinner at home; Abelone had an early evening class to teach.

'Will you be okay?' Abelone asked as she gathered her coat and books to leave. 'You could always come along? Be my guest lecturer?'

Esther pulled a face. 'Hard pass, thank you.' She looked out of the windows to the bright sky. 'Think I'll take a walk. Ahead of the long flight home tomorrow.'

'Perfect. Need a map?' Abelone asked.

'I'm good.' Esther smiled. 'Thanks.'

Esther walked along the edge of Sortedams Sø, watching the white swans glide over the lake that had turned molten in the light of the late sun. She followed the path over Fredens Bro, the

Bridge of Peace. Meandered through the gates to Rosenborg Castle Gardens. The trees were lush with glossy leaves, as if laying out their green finery while awaiting summer's arrival.

Ahead, under the pale, clear sky, Liden Gunver stood silent and tall. Vulnerable and young.

Esther stayed with her a while. Cleared the leaves from her feet. Her black swan feather was gone. She ran her fingertips over Liden Gunver's name inscribed in bronze, covered in blue-green verdigris. The same colour as the coat Aura had been wearing the day Klara had photographed her standing there with Sophus. Their hands had been clasped around her stomach. Expecting Eala.

She clenched her jaw against the pain that seized in her body. Looked up at Liden Gunver's face.

"'Maybe she chose the depths,'" she recited. Closed her eyes; saw the words written in ink across Aura's skin. "'Maybe she's free.'"

Nyhavn was aglow and bustling with the early dinner rush as Esther crossed the cobblestones to walk on the sunny side of the harbour. The colours of the buildings shone, red, mustard, navy. Moored boats rocked on the water, lanyards tinkling. She strolled, breathing in the sea. *Our ancestors didn't know their limits until they went too far.*

As she passed by the entrances to the succession of restaurants lining the harbour, Esther caught aromas of grilled butter, herbs and garlic. Her mouth watered. Around her, restaurant staff hovered in freshly pressed aprons by rows of outdoor tables filling with people. She searched along the buildings until she saw the flowerpots. At the steps leading up to the bar above Tattoo Stjerne, Esther paused. Remembered the time she'd scaled them and, later, stumbled down them, dishevelled. *Going too far is in our blood.*

'Ah, fuck it,' Esther muttered and walked upstairs, into the bar.

Inside, the English barman with the blue inked waves on his forearms was busy serving.

'Hello Dark Blue,' Esther murmured under her breath as she took a seat at the bar and waited.

Around her the restaurant hummed with the clink and chatter of meals and conversations being shared. She glanced at the empty table behind her, remembering the Australian couple she'd overheard chatting on her first afternoon in Copenhagen. They'd been planning a weekend away together and sounded as excited as kids. Esther recalled the burn she'd felt in her stomach as she'd eavesdropped and envied their closeness.

She glanced up at the barman, still busy, and snapped open her menu. Tried to focus. But all she could hear was his song in her mind. *She was the river. You are the sea.*

'What can I get you, love?' Dark Blue didn't look up as he wiped down the bar counter and lined up new coasters.

She didn't answer. Waited for him to recognise her.

'Love?' he asked again, finally looking at her. 'What can I get you?' His face relaxed with recognition. 'Oh, hey. It's you.'

'It's me.' She waited for her body to respond as it once had.

'Drink on the house? I finish in half an hour.' His smile was warm and easy.

'You know,' Esther said, standing. Her skin crawled with the urgency to be anywhere but at that bar. 'I'm fine, actually.' She bundled her coat and bag in her arms and hurried for the door.

'Are you sure?' he called after her.

She raised a hand in a wave. Didn't look back.

Outside, she took in deep breaths. Relief flooded her body. She walked downstairs. After a moment's deliberation, she turned down the laneway.

At the entrance to Tattoo Stjerne, Esther stopped by the two windows looking into the studio. Through one, Tala was bent over a woman lying face down while she tattooed the back of the woman's calf.

Through the other window, on the opposite side of the studio, under the pink neon lettered sign on the wall, a young woman lay face up on another tattoo bed. She was laughing and chatting while Lille Heks tattooed her forearm.

Esther stood back. Took in the façade of the parlour, lit candles in jars, the swinging Tattoo Stjerne sign. Under it, apparitions of Abelone, Freya and Erin gathered, arms entwined, daring each other to enter the parlour first. They giggled, then faded. The hairs on the back of Esther's neck stood up; an imagined Aura appeared, approaching the steps down to the parlour. She clutched her journal to her chest, seven stencils for seven tattoos inside and a story of transformation to tell. At the door she paused, murmured something to herself, and, after a readying breath, went inside. Esther wrapped her arms around herself. Sylvia Plath's words beat a neon-pink rhythm in her chest. *Wear your heart on your skin in this life.*

Esther dropped her suitcase at check-in and went through security at Copenhagen airport. The spicy warmth of Abelone's sandalwood perfume still lingered on her clothes from their goodbye hug.

'Come back to Copenhagen, and Gull's house, any time. We're here with an open door,' Abelone's voice had cracked. 'Don't be strange.'

'Thank you for being so good to me,' Esther had replied. 'I won't be a stranger.' She thought about the way the light fell through the dormer windows of the loft at Abelone's house. The view of the sky and lake. The seventh black swan feather she'd tucked between *Ways of Seeing* and *Fire in the Sea* on the bookshelf in the loft's living room.

'Esther. You have brought me joy. Tak.' Abelone hugged her.

'Thank you for being my family.' Esther barely managed to get the words out as she wrapped her arms around Abelone.

She settled in with a coffee at a café in the airport waiting lounge. Scrolled through her phone. Couldn't focus. Put her phone down. Watched the flow of people around her instead.

Departures. Arrivals. Hugs and tears. Grief and love. One and the same.

As she sipped her coffee and watched families milling around her, realisation hit swift and hard: in the flurry of her decision-making in Tórshavn, finding and booking flights, absorbed by the emotion of leaving, she hadn't told her parents she was coming home. Nor had she asked anyone to collect her from the airport.

She picked up her phone again, thinking of who to call first. Watched herself open her texts and start composing a new message.

Hi. It's me, Esther. This is going to seem random and I'm sorry about that, and about a million other things. I'm landing in Launceston tomorrow morning local time from Copenhagen. Is there any chance you could pick me up? I have no right to ask this of you, I know, but I could really do with the company of an old friend before I see my family.

She tapped send before she could overthink adding an *x* or not. Tried not to watch the screen. Quickly converted the time difference; it was early enough in the evening at home, he'd be awake.

Esther clicked the screen off. Tried to put it out of her mind. Sipped her coffee.

Jiggled her knee. Picked up her phone. Returned to the message. Her heart raced: his status had changed to *online*.

And then. *Tom is typing.*

Esther stared at the screen, unblinking.

Makes sense. Every great explorer needs a decompression chamber upon re-entry.

A pause.

Send arrival details. I'll be there.

Esther watched Tom's status go offline. And then come back on.

De Profundis ad Astra.

Esther chuckled to herself. Sent him a screenshot of her itinerary and a reply. *From the depths to the stars.*

As her flight was called to start the boarding process, Esther closed her texts and opened her contacts. Scrolled through until she reached *Home* and barely faltered before she tapped the green button to call.

52

Esther led the way through the blue gums to the stargazing shack. Tom's footsteps crunched through dry leaves behind her. Their reunion at the airport had been easy, but there was a mountain range of things unsaid between them and Esther knew the trek to scale it began with her.

She swept the top step clear and sat. Tom joined her. The gum trees susurrated their welcome-home song. After a while Esther glanced sideways at Tom. He looked quizzically at her.

'I can't believe you wore that shirt,' she said.

'What?' Tom asked, deadpan as he opened his unzipped jacket to show his stretched-tight, faded Space Club t-shirt. 'I'm almost offended you didn't wear yours. What kind of club member are you?'

'I don't know if I believe that's the original though.'

Tom lifted one side of his jacket to reveal a tomato sauce stain. 'Recognise this? From when we had our Space Club party for the Hubble launch, and I accidentally sat on your hot chips?'

Esther laughed at the memory. 'It was a bit bigger on you then. Came down to your knees, remember? Dad didn't do a great job with our sizes.'

Silence settled between them. Esther felt the mountains rising beneath her.

'You've done things like this, you know?' She looked him in the eye. 'As long as I can remember us knowing each other, you've always thought of ways to help everyone around you,

to be a good friend without asking how. Like answering my
text from Copenhagen, and, despite my behaviour at Aura's
memorial, saying straight away, yes, you'd be at the airport for
me.' Esther leaned her elbows on her knees, pressed her hands
together. 'Thank you for that.'

Tom leaned forward, sitting in a similar position. 'You're
welcome.'

She breathed deeply. Quietly. 'I'm sorry, Tom. For what
I did at the memorial. For just so many things. The hook-up
when we were younger that we never should have had. Not
appreciating you enough when Aura died and you were here,
day in and day out for my family. I'm sorry I wasn't as good to
you as I should have been.'

Tom swallowed. 'It's okay.' He nudged her knee with his
knee. 'It's really okay.' He looked up, at the crowns of the
gums swaying in the wind, the low-hanging grey autumn sky.
'I'm sorry too. For not making better choices with you, for
not being better at talking, or staying in touch after we drifted
apart.' He interlaced his fingers. 'Esther, we were kids. Going
through grief. Me after my dad left. You with everything going
on with Aura, and then losing her. That night we had at Baz
and Kel's wedding, that's not our whole story, you know? It's
just part of it. We did the best we could.' He gave her a genuine
smile. 'I'm not sad our first time was a drunken hook-up with
each other. It was a total mess. Kind of suited us both.'

Esther smiled, remembering Abelone's words. *That's what
hindsight is. Wishing we could make the past perfect when it can never
be changed.* She nudged him. He nudged her back.

After a while, Tom looked at her. 'This is a big question,'
he started, 'so answer it however you like.'

She waited.

'How was your trip? Really?'

Esther exhaled through loose lips. On their drive home
from the airport, she'd given Tom the basics on where she'd
been and why, what she'd learned about Aura's life, and the

phone call she'd made to Freya. Certain select details about a certain select person on her trip had been omitted. When she'd landed and switched her mobile on, there'd been a text waiting from Sophus, asking if she'd arrived home safely. Her heart had ached at the sight of his name.

'My trip ...' She trailed off, gesturing with her hands. She glanced at Tom's Space Club t-shirt. 'It was a supernova.'

Tom shook his head. 'Well, that's a shock. I gotta say. Not like you at all, to blow up your life,' he teased, but then hurriedly checked her expression. 'Too soon?'

'Fair,' she chuckled. 'That's fair.'

Tom smiled, visibly relieved. 'Maybe it'd be better to ask, are you glad you went?'

Esther looked at the sea through the grey and pink trunks of the trees and then back to Tom. Nodded.

'A successful mission, then.' He cleared his throat. 'Tell me more about it next time, when we hang out again. After you're over jet lag and settled back in. Amy and the kids and I often come home to Salt Bay for weekends. We could come here and get out your dad's old telescope sometime? I could show my girls.'

Esther took in his words. 'I'd really love that,' she managed to say. 'I'd love to know Amy and your daughters.'

Tom grinned at her. 'You're quite famous in our family. Esther from Space Club.'

'Thanks.' Esther rolled her eyes playfully. 'I'll have to brush up on my space facts.'

'No pressure. They only know more about everything than we ever did at their age.'

Esther laughed. In her pocket, her mobile phone beeped. She took it out and read the new text message.

'Mum's asking when we'll be back. Said she can't wait to see me.' She chewed on her bottom lip.

'Let's get you home, hey?' Tom said.

When they got back to Tom's car, Esther opened the passenger door and stopped to look at him over the roof.

'I've really missed this,' she said.

'Me too, Starry.'

As Tom pulled into the driveway of the Shell House, Esther's palms began to sweat. She didn't know what to expect from her parents. Would they be able to see in her face what had happened with Sophus? Would they be angry at her? For not staying in more regular contact. For delivering them more pain, about Aura. And Eala.

Tom parked. Inside the house a curtain at the window twitched.

'Oh god,' Esther muttered, gripping the edges of the passenger seat.

'Breathe,' Tom said.

She had expected Jack, but it was Freya who flung the front door open.

'Esther,' she called, running down the front steps and across the lawn. 'Jack,' she yelled over her shoulder. 'Jack, she's home. Jack.'

Esther got out of the car, unsure of what to expect. Freya threw her arms around her.

'Mum,' Esther said, taken aback. 'I didn't think you ... I mean, I thought you'd be in the studio ...' She tried again. 'You're here.'

'I wouldn't have been anywhere else.' Freya's voice wobbled as she tried to gather more and more of Esther into her arms. 'You're home. You're home.' When they drew apart Freya looked Esther over. 'You look so good, min guldklump,' she said. Her eyes were present and clear. No aloof glaze, no distraction.

'Thanks, Mum,' Esther whispered. A movement in her peripheral vision: Jack leaned against the railing on the veranda. Freya smiled, stepped aside.

'Hi Dad,' Esther said, trying to make her voice hold.

'Here she is,' Jack said, opening his arms. 'Welcome home, Starry.'

Esther held him tight. Breathed him in. 'It's so fucking good to see you, Dad,' she murmured into his shoulder.

'It's fucking good to see you too, love.' He leaned back and met Esther's eye with a smile.

'Tom, come in for a cuppa?' Freya offered.

'Oh, no thanks, Mrs Wilding.' Tom unloaded Esther's bags from the car. 'You guys need time together and I need to get home to my own family.'

Freya went to him and gave him a hug. Jack walked down the veranda and did the same. Esther followed.

'Tom will come visit again soon,' she said, pressing her hands together and mouthing her thanks to him. He nodded and smiled.

As he drove away Tom rolled down the driver's window and raised a hand with his thumb and index finger pressed together. Held upwards, towards the sky.

An hour later, Esther walked down the hallway of the Shell House, towelling her damp hair after a hot bath. Freya's and Jack's voices travelled from the kitchen, chatting as they made an early dinner.

When Tom had left and they'd come inside, Esther had fallen quiet, taking in the familiarity of home. Freya had rambled and wrung her hands. 'I wasn't sure what you'd feel like after your long journey home, so I've got a cheesy broccoli soup on the go if you need something light, but, also, I'm making a roast veggie lasagne if you need something more substantial. Oh, and I also picked up some of that crunchy sourdough you love from Banjo's. So, after you've had your shower, you just let me know what you need, Esther, okay?'

Jack caught Esther's eye and just smiled. 'Take a bath and get settled, love. We'll be in the kitchen when you're ready.'

Esther had hung back, watching her parents go into the kitchen together. Jack put his hand on Freya's shoulder. Freya put her hand over his.

She paused at the doorway to her bedroom, squeezing the ends of her hair with the towel. Jet lag and delirium blurred the edges of her vision. She gazed around. Her bookshelf crammed with old school science books. The yellowed Maria Mitchell poster still stuck to her wall. Her potted violet sat on the windowsill with velveteen leaves. Still lush, still tended.

Esther kept walking down the hallway but instead of going into the kitchen, stopped at the closed door to Aura's bedroom. Put a hand on the knob. Stalled as she remembered the varying phases of chaos and obsession Aura's décor had gone through. First, She-Ra. Then Kylie. Later Pearl Jam and The Cranberries and Ruby Hunter. Chiffon scarves and army boots. Candy necklaces and love heart sunglasses. Then the phase when Aura had turned sixteen and taken every single poster off her walls and painted the room a deep, midnight blue. A prickle of realisation: Aura had turned sixteen just after she'd miscarried. Esther balled her hands into fists. Aura's bedroom had stayed that colour, the deepest part of the ocean, the highest part of the night sky, through Aura's move to Nipaluna, Hobart, for university and then home again. It had stayed midnight blue until Aura had decided to move to Denmark. Once again, she'd covered the walls of her bedroom with the linings of her heart: photos of Tivoli Gardens, Nyhavn, the underwater Agnete sculpture; lists of things to do, places to go, Danish phrases to learn. After Aura got home from Denmark, after she disappeared, Esther hadn't stepped foot in Aura's room again. Unlike Freya, who'd found Aura's journal.

Esther turned the doorknob and pushed the door to Aura's bedroom open, expecting to find the chaos that had once been inside. But the bedroom had been cleaned and tidied. The easel and photograph of Aura from her memorial stood in the corner. The bed was made. The curtains were open.

The walls were as dark as Esther remembered; the depths of their hue reminded her of North Atlantic waves and slick basalt rock.

She walked around the room, stopping at the desk her sister had written at since she was a teenager. Esther stood at Aura's desk for a long time, running her fingers over the indents in the wood from Aura's handwriting. She traced the loops and curls of Aura's words. Written in her ink. Written in her skin.

After a dinner of cheesy broccoli soup with fresh, buttered sourdough, a glass of malbec and light conversation with her parents, jet lag started to tug Esther's eyes closed while she was sitting at the table. Her head jolted.

'Love, get some rest, eh?' Jack stroked her arm.

Esther stood and started to excuse herself. 'Thanks for dinner.'

'You're welcome, skat.' Freya folded her napkin. 'Oh, hey, if you're up for it, we're all taking a plate to Queenie's for a late lunch at her place tomorrow. I might take the veg lasagne I made tonight; we didn't put a dent in it. It'll be just family. Erin, Nin, Aunty Ro. The usual suspects.'

Esther fidgeted with the hem of her shirt. 'Do they ... Does everyone know? About Aura? And Eala?'

Freya's expression was sorrowful and strong. 'We've told them.' She reached for Esther's hand. 'Everyone is very happy to have you home and just really looking forward to seeing you.'

Esther made herself smile. Did her best to ignore the weight of Sophus' unspoken name pressing on her chest. She'd replied to his earlier text while she was in the bath. *I'm home. I'm safe.* She hadn't known what else to say.

'See you both in the morning.' Esther hugged Jack out of habit, and then realised Freya had her arms open too. She revelled in the warmth of her mother's embrace.

As Esther walked down the hall, she tried to remember the last time she'd gone to bed in the Shell House to the sound of her parents chatting into the night after dinner and wine.

The following afternoon Esther lounged in a camp chair around a lit fire in Queenie's garden, along with her family. After a bowl of Erin's kelp chowder and plates of Freya's veggie lasagne and Queenie's lemon drop cake, she struggled to keep her eyes open. The warmth of the fire, stubborn jet lag and the intense emotion of reunions didn't help.

When Freya, Jack and Esther had arrived, she'd been swamped by Queenie's hug.

'Pulingina milaythina-nanya. Welcome home, Starry,' Queenie had said, embracing her. She'd hugged Esther so hard, the points of the shells in her necklace had dug into Esther's skin. She didn't mind a bit.

'Hmmmm,' Aunty Ro murmured as she appeared next to Queenie, looking Esther up and down, running a hand over the long garland of iridescent shells she was also wearing. 'Being up there on the top of the world did you good. You don't look so sickly anymore.'

'Romy,' Queenie chastised, trying not to laugh.

'Thanks, Aunty Ro.' Esther had missed Aunty Ro's special brand of compliments. 'It's good to be home, Queenie.'

'Hello, my girl,' Erin said as she muscled in to wrap her arms around Esther.

'Erin,' Esther said, turning to tuck her face into her aunt's shoulder.

'Are you okay?' Erin asked, her silver bracelets chiming as she stroked Esther's hair. 'That's a hell of a trip you had.'

'I'm okay,' Esther said. 'Mum and Dad said they've told you?'

Erin nodded. 'I'm so sorry.'

'Me too,' Esther said. They faced each other, wiping each other's cheeks.

'How's Frankie?' Esther asked with a small, cheeky grin.

Erin made a chef's kiss gesture at her lips with her fingers. 'Painted cake never fails.'

'Oh, I know,' Esther said before she could stop herself.

Erin gripped Esther's arm. 'I'm sorry?'

'Not now,' Esther said out of the side of her mouth. Erin grinned, zipped her lips with her finger and thumb, then threw away an imaginary key.

Esther looked around. An absence nagged at her.

'Is Nin here?' Esther asked everyone. Their multiple conversations hushed.

'Ya, Starry,' Nin said behind her.

When Esther turned, she saw Nin's radiant face. The choker-length necklace she was wearing, large black crow shells accented with two shimmering green, violet and gold king marina shells. And then, her pregnant stomach.

Esther's jaw dropped.

'Oh my god, Nin,' she said. 'How did this happen?' Everyone laughed. Esther shook her head, smiling. 'I mean, when? I had no idea. How far along are you?'

'I wanted to wait until you came home so I could tell you in person. Nearly halfway.' Nin stroked her stomach. 'With your blessing,' she said, tearing up, 'the baby's name will be Romy Aurora Jones.'

Esther pursed her lips against emotion. Took a shaky breath. 'You have our blessing, of course. Right?' She looked to Freya and Jack.

They both nodded. 'Of course.'

Queenie clapped her hands as if making an announcement. 'It's so good to be together again.'

'Yeah,' Aunty Ro joined in. 'Now, let's eat.'

As everyone waited to serve themselves from the platters on Queenie's dining table, Nin and Esther huddled to the side with their empty plates. Esther couldn't stop staring at Nin's stomach, the way she subconsciously held her hands to it.

'She would be so happy for you,' Esther murmured.

Nin looked away. 'Starry, about what happened to Aura when we were teenagers—'

'She was your best friend. I get it,' Esther said softly.

Nin squeezed Esther's hand. Rested her other hand on her stomach.

'We can talk about it in time, whenever you're ready,' Esther said.

'I'd love that.' Nin smiled, grateful.

Out of the corner of her eye, Esther noticed Freya hovering.

Esther stood from her camp chair and added another log to the fire. Nin was chatting to Queenie and Erin. Jack and Aunty Ru were conferring over dessert options. Freya came to sit beside Esther. They exchanged smiles.

Freya raised her glass of wine to Esther. Esther met her mother's eye. Clinked glasses. They drank.

'I love you,' Freya said quietly.

'I love you, too,' Esther replied.

Across the flames, Erin watched them. Raised her own wine glass with a smile. 'To Esther,' Erin said. Everyone paused their conversations and raised their glasses. 'To Esther,' they chorused.

Esther gazed around the circle at her family's faces glowing in the firelight. In each one of them, her home, her story. Behind a veil in her heart, she danced in another circle, at Flóvin, with Sophus, Flósi, Heidi, Lena, Greta and Rakul.

As she was above, so she is below.

When they got home from Queenie's, Jack went ahead to unlock the front door of the Shell House. Freya hung back with Esther.

'We'll be in in a minute, love,' she said to Jack.

'Okey doke. I'll pop the kettle on,' he said.

Esther watched him walk down the hallway, switching lamps on. She turned to Freya.

Her mother leaned against the veranda railing. 'Guldklump,' she said, scuffing her boots, 'whatever burden you're carrying with Sophus, you don't need to.'

Esther stiffened. 'I don't know what you mean.'

'You can't see your own face when you talk about him,' Freya said gently. 'Or hear how your voice changes when you say his name.'

'I'm too jet-lagged to talk about this,' Esther whimpered, rubbing her eyes.

'It's alright, Esther,' Freya said.

'I feel so ashamed,' she whispered.

'Things are hard enough. Aren't they? Go easy on yourself.' Freya stepped forward, rubbed Esther's arms.

Esther focused on her boots. 'I don't know why.'

'Why what?'

'Why there's anything between me and Sophus. Is it because of us? Me? Or is it because I'm Aura's sister? I don't know.'

'Maybe there's a better question to consider,' Freya suggested.

She looked at her mother.

'How will you ever know?' Freya asked.

Esther searched for the answer in her mother's eyes. 'How will I ever know?'

Freya pressed a hand to Esther's shoulder. Moved towards the front door.

'Mum?'

Freya turned.

'Don't take this the wrong way,' Esther started.

'Geez, okay.' Freya laughed uncomfortably.

'No, it's just that, I mean ...' Esther pulled her sleeves down over her hands. 'You're so different. With me.'

Freya looked away for a moment as if considering something to say. When she looked back at Esther she just smiled, despite tears in her eyes. 'Night cap?' she asked.

Esther returned her smile. 'Yes, please.'

After Freya went inside, Esther lingered in the garden. Watched the stars. Checked the time.

The morning would be unfolding in Sophus' kitchen. Heidi would be getting ready for school. Lena would be digging Flósi out of bed. Sophus would be out in the paddock feeding Meryl, Michelle, Megan, Shagourney, Dolly, Lady Maamaaa and Frida their favourites: oats and strawberries.

Esther paced the dew-covered grass. Moths fluttered in the silver air. She glanced across the lawn at the white trunk of the birch, the Selkie Tree, almost glowing in the moonlight. An image of Kópakonan came to mind. *Esther, what do you need?*

She took her phone from her pocket and opened her texts. They hadn't had any more contact since their brief exchange when he'd texted to ask if she'd landed safely.

She considered all she wanted to say to him. How, or where to begin.

Hi Sophus, I can't stop thinking about you. I don't know what to say.

Delete.

Dear Sophus, I'm so confused – how can we possibly make this work? I don't know. But not knowing doesn't stop me wishing that we could try.

Delete.

Esther sighed, irritated with herself. She looked up at the stars. Slowed her breathing. Cygnus was swimming through the river of the Milky Way. It was such a comfort to see it in the sky again. She recalled getting out of the taxi at Flóvin, looking up and searching the sunny night sky, void of stars. The memory was too delicious to resist replaying: Sophus walking towards her through the crowd, dimples in his smile as they bantered about the flux capacitor.

An idea came to mind. A small smile played on Esther's face.

She tapped out a new message and sent it.

The thing is, as Marty McFly grew up, wouldn't his parents, George and Lorraine, have recognised that he looked the same as Calvin Klein, who brought them together at their Enchantment Under the Sea high school dance?

Esther gripped her phone, waiting to see if she'd get a reply. Her heart hammered when a text bubble appeared, indicating Sophus was typing. His texts came in quick succession.

Excellent question. This should be investigated and discussed.

It's my day off. I'm at home. The wind is crazy here this morning.

Are you busy now? I have an idea. Then four emojis: a man, a television, the Earth, a woman, a television.

Want to get online and watch a movie with me?

53

As first winter light brightened the sky from midnight blue to pale grey over the bay, seven figures walked down the cold, white sand. Headed for the seven granite boulders on the point, covered in flame-coloured algae and lichen: silent, silhouetted sentinels. The sea was glassy and glittered in the low light. The sky was heavy with dark, rolling clouds. One of the figures ambled with a walking stick. Another was pregnant. Four carried a variety of bags, two beach umbrellas, an Esky, blankets, a camp stove. The last figure carried two large bags of chopped firewood.

Next to the seven boulders, the group arranged their belongings. One person unpacked a bag: posies of dried pink paper daisies, the colour of scallop shells, were set on the sand. Each person collected a posy: two paper daisies and a frond of dried kelp bound with raffia. When all seven figures had a posy in hand, they walked together to the shore. A few of them walked arm in arm. They stood together, their feet in the saltwater, and faced the sea, the brightening sky. They waited.

The sun climbed over the horizon, turning the sky a vivid, pink-tinged gold, bringing tears to some eyes. The underbellies of the clouds were lit bronze, aquamarine. The sea shimmered, turquoise shallows to inky depths beyond view. The seven figures took steps into the sea, up to their thighs, forming a u-shape.

Each held a posy; they spoke in turn. One recited a poem. One wailed, the hands of the others on her shoulders and back. Another sang.

After they had all spoken, wiped tears, occasionally laughed, they were silent. The morning crescendoed with birdsong; currawongs, thrushes, rosellas sang from the trees. The sea swayed, an infinite story.

The seven figures standing in the sea looked to each other. One threw her flowers to the waves. Another followed. Soon seven posies of daisies and kelp floated on the sea, towards the horizon.

'Aura and Eala,' she said. 'My love will not leave you.'

One of the others repeated it. Was joined by another.

'My love will not leave you,' all seven said in unison.

The sun ascended above the sea and cast the seven figures in unfettered light. They huddled in farewell, watching the sea carry the flowers away.

When the sun was high in the sky and the scent of the tea trees and blue gums carried on the breeze down to the sand where Esther was gathered with her family, Jack fired up the camp stove.

'Breakfast orders,' he said. 'Aunty Ro, yours first.'

'Good man.' Aunty Ro rubbed her hands together.

'Starry,' Nin said out of the side of her mouth, leaning towards Esther under one of the beach umbrellas. 'Her dress and cape are done. I'm sorted. Just need to pick them up from my workshop. So,' she looked around to make sure no one could hear them. 'We on?'

'Me too. Crown is done. I've got a ladder. We're on.'

'Yes.' Nin punched the air, quietly victorious. 'Dusk tonight?'

Esther grinned. 'Dusk it is.'

Nin winked. Turned to chat to Aunty Ro.

While Nin and Aunty Ro were busy talking and Jack was taking Freya's and Erin's breakfast orders, Esther seized the moment.

'Ya, Queenie,' Esther said, going to her side.

'Ya, bub.' Queenie poured herself another thermos cup of coffee. 'Want some?'

'No, thanks, I just had one.'

Queenie took a sip of her coffee. 'Nina nayri?'

Esther kept her voice low. 'I want to find a therapist.'

Queenie's face softened.

'Can you please give me a recommendation?' Esther asked.

'I can, but your dad has plenty of suggestions, I'm sure.'

'He does.' Esther ran her hands down her trouser legs. 'I can ask him if there's no one that comes to mind that you'd recommend. But I thought maybe you'd have people you know and trust as referrals. I just … I'd kind of really like to do this on my own.'

Queenie's eyes reflected the same glow as the shells in her necklace. 'I'll write you a referral tomorrow,' she said. 'You come and get it from my clinic.'

'Thank you,' Esther said, squeezing Queenie's arm.

In the purpling light of dusk, Esther pulled her old ute to the side of the road next to Nin's car and got out. Nifty, the panel beater, had worked magic on her ute – the only evidence of damage was a superficial crack in the top of the windscreen frame. He'd offered Esther contacts for someone to fix it. She'd declined.

'Ya,' Nin said, unloading boxes from her car.

'Let me help you,' Esther said, rushing forward.

Nin chuckled. 'Luckily seaweed isn't heavy,' she said.

'Right,' Esther said, feeling the airy weight of the boxes.

'Bit different from the last time we were on this stretch of road together, eh?'

'No Tina Turner,' Esther said. 'No black swan.'

Nin shook her head. 'You couldn't make that shit up.'

Esther inched towards Nin's boxes. 'I can't wait to see,' she said.

'Do you think it's dark enough? I felt like maybe we should have worn camo paint on our faces.'

Esther laughed. 'I reckon. Our eyes will adjust. We're in the shadows here; I don't think anyone will be able to see us from the road. Just remember, any headlights, we duck in the bushes.'

'Copy that.'

'Thanks for agreeing to do this with me, Nin. Thank you so much for all your hard work to make this happen.'

'It's for our girl,' Nin said, her voice rich with double meaning. 'You right with your ladder? And her crown?'

Esther nodded, walking back to her ute.

'Let's do this, Starry.'

An hour and only one dive into the bushes later, Esther and Nin sat on the bonnet of Nin's car taking in the glistening silhouette of the Binalong Bay Girl, transformed.

'Fuck, she'd love this,' Esther murmured.

'She would,' Nin agreed.

In the early moonlight, they contemplated their creation.

Standing with her hands on her hips, the Binalong Bay Girl wore a gown of red, pale yellow, green and brown seaweed. Nin had stitched it together in a way that gave the dress its power: angular epaulettes and an attached cape that flowed down the sculpture's back and brushed the ground. Over her hair, Esther had placed a crown woven from twigs and seagrass, with a pink scallop shell at its centre.

'May her ephemeral armour serve her well,' Nin mused.

'Free the Binalong Bay Girl,' Esther murmured.

'We did good, Starry. She really would love this,' Nin said.
They lapsed into silence together. The chill in the night air
made them both burrow into their jumpers and each other's
warmth.

'Starry?'

'Yeah?'

'When I go into labour, will you be there?' Nin didn't look
at Esther. She kept her eyes trained upwards, on the stars.

Esther's face prickled with emotion. 'Of course, I'll be
there,' she managed to say.

'Thank you,' Nin said. She rubbed her belly.

As the moon rose, the Binalong Bay Girl's new silhouette
caught the light and shone in her dried kelp cape and crown.

'No shooting stars,' Nin murmured. 'I hoped there would
be.'

Esther understood Nin's meaning: when they were girls
Aunty Ro had told them that when her people passed, family
would gather at night to watch for shooting stars. They carried
the dead home. To the stars, from where they came.

She looked up at the speckled skin of the night sky. Nin
wiped a stray tear from her cheek.

On the beach, under the stars, by the seven boulders,
apparitions of three young girls ran alongside the sea, imaginary
swords raised.

When Esther got home, Jack and Freya were in the living room
reading.

'We had toasties,' Freya called. 'Pan's still on the stove.'

'Some mail came for you too,' Jack chimed in.

Esther popped her head around the doorway. 'Thanks,' she
said to them. 'I'm starving.'

In the kitchen she made a cheese, tomato and onion toastie
and a cup of milky tea. As she chewed, she went through the

small pile of mail. Car registration bill. Local bookshop catalogue.
And a postcard. From Abelone. A print of Hilma af Klint's swans.

> *An exhibition came to Copenhagen, Esther. Lille Heks and*
> *I got tickets by our teeth skin. The gift shop! I couldn't resist*
> *sending you your swans.*
> *Love, Abelone.*

Esther pressed the postcard to her chest. Tucked it into her bag.

The last item of mail waiting for her was an A4 envelope
with insignia and a Nipaluna, Hobart, postage stamp. Esther
dusted the crumbs from her hands and tore it open. It had
arrived, glossy with promise: the prospectus from the University
of Tasmania's School of Natural Sciences.

She put it down and took another bite of her sandwich.
Chewed in contemplation.

On the ledge above her, the clock chimed. Esther looked
up at Agnete's merman and children holding time for her. In
her mind's eye saw the watery figures beneath the surface of the
canal in Copenhagen. Aura's tattoo verse.

Esther ran a hand over the cover of the prospectus.

You plant seeds, to remember.

Later, in her bedroom, Esther cracked the window for cold air.
Put the lamp on. She hadn't showered. The salt must stay on
the skin.

She undressed and got into bed. Her mobile phone pinged
on her bedside table.

Morning She-Ra. How was the ceremony? I lit a candle before
sleeping last night. Tossed and turned. I'm thinking of you. Going to
do more research today.

Esther recalled the posies of paper daisies and kelp floating
on the sea. 'Takariliya muka,' Queenie had murmured as they'd
drifted away. *Sea family.*

Esther typed. *It was beautiful, Sophus.*

She paused. *I wished you were here.*

He called her on FaceTime. After she'd told him about their morning and he'd told her about his research intentions, Esther rolled over. Pulled the covers to her chin. Gazed out of her bedroom window at the trees swaying under the stars until her eyes grew heavy and drifted closed.

She sank into a dreamless sleep. Over Salt Bay, a shooting star arced across the dome of midnight sky.

A few months later, the spring morning was clear and cold. Jack stood on the driveway and checked his watch. Pulled up his collar against the chilly breeze. 'Come on, Starry, Open Day waits for no one,' he called. Freya leaned on the horn in her Kingswood.

Esther bustled out of the house, pulling the front door shut behind her. 'Fucking hell, you two, keep your pants on, I'm coming.'

'Swearing, Starry.'

Esther rolled her eyes as she opened the passenger door to the back seat of the Kingswood but couldn't stop herself smiling. Jack sat in the front with Freya, his arm stretched out along the bench seat.

'Ready?' Freya asked as she turned the key in the ignition.

'As I'll ever be,' Esther replied.

'UTAS here we come,' Jack cheered.

'Dad,' Esther groaned.

'Starry, I've told you, I promise you we're not going to embarrass you by coming to Open Day. Your mum and I have a date with the new exhibition at MONA.'

'I'm holding you to it.' Esther smiled.

As she pulled out of their driveway, Freya pressed a cassette tape into the stereo. 'Made this,' she said over her shoulder to Esther. 'For the journey.'

'A mixtape? You're cute, Mum.' Esther watched the sea roll by through the gums.

The stereo crackled. Tinkling synthesiser started. Esther closed her eyes. Drums kicked in. Fleetwood Mac. 'Everywhere'. Aura looking at her over the bench seat, her face radiant with the force of her singing. Esther sang the chorus, as Aura had once done. *I'm everywhere, I'm everywhere.* Rubbed the heel of her hand over her heart.

'So Starry,' Jack said casually. Cleared his throat. 'How are you finding Susan?'

Esther looked at the back of his head and smiled to herself. Nonchalance was something Jack had never mastered. 'She's good,' Esther replied.

Susan Albright was Queenie's referral.

'She specialises in bereavement, ambiguous loss and post-traumatic stress,' Queenie had said when Esther had gone to see her at the clinic.

'I don't think all of those apply to me, though, Queenie. Are you sure she's the right person?' Esther had asked. Queenie just gave her a compassionate, knowing smile.

It took Esther weeks to find the courage to ring the phone number of Susan's office. She'd convinced herself she had nothing to say, right up until the moment came to sit in Susan's airy office for the first time. With an encouraging smile, Susan folded her hands in her lap.

'So. To start, can you tell me your story, Esther?'

Esther had imagined herself to be an enigmatic, watertight patient Susan would have to use all her resources to crack open. Turned out all it took was someone who felt supportive and non-judgemental asking her to tell her story.

'Do you think you'll keep working with her?' Jack's voice strained under the weight of his effort to play it cool and breezy.

'I do,' Esther said.

Jack looked over his shoulder at her. 'That's great, Starry. Really great.' Freya nodded in agreement.

'Thanks.' Esther looked out of the window at the forest of gums on either side of the road. Her phone pinged. Sophus. She read his message twice. Smiled to herself.

As Freya merged onto the motorway, 'Everywhere' ended. The pause between songs on the tape clicked and crackled. The hairs on the back of Esther's neck stood up.

She turned from the passenger window and glanced at the rear-view mirror. Freya was looking straight at her.

Her mother leaned forward to turn up the piano intro. Goosebumps swept over Esther's skin.

She held her mother's gaze as the song played. Freya's eyes crinkled with her teary smile as the chorus started.

'She's a Rainbow'.

The bones of women
become aerated, filled with
bubbles of air, and thinner,
as they grow older, just like the
hollow bones of birds. This
lightness of limbs enables flight.

JULIA BAIRD, *PHOSPHORESCENCE*

Esther drove along the coast road and pulled up at the grove of blue gums by the seven boulders in the bay. It was March; the golden in-between. *This is when the veil between worlds is thin and everything you can dream of is possible.*

She got out of her ute. Breathed in the salt of the afternoon. Closed her door and walked down to the shore. Sat and tugged her boots and socks off, curled her toes in the fine, white sand. She took in the blazing orange lichen and algae on the silver granite boulders. The turquoise of the ocean. The bronze bull kelp. The colours of home. Checked her watch. Still had time. She rubbed her hands together slowly. Tried to calm her nerves.

Esther combed her fingers through the sand around her. The gums at her back whispered their afternoon stories. The sun was warm on her skin.

She sifted through broken shells, pebbles, blue gum seed pods, and pieces of Neptune's pearls, kelp and driftwood, all left behind by the sea. Gathered a few shells and lay them on one palm. Periwinkle. Black crow. Jewelled top shell. She turned the jewelled top shell between her fingers. Considered the protection and home it had once been to a life, before it became flotsam, tossed around, buffeted, at the whim of the waves. She held the jewelled top shell up to the light to better see the parts ground down and worn away. In those bare places, shimmering colours emerged. Greens, blues, pinks, purples, golds. Iridescence.

~

Freya stroking her gloved hand over the stencil on Esther's scarred wrist. 'When you get a tattoo,' she explains, 'the ink goes into the second layer of your skin. The top skin, the first layer, becomes a veil, over the magic beneath.'

Esther looks at the stencil on her arm then up at her mother's calm face. Nerves flutter through her body. Behind Freya, Erin, Queenie, Aunty Ro, Nin, and in her arms, Baby Ro, are all gathered.

'Like the shine under the layer of a shell, Starry,' Queenie says with a reassuring nod.

A shiver runs through Esther's body as she looks from Queenie's loving face to Erin's. When Esther catches Nin's eye, they exchange a smile. Aunty Ro looks on, pressing her hands over the strands of gleaming marina shells around her neck. In the window behind them, the flame of a single candle flickers.

'Ready?' Freya asks.

She dropped the periwinkle, black crow and jewelled top shell back to the sand. Dusted off her hands. Ran a thumb lengthways up her arm, over the healed tattoo starting at her wrist: a brown, gold and purple southern old lady moth, with wings as vivid as a bejewelled scarf, and fine, blue jagged line markings, like a monitored heartbeat. The jagged lines started before the outline of the moth, ran through the wings as markings, and extended beyond. Peaking and falling, peaking and falling. In her skin, she shimmered.

Esther checked her phone for the time. A new pinwheel of nerves cracked open in her chest. It would be time to go, soon. She inhaled slowly. Looked over her shoulder, through the gums, to the stargazing shack in the distance. Its windows caught the light. She exhaled slowly. Black swans dabbled in nearby wetlands.

She rolled her jeans up to her knees and stood, brushing off sand. One last thing before she left for the airport.

Sweeping her feet through the shallows, Esther walked the curve of the bay where the sea met the land. Remembered looking up into Liden Gunver's innocent face and leaving a black swan feather at her feet. Walking at night away from Frederiksholm Kanal, a feather left behind, floating on the water over the eerie figures of Agnete's abandoned merman and children. More memories came. Running over basalt rock to stand with Kópakonan, her power drawn from the sea, leaving a feather between her body and seal skin. Standing alone in Flósi's glasshouse, in the company of his night-blooming flowers, the night garden of his heart, and placing a feather with the puffling he'd been part-way through whittling. Watching Sophus walk away before laying a feather on the sculpture's ledge that joined the pregnant woman above with her reflection below. Taping a feather into his *Manly Art of Knitting* book, as if it might express everything that she couldn't find words to say. And the last memory: sliding her seventh black swan feather between the books in Abelone's loft.

Esther walked through the shallows of the sea. The colours of the afternoon began to fire in the light of the setting sun.

'Death,' she said aloud to herself. 'Reckoning. Invitation. Threshold. Discovery. Resistance.' She paused. 'Homecoming.'

Esther reached into her pocket for her eighth and last black swan feather. She'd planned to give it to the sea. Holding its quill between her fingers, she watched the waves.

'What's my eighth skin?' she asked quietly. Under the changing sky, the waves glittered, molten. Transformed. Esther glanced at her wrist.

Her heart. Her skin. This life.

She twirled the black swan feather between her fingers. Looked up, searching the changing sky. Sophus was somewhere in the air, flying over land and sea, on his way. Almost with her.

The urge rose in her chest, to say something, mark the moment. Two sisters running along the beach with swords held high. A billion galaxies in a grain of sand. A black swan crashing to Earth. Unspoken words filled Esther's mouth.

A memory surfaced, of stars above and below. A neon-blue world, all her own.

She looked down, watching herself walk through the foamy, gentle waves. Looked up, watching the expanse of golden sky.

Esther tucked the swan feather into the inside pocket of her coat. Set her gaze on the horizon line.

She breathed lightly. The line between sea and sky. Her eyes welled.

A fluttering. A shimmer and settling of wings.

'I am Esther Wilding.'

Author's Note

I dreamed, walked, ran and wrote this novel into being on unceded Yugambeh land. I acknowledge the traditional families of the Yugambeh region of southeast Queensland, including the Kombumerri, Mununjali, Wangerriburra and others. I pay respect to their Elders, and I extend that respect to all First Nations people. Australia always was and always will be Aboriginal land.

This story is set in three locations: Lutruwita, Tasmania; Copenhagen, Denmark; and the Faroe Islands.

I am honoured to have collaborated with Zoe Rimmer and Theresa Sainty on the use of palawa kani, the language of Pakana (Tasmanian Aboriginal) people, in this novel. While palawa kani is used with and without capitalisation, in this story it has been capitalised, with permission, for clarity. For more information on palawa kani, please contact the Tasmanian Aboriginal Centre.

Zoe Rimmer and Emma Robertson guided and advised me on my inclusion of Pakana characters and cultural practices. I also received immeasurable, generous support, love and guidance from Caleb Nichols-Mansell, and am grateful for the culture, knowledge and stories Jamie Graham-Blair and Emma Lee shared with me while filming our Lutruwita episode of *Back to Nature*.

I first learned about the ancient cultural practice of kanalaritja, shell-stringing, at QAGOMA's 2020 *Water* exhibition. Kanalaritja is an ongoing practice, unbroken through time. The first kanalaritja I saw was Lola Greeno's. Since then, and throughout writing this novel, I have been deeply inspired by kanalaritja made by Vicki-Laine Green, Jeanette James, Patsy Cameron, Lillian Wheatley, Annette Day, Ashlee Murray and Emma Robertson.

The story of Aura's Selkie Tree was inspired by Eastern European folklore shared with me by Aimee Fairman, through stories of her babcia.

Esther's Aunt Erin was named after Erin Montgomery, whose generous bid in an Authors for Fireys auction bought her the right to have her name used for a character in my second novel.

Neither Salt Bay nor Calliope is a real place in Lutruwita, but the areas on the east and west coast where they're located are.

In Copenhagen, a few of the places Esther Wilding visits are imagined, though inspired by real places. In particular, Tattoo Stjerne was inspired by Tattoo Ole, located in Nyhavn and widely agreed to be the oldest tattoo parlour in the western world.

Helena Nyblom was a real nineteenth-century Scandinavian fairytale writer. John Bauer and Charles Folkard were also real artists of their time. As was Hilma af Klint. More about them, and Helena, along with the three stories she wrote that feature throughout this novel can be found on my website, www.hollyringland.com

After my planned long-stay research trip to the Faroe Islands was cancelled in 2020 due to COVID-19, Faroese writer Rakel Helmsdal guided and advised me on my portrayal of the Faroe Islands. I connected with Rakel and was inspired to create many of my characters in the Faroes thanks to short films made in and about the Faroe Islands by Green Renaissance. Venues in Tórshavn, like Sophus and Flósi's bar, Flóvin, and the Lumiere Café, are mostly fictional, though, again, inspired by real places. Eivør, beloved Faorese singer and musician, is very much real, and her song 'Tróllabundin' is one of my most-played tracks on Spotify.

Three playlists from the novel – Aura's eighties memorial, Esther's Aid for Akismus and Flóvin's eighties night – all exist on Spotify, links available via my website.

Hans Pauli Olsen's sculpture *Kópakonan* was installed in 2014. I have taken artistic liberty with this date in the novel, where it is fictionally installed in 2010. The story Sophus tells Esther about the sculpture was inspired by a version written by Ria Tórgarð, for Visit Faroe Islands.

Acknowledgements

Writing Esther's story though 2020–22 kept me believing in courage, joy, hope and transformation. Though I was mostly by myself at my desk, the very last thing I did was write this book alone. I have been carried by a sea of good souls, without whom Esther wouldn't exist.

Armfuls of gratitude to my entire brilliant team at HarperCollins Australia. To my publisher, story maven and queen-maker, Catherine Milne: you are all the red thread I could ever hope for on this journey of making a writing life. Thank you to Scott Forbes, my editor, who saw me through all weathers with this book. Hazel Lam, my designer, for blowing my book cover dreams into the stratosphere, again! Mark Campbell, for directing an author photo shoot of dreams (and, I'm certain of it, commandeering the perfect sunset after a day of rain). Ryan Farrajota for big hair and shimmering make up. I'm indebted to Daniel Boud, and Jack Moran, for an incredible experience, and of course, photographs. Ben Fountain, thank you for knowing my heart and dreams in textures and colours better than I do.

Fumi Nakumara, cover artist, thank you for your breathtaking work. Edith Rewa, artist of shells and feather, the way you and your art bring my words to life leaves me speechless. No small feat.

Unending thanks to my indefatigable agents at Zeitgeist Agency, Benython Oldfield, Sharon Galant and Thomasin Chinnery. Seven years of War Room lassos, snake-flutes and lightsabers, and going strong.

James Kellow, thank you for being Esther's beginning. Your magic is real.

Thank you to Heather Rose and Julia Baird for giving me permission to use their incendiary words among my own. Thanks also to Faber for granting me permission to quote Sylvia Plath, and the estate of Charles Folkard and the National Gallery of the Faroe Islands for permitting me to feature their art and photograph respectively.

Thank you to Simon Passey, Laura Elvery and Morten Nielsen for answering my call for help on social media about the Faroes. I'm indebted to Stuart Hawkins for finding me an English translation of the ballad of Liden Gunver.

Esther has had a circle of incredible, unwavering midwives. Myf Jones, there were so many days that your belief in me was the sole force that drove me to my desk to keep writing – Esther and I raise our swords to you. Laura Donovan, Melissa Acton, Brooke Davis, Jeremy Lachlan and Libby Morgan, thank you all for being my first readers, and for your support and love that truly kept me upright throughout writing this novel. Human sunbeams: Kate Leaver, Sally Piper, Indira Naidoo, Victoria Hannan, thank you so much for reading uncorrected proofs of Esther, and supporting her, and me, with your wholehearted responses.

Samantha Smith, thank you for being the tattooist you are, and the reason I can wear my heart on my skin.

This book wouldn't be what it is without the generosity of spirit, knowledge, love and support I've received from Rakel Helmsdal, Caleb Nichols–Mansell, Emma Robertson, Zoe Rimmer and Theresa Sainty. Theresa, you are most definitely Esther's Nanny Sparkles, and, if I may be so bold as to make this hopeful claim, also mine.

To every publisher, translator and bookseller in the world, who has read my books and championed them, I can't be the author I am without you. Thank you.

My beloved friends and family, there are not enough pages to name you or say how grateful I am for you, and that makes me the luckiest one. Thank you.

Mamaleen and Dadgee, being 'stuck' with you through a pandemic is the blessing of a lifetime. Thank you for letting me sprawl through the whole house (including Frenchie taking up residence in the paddock) to get Esther written. Goose, Teapot,

Poppet, Frankie and Finn, thank you for being the very goodest dogs and writing cheerleaders.

Kira and Hendrix, Grub and Bug, you are my magic.

Sam Harris, thank you for being the reason I know how it feels to soar from the depths to the stars.

Finally, to my dear readers, every single one of you, who have read my novels, carried them with you, taken inspiration from them and had them tattooed into your skin, who have sent me messages, shown up at my events, given me hugs, time and support: Alice Hart and Esther Wilding live because of you. My gratitude will always be yours.

Holly Ringland is the author of the internationally bestselling, award winning debut novel, *The Lost Flowers of Alice Hart*. Since 2018 it has been published in 30 territories. In 2023, a seven-episode TV series adaptation of the same name, starring Sigourney Weaver, streamed globally on Prime Video. It broke records with the biggest opening weekend viewership globally for any Australian series launch. Holly's second novel, *The Seven Skins of Esther Wilding*, became an instant bestseller when it was first published in Australia in 2022, and was named by Booktopia as their Book of the Year. Holly's latest book, *The House That Joy Built*, is an open-hearted clarion call to create what brings us joy. Apple Book Reviews called it a "non-fiction masterpiece". After living between Australia and the UK for ten years, Holly has been based in the Yugambeh region of southeast Queensland since 2020, where she writes in her 'office', a vintage caravan named Frenchie.

www.hollyringland.com